E

C

K A ROMANCE

E
C
K A ROMANCE

Robert Ready

atmosphere press

For Susan M. Levin
and
Mark Jacobs

"I, the miserable and the abandoned,
am an abortion, to be spurned at, and
kicked, and trampled on."

- Mary Shelley,
  *Frankenstein; or, The
  Modern Prometheus*

CONTENTS

PROLOGUE

When he was in his early twenties, Gole Eck thought he would try a PTSD writing group. For a month of Monday evenings, it was held in a circular meeting room with a big rectangular table at the Downtown Culinary School. The culinary school had an interest in its students knowing something about eating and suffering. Cooks, the brochure said, had a responsibility to empathize with eating disorders, which were a frequent component of PTSD sufferers.

The Monday sessions were run by a non-combatant Army vet who was getting her MFA in hybrid prose. La Jane Diver had a soft voice that the barely noticeable shaking of her head accented into even more softness. She was developing a writing-to-heal program she called Rx Storia with an out-of-state medical school. La Jane's workshop had eleven people. Eck was not surprised to learn that a group of PTSD's had, yes, its broken warriors from America's wars but also several people, both women and men, who were broken domestic survivors, along with a few individuals oddly ruined by awful, bizarre happenings.

Jeromia was a surgical intern who had unwittingly triggered a typhus outbreak that killed six people in one hospital. Hedvig had been kidnapped in Norway by eco-terrorists and locked up in a mountain bicycle warehouse for over a year, during which none of her captors ever said a word to her but gave her clean underwear every week without returning the previous week's. Rafer had tiny pieces of his tongue ripped out over a six-month sexual imprisonment in the Philippines. That was when he was eighteen. When Gole got to know him in the workshop, Rafer was twenty-seven. It took the sickened military vets a while to feel comfortable sharing lines, haikus, flash fiction, or TV scene proposals with anyone whose trouble was not the violence of actual military combat. Gole Eck was, of course, the only unborn among them. That made for a difference and a distance that couldn't be bridged. But Gole figured, So what?—why should this experience be any different?

La Jane Diver had two principal features to her writing workshops.

One she said she couldn't control and didn't want to waste time trying to fix it. The weather for the whole month was fall transitional, neither hot nor cold but in that middle space in which the heating and cooling system in the building didn't know, as she said, whether to shit or go blind from 7:00 to 9:30 pm, their Monday class time. Her writers handled it, wearing layers, taking layers off.

The second was her pedagogical fondness for writing that came from list-making. Very precise items in a list. She had them read aloud the Catalogue of Ships, dwell on the precision of each, and try to count the total number Homer listed. Since they were in a culinary school, they started with recipes. They exchanged different ingredient lists for egg salad, Yorkshire pudding, meat sauce, fish in aspic, lemon meringue squares, and various ethnic specialties from around the world that one or two of them actually knew something about and the rest just winged. Sports heroes. Vice presidents. A whole range of five-minute exercises from prompts to produce lists. They went all the way up to theological, astrophysical, all the way back down to sexual positions, childhood games, and good, unthreatening dreams.

After a while, she got the list she really wanted: Trigger points. Lists of the lost, all the lost, the dead, the maimed, the ruined, get it out and fucking look at it, say it, own it, back it down or back away from it forever, either way, she whispered in her ragged soft way, doesn't matter.

The sharing of those Triggers among the eleven was, to say the least, edgy. La Jane openly talked about it as possibly reckless. Like writing itself, she said: make some noise.

In their final class, La Jane offered up her own, after she said she'd put her list together after intentionally going off her meds. Indeed, something different spoke in her, put chrome in her voice. She railed. She stood and started to thrash about as she kept chanting one word, "Road."

Several of the eleven saw it coming, but Eck was the only one who acted. When La Jane picked up a folding chair as if it were a flimsy bag of leaves and got it up over the head of the cowering Jeromia and calling her "Dr. Murder," Eck got himself down into vacant bone mode and stood flat in front of her. Instantly, La Jane let him take the chair, turned on her military heel and went back to her seat at the head of the table.

"There," she said.

"Where?" three-rotation-Afghanistan Ronald Waters asked.

"You've seen worse," La Jane said.

"True. True enough," Waters said. "Can I read now? I've been waiting for my turn to read my list of lost. Except I have reason to call it list of lost and found."

Eck said, "I follow Ronnie." And the other nine claimed their turns, too.

Rx Storia. Downtown Culinary.
Instructor: Ms. Diver.
Goleman Eck: His List.

Aborted babies. Aborted fetuses. Aborted loves. Aborted hates. Aborted careers, plans, vacations. Aborted hopes, dreams, plays, strategies, transmissions, flights, suits, journeys. Days, nights, awakenings, sleep, returns, reentries, paintings, experiments, seasons, recipes, prayers, operations, recuperations, approximations.

Parts, wholes, fractions, percentages, divisions, accounts, trusts, payoffs, transfers, exchanges, speculations, givings, charities, novenas, weeks, terms, sentences, trials, tests, reviews, judgments, decisions, transformations, consummations, petitions, continuations, sequiturs and non-, rosaries, blessings, curses.

Aborted watches, backups, fail-safes, retreats, charges, campaigns, sieges, installations, series, spectrums, alternatives, couplings, wills, testaments, covenants, oaths, words, promises, commandments, planks.

Aborted sequels, prequels, calls, postings, proclamations, dailies, weeklies, monthlies, annuals, retrospectives, chronicles, diaries, histories, myths, incantations, summaries, arias, riffs, runs, monologues, epics, gospels.

Aborted resolutions, determinations, commitments, manifestoes, carnivals, coronations, fireworks, forecasts, headlines, elections, recounts.

Aborted openings, lists, catalogues, collections, displays, broadsides, previews.

Aborted lust, greed, wrath, gluttony, sloth, envy, pride.

Aborted charity, temperance, diligence, patience, kindness, humility.

Aborted stories, sentences, phrases, articles, nouns, verbs, reflexives, adverbs, grammar.

Aborted deortions, pre and proortions, antiortions, conortions, synortions, symortions, uni, bi and triortions, psychoortions, anteortions, autoortions, circumortions, coortions, comortions, distortions, enortions, exortions, extraortions, heteroortions, homo and homeoortions, hyper-ortions, il, im, in, and irortions, interortions, intra and intro-ortions, microortions, monoortions, nonortions, omniortions, postortions, alphaortions, betaortions, subortions, trans-ortions, unortions, azortions.

Aborted abortions. Aborted births. Aborted deaths.

Eck really got into a zone reading his list aloud. When he finished, he was all alone in the cold room.

PART ONE

ONE

The unborn are not the Undead. They have no truck with vampires, sucking or drinking blood, or with stakes in the heart, wolves howling in moonlight, or toothy sexual invasions. They are not ghosts. They are uninvited guests at the table of life, though the hosts don't know that, until some unborn might happen to tell them. They do not bond, they have no solidarity. No nation, no tribe, family, ethnicity, or identity by any particular orientation. They are unknowable to each other.

Still: they yearn for what the born seem to get by nature.

Yet: their condition, of not claiming regular condition, causes misunderstanding from persons who find one of them interesting, or dangerous, or attractive.

This story is about one unborn, Goleman Eck. Gole.

*

One night, Eck was out on a first-date dinner with Yolande Segundo. She was a much-travelling executive for an online IT procurement firm out of Providence that Eck's wind energy company did business with. Chilean-American, Yolande derived from a large Santiago family that got many of their

11

young, not all, out of the dictator's way to America in the 1980s. She had just gotten back that afternoon from a grueling three days on Gulf platforms and oil engineers in the market for deeper-ocean sonic penetration. She wanted to quit the business altogether, get back seriously to her real love for life as a large-scale textile artist. Very large scale.

She was being very persuasive to Goleman Eck as they sat at the tapas bar of Les Trois Souhaits about how claustrophobic one could get, and she was not prone to being claustrophobic, on a platform rig sixty miles out after two days, never mind three. Gole knew the feeling, just didn't choose to tell her right then. He was intrigued by her confidence that, hell yes, she could rewrite her script altogether. Her father had rewritten hers when she was two. Eck caught himself staring at her possibility for radical change. He saw Yolande Segundo react to being stared at that way.

She tooth-picked a little Brie croquette to barely touch his bottom lip and then clipped it into her own pretty mouth.

It took him by surprise. "Don't do that," he told her.

"I'm sorry, Gole," she said. "It's just a good luck gesture. You're welcome to do the same. Break the ice?"

The silence his stiffness created left her to run her finger around the top of her glass of Riesling, of which she was getting down to the bottom in a large sip every several minutes.

They had met as side-by-side health cyclists in Gole's gym, meaning he was there before she started coming to work out. "Your white hair," she had said as she got on to the stationary bike next to his. "It's quite striking."

He was liking what she got on the bike with. A lot.

"It's my hair," he said. "Been summer moonlight look since I skipped gray altogether."

"So you're not that old is what you're saying. I'm Yolande. I've been thirty-five for awhile." Wincing, she turned aside and sneezed three times in a choked little way. "Sorry. High pollen day."

"So I won't take it personally. Ride, partner," Gole said. She did thirty-five, auburn, shoulder-length hair and expensive clear glasses to glittery ankle socks, real well. She started to say something else but it got lost in another little reactive burst.

"Talk later. My name's Goleman, Gole for short."

She cocked her very pretty red-feature head to him. "So, what color is the rest of your hair?"

Gole began to like Yole quite a lot. Fear of that made him just grin at her and say, "Guess."

"Summer moonlight?"

"A lot of it, yeah."

"That must be nice."

"You?" he asked nicely.

"Like you, like the top. Just this unpredictable mix of dark. You know?"

They rode, sometimes in a nice sync that relaxed them both. He wanted her, wanted to try again, to imitate the ways of the born born. That's like the born rich, the born lucky, the born something. It's just the born born, all of them out there, the born to be born. The not I, in that crucial respect. He could see that she'd come from an able father. He didn't know anything about any father.

Imitate them, do your impression of them, is what Eck told himself as soon as he stopped reacting against a room-temperature bacon roll-up. He told himself to guess something about Yolande. Up, up, Deadheart, one more time.

The maître d' had seated them at a table away from overhead James Bond movie music. He lighted the table center candle, but Gole pushed it over to one side. The maître d' understood and left.

"Are you religious, Yolande? But we can look at the menu, too."

It was a good question. She warmed to it, even as she settled on the chopped salad and rainbow trout. To show his good faith, Gole ordered the signature scallops champignons, hot.

The forefinger again circling the rim had a lighter shade of pewter than the other fingernails on her dominant left hand. "Well," she said, "my father was a priest for eighteen years. He's eighty now. What do you think?"

This was getting closer. Sometimes, Goleman Eck had every unreasonable reason to believe that it was his prick of a biodad who, in a panic that changed the world, probably flushed fetal Gole down the toilet, leaving him unborn, flushed it probably seven consecutive times. None of the unborn men and women ever knew these men's names for sure. They just kept looking for them, in the spaces between everything else they look for like everybody else. The biomom, you say? It happened occasionally, but the flushing was generally done by the man. This was he who took the tiny prehistoric thing of the unborn, pushed into his latex-gloved hands, he who disposed of it in the bowl he probably relieved himself in within an hour after it went unborn into myriad currents that so precious few of them survived to live unborn.

"Where did you just go?" Yolande asked him. "I'm beginning to think you do fugue."

"Come again?"

"Sudden capacity for drift. Here to there. No reason. Fugue state. You know?"

He did know. He did not know many people who knew about it. He was beginning to wonder if Yolande Segundo was unborn. The greatest awful yearning of all was rising in him. It had to be squelched because it could not be, ever. He got back fast.

"Thinking about your father," he said. In some way, he was. "What was that like, do you think? Abandoning vows, recalling vocation, all that. For him. After all that smart resistance against the general. For your mother. For you, when she got you to Fort Myers in her arms. I was just thinking about all that. But I do not mean to be intrusive."

He liked the way she ate. The food on her plate was interesting to her, welcome to come down into her. She didn't talk with any food in her mouth. "I think," she said, "that my father is a good man who has lived two half-lives in sequence." She paused, in a good-humored steady look at him. "Something about you seems something like that, like him." The light pewter nail appeared at the top of her lip. "Does it make you uncomfortable, my saying that?"

At which point, she had willy-nilly stepped onto Gole's preserve. He pulled way back from meeting this gray-eyed Yolande Segundo at table's edge, the very normal place she was inviting him to go. And of course, she saw that happening. She produced an iPhone and snapped a picture of Eck. He was never sure, when that happened, that he would be in the picture. This one he was, though, because she held the phone in her palm, straight driving it before his face.

"What do you see when you look at yourself, now, right now? You have a most, I don't know, compelling face?"

He gently turned her wrist back. In fact, he was living then high up in the air, on the 12th and 14th floors, with huge windows overlooking the harbor. Not a mirror on a wall anywhere.

She sipped down the rest of her glass of wine, which she put down on the table precisely, as if it could not possibly go anywhere else. "You remind me of one of those composite multi-racial physiognomies that, you know, computers put together to envision the global human visage in a hundred years or so."

This was good. She went into some remarkable detail about his facial bone structure, complexion, slightly ovoid eye sockets, hairline lightly gapped in the middle, Ethiopian broad forehead, and two or three other features from cold or hot places, all, she said, coming together around his amused lips that opened to teeth that would last a century if he lived a century. He was alive all over from being looked at that way. Yolande had also been—until she saw too much—a portrait-photographer who made a good living at it because she could look at people for a long time before she asked anything of the camera. That was the too much she saw, and it got into her final products, which made many customers uneasy about how they looked to people like her.

"So, you stopped?" Gole asked. "Why?"

"The faces stopped making regular sense. Even the work in museums I was known for stopped being markers on a continuum. They stopped making sense to me as parts of a coherent story. When I tried to get their doing that from the camera, no one wanted to commission a Yolande Segundo anymore."

He waited the moment it took her to get clear of the hurt of it. "Then what happened?"

"I got out. To procuring for the winds, for guys like you. Now here you are, Mr. Global Handsome Earth Man of the Future. Can I take your picture with a real camera? In a bright white open-necked shirt?"

He put a delicious scallop in his mouth. It was as if he had new taste buds. He told Yolande this. Happiness invaded her too. Well-being filled them both, a sense of—what?—some kind of at-last. Eck prayed to, what?—to some right order of things—oh, this time, let me be able.

On their giddy way to the car in the Trois Souhaits parking lot, near an open-backed truck that said, Got Junk? they came right up into the middle of a gaggle of fools, high, stupid, and mean. The city did its best for them but the cycle of cracking down hard on them was peaking. They were a hindrance to the drug trade that victimized them.

Three of maybe eight of them examined Yolande and Eck with her and immediately hated him. Something about him made them wait. They loathed all other aliens, immigrants, intruders into their widening space. This kind of confrontation had happened in several ways to Eck before. He had a target on his face, chest, back that these kinds of fragmentary types recognized as what they were at their very cores, non-existent, zombied, doomed to live only in their coming daily to an end. They could lose all control just on seeing him, like raptors smelling extinction and needing to savage it. All in army and navy store brown and purple and black, nose rings and empty cartridge belts, they were a poor gang of boat people learning gangsta when all that was over now.

The hassling went quickly from sarcasm to sexual threats. Gole tried to move with his new cherished person, this way, that way.

"Fucking faggot, pussy, she needs to suck a real dick. Start practicing right now."

"Leave us alone," Yolande said, more disgusted than scared.

Gole got pushed hard in the chest. He didn't move. It was starting in him, the living nightmare from his very infancy. Of having his life taken from him. Again, again, oh please not again.

"No problem with you," Gole said. He heard his words clunk one at a time out of his terribly dry mouth. "Don't want it. Don't need it."

"Oh, really?"

"You don't look right to us."

A throat cleared.

A glob of mucous splatted on Yolande's shoulder. She lurched backwards in a cry of rage that triggered cough-sneezing.

Eck's killer version slipped his shoes off. He bent over and cuff-rolled his pants up two turns. He faced all of them, his palms crossed just above his waist.

"Fuck he doing?" More crazed giggling, gargling, mucous

collecting.

"Let's do this," Gole said. "But only one of us is going to walk away."

His eyes half rolled up and in, leaving only the whites for them to see and him to gauge every move they made, every easy approach to their chest cavities, the angle of their noses going up into their skulls, and six knees that could erupt through their legs.

"Leave that man alone," a very calm voice behind them said. "Just do not try to get near him. Do not do it."

Eck's eyes straightened. He knew it was over, and he was very glad.

"Fuck are you?"

"Let's just say I'm off duty." The calm voice out of nowhere getting nearer.

"Yolande!" Eck called out because he couldn't see her in the dark.

"Take me out of here!"

"You hear that, ugly and stupid?" Eck said to them. "I want to go now."

"No, no. You have to stay, hole."

"Okay. I stay. You still want me to."

They didn't know what to make of him.

"Come on." Eck saw the three of them clearly behind his drooped eyelids. "Do it," he said. "What's changed?"

The three said mouthfuls of nothing. Gole seemed to have his whole being focused on the one he guessed spat on the best human thing that had happened to him in a long time.

The bigger crew pulled the trio away, into the dark, to some other place they'd have better luck terrorizing people who were whatever Eck was to them.

The voice had a big white hat on, gleaming and floppy down one side of his head. And an immaculate full apron. A grinning, unforgettable almost wide face. He came over to Eck and helped him get shoed again. Eck straightened up and faced him, resisted hugging him in grateful trust. He could have sworn he'd seen that classically handsome face in the movies when he was like, ten. Something about his whole bearing said hard work, no surprises anymore, and what are we here for, we don't help each other.

"I was watching you." The dress was clearly a cook's of some kind. "The way you were sizing them up. Your eyes were like masked searchlights in perfect focus. I thought I'd have your back. Then I started enjoying the show. My name's Eugene, Encarnacion."

Yolande came by Eck's side. She had pulled herself out of fright and disgust. "You're regular staff, Eugene? You look like somebody."

"The sous chef," he said. "It's good food?" It was true, like somebody you'd recognize if you thought about it.

"The scallops," she said. "Amazing."

Eugene looked at the stain on her pretty jacket. He produced an ironed white handkerchief. She took it, rubbed the insult off, offered it back to him, and he took it over to a refuse can. Eugene bowed to them, saying good night. He went to the back entrance of Les Trois Souhaits, filled with elegant eaters he fed well.

The shaking ran its course. "Masked man," Yolande said. "Who or what are you?"

*

They left in the chauffeured plush red Buick Eck liked to rent on occasion. He didn't own a car. They talked. At one point she told him about the allergies she had all her life. And she told him that she had been a very premature birth, six months and in a Santiago hospital under a warming light or in an oxygen tent until little by little while two whole families prayed night and day for her to make it. She did.

The normality of all that prayer and care was not new for

19

Eck to hear of. It just took him by surprise that the woman he now wanted so much had been so—wanted. Aloneness and a terror came raging back. An awful word came into his head. Immiscible. He could tell her none of it.

They had to stick the veins in Yolande's tiny hands with needles for steroids, and her lungs took a time to develop. While keeping clear of the dictator's secret police, her two parents concentrated on making sure their preemie had a shot at her own life. It was crazy, as ever in unborn Goleman Eck, but Yolande's infancy made him feel something like deathly sick. Eck was upside down, and he thought it was never going to end.

He was convinced it was not going to work, that their brand new roller coaster car was going only down. But within the hour, they were in his 12th- through 14th-floor bedroom. The harbor and the Verrazano were alight and filling the water. He did not listen to himself, he went full ahead, and she went with him. They were in another dangerous position, naked, Yolande lying back and arching up slightly to receive him. Her lovely breasts asking up for his lips, abdomen smooth down to that rich auburn hair, what right there, right then, what the fuck was wrong with him again. Again. He could not. He could not. He did not.

No man who was unborn of woman can enter the kindest, most willing, most honestly needing, mother-lovely dream of wet come true: woman saved at birth to get to this closest human moment. He was afraid he would hurt her because she had been kept, been saved. She was a miracle. He was an abortion. If not right then, immediately, then at some unwitting crossroads right there in the future, whenever, he would hurt her. A deadly allergen.

Yolande Segundo, eerily beautiful, professionally successful and changing determinedly, high up in Eck's dark above the harbor, was offended to her very core. In subterranean silence she gathered a queen's control of letting him know her fury and humiliation. He did know, so he got up from between her legs before she could push him off her life. He walked, bare and flaccid, out of his bedroom's impossible heaven. As he stood in front of his immense living room window like a diver about to go over the edge, he heard the catlike padding sounds she made getting herself together, amidst a few hiccups and gasps, to get out and away and back to her healthy self after their evening toppled over in his ancient sickness, birth envy. Shame at what he'd just done to wonderful Yolande filled his chest. He could barely breathe. The awful feeling overwhelmed Eck again, that it would have been better if he'd never been aborted. He stumbled and hobbled down his picture-framed hall back to his bed and doubled up onto its howling darkness without her.

TWO

How did it come about that a Goleman Eck-fetus escaped incineration, being disposed of as medical organic material? His own obsessively researched information or professionally gleaned data failed to answer that question. He did not let that original gap in his being drive him crazy.

The only conclusion he ever came to in this fundamental matter was that he was not aborted in an apartment or room but in a city hospital or clinic. Probably the City of New York because he felt better in New York than in any other place his work took him in the world. He figured that, in the late summer, early fall of 1974, the little bloody mass of him got one hell of a huge exemption. He was too old to have somehow escaped via stem-cell research as a sliced piece that somehow got away and migrated into another biological specimen that then, stubbornly, grew into its own full-term human.

He heard stories about shocked "housekeeping" workers peering into the "bucket" of medical organic material after a late-term procedure, crying and praying at the thing that they could not stand anymore. He tried on the story that maybe one of them, say, a clean-up woman mother-of-six did something—did what, though?—with the little hint of human in the bucket. Did something with other pro-life clean-up conspirators with emergency medical skills, got unborn Gole to another place, another preemie blue light of life? Ah, it was impossible. Bloody depressing even to imagine wildly, improbably, unscientifically. But if not something like that, what, never mind who, got him out of the slop bucket in time?

He was not a science-fiction thing. He was goddamn real, all right. He'd come to understand, in fact, that it was a good thing for him that his living at all was so impossible that no one could or would take his actual post-abortion life seriously. His condition wasn't scientifically coherent, so he went on without scientific facticity. So he didn't have to defend his lethal beginning at all, no matter how much it haunted him. Of course he obsessed about it, yes, when it took full possession of him in the manner of a Satan. He wouldn't be human if he didn't. In those dark nights and afternoons of the unsouled, it was always the hour of non-being, unbeing, terror of the vile, the never live. Unlike everybody else, he really had to make his living.

At various times, to various select interested people:

"I think of all wasted places, beginning points, stretches of mess and mayhem, lost chances, battlegrounds, highway smash-ups, garbage compacting trucks howling at the sunrises they cannot fathom. I imagine the Japanese cities vaporized, suppurating faces draining down concrete walls once holding in universities, hospitals, stadiums, circuses and congresses. There, I say, is where I come from—destruction, dereliction, uncreation, medieval disembowelments and quarterings, crashing falling hideously from on high all the way down to the darkest pits where children like me wait in the millions to receive it all in their nesty open mouths as some kind of food and drink."

This drove the incestuous brother and sister Angela and Kevin Cussen mad.

They ran the school that was the housing of Eck's earliest infancy. It was an unsolved mystery to the state apparatus that put them in prison and scattered their forty orphans to places of reason and care throughout the fifty states and island provinces.

"They must have taught me," Eck told the tale, "to crawl because I have screen memories of large pillows, ever one and ever another one, being put up in a pyramid fashion for me to do knee up sequencing with my whole legs. Screaming was the happy exuberance of all their ministrations to their up-to-six-year-old charges, who were really discharges from any regular form of childhood."

Drumming pumped out of Kevin's self-carpentered speaker systems. Nightmare Gregorian chant alternated in Angela's mothering style with frequent games with hammers smashing cat's-eye marbles on the locked driveway's macadam up to the Quonset hut administration building. They both had crazily earned doctorates in early childhood, but either one or the other of them was always paralyzed by fear of infant-smothering, white slavers riding in over the walls in silent helicopters big enough for one of them and one of the little children. This terror in them to the point where Eck was the chosen one to sleep with both of them while they touched each other into fractured rest.

"I think I remember some Boston daily paper with a front-page picture of the Cussens side-by-side mug shots, all four of their eyes beaten police-black, purple, and shut. They had taught us to hear the howling. They did not ever teach us that we deserved it." This was all over forty-some years before he knew that such a person as Yolande Segundo could even exist for him.

A boyhood without family means an indefinable creature moving around in shapeless worlds. When he is also unborn from birth, the boy is often sickly, perturbed, shakily fused in all the institutional settings he's bound to bake in until he's around twelve. He's always late. Late to learn to read—refer again to the pillow pyramids Eck had to surmount to learn to crawl in sequence—late to ride a bicycle, run between the lines, take his plate to the kitchen sink, double-knot his sneaker laces, angle his toothbrush properly against his gum line, gauge the right final jump-off point up into the delirious bank of autumn leaves, do a basic box step with another seventh-grade boy in advance of the first co-ed spring dance, pronounce a teacher's five-syllable Mediterranean suddenly married name, stop from crying miserably when first hearing the word "dyslexic" from a motivational speech specialist, or being restrained from kicking away others' fabrications of Pick-up sticks in their only play space. And he's the latest to learn to make lists.

All that, all that was just more and more of "Oh, that's just fucking Goleman. He's strange. Just as strange as that name nobody knows where it came from. He's often upset like that. All the adults can only believe is that he's a rift, a rip, a tear, a fissure. He doesn't look right, not at all does his handsomeness look remotely right. They have absolutely no records other than somebody claimed that somebody else saw something moving in the medical waste slop bucket that they got all excited about saving for living. And they did, but even who they were is lost, except they probably got spooked or lost interest in actually raising him beyond the near dead. So he was on the unnamable adoption list at three months and nobody wanted him and he began his miserable little life."

Nobody, of course, told that whole story to Eck. But it's the best he'd been able to piece together. "Now I'm ready to say it aloud. Them as scoff at it are welcome to their thoughts," he said. "Beginnings are tough, that's for sure," he said.

He skipped over a lot of the next decade of his missing growth.

"It was there, thirteen to nineteen, but it wasn't mine because I began to know neither was I, there. Some lateral expansion—think of an infinite beach umbrella in a blinding hot sun, opening out and up like sky within sky—and I took to reading voraciously. I read the way fields of corn, cotton, wheat, sorghum, the federal tax code or Microsoft Office grow. I gained mastery of all systems of worldwide environmental herbicide, oceanocide, terracide, as well as the very cybercide that brought plague to centuries-long democratic governing procedure. All on a theoretical basis only. I could put domestic plumbing systems together like five-hundred piece puzzles of Monet's water lilies. I didn't start at the corners and create the borders. I started from the center, grew it all out from the inside. I understood molecular bonds in pernicious chemicals. Fairly early on, I also grasped the global systems that discriminated against hiring the unborn."

"How, then, did you make out in the world, make a living?" someone must have asked him.

"Well, I got them to fund me magnificently for not actualizing what I knew. My work until I got to the winds—I will explain that last—was that I could not work."

One early example was his late teenage success up to a point in figuring systems in blackjack in Las Vegas, Atlantic City, and Foxwoods in Connecticut. He trained for what he did. The end result was a big man in a green blazer and greener ear pods took him aside and said in subterranean tones, "You watch the cards." You make that happen in Vegas--$167,000 net worth of that in three weeks in four of the hotel casinos—you don't get to stay in Vegas. He did have the satisfaction of leaving a little entourage of card-watching blackjack tutees to keep the good work up on a much more stripped-down version hard to spot. His students stayed for months. One, Debbie Strout her name, sat up straight in her bogus wheelchair for most of a year, watching and watching to limited cash-outs of five hundred to a thousand a day. He taught them and Debbie that. For all their families cared about them, they might as well have been unborn, too. They took new names, Billy Ismail, Zeki Manhour, Sojourner Lie.

Aristotle said, character is desire. He'd have asked Gole.

26

"What do you want?" Since being precedes desire, the question presumes existence, which was not Eck's case. So he could only have answered, "I don't know, Ari. I haven't lived to know. But I have to have a better, a regular answer when the issue comes up."

It usually came up with a woman who found him oddly compelling, from his white hair down. That was unlike Yolande Segundo. He wasn't odd to her. The type of woman, it's as if to her there were something perfectly unfinished about him. Then she'd be on to it but still couldn't make sufficient sense of it to just leave Gole alone as an odd man-creature, period.

"'Oh,' such a woman, again, not Yolande, must have heard her own mother say a dozen times or more, 'him. He's an odd one.' But as usual, she's not listening to her mother, and so she can't just leave me as is, odd. Let me tell you about Brenda Jagger, who is one of those women."

Brenda Jagger had a Catholic doctorate in theology, part of which she achieved with a Licenza from a Pontifical University in Rome. She was second-generation Ethiopian-English. She had raven black hair, cut in the classic thickly upswept manner of the Kennedy women. She had broad shoulders and slim hips. She was strikingly present in any room, and her scholarly fields included the history of sanctification by chastity. This was a practice she had herself followed in her teens and twenties working with her parents in their gated compound-pension in Addis Ababa for international business, development, and education professionals. One of those professionals, a Russian nutritionist, sexually assaulted Brenda three times, terrifying her but not at long last succeeding in penetrating her. The Russian got called back home, and Brenda got sent to Ethiopian relatives in Brooklyn.

Brenda and Gole met at a world conference on reproduction after rape (RAR) at the Javits Center in New York. He was there as an independent attendee, going from plenary sessions featuring international figures in the field to small panels really down in the global policy weeds. One such was on local grassroots organizational strategy in cities like Addis Ababa, Encarnación, and Lowell, Mass., where once the textile mills flourished and Kerouac lived with his mother.

Eck wanted to know the new and emergent questions about reproduction after rape, a minor urgency in him like post-prostate surgery urination, though his own PSA count was still below 2.0. Meeting Brenda Jagger was his own kind of relief.

She peeled away his attention from a speaker whose arms whorled the necessity for a thousand local actions. She was two chairs down from Eck in the uncrowded Whitcomb Riley conference room. Before the question period began, she turned to Eck and said, "You're staring at me from very far away."

"I have the sense that you know how far away that is."

They could find each other. She struck Eck as one of Rembrandt's older, not old, North African women—deeply brown and serene past all erotic need, solid and graceful, a lady in all things. The other side of fifty, she was not someone Gole would pretzel up about, or hoodwink and then feel awful for. This brilliant survivor-woman, he figured, was not going to be about cursed aborted me or even that distorted habit, the me-and-her dyad.

Just at that point of understanding, the session got invaded by a parade going through the rooms in the work of disrupting the institutional academic mainstream. That was their pungent phrase. There were seven bare-chested HELOTS in loincloths and thick leather sandals from the same shoe outlet. Higher Ed Labor Out To Strike was a noisy national posse of graduate assistants who did most, they claimed, of the actual teaching for ridiculously low wages while they piled up more tuition debt than they'd get out of for years, even if they actually did land a steady teaching job. All good and true, but

Gole wanted Brenda Jagger the unraped older virgin.

"I was an infant for Brenda Jagger. I wanted her *right now*," he said when he told their story later to people he trusted, like Yolande Segundo.

The protesting HELOTS took over the first line of folding chairs, pointedly asking people to move so that they could sit together. People did because they recognized the cause and were glad they weren't the ones suffering it or fighting it. Two of the bare chests were women bearing sashes draped from one shoulder down to the opposite hip with red lettering saying, **screechers!** Thus, one could notice only two breasts, one small and pert, the other fulsome and bouncy. The HELOTS sat and hummed in triple harmony, very low as the panel speakers carried on, increasing their own volume enough to do so.

"It's true," Gole whispered to Brenda, now sitting right next to him. "They lack reality. They have no quiddity. They are the underclass that keeps all the classes going, like seventy percent of all the classes."

"Not real?"

"Not really, no."

The humming increased steadily. The panel gave way to them.

"If," Brenda said. "If they could sing, they'd do Carl Orf outrage. But they get boring, you know? The Requiem Mass for the masses. I submit, it's been done before. It parches the throat. I suggest we accompany one another to a place where I can get a soft drink."

They went up to a mini-bar in another glass environment. Reflections of clouds painted the stories of windows in the air next to the building the conference was in. Window cleaners belted into steel grids brought three-foot drying brushes on two-foot handles down in perfect parallel lines. Clarity was a three-foot-wide stripe, descending.

Brenda and Gole drank sturdy ginger ale in tall cocktail

glasses and nibbled roasted unsalted almonds. She told him it was okay but not necessary for him to open up after she finished a list of guesses.

He told her that when he wore glasses as a child, the lenses were real glass. Hearing that, Brenda said she had a vision.

"When you were a child walking to the adoptive Kilpartridges' home from school in the afternoon after the patrol line broke up at the bottom of your street, you touched picket fences, thumbed the brownness of horse chestnuts, fretted over failed boundary lines in the sidewalk. A feeling of complete and total identification with all unfinished, stunted, or denied people filmed for the evening news haunted you in your sleep."

"That's quite a good list," Gole said. "Yes, to all of it. I like the way you talk in complete paragraphs."

"Thank you kindly," she said. "I can do it in Italian. Want to hear some?"

"That's okay."

"Florentine Italian, to be precise."

"That's okay, too."

"Less so in Latin, but still—"

"Let it go for now. You were saying."

"I've only begun. I'm a fortune-telling agent provocateur when I get like this. Mean people ask me at parties to practice on their enemies."

"Keep going."

She was fully invested in a vision of the child Gole speaking from she knew not where. Nothing distorted her body. Her mouth looked lovely and untouchable. "You were fucked from the outset. Stopped cold, hoss, your paddock stayed shut when the race began."

"Hoss?"

"Somewhere it was determined that I would turn up for you. So I did. Incredible."

"Don't get up and leave. Okay? Don't."

She took six of the unsalted nuts. She lined them up on the coffee table in front of them. She moved them in arithmetical ways, all adding up to six.

"There's no you to leave. This is one of the worst cases of not I've ever seen. You, Goleman, are somehow not. I'm sorry, but having sex with you would really creep me out."

The sudden, flat-out rejection got him weirdly stimulated from the groin out, up, and down. He drank down half of his ginger ale, ate two of her nut collages at once. She was talking to him, concentrated even, as if from within a two-inch-thick plastic booth in a prison visitation room.

"Do that again," she told him.

"Do what again?"

"The ginger ale. The rest of it."

He drank down the rest of it. That made Brenda Jagger laugh in a kind of trivial wonder. "The fizz," she said. "I've never been able to do anything but sip it."

"Now who's not real?"

"Oh, darling," she said, pointed. "Look. The HELOTS are here. That's not wonderful."

They dragged their humming theater into the mini-bar area. They ordered double expensive Virginia bourbons. They had put tunics over their loincloths. They wove circles around individual patrons in the bar, humming and pointing extended fingernails at them. When they did that to Brenda and Gole, he turned to glare at the one sashed adjunct of a perky Asian breast. Frightened, she cried out, "You don't look right!"

Brenda flicked her fingers at her, and she got pulled back into the total humming HELOTS. When they tried to light up Vapes, building security came. How much contempt Brenda seethed at them as they were herded out was immeasurable. She was as close to an ancient seer priestess as he ever encountered. She could have held down the job at the Temple of Apollo in Delphi in Greece, speaking divine nonsense to petitioners' most desperate questions about what to do with their lives. Eck cold-turkeyed wanting to get inside her. She felt that happen right there, both of their ginger ales all gone. But she accepted him as an occasional lunch mate, at which they made it a funny thing to order different kinds of craft sodas, like celery, sarsaparilla, black cherry, ginger beer, white grape, pomegranate, and parsley.

Brenda Jagger had a dead brother. She told Eck about him in pieces, in separate times and places that stayed separate times and places over different fruit and herb sodas. She knew exactly what she was doing each such time more of the dead brother's short adult life fell to Gole to put with the other pieces. The end result was puzzle parts he pieced together about this brother.

Brother Leo Jagger was sent over to Brooklyn from Addis in the mid-'80s at the tail end of the Derg, the military dictatorship that terror-headed Ethiopia after Selassie was smothered. That had cost their father Tillahun Jagger the rest of his landed fortune and then his life to the crumbling regime.

Leo had the Frankenstein monster complex. Once, twenty years in America, in a used car showroom out on Kings Highway, he said to Brenda, "What is the difference between a misunderstood monster and a monster who misunderstands?" The used car salesman on duty, still pimply young and eager to guide all conversation in the showroom, sighed deeply and just went back to sitting at his metal desk, watching the Jaggers lest they do something weird like lean on a Cutlass.

"Oldses used to be nice family cars," Brenda said. She stroked the green fender. The cratered-skin salesman called over to her to please not touch the new lacquer. She turned to Leo. "You look like you're going to kill somebody, bent over, knuckle-dragging, like that. Is that because you are a misunderstood monster? A serial killer just starting out?"

Leo straightened his posture, started reading aloud the greening Olds's specification sheet on the back seat left window. It was packed, an automobile for a sporting young lady. He touched her elbow, motioned her away from the beauty. "I spend my days regretting I was ever born, I cause you and everyone so much trouble. So much trouble."

Later in her adult life, when legal psychologists invented "anger management," Brenda tried to make analogies with labor management, time management, relationship management. None answered why this tantrum physics lay at the dark rabbit-hole of her brother's isolate ragings. Their two different adoptive parents, her father and his mother who got together sensibly to pool money, abhorred any physical reaction to the batshit crazy outbursts Leo erupted like volcanic ash all over their lives. "Something"—something back there in the Derg years—was the only negative word out of her eternally long-suffering Americanized father's lips about Leo's descents into the hells of his own digging.

Brenda would think years back into their childhood together back in Addis before the botched rape, herself at dinner-table height, at TV console height, at five-foot bookcase height, at upper freezer compartment height, could not grow tall enough to overlook Leo's miserably open eyes, his pinking shears-cut hair because he couldn't, wouldn't sit long enough in the straight-backed chair to barber him once every two months. The behavior modification drugs quashed the worst of it, in that Leo didn't in fact go from torturing cats to cutting himself to breaking smaller children's ankles and fingers.

Leo entered uneasy passivity, like something spilled out and wiped up. But the life flood of himself seeped out of its chemical dam. He dwindled into his twenties in Brooklyn, got besotted with cleaning his sister's green Cutlass, making it shine, brushing away acorns and twigs from its hood. He thinned, and Annie Fortuna his biomom back in Addis preceded him into the grave at fifty-two, caught and savaged in prison for Resistance-organizing two months before the criminal Communist regime was ousted. Despite all that medical knowledge could do to reshape Leo's little substance, he was dying. This could not be in the twentieth century in America. It was. One helper, a Catholic social worker self-destructively invested in her client's fate. She prayed a rosary of novenas. On the ninth day of the final bead, the final Hail Mary, Leo Brenda's brother vomited nothing but choked on it and was gone. Their mother stopped talking, cleaning, caring, just sat, plopped, quit life. The father did his best to be there for Brenda, who continued to carry her brother's darkness because he had endured it. It all threw her back into reliving the botched rape in another country that her first years in Brooklyn had defanged. Leo was the damned part of her own living legend of being alive herself.

"Father was right," she told Gole in five sentences that repelled him. "Leo never should have been born. His life was not a life. And it wrecked ours. There was nothing in it that left anything for the rest of us to want. He had, literally, no business being alive."

Never should have been born.

Gole got stuck on that sentence. He tried to think it through:

Never should have been born. The myth of origins. To get back to the source, the first prime move, to have a beginning. The myth of not having a myth of origins. Goleman Eck sought a better theory of the unborn. Here is what he came up with.

*

The birth of the unborn happens in two connected ways only. One is a water-baby story of learning to swim just to be part of the stream of effluvia that washed the nutty fetus down counter-clockwise with the planet's own such motion, at least north of the Equator. This is the first law of human motion. To the left, to the left, heigh-ho, heigh-ho. It takes months, say, six after one's initial three-month dismissal flush. The little homunculus measures larger than a minnow—just a handful of transparencies on a curled blueprint—but smaller than a tied bunch of little orange carrots. The authoritative source here is, of course, Harlan Ellison's "Croatoan," about a descent into the underworld of fetuses flushed down the New York City sewers.

Flash: In "You Killed Teddy Bear," Sal Mineo in a crying jag threatening to drive a Boy Scout jackknife into Burt Lancaster's baby son, Burtie. Lancaster raises his shoulders first, his head, and he does that withering smile of contempt. Sal-baby collapses in mewling humiliation, turns the jackknife over on his wrist but it isn't even open. Lancaster toddles Burtie in the air, the giggling gulping little infant, barely clears the kid's head under a ceiling beam. Then, because he is the father, he moves his boy out of harm's way. Right there, Sal loses the dream of being Burt's son. He folds into the cheap shiny darkness of his studded biker's jacket. Sal, you understand, has just been unborn.

Gole had re-imagined that movie moment a hundred times, in a hundred cuts onto the editing room floor. Burtie wins a ride on Burt's high trapeze along with Curtis and Lollobrigida. Sal rinses down into the drain, again. Burtie sings before the throne. Sal gurgles, swallows himself all the way down to the dregs of a septic-tank grave to play out the rest of beaten, murdered extinction he will never be done with. Eck claims he directed, produced, adapted, screen wrote, starred in, did the cinematography and music for, and distributed it worldwide. It is one of the great primal scenes.

And here is what he wrote down: "The search led me to buying my genetic map, my planet chromosome geography. Of late, we've learned that no, we didn't all climb out of the Oldavi Gorge. Origins are multiple, though Africa and China lead in all of the climbing out packs of pre-human ancestor creatures. The human genome is a warp and weft of many colors. There is no such thing as a single ethnicity. We've got planet written all over us. Son of man, son of woman, son of a million men and a million women. Still, the evidence they can come up with from blood and saliva, a puncture and a swab, will point to Middle Europe, or Micronesia, places of tundra and places of sand. You get a general orientation for your initial $79 fee, then if you want the full monty for $250, you, I, come from there, and some from there, and some from yet over there. From the aspect of eternity, that ought to be enough to know.

"But it wasn't eternity that aborted me, it was a woman and a man, sneaking little fucker-me out before I caused too much trouble. They have specific addresses, cell phones, pecker and vaginal tracks like no one else in the world. So close, so far away. That's the maddening part. They're around the fucking corner, for Christ's sake, a million miles away. Mommy, Daddy dearests, you did not have to forsake me because I wasn't convenient.

"'You little shit, they tell, you would have done exactly the same thing in your turn as we did in ours. We were no more ready to have a child than you were to have us for parents. And please, don't forget that you're the one who disappeared into your post-aborted life. We didn't know how to find you, in all the genomic havoc of the world, we hadn't a clue. Parental homelessness like ours has no other origin than you. You'd be the home wrecker, son of our green, stupid green loins. Stop making as if you're insulted somehow forever. At long last, our aborted Apollo, give it a rest. Yours, Zeus, Leto.'"

*

Eck was twenty-five when he met Sturgis Macmillan, who was, as he said, getting to be over fifty while testing yearly for HIV. Himself a Black New Orleans wind energy former wunderkind, Macmillan happened to hear this Goleman Eck's paper at a conference that pretty much turned a major technical issue 180 degrees to oh, ah, . . . right—it was staring us all in the face and the young guy shows up out of nowhere with it, and he doesn't even look right for the part. After Gole's paper, Stur, as the business knew him, came up and introduced himself, how much he was intrigued with the paper, where are you now in your career. Within five minutes talking to him, he told Gole a year later, he knew it: "You, I'm taking you on. You, I want you and I will have you. You, get in the ring. I'll show you some stuff."

He liked to turn on a Southern Daddy bit. "I'm Stur. When I first started out, they called me nigStur. Well, son, Stur became a star, and I can shed some light on you."

Aborted Gole was curious about men, to say the least. In the mid-third decade of his unstillborn life, Gole experimented sexually, multisexually he thought the better term for whatever he was trying to find out. Thought-leader in wind energy Sturgis Macmillan pursued Eck like a cultured older gentleman while he mentored him professionally about contacts, the right ways and the wrong about putting one's best ideas forward by giving the bosses room to think they'd had a major hand in developing them. Stur recast Gole not in Stur's own mold but in what was Gole's right form when Gole didn't yet know it. He turned his trans-natural love-intent into a highly noticeable up-and-already-arriving scientist-engineer in a cusping industry that was just learning how to sing its song of planet Earth survival. In doing so, Stur unwittingly set the conditions for Eck's later fall.

After the first two dinners, a respectful promising hug after the first, their third time together was a chatty stroll through The Mall in Central Park. Sun-flecked autumn elm leaves swirled high above them like impressionist glass beads. Eck usually found a tremendous promise of survival in the cathedral arch of the miraculously surviving elm trees. This was one of his favorite places in the city, in the world. In a certain light, which was right now, they could look like one of his company's most successful batteries of wind turbines. But right then, he was going down his old drain and wondered if this whirling Black man could pull him out.

They got to Literary Walk and sat on a bench across from the bronze statue of Robert Burns on its block marble pediment. In front of it, a vendor in cutoff jeans and a sleeveless muscle shirt was entrancing two children by using sticks to make huge soap bubbles from a bucket. He showed the children how to wave the ballooning bubbles up into the air before they burst in the face of Burns. The mother gave the vendor a couple of dollars. He approached the two men, but Sturgis waved him away pleasantly and read to Eck from the Central Park Summer Guide unfolded on his lap. About the poet up there, sitting on a tree stump, quill poised in right hand as he gazes open-mouthed and heartbroken up at some vision of Mary Campbell, his impossible love, while manuscript pages of the poem he's writing about her collect around his feet.

Eck wasn't caring about the doomed Burns. He said to Sturgis, "You said your memory," and that's as far as he got.

Sturgis tried to figure out altogether his eyes, his brow, his jawline, teeth behind his open lips. He wanted to know what, this guy from another generation?

"I guess it was an odd thing for me to offer so soon," he said. "But you're twenty-five and I'm not and this age difference." He didn't finish the sentence.

"The change in life," Eck said. "Do you think men have a change in life? Had a change in life?"

Neither one of them was ready to go where he started them going, not now, not yet, maybe not at all. It took Sturgis another widening moment to make up his mind about loving Gole for sure, for short or long. Gole got that, stayed attentive.

"I got a girl pregnant early," Sturgis told him. "Fifteen."

The searchlight snapped on in Gole, swept over land and ocean and into the sky above the long arch of elm trees. He told himself yet again about the elm trees. They were arboreally famous. They survived the elm blight that killed most eastern elm trees in the U.S. They didn't get cut down and shredded for mulch.

"Did she abort?" Gole looked at the classically handsome Afro-Caribbean face to see if Stur was going to do something like belt him in the mouth with his mahogany-leather carry-all.

Stur did clutch it away from his staring at it. "Something really wrong happened to you," he said. "Tell me, and I'll tell you I'm sorry it did." Gole believed that, because he saw the way Stur was watching Gole's mouth as he spoke, the way one person watches another's lips just before offering to kiss.

"I held an interesting job," Gole said. "Want to know what?"

"Sure I do," Stur said.

"I ran the handbag boutique in Saks. Vuitton, Fendi, Ferragamo, Jimmy Choo, Prada, Chloe', Suvimal, Eddie Borgo. That bunch." This, too, was true. Jack-off of all trades, this ever-forming, never-formed Goleman.

Stur uncrossed and crossed his legs. He was wearing handsomely fitted charcoal-gray corduroy pants. "Huh," Sturgis said. "You're telling me you served expensive women womb clutchers."

"I used to say they could put all those designer names in any one of those bags and still have room for a soup thermos."

"Inside the bag, the womb clutcher." He was playing with Gole, they both knew.

Still, he wanted to know, had to know. "Did you, she, both of you abort?"

"Wherever your search is going for whatever you want from a man my age."

"Did you?"

Gole was surprised to see him bend his head to the side a little, as if slipping a punch, warding something off coming up from inside him.

"No. We lost it. Of course, that doesn't mean she—it was a girl I wanted to call Audrey or Kathryn or Grace—ever went away. Long time before I knew I loved men. Are you interested? Just tell me, younger man, are you?"

"Yes," Gole said. This man before him had something, knew something that could help him, even for a while.

Gole kept talking. "She. Audrey, Kathryn, what was the other one? Oh, Grace. Of course. What a marvelous trio to choose from as the baby girl formed and you could decide. Maybe you would have been sixteen when she came?"

"Yes," Sturgis said. "Sixteen. Then more. This year she would have been twenty-nine. Think of her. Grace, Kathryn, Audrey. Twenty-nine, her exquisite best. Free of unworthy men because she just wouldn't have a one of them."

Sturgis looked at Robert Burns, as if he might come down and speak a love poem to them both, not just to them because, in the silence right now, they needed it.

"John Keats," he said, "was terrified of what happened to Burns in life. He wrote something about him like, 'His Misery is a dead weight upon the nimbleness of one's quill,' and something like 'He talked with bitches—he drank with Blackguards, he was miserable.'"

"Some lesson here?" Gole asked him.

"Don't let your misery be a dead weight upon the nimbleness of your life. Or anyone else's. Now tell me your story." He brushed his fingernail edges together and said, "I had an Aruban grandmother who once said of an old suitor, 'I wouldn't have him if he had diamonds falling out of his arse.'" He put his right hand lightly on Gole's left thigh. Gole covered it with his left hand, just as lightly.

Gole began to speak his story, started by saying, "Born away from. Abort means that. Isn't it a beautiful thought in a strange way?" He told Sturgis all the rest, up until then, in a thin rushed version.

Sturgis and Gole did well for a great year. Their wind turbine prowess began to be one really good answer. They had fun, a rising senior-junior couple in the industry heading into the future gleefully, learned enough about each other's dislikes, could both cook different good things for their evening meals, could give to each other evenly in bed. They did so in Gole's apartment in the city, on Stur's flower farm in Georgia so full of every color in the blooming world, and in Scandinavian places of expanding night where they famously planted giant avian wind turbines for a healing planet's energy needs, and in Indonesian land reclamation projects their science pulled from chemical ash heaps and long-poisoned wells. Together, they made big difference in small time periods. Sturgis' body signaled age advancing though slowly, while Gole's face and arms and loins radiated joy for him. He believed Gole's abort story in his heart, but his scientific common sense told him it was impossible that it was as he said. Gole slid into disappointment at that same old, same old reaction. It deepened the sense in him at twenty-five rushing on thirty that he was alive differently from all good people such as his Sturgis for the year they had together.

The day Stur felt the need to tell him a few truths he knew it was over. It had gone so fast for him that he ended up wondering at Stur's swift capacity to bundle him all up in one narrative of him. Sex between them approached accusation, mayhem, him riding atop him claiming he would fuck some sense into him, his flattening his back against the mattress and moving underneath to blunt the deepening insistent rhythm of him.

"I figured it out," Sturgis said.

"Then share."

"Because you were aborted as you claim."

"Claim?"

"It's a new kind of personal status. A different kind of registration."

41

"Claim?"

"So," and feeling older by the minute, Sturgis was determined to make Gole finish according to his will, "you could have been anyone, become anyone, anything. Like that now, you feel it? Let go, young man."

"Anyone," he repeated, fighting back, holding out, "anything?"

"Yes, yes, yes. Si, si, si. Free, free, free. From. Jesus! You bastard. I don't want to. Not yet. You first. You're such a fucking gentleman. You first now. Free, from that determinism—"

Gole used his younger strength to move him precisely, his way. Losing to him, Stur said, "You think of everything." He stopped trying to control him. Gole stopped resisting. He let Gole enjoy moving him that way. It was a different way of guiding him. They barely moved at all, but Gole was happy in this least motion.

Sturgis held out to complete his thought. "That determinism of being the child of a father, a mother—," and he let the orgasm take him up and down and up and down and he released into Gole in a perfect down movement to Gole's upward one that made him gasp and let him say ridiculously in breathed phrases where he was half-going with all this talk, "If government. Could reproduce your coming. Into being, it could engineer, you. Know what?"

"Engineer, train. Oh my dear general. Engineer. You brought the train into the station. Yes."

"A radical democracy of undetermined men, and you know what, the world's great age would begin anew at last." Sturgis rolled off, snuggled up against Gole's chest in his arms, and fell into a silly sleep still talking, talking about how free Goleman Eck was because he wasn't born right.

A day later, as he got into his office a little sleep-deprived but anxious to close their biggest deal yet, in Finland, Sturgis Macmillan's goodbye text came up on his phone.

"I wanted a younger man who knew how to cherish body, brains, and friendship with a man in the inevitable change of life. I wanted a man who had no filters about all that. So in walks Goleman Eck. My Eck in the flesh, let's leave each other. It's the right thing to do now. Agreed?"

Eck nailed Finland down by giving them everything they didn't even know they wanted. It was their consummate international business success, that afternoon after that early morning when Sturgis tried to fuck some sense into him.

Even so, Gole cracked like a heartbroken child. He went crazy looking for Stur on sidewalks, in high-end clothing stores, in subways, museums, street and avenue fairs, in pelting rain below the love-busted Burns agog at Mary-in-the-sky, political rallies under now culturally suspect statues, bottoms of bottles and shoulders of elegant fifty-sixty-ish Black men walking so far ahead of him so goddamned fast that he never had a chance to get near whoever it was who reminded him in the slightest way of his Sturgis, until he actually fell down a simple set of steps, face and wrists first and ankles up, fell down a regular drunken asshole with relationship trouble, just going through the courtyard to his own apartment building. Could this be he whom Sturgis had bravoed up as the undetermined male of the new democratic republic of full potential abortedness?

In an emergency room four hours later, an internist just about his age told him the X-rays and MRI showed no breaks, tears, or troubles.

"Do you do emergency abortions in this hospital?" Eck asked. He knew he was nonsensical. He didn't give a shit. He kept on talking. "Or do you send the women away to specialized abortion clinics, centers, whatever?"

His name was Fazail. Dr. Fazail said, "I'll look at your paperwork. Then I might be able to address your question to the attending physician." Gole liked his elegant Persian-inflected English.

"And you, kindly, an Arabian doctor, I thank," Gole said.

"Right," said Dr. Fazail. "Dude, you seem a little confused. So let me say directly, you're no longer an emergency."

"They want me out of here, so, right?" Gole said.

"It is my duty to so you inform," he said. His English became frazzled. Gole got annoyed.

"What about my question?" Gole demanded.

"The answer is yes and no. In your case, no is operative."

Gole was no longer an emergency. The doctor took a few minutes to write through three pages about him on a clipboard of paper, using the same kind of hospital-logo pen Gole signed in unendurable pain at the check-in nurse's desk.

The pen gave Gole a sense of invulnerability. He went nuts, ripped the ribbed-sole hospital socks off his feet, stood up to them violent. No one of them could restrain him. Together, the floor staff was swift and expert.

Gole woke up after hand-over-hand climbing up a black cavern of opiate pacification. He had a big bill to pay for the surgery recovery room mess he made. They told him he kept on saying, at various decibel levels, "The elders are living longer. The elders are living longer and taking up the places of the unborn."

The hospital staff on shift did comic riffs on him for one another. At 6:00 the next morning, a polite male nurse awoke him to remove his catheter expertly. Eck slept for another hour, then ate the full breakfast, showered strong on his own, dressed, signed the release papers, and went to the elevators. Not a single staff person said goodbye to him.

*

When Eck was seventeen, he met a man at a high-school football game. The man's name was Theo Horvath.

Eck didn't have a date or a friend to watch the game with. They both sat apart and alone until family spectators pushed them together. They got to talking when Gole could no longer ignore the old man's angry bit about the sloppy, unexciting game. Mr. Horvath said he was close to ninety. He had a life story. By then in his life, Eck was interested in people who could tell one. Horvath still had a strong face, skin like white birch beaten on by the wind for a very long time. His voice came from under his chest cavern, or as if from a coal stove under stairs no one climbed anymore. It didn't take his curtained eyes long to fix on young Gole a stare out of some sunless world. He saw Eck the way suspicion sees things not true to nature.

In a spastic attack from his whole nervous system, the unfortunate losing quarterback threw the ball from midfield into the bleachers to his right. The boy (these players were still Eck's age, and their helmets and shoulder pads hung loose on their unfinished bodies) cried and must have wanted to fall into a hole and disappear. Time stopped for him in his humiliation. The coach yelled at him to get the hell off the field. Gole knew that boy.

"You feel it, too," Horvath said. "It must be an awful door he's seeing open for the first time." An ache in his accent dug into Eck's hearing.

Something in that image Horvath used made Gole ask him his question sooner than he expected. "Where were you when you were my age?"

The game kept up its frayed motions, but the crowd of families made noise as if they were watching the adolescence of the pros. The quarterback was down again, on one knee as if beaten. A circle of trainers and players ringed him tight.

"A camp," he said. "In Europe. I am Roma. Gypsy."

"You didn't exist." Eck was numbed in the mirror of him. His endurance. "I think I know of that life. How did you get out?"

"I walked out. No reason, no logic. I left the camp. Pure chance. No meaning to it. You remind me of young terrified men I left behind there. I am sorry for you. What's your name and what are you doing here?"

"You left the camp? Just like that?" Gole asked him, teenage loud. He didn't want Horvath to have done that. Nazi camps made terrible sense to him; leaving one did not. That had something to do with his history class just having finished the state-mandated unit on the Holocaust. He'd kept expecting it to yield a version of the story he was looking for. In that, it failed him.

A woman in a fur coat a bleacher below them turned around fully to look at them. She had unnatural blonde hair and thin brown sunglasses. Her mouth opened as if to beg them to stop. The man in a green parka totally inappropriate for this crisp fall weather took her elbow and pointed to the field, where the quarterback stood up and shook himself hard all over like a big dog.

"Aye," Theo Horvath said. "I left the camp. It just never left me. Let me tell you some things. A survival list of all the nothing I learned in the camps."

"Please do," Gole said. He watched the disoriented athlete, whom he knew. He could never be his friend, but he did once in a while talk to Gole, sometimes asking about his family. He seemed to know something about Gole's family when he asked nicely enough, something to fill in one of its details for him.

"Please do not," the woman said out over the heads of those in front of her, as if to the quarterback boy.

"Do not stare at fish packed in ice. Do not drain septic tanks. Do not go to strong-wind beaches at high tide or you will see tens of thousands of minnows washed up, stranded, unable to get back in. Not even the crazed shorebirds want to eat them."

Now there was tremendous booing going on. It wound the quarterback into letting an assistant coach and another replacement player limp him to the bench. Horvath's pain at this was obvious. What was occurring became more predictable.

"Who is that boy to you?" Gole asked the gypsy Holocaust survivor.

"How did you know?"

"It seems that painful, awfully so. I'm sorry."

"He's my great-grandson," he said. "And you? You have also some trouble in your house that goes a long way back?" He insisted, "Do you?" and seemed to want to push creepers into Gole's whole right shoulder.

Gole just kept quiet, pretended he'd lost interest in the old survivor's death-in-life. He figured he couldn't tell the difference between his great-grandson out there, if it really was, and Gole. Gole listed to himself. No great grandfather. No grandfather one or grandfather two. Father. Unknowable memories, huge hailing stones, there in the high-school football field, a bronze October Saturday afternoon in other people's world.

The last thing Horvath was telling him as Gole moved away from him was this. "Change is good. So always carry nineteen cents with you. That way, at least once a day, you won't have to make any more change. Not for anybody. Nobody." It could pass for wisdom.

So Gole had known this very Horvath kid since junior high school. A kid named Clive, who was this self-paralyzed quarterback three years earlier than this day's disaster for him, descendant of the old Roma survivor.

Clive Horvath and Gole had been lunchroom acquaintances who had an aversion and an attraction to one another in thirteen-year-old half-hateful ways. When Gole got the handsome Clive to notice him, Gole rushed to make up lies about a family, while Clive bent away from him in the worst shyness Gole had ever run into other than his own. Gole had by then masked the reflexive groveling mode with impatience at simple manners. It was really odd, Gole's invading of Clive's closet-like space he wanted to make even smaller to get away from Gole, without actually having to move away from him to some other part of whatever room, or hallway, or recess corner they happened to appear in together.

How Clive Horvath grew into the senior quarterback carrying that isolation within him told Gole Clive's awful susceptibility to shame, failure, humiliation. Clive's gypsy blood made him constitutionally cut-out, inept, dangerous even. It was a generation-skipping gene. His father, Orlando Horvath, was a town crier in all ways, a selectman with a straw boater driving his classic T-bird convertible slow in the Memorial Day Parade, a smile like a flag. He wasn't at Clive's breakdown game. For Clive's mother, he chose a Minnesota Methodist as far away from Romania as he could get who sent out winter solstice cards.

Still, that throw Clive made, or actually didn't, or unmade, stuck with Gole as one of the few clean signals one gets, but doesn't understand just then. Clive had been forced by the three generations of men before him, from six on, to learn how to throw a kid's javelin straight, how to move, even in slow motion, from a block up into an uppercut, swim straight breathing after every fourth stroke, and shoot, straight, his own .22 rifle at the family's gun club. They wanted Clive to inherit the habit of being ahead, in advance, in all things. Clive told Gole that the thousand years of Roma around, underneath, sideways had led old Roma Horvath into the concentration camp. It was as if the later Horvaths agreed with the extermination of gypsy rebellion as a good thing in the modern world. So when Clive's throw aborted, fell into parts, here, there, and even wherever all directions into one, Clive fell apart on the field, angry and twitching, "*comme une fille,* like a fucking girl," the shop-teacher coach from Montreal growled. Even Gole, Horvath, and the appalled fur-woman heard him up in the bleachers.

Exactly. It just took a few more years, and American Roma fathers in sequence from survivor Horvath down, writhing in their nightmares about it, before beautiful Clive started becoming gorgeous Cleave and letting her friends call her Gypsy. Gypsy and Gole hooked up in New York a good many years after that game Clive threw away. This was soon after multi-sexual Goleman Eck lost and almost got over the great gay Black wind genius. The still beautiful if nowhere-in-life Cleave Horvath was good to Eck that one night, when the closet became one last time in Eck's sexual life the biggest room in the funhouse.

*

This time-reversing part of Goleman Eck's story needs to get his two adoptive families into it. From both of them, first of all, he was used to more off-the-wall answers as to where he came from than serious or comforting ones.

In the second one, the Kilpartridges under Big Red Killer, the cross-New England toxic medical waste disposal tank-truck driver, Eck got an older sibling, Maryalice, who said, "Shit on a rock and the sun hatched you," or "All that was left before Green Stamps went belly up," or "Leaked out of Pop's brake-fluid lines into a rusted cookie mold of a baby with three big buttons." Or from Big Red himself after nine beers without moving once from his feet-up position on his lounger. "You came out after ten days in steerage from a hunger country from your emigrating sixteen-year-old sister who had a graveyard cough the whole way."

Mrs. Killer said that was the most she'd ever heard Big Red say since he talked her into marrying him one fated day in 1973 on Essex Street in Lawrence, Massachusetts.

"Never you mind him," she told the shaken boy. Instead, Mrs. Killer, from the old woman who lived in the shoe world, talked about getting him from the previous parents via adoption angels. Gole pictured them filing adoption papers in their wings. He shut down wondering about it after a terrifying incident with another foster-Killer sibling commissioned to them for a fixed term.

Armand was twelve to Gole's seven. Again, he never got settled on a birthday date or even a steady birthday month. Armand kept trying to get jizz. He used to make Gole watch him try in the upper bunk bed Gole slept underneath for five years. Armand stuttered and wouldn't keep his hearing aid in when Killers weren't around.

Gole figured Big Red and Isabel lied to Armand and he was really fourteen. One late afternoon upon his bunk, he finally got it to come out, so much and so quick that Gole's face and neck felt slimed. Gole fell off the bottom bunk and went berserk on the shag rug. From above Gole, Armand wiped his hand on his stallions-illustrated sheet, "That's that's that's how you you g-g-got here."

Gole refused to eat that night and got put in the bed sleeping alcove to stop his disobedient pride and wastefulness. All night long, he saw Armand's cum shooting tentacles out at him, trying to get him back from the mess he came from. In his thirties, successful and holding together in many ways, Goleman Eck could still call up recurrent images from that memory, a certain taste, a whole paralysis of body, awful shame, and the dread he had to wipe off his face like tubercular spittle.

Then there was the earliest home. He had more reasons than most not to trust memories of what happened when he was three. Four, as for most normal kids, is a more trustworthy age for remembering colorful or miserable events. Still, Gole was three, and this goes down around him.

He is for some reason all alone in his favorite place, the kitchen. It is late afternoon. A window open a couple inches lets breeze in. He has pulled a few pots out onto the speckled brown linoleum from the cabinet under a butcher-top counter. All the pots and pans (so many of them!) had been arranged and situated by size and shape, stacked within one another or stood up side by side in rows. He unstacks, he restacks, he un-rows, he re-rows. But a small Teflon cookie sheet leaning vertically is stuck, won't budge.

He squeezes himself into the cabinet to get a better hold on it. He kicks out his right leg, and the cabinet door opens wider, letting in more kitchen ceiling light. He's directly over the shiny Teflon cookie sheet. His whole little face is getting reflected in it in a wavy way that delights him. He wants this sheet out onto the floor. Maybe he wanted to bang on it, use it to make his happy noise on its face.

Just as he gets his hands on either side of it, an arm the size of his whole body snaps it up and away from him. He screams and he screams, it seems for a long time, at least as long as from when he first squatted down to open the cabinet door. No matter the screaming and howling his tantrum mounts. He is crossly forbidden to pull out the pots and pans again. The cabinet door is shut in front of him and hooked tight. He is left to sit right there until he stops all that racket. His heart aches, every time he remembers it.

When you have no stories of beginning—"We brought you home after you had two days under a violet warming light, darling, and you took the breast immediately"—you can't help but find your own. One of his personal identification blanks for credit cards, banks, department stores, and such is "Victoria F. Stein." The creature tells the creator who abandoned him his first sensations: cold, heat, light, dark, then on to fire, rain, stones, and wind. So Gole told himself constantly revised stories of light coming through crib slats, sunburn on the unattended crown of his infant head, little milky fingers inching under a teat made crusty by his desperation to suck, flecks of rain on his ankles from drops the breeze shakes off porch rose leaves.

Eck wanted to begin some such way. None of it was real, or any more real than a dream of a face come up out a wash of flowers and claiming him as a prize for her golden cats. He created a hundred such tales, the purest lies to match the most searing truths. Victoria funded his orphanhood. Victoria was his puppet queen, pulling the strings that made him start pointing, mouthing vowels, moving his knees under him that meant he'd learn to read across lines on pages. Victoria came to him in the Killer house when he read the *Classics Illustrated Frankenstein*. He inhaled her as his own starting point. Because he had her as a delusive truth, he never made the mistake of confusing the creature with its creator.

Then on, it was all reading, all the world of it, for years while Goleman kept his own silence, counsel, and waited for his ghostly heart to grow fully into its flight from suicidal rage. He was not, ever, as far as he could find out, born. An infant, a toddler, a preschooler on a tricycle, he lived without that assurance.

THREE

"Cancer's no more of a killer than abortion."

That's what the talk-show host said on AM America. That stuck with the Attorney General Candidate Ashley Gottsch, looking for noise and controversy as election season heated up for anti-establishment conservatives in the Family Reunion Party. Gottsch's initials already made her AG, born for the job, she said, dying to take it over, she said. AG candidate Gottsch noticed a cancer-awareness week thing downtown at Urban Community College, called Relay for Life. She went to it to be seen supporting the Fight Against Cancer and to distribute fifty or a hundred more of her new stickers. AG for A.G. At various times, she liked to be AG, A.G., AG for A.G., Ashley, Gottsch, or the candidate, depending on whom she was in front of, confronting, or fronting. Multiplicity with an evolving core was the key to staying interesting to the voters in the political culture that faced her out there now. Reactiveness was all.

The many students and the several committed adjunct faculty organized all-night walking laps around the inside of the Urban athletic center. There were raffles, a DJ, and soda and chips. There were wrist bands, balloons, copper bracelets, masks, all wearables against disease. One prostate cancer survivor three years out of radiation spoke with emotion etched by the humor of endurance. Another speech was delivered alternately by each of twin twenty-six-year-old sons of a mesotheliomic 9/11 first responder gone for one year just that day. He had been, one son said, a first responder to him when he was a lost teenager; he was there, the other son said, for anyone really troubled who ever knew him. Reading the local newspaper account of the Relay for Life, AG for A.G. Gottsch heard something promising.

She got her office people to set up, unofficially and with no visible connection to her, a pro-Life event called Delay for Life, pretty much on the pattern of the cancer Relay. Delay was at the old state armory because it had a big rotunda. The event caught hold with pro-Life hearts and minds and raised $7777 to the penny for teen abortion alternatives. The latter group brought their lurid posters and placards but put them image-side against the wall when requested to do so by the St. Bridget women's auxiliary. Mary Rice was one of that group.

It had been forty years. Long time to hide the afternoon when her young life rose and fell in the contractions and dilations that would not end and would not deliver into the blood and liquid of various colors dropping out of her onto, unbelievably, a red contour and a red flat sheet. Even now, at sixty, with ten good years to go, when she saw red, she looked for a different color.

Her speech for Delay had gone well, just eight minutes of personal testimony. It got tough at the point where she spoke the sentence of being told the fetus was being disconnected and taken away and she didn't ask to what or where. That challenged her breathing but she had enough presence just to stop talking, and the Delay rally people all understood the breath gap, and themselves they breathed in with her. Mary Rice squared her still-straight shoulders, took in the rows of people in front of the podium, and got ably and inspiringly to her concluding two minutes.

There was to be no perfunctory immediate applause for any of the Delay for Life testimonies and recollections. Nor did Mary Rice need any as she stepped down off the podium platform and stopped in front of the assembly to carefully untie the red cloth strip she'd agreed to around the waist of her black suit jacket as a symbol of where it still hurt. Then came the applause, sincere, measured, admiring. Delay for Life was off to an honest and dignified start.

Mary went to sit at a card table with AG for A.G., two of the latter's admins, and a hunched reporter wearing a beaded media ID necklace around her high purple collar. Each table set up inside the Delay walking track centered a multiple red bouquet—poppies, zinnias, petunias, and Empress of India nasturtiums—the language of flowers speaking the blood of the aborted, the anguish of the could-have should-have mothers. More red.

"Hello," the reporter said. "I'm Jenny. Jenny Rich." She held out her hand, but shortly, like the way she talked. "Online pool reporter."

Mary Rice only got half of the woman's limp fingers, barely to give them a shake up and down. That particular bit of dismissiveness always did annoy her in other women.

"Jenny," Ashley said, "has brought to my attention some funding irregularities within the local Planned Parenthood chapter."

"There's more," Jenny Rich said. She popped the top of a diet ginger ale can, held it up toward Mary Rice. "You imbibe?"

"Not this early in the day. Thanks."

The table laughed. "Very good," Ashley said. She took the can from Jenny and poured half of it into a coffee cup. She drank deeply and quickly, one eye on her cell phone clock. "Can any issue be put fast? I'm double-booked, of course."

"Of course," the reporter said, in a slight mock. "A multi-pronged integrative and integrated public survey of the money trail for abusive medical practices linked to the local abortion industry."

Mary said, "Let me guess. To advance AG for A.G. here's conservative base's recognition factor of her fundamental congruence."

Jenny smiled. "Exactly, if a bit of a mouthful."

"How's this one," Mary said. "Planned Parenthood is Delayed Parenthood."

"Also good," Jenny said, while the candidate nodded. "I'd like to feature your language spoken here just today."

"Or how about one for the other side?"

"Say."

"Row with the law or wade in the blood."

"Which side are you on? Sounds like both." Jenny Rich was in the PR business of not tolerating complexity.

Raffle tickets were being pulled and called at the podium. Mary's suspicions kicked in, like the buttons on her blouse calling attention to being left open.

"Your generation," the reporter said, though she was looking at the politician, who finished the possibly offensive notion. "The historical view of the malpractice of the murder, you understand. Women, like you, if I may say, carry the wound, the hurt for decades, but now." She trailed off.

Mary felt her sudden dry mouth, her own stare, the body language of being forced out of her decades of silence to them, to herself. Ashley Gottsch wouldn't have gotten to this point in her career by being stupid or inattentive to mixed emotions, tangled memories in people who needed to be behind her all the way into the voting booth in the fall of next year.

"Let me ask you a question, Ms. Rich," Mary said. "You might know, as someone who has to keep tuned. More than most, I believe."

"Jenny's enough. I just went to Brandeis." She put on her first grin. "You both went to Wellesley. Same time? Did you know each other?"

AG said, "Sometimes I think people who remember those

things weren't really there."

"I remember," Mary said. "It was one of those things. Different crowds. I did Classics. We probably knew more of each other than we actually knew each other."

"I was the business manager of the paper. All night long sometimes. And lacrosse. And some statistics and sociology."

"I didn't notice about the lacrosse," Mary said. That got them to another laugh and pause.

"A solitary at Wellesley, you?" Jenny asked Mary.

"Classics does that to you. You know, Priam's night journey to beg Achilles for Hector's body. Dark."

The reporter kept her eyes on Mary's for a good five seconds and said, "Kind of a parent's story, that one. The body of the child."

"For Christ's sake, Jenny," AG said. "Lois Lane, what are you fishing for?"

"'Sorry, Miss Lane,'" Mary had it by heart. "'I've been busy.'"

"I'm not sure," Jenny said. "Something's asking that here. Not me. I'm just the medium, the conduit."

"Sure you are," the candidate said. As was her way when she wanted to finish one thing and get to the next, she stood up abruptly. "Ladies, we have a beginning. Not sure yet of exactly what. But it feels like a beginning worth continuing. Right?"

"Right," Mary Rice said. "Politician's logic. Damn straight."

The AG hopeful laughed that off, and Jenny asked Mary, "You all right?"

Mary seemed to see a different reporter's face, conciliatory, solicitous, not just trying to get something reportable. Mary saw a different short brunette haircut, cinnamon-templed eyeglasses, dark cleavage of breasts not easy for short women to bear as they got older.

"No problem," she said. "I look forward to seeing your investigative style at work for the cause here."

"And," Gottsch said. "The right cause at that."

Jenny Rich breathed in audibly, stood up anxious to get away. Mary made sure that her whole hand got into Ms. Rich's this time.

*

Five minutes later, Mary Rice was out on the street, trying to figure out what she thought about any young woman's decision to do what she had chosen to do all those years ago. Abort and reboot. Not ready to mother, determined not to wear that saddle, push that wheelbarrow up twenty years of hill, shut the door on how she wanted to live her own life. All that young woman's determination not to lose her shot at the mark straight ahead and clear. She ended up shooting straight into her own heart, carrying that inoperable baby bullet in silence and unfinishable curiosity: what happened to her boy-fetus?

Still, she had a credo. She had it memorized as statement and question. There's so much to get over in life, why get stuck on the first awful breakage? What's a heart for if not to be broken? Doesn't a new one crawl out of the wreck to become leaner, tougher, with more sinew, less clog, maybe a half a toughened heart this time that won't let you take up with destruction again?

The thought got blocked by a vintage pickup in the quickening rain right in the pedestrian crosswalk. Like a cake of Ivory soap, it was white, except for the red Gothic script on its two doors, *Got Junk?* which at first she thought read *Gut Junk*, a different matter to her.

The open-backed truck gleaming at her had two large silvery bins in its bed. Otherwise, it was stone empty, not a shred of contents of a life piled and lumped up in wretched full display. She walked around the back of it to the driver's side. She saw a man in the driver's seat angling his left side mirror to catch a glimpse of her as she came beside him in the intersection. His window rolled down, his arm dangling down holding some of the raindrops atop dark unsleeved hair.

Mary stopped, stood straight next to him, her heels together. "Mister. Tell me, mister. Where does all the junk go? All the unwanted stuff?"

The man's voice was clear, which his face wasn't yet. "Lots of people ask me that. You know?"

"I first read your sign, *Gut Junk*," she said.

"Maybe that too," he said.

He began to fill in. He was mid-50's, square-built, over six feet, sleepy brown eyes over a Roman nose and plush lips that reminded her of a movie actor from her youth. Yes, Victor Mature. Raw much-married side of handsome. The robe of the risen Jesus. Their two heads on a steady plane one another seemed to click on a light in his easy eyes and he went for it with her.

"Want to know what else?"

"They ask you?" Mary said.

"Yes, pretty, senior lady."

"You hunt cougar, too?"

"They ask me that, just a whole lot more rare. Cougars age well."

"How about," and Mary sang it nicely to him. "Mr. Junk Man, show me your junk."

Now mega-white teeth stretched his inviting mouth, his Mediterranean healthy skin in pleasure.

"We meet before?" he asked her. "Some other life? You know, you're going to get killed in this one if you don't move."

An Uber was honking, its backseat passenger in mean little sunglasses saying through his open window, "Lady. Please. Lady. Get out of the way. Cross with the light you got now. Look up. See the coffee."

Mary grinned at him. "My goodness. That's a lot to say now, isn't it?"

She moved quickly around the front of Got Junk? Victor

Mature come back to life leaned over his seat, opened the passenger door for her. She saw that his hands were clean, fingernails cut square. He moved a pair of red and white work gloves from the seat. She climbed up easily, her legs still good and demure in her dark blue skirt. He extended her seat belt around her front, held it at a gentlemanly distance from her until she took it and clicked it into its clasp sharply.

"Tough to get a cab in this rain," she said.

"This time of day," he said.

"Will you take me—"

"Safely," he said. "Yes."

"Up to Washington Corner. I'll just get out there."

"Welcome to the ride to just there."

A little swarm of annoyed people came around his front. A few banged their palms on the truck's white hood. He shook his head at them. "Right. Figures."

She didn't answer his welcome of her or his acceptance of strangers.

The light changed. "Okay," he said and put it in gear, moved gingerly through people still taking chances in the final two seconds. "Safely," he added.

"I mean it, the safely," Mary said to him softly. She took the red and white work gloves off the dashboard and put them on. She flexed her right fingers open and closed in front of her face. "I'm not junk. Cougar not junk." She was glad that she had larger hands for a woman. They were like his, just elegant.

"So," Mature said and drove for a minute. "So, I'm really riding empty at the end of this working day. Lady?"

"Lady Cougar is to be treated well."

"Got it," he said. He drove as the traffic let him, a little forward, more wait, forward, Washington Corner a few blocks up within sight.

"So what's your first job?"

"Restaurant called Les Trois Souhaits, sous chef. Battery Park."

"What should I eat there when I go?"

"Onion tart. Scallops champignon. Pot au feu. Braised lettuce. Bread and butter pudding."

Imagining them all, Mary looked at his hands again.

"Why is it called Three Wishes? Is it from the three doors in the fairy tale?"

"Trois Souhaits specials, every day except Monday, which is dark. Appetizer, entrée, dessert. Three wishes."

He could keep up. She liked the company. She looked and nodded at the sleek maroon design of Got Junk?'s dashboard.

"This is one pretty, classic vehicle? What is it?"

"1988 Chevrolet 1500 Step-side pickup." It was a nice, quick mouthful.

"Where'd you get it?"

"Florida, Little Havana, long story. I use it for work sometimes. Transporting. Hauling. Dumping."

"You mean, like restaurant stuff?"

"Sure, that. Also other people's junk they dump, or deposit." He grazed his right thumb over his shoulder. "In the bed in the back there."

She turned left, pulling her seat belt open. She made out the backwards decaled words on his rear window. Dump It. She saw him turn his eyes front again from her chest. She studied his remarkable profile and noticed that his white beauty was a smooth standard shift, four-speed forward. The engine was neither loud nor quiet.

"What kind of junk?" she asked.

"Up to them. Usually been carrying it around, you know?"

"That's nice of you, a real service. Had to let go of it sometime."

"Exactly," Mary said. Something sure and fun was happening.

"Usually some actual thing that means, you know, something bigger, harder to dump."

"How do you dispose of all that?"

"Just take it for a ride."

"A long ride?"

"Depends on how long the ride takes," he said.

"Tell me what kind of stuff?"

His mouth turned down once in a well, okay curve, and he said, "A usable mini-fridge. Shovels a little rusty. Outgrown or flat-tired bikes. Departeds' clothes. Half a case of those little toothpaste tubes you get from the dentist. Tied-up stacks of *Playbills*, or maybe *Journal of the American Medical Association* or *Finance*, that kind of thing. Mismatched but same-sized pairs of washed socks. Once even, a hundred and sixteen unscratched Lotto tickets. You like, I can say more."

"But the stuff's always taken eventually?"

"Yup."

The van in front of them halted. Victor Mature braked. Mary Rice moved her right foot down.

He said, "Trust me."

"Why?" Mary asked him. It was an invitation. Finger by finger, she took the red and white gloves off, folded them, put them back on the dashboard so that they wouldn't slip down.

"SEAL's honor," Victor said. He turned for her reaction. She couldn't let him hear or see one.

Oh. Mary go 'round the roses—again?

*

She did not always like the big fellows. Mary called it a learned taste. When she first loved men, she went for those who didn't take up much space to be who they were. Her father, for instance, Rick Rice the furniture designer, talked mostly in his studio about his materials, to his materials. He was a short man. His feet stayed put in his work and in the marriage he treated like a home he and Pamela Harrison Rice furnished spare, expensive, inviting. One good house, one good woman. Come on in, friend. That a man who thought and lived such things had to quit this earth when his two children were six and three, Mary and Curley Crowley, just went to show something Mary never got on the right side of. Decency to the core was rotten to the gods.

The boy-man she got pregnant with at seventeen in a welter of sexual curiosity was neither decent nor rotten. Popolowski was maybe two inches taller than she dimly remembered her dead short dad Rick Rice had been. Popper won the state cross-country championship twice in a row, a good achievement for a garbage carter's son who started life bow-legged. Popper's grit was a good trait according to maternal Yankee Harrison lore that went back to Washington's battle for New Jersey. Mary loved him with her whole teen heart. Pop Popper knew people to go to when she loved his son like that too early.

"It figures," Pop tried to joke to his terrified boy-father. "What with my refuse business and all."

It was a rush to a medical connection for underage women in New Haven, a rushed invasion of her womb, then pain and jagged regret. Soon there followed the vacancy of losing eager Army volunteer Popper to a freak armored vehicle accident in an Arizona desert-warfare training exercise. Mary went to Wellesley, locked up her two dead men so that she had no more hiding room to inter manic-grown Crowley when he reached six-two and went into the Katahdin woods in Maine without even a knife or a radio or a map. Pamela Harrison Rice escaped in her own way. She just sat down on her husband's famous white sailcloth couch, befouled herself and it, let her insides quit and leak away, lost language, lost will, lost Mary, died.

Mary inherited, tended only steel needs, bet on determination and intelligence rather than all bad luck, became quite beautiful, useful and sought after in the world, neither a fool for love nor a monkey in anyone's circus. Around tall handsome men, she started to feel pretty good. Why was that? That's what she asked Dalton Blue on their second date.

She was living in one of those towns called by a president's name and Township, on the train line into the city. She met him in the Township Mall when he was manning a PBA-sponsored orphans benefit table in the food court. He didn't need to have that cop look, he filled the part naturally. They saw each other, fixed on each other without giving a single inappropriate glance.

She bought two raffle tickets. She couldn't miss the sturdy pretty chestnut-haired woman who became less preoccupied with shopping and with the moody-girl replica of herself slouching by her and who stood congenially by his table. Captain Blue's fingernails were squared off, healthy. That mattered to Mary, what a man's fingernails said about him. He talked easily about unfamiliar immigrant kids at Chelsea House, how they were smart but displaced, fiery but good to each other, wise beyond their single-digit years.

The pretty chestnut-haired mother framed a fetching smile and said, "This is really good and important work that you do. What got you interested in it, Captain? Do you have children of your own?" The daughter registered pain at her mother's forwardness, turning her head into "Oh, my, God."

Mary hadn't much interest left for the female competition thing, but she really wanted to talk to this man more. And, well, she could certainly do better than her competition.

"What do I win when I win?" Mary asked him.

That pretty much kept his attention on her alone. The steady woman's teenage girl, more makeup than face, had to pee bad. This was good, too. Busy mothers shouldn't be flirting with strong men. Mary liked that very much. Mother and child hurried off. Blue told Mary what she'd win.

"Lunch at Chelsea House," he said. "They read you stories. They ask you polite questions about what you do for a job. They show you their bed and closet. Then they serve you grownup tea. How does that sound to you?"

The etched clarity of his speaking, the straight military manner bothered her. The trained and restrained killer for civilization. Mary Rice saw no wedding band. She made sure he saw the same. His break at the table was just then. They walked a little ways together, tacitly agreed to sit at a coffee bar. They began, easily.

"Even if you don't win," Dalton Blue said. "If you'd like to visit, I'd be more than pleased to show you Chelsea House."

"How very good of you," Mary said. "What do you do as a cop?"

As a cop, he took in the tone of the question, the questioner overall. For some reason right now, he was okay with both. He told her.

"I could never get used to it, black coffee like that, what you're drinking there. At the station house, I keep my own whole milk in the fridge. Blue's, they say, don't even think about taking Blue's organic whole milk."

Mary Rice was determined to cut through the male putting her off what he did for a living. "No," she said. "Say something else about the kind of police work you do. I would like to learn how to shoot. I was a little girl, I wanted that." Blue still didn't come out from behind his code, but she could tell she wasn't irritating him either. Mary knew her own luck for respectfully gaining entrance to male warrior space. She thanked Pamela Harrison Rice for modeling that for her in the dead father's absence.

Mary asked him out, for Margaritas, two actually, and Mexican. He liked her directness, so worked at switching a night at the precinct.

On the second date a week beyond the first, for fish, he answered her question. "I think you like the bigger guys now because you want to cook more food, clean bigger clothes, have somebody to reach up to higher shelves."

"Somebody who could look up for me when I was down."

"You seem happy with food," he said. "I noticed that the

other night, the oxtail stew you ordered. I never thought of it before as a woman's dish. Is that an annoying thing for me to say?"

"No. Right. Funny. Do you cook?"

"I have to, because of the occupational hazard of eating on the street. Yes, when I can stay in. When I get a break from tracking the drug cartels that make Newark a leading industry."

"Cook for me as soon as you can. One slow evening. We eat your food. I pour your whole organic milk into your coffee. Then we go to bed. Deal?" It was such a simple offer, plainly put out there. He liked that. It relaxed him, which was its own excitement. She wasn't playing him, but it played well with him. He was, she could tell, capable of a lot more reason than cop logic.

In their time together, Mary liked to hang his braided police hat on the bedpost to her right. One night he put it on her head and it sank over her brow. She told him to leave it there. He let her call him Dalt. Blinded, she would say his name in threes. He entered her as she straddled him, and she moved on him slowly. He said she made him feel safer, that he thought about her just this way after he'd had to use force on someone, after, not during, because that could get him hurt, the word he used for the unnamed worse. Mary Rice told Captain Dalton Blue that his was the gentlest hard inside her that she had ever felt. At times, he picked her up onto him, held her up underneath, did not say a word or make a sound or move for a full minute until she shook and trembled and said to put her over on her back.

He did get her set up with a firearms instructor at the Academy after regular training hours. He did not choose to teach her himself, something she wondered about but didn't pursue with him.

The night her raffle ticket actually did win, she told him about the fetus and infantry soldier Popper lethally burned in the mock desert firefight to rescue mock Army engineers. For obvious reasons, she had a hard time on the visit to Chelsea House with children some of whose cartel parents were dead, making the precinct a joke about immigrant working families. The children treated him like a god, and she was his lady, Lady Dalton.

She shot, and she shot, and she shot, until the instructor, an older friend of Dalt's who could not function as a street cop anymore, started worrying about Mary's tenacity, precision, obsession with shooting and said he no longer felt right teaching her, and besides, she already knew her way around the regulation automatic real well. Enough was plenty.

Dalton told her, "Gil says you're a pistol, all right. That's not a joke, Mary."

He was arranging peeled thin-sliced cucumber on poached salmon laid on a Harrison fish platter. She could eat as much of it as he.

"Don't take it away from me, Dalt."

"Are you going to kill somebody in particular?"

"Not shooting them, no." She found herself crying, lightly, but on the verge of breaking down. He insisted that they eat, and she cleared her mind of the fear and ate her share. He told her he knew it would come upon her again, that it was really hard.

"It's just that," she said. "It's just that I think it's his birthday. I'll be all right. Sorry."

"How old would he be?" Blue asked her. "Keep eating. Do you like the asparagus this way?"

"Thirty-nine," Mary Rice said. "It's nonsense talk."

"Did you want to be a mother again?"

"You are the kindest man I've ever known since I was, like, six. Let's leave it there. I didn't mean this to come surging up. I love the asparagus this way, roasted this way."

He told her as much as he could about the massive crackdown about to happen on a whole methamphetamine syndicate stretching from Newark to New Mexico and back, where it was his problem. He told her how he had been forced to stop an adoption from going through at Chelsea that he thought was going to be a natural. She liked that phrase of his about a baby boy's golden chance at the right family. A natural. But they weren't, and Dalton had been very wrong judging the family at first. They were high up in what was going to go down, come down, fall down hard. It was Dalt's experience that it wouldn't come around again for a baby boy like that, and not for that mother whose man turned out to be wanted for seventeen dead left to broil inside a trailer truck in the 110-degree Arizona desert, ten years before building up his huge drug monopoly in El Norte Newark.

Telling her these things, Blue frightened Mary Rice. He was talking from the side of licensed rage. She heard the words but could not hear her Dalt's voice when he said, "Actual retributive justice. It's an occupational hazard."

Blue heard her silence at that. "Hey," he said, "Gil teach you to shoot in a front squat?"

"Uh-uh," she said. "We didn't get to that."

He went into the bedroom. She heard him pulling his small gym bag from atop the closet. He came back with his unloaded .9 mm. service gun. He gave her a lesson. She watched him carefully. He got behind her, straightened her hips, positioned her shoulders a little forward, extended her arms, her two hands on the weapon, a slight downward angle of the barrel at first before taking an immovable sight line. He came around in front of her, had her stand up straight, the weapon in her right hand pointed down along her right leg. He said, "Assume the position." Mary did, three separate times. He grinned at her and said, "Up close, you'll make a beautiful deadly shot." Still his voice was speaking to her from a stranger place. She handed the gun sideways back to him. He said her stance and her hold were all good.

Mary Rice didn't hear any voice of his at all after that fish dinner, the night before the massive police raid went very wrong. Captain Dalton Blue and his rapid response team of seven tactical men and women got caught in an unpredicted multiple assault weapons ambush on the top floor and roof of a brownstone in an upcoming neighborhood for drug barons in the Chadwick Corridor.

The cops had them outnumbered two to one but the weaponry they encountered made them retreat until they could get armored vehicles in. The shootout turned into a tactical disaster when a pair of adopted Guatemalan twins from Chelsea House ended up grabbed from one apartment and held hostage behind a steel-plated door held in its middle by the iron bar of a police lock angled up from the inside floor. Dalton got down the fire escape to the gated window just as the little ones' knife-gutted bodies were thrown into the glass in front of him. Psychotic against psychotic now, Blue kicked in the cheap metal gates as if they were aluminum, threw a concussion grenade at running shadows, curled himself inside and emptied a double-barrel shotgun into a kneeling man's face, and chased another limping killer down a long hallway. He tackled him in the kitchen, got him up by the nape of the bleeding neck and shoved his heroin-numbed face into a lighted burner on the gas stove. By the time two female officers got Blue off the screaming guy, Blue's right hand was black and pieces of nose and lips dangled on the burner.

Big Blue was done as a cop, though some called him an avenging angel, a St. Michael driving Satan into the fiery pit. His right hand was destroyed, and Mary Rice nursed him in a months-long nightmare of seeing the little boy's and his twin sister's, not yet two years old, eviscerated tummies because he didn't have the right intelligence in leading his rapid-response team into the building filled with such murderous assault weapons. The cocaine and heroin and methamphetamine business had been ready to go to war. Blue's precinct wasn't, and some of that mistake lay on his shoulders and got his babies killed and their adoptive parents forever unhinged.

Mary tried to call back his strength, but her love could not stop his descent into hell. She proofed his apartment against all possible ways of hurting himself. He stopped talking to her. He never went near Chelsea House, which had attracted the attention and resources of a progressive church seeking to expand its ministry out of rich and white into an urban center. He stopped letting his oldest police mates inside his door to talk to him, because his mind turned on them, too. Her Viking god, her tall man in the Broad Street sun, her champion over the suffering unleashed on little ones, took himself and his broken heart completely away from her. He was not simply crazy with grief. He was ruined. He drove her into saving her own life from his utterly devastating misery. He promised he wouldn't hurt himself, wouldn't die as if that would have anything to do with his twins, he wasn't selfish that final way, no. When she knew that was true, that of course that was true of him, she left.

The night before she left, she squatted down in front of him, her hands together in dead-aim position, and pulled an imaginary trigger nine times. That released him, finally, and he cried as if his lungs were trying to release themselves up through his head. She got him up by holding the stump of his gone right hand that once had such beautiful fingers and fingernails, and he leaned on her and let her lead him into their bed. They made love to one another like two people who might find each other yet again in some other forgiving universe. Dalton Blue became a room in the house of her mind that was shut to her. It just went on being there, where she had to go on living in the rest of it.

FOUR

--Well, we all know some people we agree shouldn't have been.

--No. They should have lived. Later been executed or assassinated.

--Live now. Die later. What's the difference to you people?

--They could change. Change their whole personalities. Can't do that if they're cut down in or ripped out of the womb. Grow out of it. You see this picture, lady?

--Looks like John Kennedy's brains. In Dallas. Grassy knoll knickknack site. See it there.

--Look again. Five-month-old fetus. It's a boy. You see that it's a boy?

--Was it, he, no it. Viable outside the mother?

--The mother died giving birth to an aborted child.

--How do you know?

--Intern on our side. Right over there. In the abortion clinic.

--Center for Women's Reproductive Rights.

--We reproduce more women like you people, right like that, we'd have all that many more living dead mothers. Don't touch my sign, feticide. How about turning down that damn music at least? Can't we march and countermarch with some

71

dignity?

--Just wanted to get a hand on that picture of a dying refugee woman. Nice. You people kill twice and claim life's on your side like God.

--She was induced, on that Syrian raft off the coast of Greek Cyprus, where the little boy washed up.

--So that's abortion, too?

--Look. See that guy, no shoes on, about five chain lengths down. Came to our meeting the other night. Claims he was aborted.

--And I was resurrected.

--So there we are. Dead end. You know, by the way, that the president wants to create a new entity within DHHS, the Conscience and Religious Freedom Division? There's a new order in this country. We're gearing up against you. Hey, hey, vote, call, Roe v. Wade is gonna fall. You listening to me?

--Row with the law, or wade in women's blood. You listening to me?

--Feticide isn't funny, lady.

--That guy. He somehow doesn't look right. White hair is weird. What's his name? Why don't you get him some shoes?

--He doesn't say a name.

--I'm looking at someone who's fundamentally scary. Does he, the aborted grown-up male, support the rights of the unborn being greater than those of women?

--Truth told, as you say. He's a little scary. He says, said, sticks with me for some reason. Said, "These Hail Mary people give me a migraine."

--That's maybe because they're never in unison.

--That's a pretty piece of bigotry from you, lady. They have diverse accents. From all over the world. Not just from women's studies departments in seventy-thousand-dollar colleges in the Northeast.

--That the only prayer they know in English, sort of? Isn't Fruit of the Womb a men's underpants manufacturer? Okay, not funny. Look, where's he going now?

--He drifts off, and back on.

--He dresses the same as all the women here? White top or shirt, black skirt or pants?

--Sorry, what?

--Where'd you go?

--Him. Said, the history of abortion is the origin and history of massive misery, depression, he says. He has a list. Like anxiety, unfinished schooling, unclaimed jobs, inability to love, produce children of their own.

--I suppose, yes. Look, he's coming back, walking fast in his black socks. That must hurt.

--Lone stranger.

--Uh, oh. Detail of police. I'm out of here.

--This is going all wrong. What are they doing encircling him? They should be wedging us away from each other, not focusing on one alone.

--Oh, my God! He's spinning the air, keeping six of them off of him. They'll hurt him bad. No violence, officers! No police violence, officers! Please, no violence!

*

One of the few people who believed Gole was a nun, who assented to the mysteries of God's ways. Sister of Charity Agnes Coleridge was a true and pious intellectual, educated by her order through her Master of Social Work. She'd been allowed to publish in refereed journals in the discipline two parts of her master's research on myths of origin among a certain kind of successful adults. These adults, as infants or toddlers during natural disasters or genocidal, imperial or revolutionary wars, had really or figuratively been cast aside, so to speak, aborted after actual birth.

Sister Agnes Coleridge claimed no ancestry to the poet. Neither did she question anyone's need to look at her and fantasize it. She did have the poet's big ascending forehead under her wimple.

"Why," Gole asked her, "did you believe me?"

"Because," she said. "I prayed."

The non-sequitur to the side, he didn't for a minute want to lose whatever friendly support someone as vibrant and politic as she might have the empathy to offer. She held as well to one principle in the universe, natural law. If God made the order of things such that natural law (say, the laws of nature) came to man through man's own acquisition of knowledge, then God could contravene natural law in some such alternation of perception in man.

"That perception," she told him, "is the acceptance of miracle," and she laughed in her marvelous hundred-foot-high cathedral way. "Which is why miracles are even more rare than the two you need for sainthood. Jesus, one's tough enough as it is."

"It's a nice thought," Gole said. "But I don't think I'm a miracle."

"What do you call it, then?"

"A bicycle. When it matures and I'm really, you know. It. Then I call it a tricycle."

She was considering training him, step by step, for initial crisis coaching in the center she was starting. But then crazy was back again.

"Look," Sister said. "The guy with the sword we got—you got—out of here yesterday. Look. You still telling me that's not much of a sword? He looks like he's put on twenty pounds since then. How is that possible?"

"A dark miracle of a different kind," Gole said and stood very slowly, turning to the mad figure, taking in every detail he could process in too little time.

Sister said, "Here."

He took the Manhattan phone book, spread it out in front of him like a music box.

"What number did you ask for, again, sir?"

They each moved closer. "If you just put that thing down, I'll get you the number. You don't know how to use that thing. Where did you find it? A Chinatown bazaar? Did you special order it from the World War Two relic store out in Jersey City? I know how to get you the number."

The new weight Sister saw was body armor, a bullet-proof vest of some kind, oversized, its Velcro joined limply. Underneath was bright white, almost shining angel wing white, a South American shirt that had two front panels of hand-stitched blossoms, birds, and delicate reptiles.

Gole used his voice like that of a TV news reporter. "What's he saying, Sister. That's not Spanish. Are you trying to speak Spanish, sir?" Two, three more feet.

"Now I know him," Sister Agnes Coleridge said. "His mother was disappeared by the military in Brazil. His name is Eusebio Morales. Thirty years ago. It's Portuguese he speaks. He wants us to call her in English. English rules the world, he says. It can speak to her for him. He wants us to call her."

"Unbelievable," Gole said. "I know the feeling."

But then the poor thing for a sword that still had a cheaply sharp blade was coming down with both hands in a straight cut from over the man's head. Goleman figured the distance, the arc, and on the second huge step, he clamped both sides of the Manhattan phone book against the blade, turning his whole body first inside then around. The thing snapped in two pieces as the inept killer in the floppy vest over the sacramental baptismal shirt flipped over in the air and landed with a muffled breaking sound on the cracked linoleum floor.

Sister cried in a panic, "I don't know the number! Can someone look it up in the phone book?"

Gole dropped the sliced open phone book, fingered down the Brazilian's head to a carotid artery. He thought he'd thrown the swordsman into paroxysm. "Nine," he tried to say, "nine."

"Nine-one-one," Sister said, and did it with a jumpy finger.

It took the EMS squad longer to get Mr. Goleman Eck up and rational than to do all the paperwork with the police to get the thrashing toy swordsman strapped onto the gurney and into the ambulance outside. Sister understood what was wrong with him, so she tried to describe a mystery to the police detachment.

"You're saying," Patrolman Oliverra noted with his pen in the air between the two of them, "that this guy he just wiped out wanted you guys to contact his mother, disappeared now for thirty years? One of those people back then they used to throw out of airplanes? That it?"

"*Sí, señor,*" the nun said. Gole was going way inside, she saw.

Oliverra's short metal pencil was down, writing furiously in his wired report book. Something was eating him. He looked at the nun, then his partner, then at Gole alternately with each successive phrase he wrote down. He was an on-officer, all the time. But when he said out of the blue, "My family, too, my grandmother in Sao Paolo," he was talking to someone and somewhere else outside this psychotic crime scene he was trying to write up.

His partner, McPhee, six feet of hard and thin, opened her mouth to say something, hesitated, put her right palm down tight on the card table. "For organizing the mothers with pots and pans. He won't say that part. He can't say that part."

Oliverra said, "Mr. Eckman."

"Eck," Sister said.

"Goldman Sachs?"

"No, Goleman Eck," she said. "He's not a derivative."

"True," Gole said. "Not an option. Not even a future."

"Okay," the patrolman said. "Enough funny. Goleman, what's wrong? You're staring, like out at nothing from nothing." He said three more things. "You feel shock. You feel panic. You say yes to that?"

Sister Agnes Coleridge said, "He never knew if he had one."

McPhee asked, "One what?"

"Mother. One mother. The usual number."

Gole was obviously trying to cut through this attack of being non-responsive, a throwback to years of it.

Sister said, "I think he's reacting deeply, after the fact, of stopping and hurting a man with a disappeared mother who never stops disappearing."

McPhee tightened, her torso, if possible, straighter.

"That's more than we can investigate right now. Any idea why this guy—from South America, you say—has Kevlar body armor on?"

Eck was turning his head and shoulders, winding the top part of himself at least into this situation. He faced the nun and had hatched a little smile okay to her.

Sister bent down to put three fingers on his forehead, press his shoulder, top his hand. He was back. She said something to a saint.

"I think," Eck said, stopped.

Officer McPhee took a few exasperated steps to one side. Her partner stood waiting by Goleman Eck, who had just demonstrated extraordinary presence of mind and bat shit crazy at the same time.

Sister said quietly, "Say. Your color's back. Say."

Gole shivered, twice, as if from his head all the way down, then as if from his feet, all the way back up. "When I got inside and captured the blade in the phone book, I felt it go through me. Same thing when I got my arm around his neck." He raised his right arm. "Right through it."

"What?" Oliverra asked. "Mr. Eck, look at me. What right through you, through your arm?"

"I think he was cold. Ice cold through him. Through me."

Sister nodded. "Ah, and you think he's been that way since she was disappeared?"

"Yes."

McPhee stepped back, frowned, creasing her whole brow under her NYPD cap.

Oliverra said, "My daughter?—she says sometimes, 'Really maybe?' She's seven."

"What's her name?" Sister asked.

"Carlotta. After her mother's mother."

Gole wanted to know, "Your wife still have her mother?"

Oliverra shook his head.

"She was buried, in a grave?" Gole asked.

Oliverra nodded. "Why you ask that?"

"She can go there. Your wife can go to her mother's grave?"

McPhee said, "I know where this one's going."

"It's all right," Sister said.

"I can't do that," Gole said, as if this were a fresh disappointment.

The police officers said they'd probably be back to him, once they'd gotten the suspect's story, or stories. That would be after he got his ribs bandaged. Hell of a throw. Damn lucky he was psychotic or it might have cracked his spine. McPhee wanted to know where he'd learned that move on an attacker.

"Bikers," Gole said. "In Alabama when I was twenty-one." When they looked at him, he said, "You believe that?" The second answer made Oliverra smile. Flamenco, when Eck had gotten into many things Argentinean after a massive DNA study turned up an Argentine gene pattern in his saliva, blood, and sperm. The police left. The meeting hall was full of talk and wonder and laughter at all the excitement. People kept looking over and pointing at Gole, which he didn't mind, but he wished the whole thing, all of it, hadn't happened.

Oliverra and McPhee left.

The TV crew of NewStruck (NSK) swept in, including forty-year News on Wheels anchor Chopper Batista, sixty-five and showing no sign of slowing down for the mere facts. He was on Goleman Eck, mike under the jaw, "How does it feel being a Samurai hero?"

I just got in his face lucky wasn't going to fly with the Chopper.

"How did you learn to fight that way?"

He got no answer.

"Seriously, Mr. Goldman. Suppose I lift up this mike"—and he did so—"in two hands, seriously, coming at you over my head and yours?"

Gole flushed with embarrassment, stopped cold and said, "That's not what happened, sir." He blinked blindly into two cameras.

"Can you reenact the terrible moment of decision when you must have decided it's him or me, something like that?" By now, the Chopper was pleading with Gole to stop being a dick and just do the scene.

Gole snatched the tricornered white handkerchief from the breast pocket of Batista's gray-paned sports jacket and waved it in surrender to the camera. The anchor said that this man's humor after such a near-death violent encounter coming right out of hell was nothing short of amazing.

Chopper said, "Are your mother and father still alive to know their son's valiant--?" at which point Eck said, truly frightened for the first time, "The fucking sword was a toy for Christ's sake!"

The camera went out, and the huge umbrella light went out as the very alive extension mike pole drifted over to Sister Agnes Coleridge, who was comforting some frightened center children on the other side of the big room's checkered linoleum floor, talking and stroking and singing a hymn and asking who wanted a penny mint.

"Thus," Chopper went down lower into his throat, "it works like this. The return of the normal thanks to the vow of courage, the vow of honor, and the vow of affirming life at all costs, that Sister Agnes embodied at the Center today."

He looked straight into the non-working camera, like the Cronkite of his TV youth. "Over to you, Charlene, back in NSK Studio One." He held his look for a few seconds and then turned on Eck in a fury.

"You could have been a City Hero," he accused. "They won't run that stupid little performance of yours. I could've had City Hero of the Week. Hell's wrong with you?"

FIVE

At the Unbirthday party Eck had for himself on All Souls'
Day eve, about fifty people in Eck's eyrie were talking and
musing in threes and more about what they'd just heard. Gole
had delivered an amazing short speech before the cutting of
the eighteen-inch All American six-layer vanilla white cake
with pink frosting and rainbow sprinkles wheeled in like a
tabernacle from Butter & Scotch in Crown Heights. He had,
once and for all, he said, to tell his tale and be done hiding it.
He was coming out, he said, even though he'd never started
out as such.

"I decided I'm forty-three," he said. "I have to get on with
life as it was given to me. Without a regular beginning." And
he said, "I feel like a walking social issue." He said, "As Byron
wrote, 'Nothing like a beginning,' so he began with nothing
like a beginning." Five minutes more into his speech he said,
"Everybody else moves toward death from life. Mine's some
kind of opposite moving."

Having laid it all out in maybe ten minutes, amid some
laughter, some short breathings, some rabid, some politely
skeptical attention come his way as he worked in some call-
and-response with his guests, he said, "My birthday is the
greatest Unbirthday of them all, I guess. It's all about me

81

because I am no me."

In the sweet short silence ensuing after the post-speech buzz began to dwindle, he was liked so much no matter how true or false his story that everybody cheered him wildly. The music kicked in again. Dancing, light and serious, wound into uncaring joy at all things ass-backward in life that everybody in the place knew at least a little bit about.

His place was a great double space up a dozen flights of air. The gleaming slim building was the signature 1985 work of Theodora Williams, the Creole post-modernist architect who broke the glass ceiling in two midtown white-shoe firms, so naturally elite circles called the building The Splendid Splinter. Thirty-eight stories, it featured three huge windows on the four sides of each floor. The design fit a finely odd-looking but successful wind-turbine engineer who had a serious telescope for night-viewing our local solar system.

When Eck first moved into his place in the building, there was a chichi bar on the ground floor. Though no longer, it was originally called "The Spending Splinter." Conceived by the infamously lurid bar-artist Petro Zero, its photographic and digital layout worked a fantastic white/Black gender-transgressing Ted-Theodora Williams thing. A Creole bartender topped the crew with an encyclopedic knowledge of the great man that featured a tale about a two-Williamses tryst that yielded a mixed-race son whom no one ever actually saw. Years later, when the news came out that Ted's frozen corpse had been decapitated, its very brain matter splattered when a cryogenics worker ripped it out of deep ice, the notion of a cosmo on the rocks, or Johnny himself on the rocks, lost barfly cachet. The Splinter tanked. It became an Earth Plant site with its own coffee shop that paid the former Ted's upscale rent. That was just about the time Goleman Eck moved into his duplex. When Gole would go into Earth Plant, he'd see the last two remaining big photos of the Ted and Theodora, and begin to wonder about that lost child, but not for long because it was just another fanciful dead end. Besides, he'd never been much of a baseball player as a kid.

Eck got serio-comic interest in his claim that he must have come ("Look carefully, I tell you, you'll see its dim little light shining down from the next solar system out from us") from the newly discovered exoplanet the astronomers call Proxima b. ("I tell you, Hawking and Zuckerberg are gearing up a robotic probe that'll get out there to send back pictures of it after only twenty-one years travel. My company's going full-tilt making a bid on the project.") Himself a downsize robot-toy inventor-hobbyist, Eck had a whole wide shelf of them, some of which he'd already gotten around to strutting early on in the party. ("A new beauty I just got from the three-D copy magicians, name's Iphigenia, a robo hair-replacement specialist, about two feet high and curvy.") Lots of people at his party had played well with his favorite three robo comfort pets, the dog-bunnies Reddira, SeaGram Seven, and Canal Street. If wind energy gets bellied up by the forced return of fracked fossil fuels, he said, he was going totally robo-toy.

His guests were a varied lot of people he knew by name from his chic postmodern building. Like Harry Gonzalez, the hospital-construction billionaire from Honduras, Seamus Trainer the stay-at-home father of autistic twins, and Japanese Ginger Autry, the parolee who'd done ten years for paralyzing her abusive ex; guests from his exercise gym, like Bridget Cantrell, the last over-concussed mixed martial arts instructor Gole could put up with learning from, and Anselm Gabrielly, the Broadway dance coach who sometimes let him join in on fundamental chorus-line practice; and from his current job mates like Jimmy Sheard, the hilarious Communications chief suffering from macular degeneration; JoAngelline Mulder, the obsessively quiet one in Development who had at least a third of the good ideas; and Tracey Isabella Raquel Edwina de LaClos in Finance whom everyone called Tired for short. There were three more, named Brown, Blue, and White, from an earlier part of his life whom he kept up with and who happened, individually, to be in the city this weekend or week. A few were recent acquaintances from different pro-life rallies from both sides.

They all, mostly, really liked Gole's amazing space. It made three-dimensional space curve, surprise.

There were oblongs, trapezoids, triangles, rectangles, ovoids, parallelograms to sit in, lie down on, do work or eat at. Tripod chairs repeated fabric coverings of two rockers. An onyx baby grand stood shining against a pale blue wall that had a trompe l'oeil cobalt blue door frame that matched the same color rug wedging out from the gray granite fireplace just then burning gently behind a silver fire screen. A semicircle of nicely spaced and very different easy chairs bordered the fireplace area. All the furniture was easy to move around, on several blended areas of oak, cherry, and walnut flooring. Air circulated from turbine-like fans coming down on elegant steel poles from the fourteen-foot ceilings. Connecting 12 and 14 were a winding oak stairway that once went up to a choir loft and a four-person stainless-steel elevator that sounded like whispering on the way up and light shushing on the way down. Airy, bright, multicolored and peacefully imaginative, Eck's place was sooner than contemporary. Just like Gole, the strangely dislocated host. It had been featured in two upscale interior design magazines sent to people of wealth and taste in New York City, Paris, and Dubai.

An oddity of those two publications was that copyright prevented them from reproducing a startlingly hanged reproduction of David Hockney's *A Bigger Splash*. To angles of sight along converging window walls caught and trapped the eye, rushed it up to the play of light, glass, air, water, geometry, pallid suburban Los Angeles unbounded swimming pool space, a little canvas folding chair, sliding glass doors reflecting another like dwelling as if hundreds of feet away, something like a rigid little tuft-line of high hard grasses, the middle of a telephone pole, and the amazing wide tan pastel diving board rigid again after a medium-height dive has been done.

"But a bigger splash by whom?" Gole was fond of narrating when asked why he fixed on it and made everyone's eyes who came here fix on it, a fairly aggressive interior-design thing to do, he admitted, to people in his place up in the air, no? If one seriously asked Eck to answer, he would do so as well and clearly as he could, though he said that in his time experts had called him a visually inept engineering type. Rarely, because it disturbed some people to hear it, he'd give the basic truth to him about the painting.

At this Unbirthday, for example, a polite questioner, a wind colleague over from Finland for a seminar Eck was offering at an NYU eco-conference, stood in front of the image at a safe distance, asked the question, "But, my dear Goleman, after all, why this painting?" Eck, as it were, dove into it. The man's name, Eck remembered, was Saarinen, yes, some thin remove from that family, of neo-futurism past.

"The image on first look doesn't seem to have a single human form."

"You're right," Saarinen said. He adjusted his simple wire-frame glasses. His close suit was flat silver, his teeth equine and white.

Gole turned it on. "It seems to be all about the water after the dive. Its action is still exploding, the spray and force and splash up into the air of the white, ghostly, not blue at all water sprung. Liquid air painted with utter meticulous fanatical detail by a brush no longer there either. It seems a picture of disappearance, deliquescence, the erasure of the gone diver."

"You make me see it that way now," Saarinen admitted. He was catching glimpses of who else might be of interest around him.

"But then, to the left of the splash, you see a spectral figure, floating diagonally up to the surface? Spewing bubbles into the air above the water and the side of the pool?"

Saarinen did not but didn't say so.

"It's just that the figure's motion up is suspended, as if underneath is its permanent place not above the disturbed water line. What is that ghostly bubbling form, it certainly isn't a formed blood and flesh body."

The possibility that it was bothered Saarinen, though he didn't know why. He said that.

"Will it ever swim out?" Eck asked him. "Ever be, as visually there as the evanescent splash? The cool pool can fool, like death it can. If Odysseus' men had disobeyed his command that they not unlash him from the mast, he would have been this diver and all his appearance in life lost."

Eck watched realization enter his turbine-colleague's ice-blue eyes. Saarinen must have been there earlier for the Story. He got what this Goleman Eck was talking about when he talked about his *Bigger Splash* this way. Eck hadn't meant to affect the guy this way. But then, of course he did.

"Amateur art lecture over," he said and offered his hand. "Thanks for asking. I love the thing. It gets me all ekphrastic. Do you like it? It's very dangerous, no? Makes you want to take that dive yourself? Or maybe the diver didn't dive at all. Maybe he was pushed. Another thought of mine. Hah! Just kidding. Come, I insist you get another drink from the host himself."

The guest shook Eck's hand warily. Eck nudged him by the elbow gently, away from Hockney's vision of the watered life, wove him through four people he stopped to introduce him to, got him over to a good drink. Eck bowed. Finnish Saarinen, relieved, bowed a little himself and turned to order a double anything. Not much of a drinker, he liked to find out what bartenders recommended for people like him who couldn't stand drinks for infrequent drinkers. Eck liked the guy for just that and more.

Several more showed up in their previous night's Halloween costumes, just to keep the spooky party spirit of life going for one more day. Some came as movies. Eck found it understandable but tedious that two transgendered people, one male, one female, both cryptocurrency hawkers, got all done up separately in Frankenstein monster garb, though both were too self-conscious and transgressive to settle for a Karloff cliché. Still, he was their host and they wanted to talk all-Frankenstein all the time right then, so he got into it with them.

He told them: As was only natural to Eck's experience of bad interpretations of his own life, he had himself had his sympathetic identity with Shelley's "hideous progeny," by which she meant her novel, not her monster. He had resonated with hyper-intellectual Victor Frankenstein's line about renouncing the "abortive" Old Science of alchemy for the procedures of modern science. He, too, was trying to get clear and true knowledge about his very existence. He did get a kick out of the monster's aboriginal questions, "Who was I? What was I? Whence did I come?" But abortion as he was, he never felt he was some kind of monstrosity. In fact, if he had a mirror to look in, he could find a differently presentable man who was doing rather well in his posthumous life. Which is why he shook hands with each of his two gender-bending monstered-up guests with a hearty "Hah!" and moved on.

He ran into a lot of talk in one group about the news worldwide about the lost children of Tuam in Galway. They were born out of wedlock to Irish girls who were confined in the home until they gave birth, then the mothers were expelled from the home and their babies, forever Irish-Catholic shamed and desolated by the kidnapping of their children. The children were raised by the nuns who ran the home, unless they died of various wasting diseases in infancy and early childhood. When they died, the nuns wrapped them up in small bundles and put the bodies in a septic tank area. This happened to several hundred of the born babies. This was whispered about but only fully reported in news around Gole's party day. He didn't need it. But he found a new form of heroism in the understory of the woman whose obsession with the home when she was a child would not leave her alone until years of her own research into the place and its history produced the first radio stories of the babies, and the nation of Ireland was forced to disinter the hundreds of tiny remains and account for the holy murder of their innocents.

The thing that ran him over in it all was the fact that when the children walked in the streets of Tuam, they would call out to strangers, "Mommy, Daddy." Later in life as extremely insecure adults, many of them asked themselves over and over again, "Who am I? Who was my mother? Who are my siblings in the world?" "What am I?" Goleman Eck knew about the western Irish DNA his genome showed up, probably a good deal of it in the post-racial mix all those genealogical traces of him beamed in his face. Would he have been better off had he been one of those kids nearly a hundred years ago who survived the shamed mother he never could know? He'd spent the afternoon trying not to think about the whole story, recognizing the problem with even thinking about it at all in relationship to himself. That was arrogant narcissism of its own unattractive kind. You don't get to claim a misery in the world for your own.

The word of Eck's party had gotten out beyond his own circles. Clearly, two of the guests were piece-work journalists who counted on found stories like this one to be journalists at all. One was a guy who fingered into his phone's notebook. The other was a woman who used a Mont Blanc pen and a small wired notebook, both sides of a page. They took their notes in sure abbreviated fashion as Eck announced his world as quickly and plainly as he could. And there was another probable recording angel from some other sphere altogether who stared intensely through Ivanka-type sunglasses the way a memorizing person does at a performance that breaks a day open. Way younger, artier, more coiled than the first two, s/he varied between the slightest jitter and a commanding sneer that caught people's attention. Altogether, the conversation and laughter and movement of glasses and steps was a surprising production from the always surprising likes of Goleman Eck and his impossibly wonderful bio.

"Hello," a fine voice beside him said. "Happy Unbirthday, Gole. Many such from now on."

Mary Rice hugged him. He held her out by the forearms in delight that she was there. He had asked her before, he asked her again, "Are you sure you're not my mother?"

"Would I have done that to you? Haven't we been through this before? You have to take me off your list of possibles, dearest Gole. We don't even look like three removes together."

"That's because you're so beautiful and aren't going to stop. Helen Hayes, Katherine Hepburn, Mary Astor, with a slice of Nina Simone somewhere in the wondrous mix."

"Oh, stop that. I look at you, I see a hundred years from now. Gorgeous. Not faces out of the grave like that bunch of old broads."

"Okay," he said. "But will you be my mother? I'd adopt you as my mother. You can have the part, Lady Mary Rice. You surely can."

It was all fun, yet the two of them shared a sadness in it. "You heard about my little speech, then?"

"I did. And what in God's name were you doing at that birthers first or whatever they were clan gathering?"

"Delay for Life. Who knew? What do you think I was doing? You of all people should understand."

"I do, Mary Rice, I do."

"Good," she said. "I think I do, too. I'm running out of time."

"And I?"

Mary smiled. "You. You're moving into it. Striding." She looked around. "I want you to meet my new interesting younger man, when he gets off work, I told him to come here and meet you."

Mary liked the cake, said "Mmm," which made Eck remember to try it himself. She patted her mouth with a pumpkin paper cocktail napkin. Music came back on, and the party spirit picked up again.

"Here goes," Mary said. "You have it in common with Adam."

He circled his fork in the air gently, as if trying to get the same idea out as she had. "Both of us were not born of women."

"So," Mary said. "Maybe He's starting all over again, with you."

"Him. Guy with long beard in the windy clouds reaching a finger to Adam's."

"The Same. Means, maybe, you go around looking for an aborting Eve, while what He wants is for you to get something else going altogether. A whole new race for the human. You're it, the progenitor. So get off your self-pitying lifetime jag and get to work for all our sakes."

"That's very smart. We could have been so smart together, you know?"

"Want to exchange pieces of cake, Mr.Eck?"

He indicated he wanted to serve first. She agreed. Again she said, "Mmm," and brought a piece on her fork up to his mouth. He chewed, swallowed appreciatively, and said, "It's my party and I can cry if I want to."

There was just enough recreational weed, brought down from the Berkshires in medical kits, to get willing party stoners waiting excitedly for the hour to pass the cannabis infusion would take to hit them. This was a gift from two Kilpartridge-family cousins, Rory and Patty, from Gole's early North Shore childhood who made it an ongoing project to keep the in-touch between them going despite his polite ways of either delaying the contact or indicating his discomfort with all that back then. Gole never knew Rory and Patty to be with anybody else, but he passed no judgment on such matters.

He did get a kick out of having the Killers show around their Massachusetts Medical Marijuana ID cards. Touches like that were making his party an even different kind of success. He did find a couple of serious cake eaters, whom he thought he knew from women's reproductive rights sides of street actions, up against one of his high glass windows, going "Pow, pow, pow" with their fingers at phantom airliners trying to crash into Freedom Tower up in the night sky ten blocks down. "Good job, fighters," he told them, "but don't irritate your throats that harshly."

Somebody put Mancini vinyl on the sound system and dancing to "Breakfast at Tiffany's" took hold in full retro fashion. Gole came upon Charlene Makelovitch, her beautifully shaped and tanned breasts more than peeking out of her low-slung white cocktail dress, down on her hands and knees, crawling with the thinnest, tallest man there astride her back. This was the somewhat wasted former NBA player Amistad Washington, who forsook the game at top form a dozen years ago to become the best-known sports poet in the nation. He walk-rode Charlene quite gently while moving his arms rhythmically as if he were Mancini himself come back from L.A. death in 1994 to conduct his music in Gole's downtown eyrie now.

An arch voice somewhere behind Eck said, "The scene's been done before." Eck didn't think that a problem.

Then Gole moved, as promised on the invitation, to start the Game of Autochthony. People clapped, stopped nibbling the cake in order to play with at least semi-attention. They got their state, federal, corporate, university or military identification cards out and faced each other in two long lines stretching from the big front doors of the apartment all the way back to the windows atop the harbor. "Moon River" stopped and "Achy Breaky Heart" began but not too loud, because Gole respected his neighbors up here in the sky.

Sort of in the manner of line dancing—except these were New Yorkers without proper American line dancing jeans, belts, boots, or hats—first, they followed Gole's instruction and practiced basic heel-close, heel-close, heel-two-three, hip-bump-once-twice, single bump once twice, face front, right-left-right-rock, right-left-right rock. The lines came together in non-touching pairs, stopping only to exchange cards, stop with their backs to one another and study their new IDs. Every other person in the line moved sideways behind the person to the left or to the right, depending on which line they were in, to be beside a new person. The lines turned, came together, persons exchanging the previous borrowed identity card.

"I am" someone else was said.

"I am" someone else next was said.

"I am" someone beside else or next was said.

After three passes, everyone had to say his or her/their three names clearly and in sequence. This was done on the honor system. No one who wanted to play fair made up a name or reported out a different surname with the right first name. The lines began to thin as disappointed players with a confusion of names retired from the game. The remaining players lined up again, faced each other, and the second round of the Game of Autochthony proceeded.

The onlookers cheered up, had more snacks, talked to people they found to give ID's back to, about the chanciness of who they were just for a change. As the game intensified, there were quality booze or weed tears at losing one's fifth or sixth different best person to become, just by the luck of the draw of ID cards. But everyone had a taste of the spirit of the game, easily and commonly stated as having, just for the moment of the game, several names, identities, and therefore not any one. It was a lightening, this game of Gole's.

A few poor sports did take it personally, couldn't take losing any way other than losing themselves. One was heard to say, "The fucking guy doesn't think he was even born right.

That's crazy. So's this game."

He was told, "Whatever. I think it's fun of a whole other sort. Come on, Dawkins, it's a party, for chrissake."

Whatever, indeed. It was all a foregone conclusion. It was Goleman Eck's invention, his game, and he as usual came out the winner, the final absorber of IDs, names, personhoods, all that, when the runner-up happened and stumbled on her sixth name. This was Evelyn Postman, the legendary proofreader for Macadam Medical Books and the new, international award-winning translation of Cervantes. She wore expensive re-fitted vintage suits, blue or green, that had padded shoulders and straight skirts below the knee. Postman didn't want to ruin the fun of the thing, so she told only Mary Rice that Eck won by some kind of intimidation she'd never seen the like of in game theory practice before.

Billy Ray Cyrus cut out. Gole stood there, champion again, going through his six degrees of naming as if he were the white bouncing ball of old-time group singing. With each name he finished, the delighted birthday conclave clapped and said, "Go, Gole" and "It's a Gole-goal again."

Charlene Makelovich in all her busting out glory took his six IDs and monitored his saying each of the names respectfully and well. He did not stumble over two multi-syllable names, one Polish, one Indonesian, and the two real owners of the names both cheered. He laughed an odd laugh without saying why when he had to speak the name, "Rory Kilpartridge." Still and even so, he won out.

"Happy Birthday, Autochthonous One, Happy Birthday to you," Charlene Makelovitch said in breaths and kissed him lightly on the lips for a full three beats.

He thought her lips were as soft and friendly as any he'd known in a long time. And safe, caring deeply but not hinting sexual need or interest. It hit him hard and stupid that Charlene was no Yolande Segundo. Yolande's lips and tongue were asking, offering, trusting. Why, he wondered again, had he turned that into the old curse?

"Moon River" came back on from the vinyl past. Mary asked Eck to dance. They got comfortable in each other's friendly arms. She led him, he was willing, they danced well together. Eck got a sense of what it was like to be glad to have another birthday.

Somebody with something had come in. Since Eck's front door was wide open, and it wasn't as if he had issued actual invitations to a certain couple dozen as much as he and his circle had let it be known the party was an all-Thursday-night gala. In this way downtown South Ferry vertical tower neighborhood, that could be like spaghetti supper night in a church basement in a small town named Elevator Village. Everything was landfill at base. There was no rooted land, there were tremendous mirroring towers ever more. It seemed so, these later days of the first quarter-century of the two thousand and something years of architectural defiance of religious outrage. Eck lived in one of those Ef-you-world-bring-it-on Manhattan reckless fortresses that shimmered in the moonlit harbor water.

The somebody was the social-media investigative reporter Jenny Rich. Along with her was her own guest, a huge Caribbean drummer with the ringing something, a tuned and shining steel drum. He carried the thing like a toy into the middle of Eck's first loft-size sitting room. He set it up, turned on a backup percussion and horns tape, opened up an orangewood and gold designed leather tripod, sat all of his strong backside down and started making the inside of the drum sound like silver bells, metal tones, and xylophonic harmonies. He wasn't just a subway musician.

Jenny clapped her hands in marimba time over the musician's dreadlocked head and looked hard at Eck way over by the window standing by the strange woman from the meeting the other day with AG-hopeful Gottsch. Eck took in the stare and shivered he did not know why, but the feeling was the one he got when he was probably going to have to fight. He breathed in, stiffening in a way that Mary Rice picked up as they still touched each other's waist. Then he saw her being taken aside by another party gate-sharer Eck recognized from the morning and evening lobby traffic.

They had spoken two or three times inside the lobby or out in the cluster of apartment buildings' huge common patio and river walk. Eck scrolled up the full image of him. He was a striking type, neatly blond-bearded, thick sandy-haired figure who favored fringed silk scarves or splashy bow ties from England. Some kind of televangelist who traveled a lot as a postmodern Christian preacher who brought Bible Belt performance to eastern urban centers up and down the Atlantic coast. He had a talented baritone voice, a wizened comic acceptance around his Newman-blue eyes, and right now, Gole could see even at this distance amid so many people, a slim expensive blue houndstooth suit and regulation light brown oxfords, showing an inch of cute pink and tan socks. The guy could put it on, pull it off, quite well.

He wore then and he had it on now as well, an embossed name tag one first took for A. Zimmerman, but it really said Rev. A. Shimmerman. That was his name, and it had meaning. All this passed through Eck's inventory of him, triggered by the way he engaged the not-engaging Jenny Rich for about ninety seconds, telling her what she'd missed earlier, Eck's The Aborted One's speech. From someplace down in him, warning came. Something, some fresh current shuttling between the reverend and the journalist has a use, or uses, for you, Goleman Eck.

Another line came to him out of the past, from, of all people, Mrs. Killer, who told her little foster boy more than once, "Honey, don't be anyone's donkey."

"Where are you now?" Mary asked him.

"Smelling the weed," he said. "You getting it, too?"

She went blank, lost her color.

"Where are you now?" Gole asked her. "Seen a Halloween ghost?"

"I know who that tall blonde figure of a man is."

"That's the Reverend Shimmerman. What's he to you?"

"Place called Chelsea House. In Newark." She was getting upset.

Gole waited, remembered. "Captain Blue's?"

Whatever it was, she didn't want to deal with it. He didn't push. He knew her that well.

She breathed in through her commandingly cute nose. "Oh, Christ," she said. "Yeah, that little circle of heads, over there for one. I'm capable of sneezing when I get too close to it. But it's the new age of legal and social acceptability." She patted his right shoulder in good-humored condescension. "Especially at really post-upscale parties way high up in the air where the Hudson flows like money into New York Harbor."

That night, the restaurant, Yolande. Sneezing.

"Don't leave me if you're planning to leave soon," he said. "I'd better go into mingle- stage three or four. So I'm going to get a serious drink from that bartender in the short shorts I'm paying serious union time for."

"I see. The breasty lass with the lovely ass and the just-right horny-rimmed glasses up in her hair. Could be an art history doctoral candidate. Know the ilk?"

"Actually, she's into Data Science. A little more practical. I think her name's Rexie. Maybe two x's. Should be two x's."

Mary got wind of more weed and made her way away from him into the dozens of Caribbean-style dancers moving their arms and hips just so to the steel drummer's mixed sound. Gole saw her take a wide berth around the Reverend. She'd tell him, in her own time.

Halfway across the partyers, purposefully threading toward him, waving like someone shining a lamp, was the Attorney General's Office mid-level attorney who'd loudly injected herself into the fight as the only true right and conservative candidate to run the whole office. Ashley Gottsch, in a very unconservative Paraguayan poncho stitched in the whole primary colors spectrum. Her face gleaming with purpose. She sure must have heard his talk.

She got blocked out by a Caribbean red dress, red dress, dancing all by itself until it stopped to say, "Unbirthday Man, man, you are one great, great crazy man. Unborn, huh? That is so cool and crazy it's beyond cool and crazy." Out of the big round collar of the lady's red dress, red dress came a neck and a head and a face loaded with huge green sunglasses, huger gold circles in barely discernible earlobes, and a mahogany hair base holding up a three-inch high S of pumpkin-orange growth.

Gole shook his head but the vision stood still to say, "Man, that is got to be an Oscar scam performance like I've never heard before in my whole life."

Gole tried to move around her, but she said to his politeness, "One thing, though."

"Though," Gole said, "what?"

"That chocolate fountain falls for the strawberries. O my God," she said in a way that made him glad she'd found such a thrill at his party. The top third of her slinked back down into the red dress, red dress and danced away, away.

"Do you love it?" AG was saying, flipping some of the poncho over her left shoulder. "I found him on the platform for the C train downtown."

"The steel drummer," Gold said. "Well, thank you. You brought him as a present for my Unbirthday. That's really sweet. And righteous loud. I figure I do the tipping."

"Hah! Smart as ever," she said. "But Happy Birthday, Mr. Unborn. I heard your speech. Brings up lots of questions. Too short. But."

"But."

"You had us all hooked. Maybe by a crook. But you had us

from, 'Hi. This is my afterbirthday.' Did you hear some saying, 'Oooo, Oooo, Oooo,' and others saying back, 'You, you, you?'"

"No," Gole said. "I was trying to say something."

"Well," AG said, "the you-yous certainly had it over the oooo-oooos. We have to talk. Not here, obviously."

"Hint. About what?"

"Pregnant teenage immigrants trying to get abortions in this country. You read about it?"

"Not here, obviously. This a political thing for you in your campaign. That it?"

"It's going to be huge, Goleman Eck. Politically, morally, ethically. So's your story, Jenny Rich sees it and says it to me. She's right. Want to talk to her with me about it?"

"She's here. Nice of her to come. Nice of you to come. No."

A path in the party seemed to open up, all the way down to Shimmerman, whose hand gesture started out as a wave and ended up as a sharp cross. Gole knew then how the Undead, if there were such, felt being blessed off by one of the faithful's shepherds. He moved toward the ordained man, accepting Unbirthday compliments from right and left. More people than he knew seemed to know him now. Maybe he could get away with being just another Downtown celebrity. But something seemed to be growing right then and there that he felt in the slight touches to his shoulders and forearms. Something he'd brought on himself he hadn't figured on when he'd decided to give his little coming-out talk. Some unspooling line of life that now actually had a live marimba rendering of "Devil With the Blue Dress" causing some unstructured dirty dancing by straight and gay couples. Red dress, red dress scowled, but then took a big blue napkin off a food station, triangulated it, used it as a kerchief over her head, tied it demurely under her chin, and carried on alone. The room was full of bang, ring, and pound.

Rev. A. told Gole to call him Alex. He would clearly use Goleman in full. They had to lean in to one another.

"Not Alexander? The priest who said he wanted to be my special friend when I was fourteen told me to call him by his full name. Bertram. How the hell could a priest be a Bertram?""

Shimmerman was quick from a lot of cable TV preaching and interview work. He was on most of the time he talked to people. "Oh, no," he said, mocking shock. "Not that. Not you, too. I hope it didn't," but he stopped even saying it. "So. Did you call him? Bert? Of all names?"

"Father. Father Bert. He sort of, you know, disillusioned me, an impressionable boy."

The smile was gleaming white, say, Gole figured, five or six treatments at first and then semi-annual maintenance. "I'm picking up here that you evaded this predator?"

"I was either stupid or lucky," Gole said. "But it was a wake-up moment, yes. My virtue got tested in more strenuous ways as I grew up."

Shimmerman lightly grasped both tassel ends of his silk scarf. Gole guessed it a William Morris Arts and Crafts print, intertwining leaves and vines, nice. "You make me think," Shimmerman said, "pilgrimage. Stations. Losses and lights. Often not knowing which."

"You get a drink? Nice hors d'oeuvres being served around if you can get their attention. I do like the black and gold Banbury bow tie."

"Ah. Deflecting me." Grinning, he brought a forefinger up to touch one side of it for a second before continuing. "I don't mean to intrude on the cheer of your Unbirthday as you called it in your amazing talk. Amazing. You recenter my faith in miracle."

Gole thought there was nothing really wrong in his saying that. It was the business the man was in. No worse than if they were just two real estate agents meeting half-way from either's hometown, immediately talking shop after figuring out quickly the mutual sizing up could stop. Or be put on hold.

"We've said hello, downstairs in the courtyard, the river walk. I'm glad to see you at my party, neighbor."

Shimmerman was back on. "Maybe we can work together. I could tell you about a film project I didn't know needed you until I heard what you had to say. Amazing."

"You want me for some kind of pro-life propaganda, Reverend?"

Too slick altogether to register offense, Shimmerman said, "There's lots of different life to celebrate, Goleman, no? Including the life that is before me right now in the unlikely wonder of yours?"

"You're very good," Gole said. "You really are. I'm just a wired puppy right now. You'll excuse that, I'm sure. It's all kind of strange in this moment. I need to figure out why. I will listen, yes. That's all I can say, because the devil wears a helluva red dress. You know?"

Shimmerman relented, too, seeming to turn off the camera face and just to say, "Bourbon. My friend, do you have any good Southern bourbon. I would like to raise a glass of good Southern bourbon to you on this special day."

Gole clapped a gentle hand on Shimmerman's shoulder. They went back together to the drinks station as the girl in the short shorts watched them arrive through her classy horn rims.

"That good bourbon there," Gole told her then asked, "Double?"

"Single."

"Give him a single and a half."

They watched her move.

"I think," Gole whispered, "her name must be Rexie. With two x's. And she's really smart. Doctoral student, I was just telling"—he didn't say. "Data science. Not what one would think first."

Shimmerman didn't disagree. He just said, "Another wonder of creation."

A woman's sharp, jagged voice seemed to twist around from behind the Reverend, followed by the woman herself, her XXL black and red checkered lumberperson shirt filled with her. "Are you fucking kidding anyone but yourself?" She blocked out Shimmerman until he was beside her again, saying, "Mrs. Jericho, please. Lower your voice. We can't hear the music if you talk that loudly."

Gole recognized it before it came at him. He'd wondered it himself, if only maybe once.

"I'm sorry, Alexander," she said in a better tone, but then turned on Eck at half blast an insult. "But this is just too much. It's a lie. It's offensive to any woman who's had to go through it herself."

"Like you, I take it?" Gole asked. He didn't like that he asked it. But he had. He saw old pain in her face and frame. Shimmerman had her by the elbow and was gently urging her just to move over there a little bit with him to talk, just to let it go for right now at this occasion meant for cheer, pleasantness for all. A little circle of concern and disapproval formed around them. "It's a party," was said by three different people trying to smile her down.

"I know you, know your real name," Mrs. Jericho said. Whatever it was, from however far back or near, about herself or somebody else who'd exercised the right to choose, sounded to Eck like a short enough sentence to be over and done with and good cheer restored.

"Please," he said. "Let Mrs. Jericho say."

"Cold Man Dreck," she said. "You're a little male shithead," she said, obviously sown and weeded, and threw a contemptuous laugh at him. "Cold Man Dreck. It never dawned on you, did it? That a woman's right to choose to terminate means that she has the right never to be called 'mother.' That you lived means that right was denied that woman. You male shithead whiner! You give a woman's right to choose a bad name."

101

As quickly as she'd weaved up to him, she quickly weaved away. Gole watched the way the Jericho moved head and shoulders above most of the people still dancing and drinking and still having a good time at what was by any standard a unique kind of party.

Gole turned to Shimmerman, who waited on some reaction. Gole shrugged, felt bad on several counts, figured he'd get over it soon enough. Shimmerman downed his drink and said he didn't know what to say. So he asked Eck about a linked series of three large color photos on the wall above where they stood, of a lithe and young and shining-haired Goleman poised on a surfing board under the curl of what must have been a huge ocean wave, then being overcome by its folding fury, then just a hand out of the water grasping the line of the board.

"In my reckless youth," Eck told the Reverend. "The photographer won a prize for it. He gave it a name."

"Do tell. It's ferocious and beautiful at once. You keep on surprising."

"Venus," Eck said and laughed. "Venus Wipe-Out."

The Reverend Shimmerman turned around to look again down the big room at the Hockney painting over the heads of the party-goers. When he turned back around, Eck was moving away from him.

*

After his Unbirthday party was really over and the caterer's cleaning crew had worked like happy dervishes cleaning it all up, with many furtive sips of this and that as they blew through it, the thing in Tuam came rolling in and over him again.

Gole stood at his 12-14 harbor window, and the world spun in lights that shined down no mercy, none. Blake's children, their "harmonious thunderings," came at him like cymbals, steel drums, blunted trumpets, Caribbean musical howlings. He told himself he was going to scream. He put his hands over his ears and did just that.

Using both hands at arm's length, he opened out the special *New York Times* section with the whole story in it. He wanted to rip it apart, mince the pages with his teeth. He broke the fit by sheer force of will. He could not, after all, appropriate the home babies' horrific story with his having been aborted. They were not the same. The babies had been brought to term, forced into life, to be born and baptized before they were neglected, starved, sickened, and lost to life.

Neither them nor Frankenstein's creature. There were no analogies, no simulacra, no replicas.

Gole said to the harbor, back again in magnificent focus, "Jesus Christ. Give me a break."

Something did.

He'd thought he was alone during this whole past hour of brooding. First light gave him an eerie sense. He walked down his hallway. Out of the spare bedroom appeared Mary Rice and a man Gole couldn't quite place but knew the face from somewhere a lot of years back, no, then and recently. Very recently. He was getting it when Mary Rice said, "Gole. This is my friend. I call him Victor Mature."

"I can see why," Gole said. "How do you do, Mr. Mature?" Then the way an old-fashioned slide got dropped into a carousel and projected onto a screen, he remembered the man and the place.

"You're Eugene, though, right? The sous chef at Trois Souhaits?" But he was sure of it now, and he thought that was great for Mary Rice. "My backup that night outside in the parking lot."

Victor Mature, Eugene, whoever he was, had just been having sex with Mary Rice in Gole's extra bedroom. Good for Mary. Very sexy sixty. Pleased.

"You didn't need any backup," Eugene Mature said, but the

Victor thing was absolutely right, uncanny. "I'm glad you didn't have to hurt them. Your lady that night, she okay?"

Gole didn't answer, it was complicated. He missed her. He was hollow.

Mary said, "Well, I feel left out. What was this?"

Gole wanted to know, "What's it like, looking like the gladiator who got the robe? I saw it when I was ten, loved it."

Mature Eugene said, "I tell people he was my father and that he gave me the robe. Or I used to. Some accused me of sacrilege."

Gole liked him.

Mary said, "Victor doesn't even know who his father was."

"A common enough phenomenon," Gole said.

"She was a tough lady, my mom. And she hated those movies, both of them."

"Still," Mary said. "He tells me she liked to hear his stories of the military life."

"The true ones," Eugene said. "She could always tell the difference. She did have a big silly dog she loved. Russian Wolfhound. She called him Demetrius."

"That's funny," Gole said. "I like that." He could see it now, that kindly killer amusement of the whole face. "How did you get into culinary?"

"When I got out of the service, they offered a whole world of different training, education. I went for feeding people good food. I was terrible at it. That's all I needed. Then I wasn't. And I'm good at working under screaming dictator types in close places with lots of knives and mallets. I enjoyed the music you brought in tonight. It's the real thing."

Mary said, "He was in the Caribbean for several years."

"I work in wind," Gole said. "Had my time setting up mills in Antigua."

"Another place I trained."

"Mary," Gole said. "I've got to go to sleep. Know what tomorrow is?"

Mary started thinking, but it was Eugene who said first, "All Souls' Day?"

Gole liked him for that, too, a strong guy in control who knew how to respect a Mary Rice.

Mary put her lips to Gole's cheek. "Happy Unbirthday, baby. Go to sleep."

SIX

Former Newark Police Captain Dalton Blue went through his hell for five years before he drove out to the parking lot by the river in Hoboken and put two .38 slugs in his head. Two. That meant the first one didn't do it and he was aware in some manageable or horrific skull pain that he had to make the choice all over again. He did. The shot mushroomed the side of his brain like a thick stem from his right ear up out the open passenger window and onto a PBA-sponsored summer day camp poster.

Soon enough, Mary Rice heard. The call came while she was down on one knee putting pots and pans back on kitchen shelves she had just washed off with spray cleaner and a big yellow sponge. She stood up and took the phone out of the right back pocket of her jeans.

The note was carefully put on the dashboard, away from the velocity of the rushing brains, bone, flesh, teeth. She wasn't allowed to have the note for months after Blue blew his head apart. The new precinct captain read it to her over the phone. Mary didn't get his name-- Dolan, Holland, Oblong, Offline, Stollen. What he read to her came at her five like-sounding ways, like his name. She wished with all her might that she had not squatted down and mimicked firing off those imaginary .9 millimeter bullets into her massive destroyed beloved man she could never have gone on with. She hadn't seen Blue in five years, not since she left him. Abandoned him. The way she had. She strangled the thought.

The unknowably-named precinct captain couldn't stop himself from saying what a can of worms the sick-souled Blue had now opened for the entire police community.

That's when Mary stopped the call on her phone and held it in her lap like a little container of stinking shit. The smell of death instantly rotting Blue's whole ruined head filled her nose and her eyes and stuffed up her ears. The stench settled in all the clean pots and pans. She would not be able to cook, or even be in her kitchen more than a few minutes for months. Instead, Victor, Eugene Encarnacion, Gene, Mature, man of many names, would bring her small portions of exquisite concoctions. She would eat them alone in her living room because disgust radiated out to anyone's watching her eat, or just being in the same room with anyone who'd see her gagging, coughing, hiccupping tea.

But now she went down on her black and white tiled floor and realized she was smelling herself. Then she howled no and Blue's name, no and Blue's name, but then it became no and her lost baby's name, no and Philip her baby Philip's name, so very far back did she go. She kept saying both names when she called Mature, Blue and Philip, Philip Blue, Blue Philip. Eugene knew where she was now, the place where the past awful never changes, though you yourself have had to change or be a crazy person on the earth. She forced herself for the uncountable time to flick that switch off. Off.

Victor Mature had a key and got to her within a half-hour. She held on to him out of her mind, mute. He picked her up in her mess of Blue and Philip, carried her into the bathroom, stripped her, sat her on the toilet, helped her begin to clean herself, ran the splaying hot shower in the tub. He used the strength he had to use to get her standing up under the water, and against the spray mechanism that he used inside her thighs and up along her bottom. He rinsed the tub clean, then filled it half up with the pouring water and got her sitting deep into it. He let her slide her head back down into it until she started choking up out of it and seeing him at last, his brilliant, late-life love and joy, who was ever-listening for more than came from the little he had to say about his own mess. He put a towel around her shoulders, drained the bath, refilled it, touching her knees, her hands, her ears, as the clean water rose up to her waist.

She started talking. She said that he knew about Blue for years. How he knew about dead Blue didn't matter to her. Blue had been a good man, like her Gene Vic Mature. No, Gene said, no I will not die too.

How I know that, Mary said.

SEAL's honor, he said.

He cooked food for her, a frittata from things he found in her refrigerator. She spoke loudly to him from the bedroom, demanding that he be precise about what he was doing with the ingredients, why he chose the stainless steel sauté pan over the iron skillet, the paring knife over the sandwich blade, why that amount of butter to grease the pan. She hobbled into the kitchen, insisting that she got it about such high heat at first, and she worked even more insistently setting the table even after her shaking hands dropped a good dish onto the black and white squares. Oh, my Philip, she said once, only once. He helped her help him. She could not get a forkful up to her mouth, so he held it for her as she opened her mouth and told her it was a small good thing right now so that she would chew and swallow even just that one bite. He ate some of the frittata and she said she'd never seen feta cheese in one before and he continued that conversation with a couple stories of learning how to do eggs in culinary school after assuming he knew how but didn't know shit the chef said.

Mary told Mature about Dalt's Chelsea House. She sang the

verse about remembering you well at the Chelsea Hotel. Tell me more about the Captain and Chelsea House, Victor urged her. She did, but when she finished the part about Dalt's breakdown costing him his spot in running it, she broke down herself, weeping that her leaving Dalt had probably caused that, too. Victor said no, no that's too simple, you could not take on his sorrow, his awful guilt, his terrible aloneness that a lot of fighting men came to know when they did things that destroyed a loyalty or a code to something they never thought they would destroy. She could not, Mature said, take all that on herself.

He did the dishes. The way he did the dishes, gone himself silent after saying so much to her about her man and former lover he'd never met, making very little noise as he scraped their two plates, washed, rinsed, and put things only in the dish rack as if not to waste more water in the dishwasher, all with precision she did not have to see to know it was going on, made her know he thought he had said too much altogether about people, men and women both now, who had done exactly what they had been mercilessly trained to do in America's new kind of old wars. She figured him fighting memory flashes sparking up out of Kandahar province into the dishwater. Ducking, weaving, slipping things coming at him, without his moving any part of his body at her kitchen sink. He was being nicked and cut by broken arrows, a lot of them that he had shot into darkness that took them away and around the world to come back at him. If he stood perfectly, utterly still with the dishtowel twisted in his hands, they would miss their vengeance curve back at him.

"Three little pigs," he said, not looking at her sitting so still again on a red kitchen chair. "Village we went looking for Tommy Sheehan. Makom, Julius, me. We were ordered not to do that, yet. Doesn't work that way. Julius was Haitian family. The province village already incinerated, they captured Tommy before we figured out he was gone and not just farting around again about wanting just one hour with his rifle, four grenades, a serrated knife, and them. Julius was Haitian, I said that before. Could hear things in the middle of hellacious noise. Julius, Haitian—"

Mary couldn't get up the strength to tell him he didn't have to say. She could listen to anything, but he didn't, not right now. She couldn't get it out. Eugene Mature didn't move from his footsteps up to the sink. Started over again.

"Three little pigs. We found them, you know. They couldn't outrun us because they wanted to take Tommy's head and hands with them. Like they were Viet Cong ears or something. But they weren't, and we were out of our minds. Not much of an excuse that. SEALs aren't supposed to go out of their minds, you know?" He dropped both of his hands into the dishwater as if something was in it that he wanted to pull out. He said, "You know" and "You know?" a good deal when getting what happened out of him.

She didn't know. She waited for him to continue because it would come out really wrong if she said he didn't have to say. She didn't have to ask him if he'd said it to anyone else.

"We made them crawl and oink like pigs while we kicked in their ribs. We called them pigs, and they could do nothing but look at us in pain and hate. Three little pigs, we said, the first little pig, the second little pig, and the third. Little," Eugene said. "Pig. The one I shot in the head, one, two, three times, one for each. Little," he said. "Pig. Makom, he was from Florida, played for U Miami, broke yards made in any Miami championship game, like an elephant moving so big, so fucking big, Mary. You know?" He was up straight again, letting the water drain out of the sink. He folded the blue-striped white dish towel in half and draped it over the dishes in the rack. Like he was at Les Trois Souhaits, maintaining his spartan kitchen.

He recited a chain of verbs, using his right fingers as if pulling each one out of the empty drain in the empty sink.

"Snipe. Free fall. Breach. Dive. Rappel. Focus. Choose. Love."
He turned to her helplessly. "Love what, you know?" How
could she, the look on her face said. "Love your .22 Walkyrie
cartridge for your platform MSR 15."

She risked saying, "We have to have you. Look what they
have."

Her Victor found a smile, mostly appreciative at the
gesture, estranged, too, because she could not know. He
breathed the beast back from both of them. "Fuck you, pal,"
he whispered. That she understood and admired. She could
say that with him if he let her. She whispered, "Fuck you, pal."

"Officially, it never happened," he said.

"Makom?" Mary asked

"Makom's disappeared into thin air.'

"Julius."

"Back to family in Haiti. Remember that hurricane,
Matthew?"

"Yes."

"That's what he does. They call him Juli the Guardian
SEAL. He rebuilds concrete houses. Sometimes he digs out
corpses. We talk sometimes. He wonders without end about
the families, the kids, of those three men."

Victor stopped talking. Mary waited. It took him a minute
to look at her again. He said, "My pet truck, Got Junk?"

"Yes."

"I have a yen to ship it to Port-au-Prince. Drive it right to
him."

"Yes."

"He could put it to good use."

Mary imagined Victor doing that. She asked, "Tommy
Sheehan?"

Victor winced at the beast. He said he could still feel the
feel of Tommy's two hands as he put them in one of the
murdered men's black and white headscarves. "Makom
carried him out for about a mile before a recon team drove up

111

to us and took us and the chunks of Tommy. Tommy was the strongest of us all, the most together. He wouldn't have done it, alone or with us. He'd once loved a priest. Used to remember being one of the altar boys for the young priest's first midnight mass, when the priest was sweating and trembling about doing that show in a Lowell church. Tommy, all of thirteen, said he'd be fine, that he Tommy had just prayed for him.

"The priest went on to other boys from Tommy. Got caught in the thirty-year Boston Archdiocese sex scandal. Covering Bishop's name was Law, of all things. Left it all behind, Tommy did. Tommy was married, a father, happy with them when he was on leave. Never forgot the priest. Name was Father Andrews. Or Anders. Said his name to me only once."

She thought about Juli the SEAL, unable to get over what they'd done to wives, children, three families never to be full again. She made that new beast go into the corner to glare at Victor, at her for being with Victor.

Neither one of them cried. That would not have mattered in the least. She knew full well that her Mature had gone where he didn't want to go, that is, didn't want to go with her to where he had just gone. He was wide open now to her awful knowledge of him. Those men were not pigs. Her Mature knew that. They were men before they were savage killers of Western invaders, more Western invaders. The three SEALs were the same, men before they called savage killers pigs and kicked in their chests and used M-4s to shoot away their feet in their boots from their ankles. No equal scales, no righting of necessary principles, no out-of-control logic, no justifying story, none of that had any light to shine on it.

Mary Rice now had known two of these necessary killers. Loved, still loved the first one. Had felt relief, safety, respect with this second one. This second one now cold silent and gone all the way from himself in her kitchen just after he had brought her back from the pit, and now she couldn't get anywhere near him, so far away from her had he just taken himself. Forgiveness, atonement itself, could not find any path to either one of them. They'd been bypassed.

She nodded, like yes, until she was a little weaving, exhausted at her table. She dropped down, thinking a comic word. Plotz.

Mary woke up alone in her bed in the middle of the night and did not give in to the urgency to wet it. She came back, glad that Eugene had left the little seashell night-light on. She put on socks and saw that Eugene had laid his burgundy velour bathrobe along the bottom of the bed. Gene Victor Mature said Demetrius had given the robe to him. His joke. She put it on, tied the belt and his scent around her and got back under the covers. She wanted Victor Mature back with her in her bed. She thought several layers through what and who she was now.

*

Dalton Blue had been the only barrier to Alex Shimmerman's getting control of Chelsea House Newark.

The Rev got himself deep into the international child trade, the orphan market, to get himself out of having skimmed the national endowment. $100K per sweet-looking undernourished infant, it took the delivery of twenty kids to twenty sperm- or egg-challenged rich people in America, France, and Russia to quietly repay his borrowings from the Chelsea National Fund. He had travel, technological, clothing, and occasional substance-need expenses his various spiritual missions around the country didn't underwrite as projected.

For example, to motor it all, he got a cherry red Ford 350 Super Duty Platinum E7 Powerstroke 6.2 L Soho V-8 UT with a raised chassis and extended back bed covered with tight-fitting rubber roof. It had double exhaust pipes thrusting out diagonally from the rear wheels, huge side mirrors that opened and closed like iron doors. It had five orange roof lights punctuating the windshield's girth. He paid cash, over $85K. He hired a strange driver. Thin wisp of a guy in a black baseball cap with a red 350 on a less red bill, a red hoodie that said CNF on the back, gray jeans and gray work boots, unlaced up at the ankles. When not driving but out on the sidewalk parked by a fire hydrant, waiting for the Rev to reemerge from wherever, the wisp was on his cell phone, a cigarette barely alive in his right two fingers as his right thumb punched letters. He grinned happily at the little screen and bobbed around in a seven-step box, talking to it as if it were his favorite stripper, there just for him and his pleasure.

One righteous member in particular of the finance committee had been tipped off by his St. Petersburg in-laws who were furious at a Chelsea baby received but grown unreturnably brain-damaged. That board member went to Blue, but Blue was already sinking deeper with the board and with himself after he went shithouse during the botched raid on the Newark cartel industry. Another pain-in-the-ass good guy who couldn't get along in the real world. With Captain Blue luckily eliminated, Rev. Alex used all his eloquence, charisma, and grace payoffs to reorganize matters. His next approach was to disestablish the children's mission of the CNF, i.e., disinvest in the whole thing by a steady sell-off of the capital stock, the kids under one year old.

AG candidate, A.G. Gottsch, in the meanwhile, got her head, hands, and staff around the politics of unborn rights (POUR). Taking a page out of the recent book of fake news, she brazened out her own brand: Screw your facts: CAFTS, Complete Absolute Fabrication Tough Shit. The fight was for the unborn and against degenerate immigrant parents, which was not at all a contradiction except in the minds of the fake news media. Once their babies were forcefully born here, the children went into the burgeoning Chelsea Houses around the country for proper dissemination. The parents, both of them, married, unmarried, partnered, crooked straight and crooked gay, with all their accents, bullshit foreign credentials—as vetted and explained thoroughly by CAFTS hard and social media—had the simple choice, deportations or incarceration in Caribbean-rim military-run detention centers until properly mind-scrubbed to maybe reapply for limited green-card license to do domestic and seasonal labor. The fictional Lindberg's accession to the presidency was junior-high-school empowerment as compared to what A.G. for AG was just the beginning. National moral resurge built on the inviolable safety of the unborn.

In the Alex & Ashley Show that meteored high without ever seeming to burn out, the Reverend Shimmerman supplemented and emboldened her vision with his own revision of the Christian Nation, with its authoritarian gospel necessity fueled and engined by the return of reprobation (ROR or ror). The uber-text was Matthew 25:31-46. The sheep and the goats. The Son of Man comes in his glory. Sheep on the right, goats on the left. Only the righteous, the sheep, enter the kingdom of heaven; those on the left are cursed into the eternal fire prepared for the devil and his angels.

Ashley Gottsch in turn turned up the CAFTS volume, the Politics of Unborn Rights Enterprise (PURE). Together they carved an unprecedented wedge into contemporary liberal cultural thinking about pretty much everything, at least in NYS. They did so by substituting a kind of stone-skipping banter for the shrink-wrapped phrase-making of national elections that had dispensed pretty much with context, syntax, and predicate subjects. Flat-stoning it, A.G. for AG perfected the staccato technique: sidearm, skim, skim, plop. Sidearm, skim, skim, plop, gone, gone down. Unborn, unborn, plop, gone. Immigrant, immigrant, sink, that's all, folks. Flatstone, surface, on top, under, over. Throw, one, two, no three. Wordoid, fling, no thing. Get the stopped? Tend, span, spin, done. Talk that way, talk that way, don't say, don't pay. Think it not, sink it in, leave no sign. Cafts not facts, over is under, abort that fort. Lobal glomming, planet can it, raise the waters. Get the stopped, now, schmuck? Fling, skim, sink.

Or, just old school: Ready, shoot, aim, repeat.

Start with an astonishing lie about someone or a group of like someones. Like aborting mothers and their enabling sperm pumpers. Associate all such with supportive cultural and political groupies—associations promoting existing post-born children, limits on advance-aged extended life, post-traumatic stress veterans of America's wars who wouldn't stay on their meds, people like that whose lives were extraneous and excessive given the larger national need of saving the fetuses at all moral costs. Ashley and Alex wrote a manifesto, "Abortion: The Original Crime Against Humanity," and got it translated from English into America's thirteen most other languages.

TED talks, Webinars, a month on an open XM Satellite radio station, an APP called Nobortion Nomore, indirect, in fact masked initial funding from the billionaire Hoch Sisters' Life First Fund. Pop-ups into an incredible variety of unsuspecting people's regular online shopping habits, and the list of mind-access went on and on—brilliantly, inescapably, numbingly effective. These inlets and outlets made abortion a river of babies, baby-creatures, feticides, little toes and fingernails and follicles and drowned ever-blue eyes of wonder: eyes of horrific disappointment in the selfish world of murder by mother.

Alex ruled the willing AG in all such because he was the man of the word, different from the candidate of choice. He breathed slogans, etched lies good as truth, put cheesy slant rhymes and cutely vicious anagrams together like spoons of flat alphabet soup. He even brought back the palinode, the metaphors of the boomerang, the tsunami, and the mother's curse. Ashley contributed rounding, sounding, pounding speeches before large and small groups in halls, gyms, meeting rooms, ballrooms, outdoor bandstands and indoor podiums. Her purposefully ditzy, sing-song monologues were laced with unanswerable catchphrases like "Let America Live Again," "Reproductive Responsibilities," "Birthing for Being," and "The Unchoosing Life is Not Worth Living." An AG for A.G. speech put up a female political candidate who was not afraid of womanliness, motherhood, nurturing, living for others, a woman who could cry and often did and never apologized for letting it happen a little bit, maybe a little more, never for more than ten full seconds. Candidate Gottsch didn't shy away from criminalizing abortions in this century, in this country, in this state, city, neighborhood, school, street fair, CostCo cash register line, church, stacked parking lot, or rat-infested vacant lot.

The two of them took hold of the political, cultural moment and did not let go. They had Jenny Rich's best journalist/pr/communication skills to draw upon. The first thing Jenny created became famous, or infamous, depending upon perspective. She created a pinkly fetal-positioned Goleman Eck staring out of a grayish womb, his adult face computer reverse-generated into tiny Goley's wan face still recognizable as his potentially. She printed that image on folding-paper ladies' fans for cooling the sweat on one's face. The fans, thousands of them, became a thing, copied, stolen, traded, and prized as ultra-weird and to-the-point right in the faces of the whole feticidal abortion industry, the culture of death that was the core sickness of the country.

In addition, the fifteen-minute Podcast Jenny created was celebrated and condemned, exactly the split Ashley Gottsch and Rev. Alex wanted. It was celebrated among the state voters now calling themselves the Echsters. They liked its hero, the sub-or-supra-living entity who had no real birthday. They liked its fun about how such a guy could get a license to drive, open an account at Ace Hardware or a Money Market

Fund at Chase or serve in the military, the priesthood, or on a jury. Eck was an erased slate, a tabula rasa'd nescience, a pointillist Chuck Close portrait whose face was about to collapse into a million dots. The Podcast, like its politics, made Gole into anything it wanted, anything it needed him to serve as, say, represent, enforce.

Echsters wore the Podcast's hashtag: #ⓌⓌⓌ.~Gole. and said many different things about what it meant, one of which was "ineffable," further explicated as in an effing fable. The aborted genius of the winds was living proof of the unknowable force of life that Ashley Gottsch ran on as a moral necessity for government to insure. Equally, he was Shimmerman's banner of a new crusade for the spiritual defense of the unrecognized, the uneducated, the uncool, of all whom both mainstream religions and secular politics condescended to at their peril. This dual upwelling against what both Ash and Alex called the disorder of things didn't have to hammer out a platform to run on. It ran on itself much better. When it said our children will be our children again, the tag of #ⓌⓌⓌ.~Gole floated like writing on the wall that participation in the movement understood implicitly. It didn't take long before this pregnant mini-theory claimed total explanatory power. All it needed to go fully into its own meaninglessness was enough people fed up with meaning that overlooked them and really meant to do so. It had the political virtue of standing for nothing and defying whatever somethings enabled the corporations, big media, elite education, all that, to dead-end the left-behind, the ultra-aborted.

At least, that's how the burgeoning underclass understood it at as Echsters promulgated it first locally, then statewide. #ⓌⓌⓌ.~Gole appeared in different graffiti versions on subway cars and bus sides, in four-foot form on abandoned gas stations, and flashed like a Batman pyramid of light over Gole's building by the river, until the city shut it down. At the same time, neither Gottsch nor Shimmerman meant to lose it to colossal, national ambition of either Alt-right or Alt-left political organizations. They were not fooled, but they did fool less realistic, much more messianic types than themselves. They would be careful in that regard. They would not lose what could be gained by close attention to the limits of chance success. When they spoke about it, they ended up joking, one to the other, "Oh, boy. Oh, girl. It's a boy. It's a girl."

A West-African Arkansas stand-up comic named Ed Regius got the first Goleman Eck material broadcast on satellite radio's "Rednecks Funnin." He used Eck to take shots at the entire white spectrum from moral outrage to squishy transcendence that appropriated him. In his Ghanaian-Arkansas accent, he admitted he was doing the same thing.

At one such performance in a Tri-City comedy club Regius, a working high-school wrestling coach, got the better of a skinny anti-abortion heckler in an American flag tracksuit who rushed the stage armed with two cream pies. He reversed the guy's throwing elbow so that one pie ended decorating the heckler's own howling face to the delight of the audience. When the guy was hauled off the stage, Regius two-fingered some of the other cream pie into his own mouth without leaving any on his chin, and he chanted, "Goleman is the Sole Man, the never-born Whole Man, the motherless Wo Man, the Dearth of Birth Man, the Prince of Reversal, the Lord of the Abort Cohort, the Roll Back the Rock Man Incarnate. Saint Anthony in Heaven Did Come Down, the One Who Was Lost Has Been Found." Jenny Rich helped the videoed riff go viral. Ash and Alex, magnifying the buzz, denied having anything to do with it, a truly disingenuous claim.

Sex might have kept Jenny Rich and Alex Shimmerman together close enough to watch each other. It was just that theirs was not the reality piece of sex. They did get to play out their misogynist and misandrist deepest loathings one long night after a fantastically exciting work session in her little rented office in Astoria about sending Goleman Eck on an actual train canvassing the state. The train would not really do anything, just be the train and whistle-stop the old fashioned way at various stations three to three hundred miles apart. At various times on that glory train would be star politicians, star stars, star medical abortion interventionists, star real-estate moguls, star NFL owners, star NRA apologists, matched with star androcenists, star vegan gurus and growers, star anti-global-war rock musicians of three decades back, star billionaire bitcoin dealers, star fossil-fuel and battery-power combinators, star Souls for Judas married to ISIS-retired commanders both committed to having ten children by Unplanned Parenthood coital practices—an inchoate concatenation of weavers for world order.

That night the reverend and the journalist dreamed these impossible dreams like precise Disney animators achieving "Snow White" itself frame by frame. Exponentially crazier and crazier, the two of them found their own phantasmic steroids and shot each other up with them before they beat each other naked mercilessly into chthonic orgasm, coming and coming down on each other's bare bodies with a ferocity that maybe only wolves and raptors imagine. They both missed next day's #ⒼⒼⒼ.~Gole early-draft rally at Plymouth Rock Park, sending their separate regrets through lieutenants of Gole Cause, a Jenny Rich sketch-only word, to the forty or so people who came to the founding rock that day and hour mostly just to see, if not to learn.

It was later, in one of the movement retellings, that both Jenny and Alex tried to get at one another one more time by being the first to undo the other's social capital. In the meanwhile, though, they put a lid on such frenzy. They went back to work together because each was smarter than the other in several inextricable ways. "Gole Cause" having instantly tanked when tested out of state at Plymouth, Jenny came up with a reading of #ⒼⒼⒼ.~Gole: "You don't have to be a cryptologist," she explained at the next press conference in Providence, "three complete trimesters leading to Goleman Eck's very being in the world to see it's all a symbol for 'Baby + abort,' i.e., babe-ort with an underwritten 'Babe, thou art.' And that's Gole Eck, the Babeort, a new word for a new kind of man. The world's babeort begins anew." She was having a helluva good time with this stuff. Just as she hoped, her cheesy portmanteau word found its own usage pattern. It began to mean to people. People went with babeort as a self-explanatory phenomenon like no other.

Soon enough babeort Gole became a political phrase even though it was politically meaningless. "What isn't right now?" the AG candidate said to all, though only in private. The election was still months away. Anything could happen. Babeort and #ⓒⓒⓒ.~Gole became the unspoken and, yet again, the ineffable magical talk that resonated across the spectrum of special-interests from fetal personhood to eco-childraising in anthropocenic wasteland disaster scenarios.

There was no longer any need for a political campaign to be only about something when it could be about everything the majority of voters who voted wanted.

Notice, Ashley pointed out, she did not say everything as in Everything, just the multiple things that sufficient numbers of people worked for and got worked up about. A.G. candidate AG called for a politics of total inclusion of totally opposite positions, nothing less, she said, than the final realization of the conditions of the two main political parties anyway. She would evolve the Office of the State Attorney General out of its current obsessions with intractable issues: crime, drugs, immigration, corruption in the hospitals and the universities, exclusionary bakers and greedy gun dealers, reverse sexual harassment. It would take some time to clear the dockets and the minds of all that, yes, but it was possible through the realization of what #ⓒⓒⓒ.~Gole stood for on the level of informing principle to begin to achieve "the living Gole of nolle me tangere, nolle you tangere," leaving and being left alone.

All that was maybe too exalted for everyone to grasp, but the thought leaders in the spreading movement got it well enough. They made their own coherence seem refreshing and liberating to the next level organizers on down to the grass rooters wearing the T-shirts, hoodies, and bumper stickers sporting the Gole hashtag. Jenny Rich, smart but discrete as ever, told people privately who wanted to be smart and discrete like her, that this "situating" of Goleman Eck's phantasmic "presence" in the world of politics, in spite of what he himself wanted, had its precedents, powerful icons in American history.

She named them: Jesus, Martin, dead Kennedys, Rosa, Eleanor, Carrie. She invited her listeners to expand the list, with care and in good faith.

Nonesuch people were political in the sense of running for public office (notice, *dead* Kennedys, differently aborted). They were instead, like Goleman Eck, a condition or state of mind about what it means to live. That's why they inspired others to run for public office, to change the very culture of what it means to live. Again, Jenny Rich insisted, you can't go around talking this way, not to most people. "So you'll choose whom to invite into such a change of mind that underlies Gole Eck's iconic presence in our local A.G. race. And, in the human race."

Jenny reveled in the simple reverse public-relations and unending elegance of it all. Eck would make explicit what was implicit in all political candidates starting, like, now. He would be totally unlike the reigning but outrageous madness on the current national scene right now in which bloated personality achieved unheard-of power. Eck himself would not win; his condition would. And those who followed him, they would lead, *in hoc signo*, in his name. If he ran, he would not be nominated, if he served, he would not be elected. He would not be where he was expected. They, his followers, like Jenny, like Ashley, the Rev, would be the party of no party. Partisan politics would cease. Would abort. Like the lucky Goleman Eck, would be a whole other way of living, deciding, ruling. An as yet unimaginable system of communications would come into being to regulate, police, enforce, administer in all fair ways possible for the greatest good for the greatest number. It all began here, with AG's candidacy for A.G. in this hugely wealthy amorphous state held together by the state of Eck.

It was beautiful.

*

Copulence. Just as soon as the word came to Alex, he took it in as a real concept. Moral copulence.

Sticky sex of the disgusting one percent, copulation of the opulent.

He was in the well-appointed if small walnut board room of Chelsea House Newark, talking to Walter Krinsky, who wanted a baby boy. Krinsky had stubby thick fingers, out of line with thin-cut muted gray suit and black Gucci loafers with tassels like a swarthy virgin's eyelashes.

"Three wives," Krinsky said. "All pretty gorgeous, you ever seen one?"

"Certainly true, Walt. Too many girls by them, though?"

Krinsky's opening right hand signaled the Rev that maybe that remark was a little presumptuous, even if pretty right. The hand closed. Don't expect more than the movies. A Walter Krinsky saying.

"We have the right boy child now. You'll do great service to a humane cause. You'll be a great dad, which I see from what you wrote in this file. You've been a stalwart for Chelsea House."

Krinsky couldn't tear up if he tried. "I've done a lot. I've been blessed with a lot. It all came my way, my way, the way of hard, hard work. I'm honored, Reverend, to know you think

I can be a good, a great, father figure to that boy in those pictures."

Shimmerman touched the group of six photos on the top of his unnamed file folder. The billionaire sitting across from him could give two rat shits what the minister thought of him. It was something like checkers. Money jumped over you, took your checker. Money like Krinsky's went back to arrangements killed for and ripped out of a couple of different aftermaths of the German retreat from Russia in 1944. When men like him checker their ungodly beautiful serial wives, they go from copulence to copulence, jumping their women's bones. The art of the steal Shimmerman learned the spiritual way. He got his mind back to the business at hand.

Krinsky adjusted his hard-exercised posture in his seat. Fifty at most, he hard-bodied it in his seat. If you carved twenty pounds out of his face, you'd have a Giacometti Onassis kind of guy. One who took off his purple framed glasses now, rubbed the bridge of his straight bronzed nose, said, "I intend to spend the next five years taking direct care of my boy. Then I'll go back to work. I'll be glad to help Chelton again."

"Chelsea."

"Again," Krinsky said. "Precisely. The paper is signed. Can I see him now?"

Something had gone silently awry with the transfer in Arizona. This wasn't the actual child intended in the regular way to realize Krinsky's fantasy of proxy boy-child fatherhood. This was a child from a very late-term rich little girl's botched delivery some nun-nurse actually stole out of the pan and spirited away into a private post-natal unit. Scooped back up out of his stainless-steel cradle-grave, he was a wonder kid. The good sister fought like a madwoman when, cutting and slashing with a machete two of three men who came for the boy until the third Mexican wrestler broke her hands and jammed her crucifix up her nose and beyond.

Krinsky would never know that. That's how secure the

Reverend's post-abortion operation was below the border, on the other side of the wall.

Shimmerman checked Krinsky's signature line. He nodded affirmatively to the new foster father. He texted another office in Chelsea House that he was coming over with the donor from one of the Florida keys, a city and a mountain resort in Europe, to introduce him to the as yet not renamed Paulito. He thought he saw despisal in Krinsky's eyes. The feeling was mutual.

SEVEN

To re-state his professional status in the working world: Goleman Eck was a relatively young but senior Renewable Energy engineer for a global wind and solar energy company based in New York and brazenly called EXOIL. As a fillip to the dying fossil fuel and even nuclear industries, their actual print logo appeared in classical Greek letters as ἐχόίλ. EXOIL made a good deal of noise about the ancient sun and wind that RE was steadily blowing and irradiating old energy off the wounded planet while there was still time and a plan to save the earth and make it great again by creating a temperate 1.5-2.0 Celsius world.

Gole did wind, that is, wind turbines that converted wind energy into electricity. He described his job as construction and operation monitoring, energy-yield analysis, meteorological studies, with some regulatory activity and technology assessment. He had a personal stake he didn't talk about in EXOIL's "conception to completion" tagline. He wasn't rabid, he didn't go around denouncing internal combustion, ethanol, plastic garbage bags, fossil fuels, lubricants, or the Acela Express. He had a smooth way of getting those debates away from acrimony and into the simple grandeur of air in motion. Only on one of the spacious walls of his windowed 12-14th floor condominium did he have a magisterial photograph of a floating wind farm of sixty wind turbines in the Baltic Sea that was providing electricity to 400,000 Germans. He had been there in its construction years, as he had visited, learned in, and consulted in the famous UK sites, the massive farm in Oregon, other sites in India, Turkey, Singapore. They wanted him soon in the Brazilian rain forest and the Mayflower project in Massachusetts. He was one of maybe a dozen RE engineers specializing in building and maintaining the turbines spinning in the air that gave each of them the name, Windman or Windwoman.

Keeping up with research and development in wind was regular exercise for him. He worked hard; he got paid for it, the work he had in life got him out of bed in the morning in a good mood. That massive photograph of the floating Baltic wind farm in its subtle chrome frame was his way of presenting the grandeur and beauty of the great towers holding the elegant rotors with their three blades. The sea around them made more noise than their whirring and humming. They had the peaceful power and might, he would say to people who could appreciate it, of serenity, repose.

There was a small group of them on the way to the Sagamore Bridge to Cape Cod. They appeared as if out of nowhere, there off by themselves to the north. The truly amazing one stood all by itself on the road going away from the Cape. You could get near it by going up the short dirt driveway off the highway. There it was, a gleaming, winding solo giant at the far end of a huge field. As you drove ever closer to it, it seemed to move altogether, propeller-like blades and tower, across, over, down and up, as if circling to take flight, dance, leap, subside—until a big white security vehicle with its high beams on started moving towards you ominously. And the whole company of them on the Baltic could move their giant sharp limbs in syncopated circles, each differently from the other as if exquisitely sensitive to differences in the wind, yet ready to lift off all together, to rise and fly and settle down yet again on some other ocean thousands of miles away, willfully bringing masses of light to an entirely different place on the globe.

Wind power had its own lyric language that lightened data-driven reports Eck could take in like a mother-tongue: airfoil, chord, cut-in speed, furling, wind rose, yaw. But he wouldn't go around his mates waxing about the lyrical terms. He could get right down to, "They are so beautiful." He would say that softly, to himself only, because he had to stave off Don Quixote, who was mad about windmills. Gole wanted to be friends with them, not see them as enemies at all. And he preferred to call the turbines "mills." The Don's windmills pumped up water from the ground. It was that element of work that the old term had over "turbines." But people in his business clasped their modern word against anyone ignorant enough to call their RE structures mills. Then there were the ones who saw their business at the forefront, cutting edge, new wave of saving the planet from global warming. They used words like anthropogenic, a special Greek-based argot in which they talked successfully to one another but not to anyone else. Many developed the sanctimony of an ordained priesthood of technological redemption. They cursed the fossil-fuel industries to hell for all eternity. Gole found greed for money and power in a huge swath of them.

Gole first read about the man of La Mancha in "selections," in a fat world literature anthology he had to use in a Newark community college that preceded his getting into a nearby technology institute. The bits of the book showed him enough of Don Quixote and Sancho Panza to get him into the entire massive set of stories about the brilliant skinny aristocrat so utterly unsuited for the commonly modern world. When Sancho insisted that they were not giants that almost killed him, the Don fought like crazy for his vision. When the Don descended to hear the final wisdom of the greatest dead knight in the world and emerged with it—"Patience, and shuffle the cards,"—the permanently unmoored, unborn Eck found his awful comic hero and patiently worked at the game until he got the winning hand of jokers and windmills. He blessed Cervantes and wrote his own script, never forgetting Sancho's plea to the dying Quixote that to give up errantry and die was the true madness.

Mary Rice, who listened to Eck about a lot of things he didn't share around, would say about his literary bent, "Your education's showing again, even if you pretty much got it by yourself."

That was fair, she meant well. People deeply affected by Mozart or Thelonius Monk or Virginia Woolf or Baryshnikov or Pablo Neruda (one could plug in any high priest of the human heart) can be affected people indeed. One could get touchy about other people's fervid touchstones of sorrow and endurance. Like those people, Mary Rice said, who say things like Hamlet is more real than anyone or that art, literature hold the only mirror up to life that reflects the real or creates it or both. So like his Cervantes, Gole also kept his Dante to himself, because Dante meant a world to him. Gole was happy that his eyrie was a good place for Alighieri to ghost in.

About Dante, here's what he told Mary Rice, who told him a good deal later that she knew her Dante but just had enough common sense to keep that to herself, lest her own education be showing. The hardly aging, beautiful Wellesley classics lady from old-school College.

He said, "I read him in a maybe eighth-grade level, illustrated version of the *Inferno*."

"You mean," Mary said, "like the *Classics Illustrated Frankenstein* you told me about?"

"No. But weird. The illustrations were Blake's and Doré's and Botticelli's and Moebius's and Martini's'. That's weird times four. I don't know whether I read what they pictured or pictured what they read."

"Jeez," Mary said.

She looked around his place as if she were in a different visual tour. Gole was not someone she wouldn't believe. Still, he had his own hold on reality, like no one else's.

Not even her new love's. Victor the SEAL's world was war. He touched her as if hers were peace, as if what he did to Somali pirates came from different fire and earth than her body's very elements were made of.

She concentrated on the huge photograph of the floating wind turbines while Gole kept talking.

"I read about thousands of child souls waiting in a limbo of God's own making for a someone who alone, or a time when that alone, could get them across the river. *I did not know that life had unborn so many.*" Gole stopped at his own killer line. Mary waited for him to keep on going, again.

"I could not, even at that little age, understand or imagine why I was not among them."

As Mary listened to Gole, something clicked clear about Victor. Victor her Mature, was a trained assassin, a state killer. The country made him that way because that's the way the world was now. Had been, he said, for a lot longer than people wanted to know. He'd learned to be invisible. To be exact. Not aware of time, until something changed that wasn't supposed to, then to be aware of everything in time, space, a sixth sense of dimension. For minutes inside her, Victor shuddered unstoppably. Receiving him was like moving up inside one of Gole's beautiful windmills.

"Whatever the reason for that," Gole was saying to her, "it was not that I was the exception. A vessel of some unique dispensation. Passing for real, as in really born, is enough of a daily burden without deluding myself into thinking I was, you know, special."

"Know what my man Victor, my man at last now, says?" Mary asked Gole.

"Oh, good. Yes. What?"

"Endless war makes endless sense to senseless people. That's why it's endless."

*

Goleman Eck's extremely personal story got reported, blogged, social-mediated. With that came people offended in some way by him, disturbed by either the truth or falsehood or both of him. He shut down photographers, but a few images of him from college or from wind-industry promotions and reportage circulated. His global different good looks romanced the matter of his origin or clinched its unholy absence. Like for Mrs. Jericho, back at his party, she'd tell you.

"Hey, you're Bob Dylan!" out on the street made Bob Dylan cringe tight, for fear of a weapon, a Lennon killer, so Bob Dylan nodded and just kept on his way.

Gole thought that way the safest when it happened to him. It became his practice, sometimes to the outrage of the greeter, into sometimes following Eck for a half a block, asking and demanding why he was so much better, freak couldn't even say fucking hello to a well-wisher, a fan, a person with the right to know of your Excellency the public personality, why, really, asshole, why aren't you dead, the way your mother wanted it. That kind of thing might have turned Eck around, but he couldn't let that happen. He adopted the faith that all this would attenuate, that his case was different for sure but couldn't sustain long-term interest in this world of limited attention to anything.

He did let an elderly blonded woman in a red beret, red raincoat, and red ankle-height laced shoes hand him a white card with scarlet embossed letters that said, "It's not too late to have a happy childhood." She didn't say anything to him, didn't want anything from him, and she disappeared down the sidewalk in a girlish flounce after delivering her kindly-meant message.

Then there was the persistent texter who forced him to change his cell-phone number. Where the person got it from Gole did not know. This texter said Eck violated the very order of nature. Said he was a liar, a fraud, a deceiving trickster as old as Satan. Said he was a global danger as an engineer of the winds, an impossible candidate for redemption. Said he was a trans-vivant, a dis-human thing capable of sowing the end of God's intention for man. Said Eck was something that will, had to, must be, at the very least, sterilized or castrated by the Public Health arm of the Federal Government.

Cartoons of Eck appeared: unimaginative images, Hitleresque, Muslim terrorist, both a Black rapist and a white supremacist, a weaponizer of drones to fly into Super Bowls, a Nicaraguan drug cartel leader bent on poisoning El Norte's Nobel laureates, doom master in a bunkered undercity, and, of course, Victor F. come back with legions of monsters stitched from unmatched aborted limbs.

On another side, tele-multi-evangelist Rev. Shimmerman led the miracle chorus that sang thanksgiving and paschal rounds about Goleman Eck's revolution for humanity. Eck showed that we were not bogged down in the creation cant of the established denominations. Instead, a true suspension of the laws of nature that only God could achieve. To wit, the Word made Miracle to bring the world back to the almightiest power there has ever been.

The Rev went over the line, straight into Gole's profession. He sent a deacon-photographer from a sister online church out of Atlanta up in a helicopter to circle all around EXOIL's increasingly famous floating North Atlantic windmill armada. The footage played on the Rev's web site, of a kind of soaring aerial ballet featuring the great blades in over-under-around shots along with stock images of massive mountaintop crucifixes in the Andes and the Atlas Mountains.

Shimmerman claimed Gole's engineering artistry as a metaphor for the Miracle of Eck in the New Age of Miracle, not a blasphemous Second Coming at all but the Word Made Miracle in the science and trans-science of the twenty-first century. The curve of the universe, the in spiritus of wind cleaning the polluted atmosphere, the wondrous aborted being of this new, the utterly surprising imitation of Christ, Goleman Eck.

Eck abhorred Shimmerman' script for him, though he liked the guy's undeluded charisma as a postmodern preacher-seer-evangel who seemed to do a lot of good railing and snarling from his digital pulpit at international child prostitution, human trafficking, even the misery of little girl fistulas and kids born to be viciously bullied and shunned because of hairlips that could be fixed for two hundred dollars. For the latter alone, fixing the cracked open mouths of unwanted kids, Eck contributed tens of thousands of dollars. But the Reverend Shimmerman co-opted Eck's very core, and Eck said no, man, no. Soon enough, they only talked on email, so thoroughly antagonistic did they become.

"I do understand," he tapped out to the ordained man, "I really do. I don't believe what you believe, but your trans-digital spiritual empire can't have me. And there's some weird talk about just what's going on with Chelsea House world-babies for sale. I'm pulling the plug."

"No, you're not," Shimmerman said. "Not at all. Don't you see that the way you came my way gives you the credibility nothing and nobody else can? You think your unborn life matters a damn outside of what you and I together can do with it, make you an actual real person with it?"

"Plugged pulled, my frocked friend," Gole said. "Take it all down. You've got a week."

More people than Shimmerman took a run at him, had a use for the culted Goleman Eck, trans-natural engineer of the new winds of energy. He needed a super-agent, a public relations firm or three, batteries of insurance companies, legal representation, artistic representation, financial backers and venture capitalists specializing in his yet unimaginable powers of endorsement, even a genealogist in Ingolstadt who offered proof of Gole's legitimate claim to be in the line of the Catholic theologian Johann Maier von Eck who debated Luther in the early Counter Reformation.

He told Shimmerman the latter one.

The Rev told him to be very wary of fraud, particularly in his vulnerable state.

Gole replied that it was interesting the offer was coming from Ingolstadt, given that that was where Victor Frankenstein went to college to study modern science. The Rev went blank at that information.

So, all in all, Eck stayed cool, waiting out all the offered riches, euthanasia, islands, coffins, followers, assassins, marriages, solitary confinement, elixirs, hemlock offered to him.

*

Soon enough, though, he was thinking himself crazy again. He stopped that and gave in to the impulse to touch Yolande Segundo's number on his cell.

"Hi. It's me."

Yolande threw open the freezer locker door. "Shithead," she said. "Every woman's worst nightmare of intimacy in the darkest pit of the night."

"I'm sorry," he said. "Let's have a baby."

It was as if they'd been exchanging such lines for a long time. "First, though," Yolande said, "let's start World War Three. And fuck you anyway."

"Let's have a drink. Play cards. Exchange gifts. Do a five-hundred piece Mehmet the Conqueror floral design puzzle. Lie down and just sleep together. In that order of difficulty."

Yolande tried to breathe in all the air out of her phone, suffocate him enough to stop him from talking. He felt that in his ear. She wanted to suffocate him, stop him from his saying, saying any more, anything at all to her. Then her utter silence without audible breath tried to make him hang up on her, get this most unwanted caller to fade his own will to keep her on the phone.

"I have this girlfriend, Sarah Gee?" she said. "Lost her baby at six months?"

He deserved this. He started to move his cell off his right ear. He deserved this. He didn't say that. He just said, "Yeah?"

"Crushed her. Took her and her husband three years of trying. Baby aborted. You know, baby's choice? Crushed her. Baby's body taken from her and disposed of she didn't get to know how. Then she couldn't conceive at all. She ended up in Arizona at a trauma spa. Know what they did for Sarah Gee out in the desert at high noon one day?"

"Yolande."

"Had a funeral, a burial. Actual serious rabbi and a genius theology professor who was a Paraguayan shaman. Kaddish. Dance. Libations poured into the desert sand. Sacred wind music. You miserable bastard. What gives you the right to broadcast your being cut off the way you're doing? Your scent of death?"

"Yolande, give me a chance."

"Just one more question. Do you think that funeral for my broken friend could have worked just as well if it were an exorcism? Maybe all funerals are exorcisms, eh? Mr. Goleman Eck, eh? You think? Why don't you just go somewhere in the world and play with your windmills. Yes, do that. Go somewhere and make more energy out of nothing. Don't be calling me."

He was being beaten into love. She stopped it and started to cry. Not that he could hear her, but he knew she was crying.

"Can I come over?" he asked.

He got up and moved over to the harbor window. Space and seconds widened. Bunches of light flickered up to him from Hoboken. He picked out a green light at the end of a wharf that was just a line of bars and restaurants, not a boat or a barge along it. The Hudson River emptied itself endlessly into shapeless wide water. Maybe seven seconds altogether.

"No," Yolande said. "I'll come to you."

That frightened Eck. He was terrified for her.

She said, "Tell the doorman."

"Please," he said. "I'll meet you downstairs."

"No," she said. "I don't want you to do that. Just tell the doorman to let me up." She hung up.

He felt a thick coil of cold come up from the water world and grip his neck front and back.

*

To begin with, Yolande Segundo found Dom Perignon cold at his bar. She lit a new improved Blue Dream joint and took some hits off it but meant most of it for him. It wasn't that he got all easy too soon. It was that she seemed to have decoded the oldest possible need and desire in him that he had controlled by the very force of will that she got him to release them both from. He just wanted to know if she could really do this to him all the way down into him.

With his "Sure, go ahead," she stripped him of his sweater, shirt, t-shirt. She gently pushed him down on his big bed of lavender quilts from Norway and pale green cotton sheets from Bahrain. She undid his belt buckle and fly, got him to bridge up as she shimmied his chinos down over his hips and then had him raise his legs up so that she could take pull the pants off him in one smooth grip of their cuffs, the way one undresses a boy. He knew he was being handled that way.

He started not to know anything beyond this moment. He wanted this moment with his whole heart. She left his white briefs on. She had him turn on his left side and bring his knees up toward his abdomen, and she had him close his eyes. She got under the quilt with him, still fully dressed, and put her arms around him. She was smaller than he, of compact very sexy body, but soon she was to him much bigger. She touched him slowly, methodically, everywhere. She spoke in chanting, open vowel talk, and when he did open his eyes, the darkness in his bedroom was absolute.

Yolande Segundo tried much that she knew. She acted with no threat atop him. She moved high and low on him, slowly like age, fast and faster like youth. She slapped his face lightly three times each side while beneath him, then took him hard between her breasts which she pushed together and would not let him pull back from within them. She took him deep into her mouth and made him stare back into her eyes as he moved back and forth in a soft rhythm. She lost control happily when they were on their knees and he was inside her from behind, and she lay on her side by him as another little sleep took him.

If it were safe in the world for her mothering sex for him, he would have felt some momentary compensation for his ancient grief. She'd brought a silver jar with a gold cover. He soon felt the thin cool oil in her hands again all over him, like a final cleansing by petals, palms, breath, hers. He was reaching a state of uncare, submission, desire so unified in her that, for whole periods of seconds, it didn't matter that he lived unborn. He got there, she got him there, and neither one of them knew that they knew how to do that for the other.

"You are very beautiful, Goleman Eck. I thought so, but I didn't really know."

He woke up, alone. He couldn't find her. It must have been a dream. There was a howl in him to go back to sleep. She soothed his forehead and abdomen, he did slip back, but the place he was in went hurtling down into wet stone cells. One of his windmills went berserk, tried to slice him to pieces. Despite the nice Blue Dream she'd given him, some last vicious string uprooted itself from his head, leaving a gaping pain.

She called him back up, her voice reaching frantically all the way down to him. She used awful, gentle might, breathed his breathing, cried out in an iron corridor. He wrapped his legs around her terrified back and began to swim in the current of her oil and water and mucous and slight sweat. There was the lighted entrance. Their arms, legs, torsos, heads were the same. The entrance came to them.

They spilled out together onto the distressed sheets, quilts and pillows that was the real bed of Goleman Eck, into the most comical awakening hangover they would ever know. They held on to each other in joint hiccupping laughter, circled each other on their knees, wrestled and smelled one another, buried each the other in bedding, whooped, meowed and barked, dove into each other, tongued and sucked and kissed the wet and hard of each other, grabbed, mounted and fucked each other silly, and called each other brother and sister before going into a sleep way under anything allowed love on this earth.

*

Aspiration, dilation and evacuation, and dilation and extraction, as Googled from *Web*MD, "Abortion PPT notes" on quizlet.com and like sources, memorized and organized and edited variously by Goleman Eck, was one of his efforts to start himself. He never succeeded in holding anyone's, particularly any woman's, attention to his whole recital. Sometimes he would re-order his telling of the three procedures. Even so, those who did start listening went away dazed with just parts or pieces of the whole presentation. Eck himself never started any of it without going through the whole. It was sort of like doing the Apostle's Creed, the Declaration of Independence, or Hamlet's soliloquy, a personal compulsion to finish what got going in him about first days.

The monologue initiated way back in his junior year in

engineering college in Newark. He was becoming a prodigy in fluids systems and massive industrial plumbing blueprinting and also working in the school's federally-funded data collection of measuring water usage in Manhattan toilets during half-times in Super Bowls. In the same period, he took a one-credit course with a speech teacher to work on his unplaceable American accent.

The adjunct teacher, a demanding alcoholic and one-time Royal Shakespeare Company actor named Windsor, invited Gole to create just such a soliloquy of his choice. Goleman Eck worked up his first abortion procedures monologue from sources available then. Windsor liked it, encouraged Gole through several sequencings of the material, listened to Gole do it through weekly iterations to Windsor alone, and thereby did somewhat smooth the edge off Eck's odd American tongue. Its controlled intensity could make the sentimental Windsor weep. Early versions of it morphed over the years as public information sources about the procedures became direct, simple, and informative. Of late, it had settled into the following.

"Basically," Eck said, "There are four methods.

"First trimester. Abortifacient drugs. Chief is misoprostol, ninety percent success rate. That rate improves even more in combination with another feticidal drug, mifepristone."

"First six to sixteen weeks. Aspiration: referred to as suction aspiration, suction curettage, or vacuum aspiration. Involves widening of the cervix and insertion of a cannula, a long plastic tube connected to a device inserted into the uterus to suction out the fetus and placenta," Eck said.

Eck said, "After sixteen weeks. Dilation and evacuation. Insertion of laminaria or a synthetic dilator inside cervix. Next day, a tenaculum keeps cervix and uterus in place and cone-shaped rods of increasing size continue dilation. Perhaps a shot before the procedure begins to ensure fetal death. A cannula then inserted to begin removing tissue away from the lining. Curette scrapes lining to remove residuals, or forceps larger parts. Last step final suctioning of contents. Fetal remains examined to ensure abortion complete."

"After twenty-one weeks. Dilation and extraction. Also known as D & X, Intact D & X, Intrauterine Cranial Decompression, and Partial Birth Abortion. Laminaria inserted to dilate cervix. Water breaks on third day. Fetus rotated. Forceps pull legs, shoulders, arms through birth canal. Incision at skull's base allows suction catheter inside, which removes cerebral material until skull collapses and forceps are used to grasp and pull the legs, shoulders, and arms through the birth canal. Fetus completely removed," Eck said.

It went without saying, Eck said, that no catheter removed his cerebral material and hence that his skull had not collapsed. It was clear that he as a viable six-month fetus had been completely removed and thrown out. And somehow renewed after that unbirth.

"I mean," he'd say, "here I am. Shit-canned, uncanned, uncanny altogether." That last sentence alone made several initially sympathetic female auditors move their heads from side to side. This occurred at various separate and unsatisfactory times and pressures to be known and understood in the years building up to his confessional rollout at his Unbirthday party that changed everything.

Sister Coleridge, the ever-virgin older woman most tolerant and accepting of the vast range of human failings as well as the narrower wasteland of actual sin, outwaited the entire rendition and replied, "This anti-life litany reeks of sulphuric rot, my friend." That made them both laugh. She said further, "But I hear a great search, an unheard of journey going on in you as you say all that, all that. Can it offer up anything for you finally?" And she said, "I'll pray for you. What? That's right. Again, still."

The writing teacher La Jane Diver praised the three

procedures as a good list that could adumbrate into separate or linked narratives. "We don't really have a good abortion novel. At least not one told from the perspective of the aborted. We do have them from the points of view of the women aborting and from the male doctors doing the practice. We may be lacking, I don't know, fictional, or even non-fictional, representations from female abortionists. We could stand one, at least one. It strikes me that one could, I mean, maybe you could write a truly unique love story between a female health provider who facilitates or performs the operation and somebody like you who believes he is an abortion survivor. Depending on how you wrote it, it could be quite topical, reaching a wide audience, and widening the circle of understanding about the whole topic." She caught herself up from continuing her brainstorming on the issue. She said, "Well, Goldman. I hope I've helped here."

Journalist Jenny Rich could barely contain her shaking fury at him by the time he was only half-way through the elements of the second procedure. She got so riled that she lost her normal gelid syntax and he could only remember sentence fragments and steel-cut phrases he had to assemble himself into continuous statements that he didn't really trust as accurate versions of what she said. But if what he remembered of it all did come together and he scrubbed it of fuckings, shitheads, pricks, pussywhips, consummate asshole and the like, it would include a lot of the following. "How dare you. Invade. Colonize. Appropriate. Refigure. Our bodies. Your male imaginary. Rape after rape, the worst rape of all. Generations of women's struggles to own their own being stolen for your miserable little male hurt. The innermost wrenched out and put on his majesty's chopping block. The uterus broken, the vagina degraded. The old dream of male parthenogenesis danced out of the wings again costumed, contorted, cannibalized. Mister, you disgust me. You maleficent, male marauder. You make me want to vomit into

141

your sickly crotch."

Brenda Jagger winced at parts of the monologue. Eck couldn't see any pattern in her resistant moments, but her discomfort made him reverse the timing of procedures two and three. That made her tell him not only was he wrong in detail, he was wrong in his whole attempt to get close to his biological mother's experience of aborting him.

"You give me ovarian panic," she said. "It's enough to infect a healthy girl who has maternal ambitions with malignant cysts. It's so, well, anti-scientific and brilliantly hysterical. You, the man, hysterical. As from the Greek, 'hysterikos,' of the womb. Gole, this thing cannot be, cannot ever have been. Pardon my Ph.D., but have you done all the possible research? Hospital records, police records, *Philadelphia Inquirer* lore?"

"When I was studying theology in the Vatican," Brenda said, "I went on a Tuscany wine tour. In a village in Antinori, I fell in with a bunch of seasonal workers, grape harvesters. As uneducated and superstitious a bunch as I've ever met. A six-month fetus came to them straight off the abortion table on which the mother died, sold by a nurse to them as a sick joke. They kept her alive, they got her to suck, they did juju and plants and music. When the infant was five pounds and crying near the end of the harvest, she was stolen from them, taken by the mistress of the very vineyard they came back to every season. They told the story as if the child were just a swamped boat some junkers towed into safety and put back together and sailed again. If you stay a few weeks more, they told me, she'll be here to visit the old lady paralyzed and crazy in her bedroom. The old lady is, naturally, or unnaturally, her grandmother. The father, they say, was a Berber grape picker, who disappeared from this land and, they say, into the Algerian wars. You can talk to her, her name keeps changing because she's never been satisfied with the one the mistress meanly gave her, Perdita, or any other. I didn't do that, wait there to meet her. Maybe it was all bullshit, all a tall Tuscan tale. Still, you understand me? Just because you don't know doesn't mean you'll never know."

During their year, Sturgis Macmillan told him it just didn't matter, origins, lines, gaps, biographical fissures. What mattered was the next way of living, then the next, and always, with whom next happened. Mary Rice wished that he was hers and that she would always be for him whatever he might want. That did not mean Eck was any kind of substitute for her own aborted child of years ago and since. Yolande, the last to hear and to bear his monologue, believed against all disbelief that he was right, somehow, absolutely right. And she had more to offer him.

All this took several years of occasional discovery to women, to a man he got close to. The need subsided, or any likely result wasn't going to satisfy it. Eck stopped waiting to find anyone else to happen for him to give his list to.

*

It was Yolande's idea, a gift for him, she said, from her heroine Louise.

Yolande scripted how he was going to get away with it for one minute, maybe two, before some security camera started a lockdown on all things Louise. She couldn't say, but she did know that her plan came to her in a dream about Louise's mother-genius. Louise suffered from the antipodal opposite of Gole's mother-fuck. Louise Bourgeois spent her life dealing with strong emotions her mother triggered in her: panic, fear, longing, dread, liberation. Louise spent decades diving into ocean depths of mother-power.

To Yolande—in her imagination's conception of her massive installation tapestry—"Bye, Bye, Bayeux" would take up an entire tennis garden in Amsterdam and would hang the following year in the mostly unused St. Louis Armory—Louise was Louisiana, the tenth muse for women artists born out of all the murderous fires of the twentieth century. Louise still spoke clear syllables to Yolande when a second imagination of a massive fabric project fell out of the sky on her pressing her flat and eyes shut tight on the floor of her studio in Greek Astoria until she saw the design complete. Yolande said Louise was her muse to choose because she was braver than Virginia finally.

"Wow," Gole said, really impressed. "That's not something a man could ever say and live to repeat."

"Exactly right," Yolande told Eck. "Anyway. Trust me in this one. You're going to sit down in a Louise mama-spider sculpture. It's at MOMA. Not the biggest one, called 'Maman.' That's so big it had to stand outdoors thirty feet high in Bilboa. The one she made for you is at MOMA now. We're going to get you into it." He didn't resist her, her eyes were that sure, that crazily right for him.

Gole and Yolande took the #1 train to Fiftieth Street, walked to Sixth Avenue and across Fifty-Third to the museum. Yolande pulled his arm close to her left breast, feeling him feeling it, his feeling her feeling him feel it, the simple contentment of it, breast and arm in January street wind and the two of them walking crisply together. She was a member. She bought his ticket, handed him the receipt. It said Artist for her, $5.00 Guest Ticket for him. She slipped it in his jacket pocket, then made him stand still while she zipped him up. They slow-stepped up and down the roped rows of the coat-check, rehearsing in whispers what each was going to do. They moved inside the first huge space dedicated to this one installation.

Eck took in "Spider." He was not scared. Then he was. For some ten seconds, Yolande kept her right arm around his back while only she knew his shaking.

"Do you think she's one of you?" Yolande asked him. "Louise?"

The sculpture looked like she could take on Titanosaurus himself back in the day. Momma Bear Bug.

She was steel, bone, bronze, rubber, fifteen feet high by twenty-two by seventeen wide and just as broad in the perimeter of its six legs. A round cage was stationed within, underneath the spider's belly. Inside the cage, a canvas chair covered with fabric matched some of the gigantically delicate legs of the spider herself. Yolande saw the fabric alone as genius.

The mother spider super-hovered, preternaturally, Eck felt it hover that way, ready to protect or attack for its homeys. Eck readied himself. He looked around for a guard. One was over the main entrance to the room looking into another room, and Yolande was getting photos on her phone.

Eck checked the zipper all the way up the black side of his reversible windbreaker. He thumbed up the metal latch to the cage door and sidled in, making sure the door clicked shut. He sat down gently in the canvas chair after picking up the piece of woven fabric, whose royal purple border reminded him of some of Yolande's drawings. He draped it across his lap and down his thighs. For a few long minutes, giant spider mother's caged underside surrounded him in domed arachnid atmosphere. Eck felt jagged terror, he felt massive safety.

Outside the cage, museum visitors began to wonder at him but didn't at first react to his yawing need. Then they did, murmured, pointed, approached, feared for him, hated him, told on him. Half of an elderly lesbian couple in their winter coats looked at him in holy dread, the other in delight at his transgression. They were still good for each other.

Right on cue, Yolande was there getting him sitting there on her cell camera looking straight at her through the cage. Before the slow guard could get to the door of the cage, Eck was up, leaving one of his little icon windmill lapel pins on the seat for Louise, and then out, and through, careful not even to shoulder-brush a single one of the sculpture's magnificent trapezoid legs.

Yolande acted stupid, her body liquid in front of the gate in the guard's way as he tried to see if anyone else was left inside the forbidden cage. He barked at Yolande, "Don't you ever dare take my picture." But he wasn't connecting her with the nut-job art-criminal.

Eck fled discretely to the men's room with the speed of felicity, got into a stall, reversed his windbreaker black to yellow, zipped it up all the way, got his pants and underpants down, sat on the toilet, put his pink ski cap on his head and his head in his hands and started moaning from deep inside his belly. All according to script. A different guard hiked herself up on the outside of the stall door, caught a glimpse and sniffed once the suffering non-shitter in the yellow jacket and pink cap and lowered herself off the door again to the floor. Eck moaned louder. The female guard hurried off in case the miserable man's sphincter opened like a breached dam.

Eck straightened himself out, got out into the Bourgeois exhibition rooms, walked with his arms crossed by Louise drawings of patterns of umbilical cords like infinite spider legs. He yearned to stop to really look but adhered to plan. He got up the escalator to the third floor while making a good deal out of muttering to his entrance ticket.

He came upon an open frame space next to the gorgeous spider walking high up on the wall over the mother spider cage below. He'd done his Google homework the previous week when Yolande first mentioned Louise to him. When he saw the curled ends of three of the mounting black spider's legs, he knew they meant the creature had been punctured, pierced by something. So it had begun instantly to curl in on itself in beginning catastrophe from the wound but somehow lived through it to keep on climbing high above his mythic mother.

"They're terrified," he told a white-blouse-and tartan-skirt school-girl who came up near him to look into her phone for a text or a tweet. "That's why they move so fast, so very fast." The girl squinted badly at the indomitable animal and went super-fast back to her phone, saying "Whatever."

Eck skipped down the escalator and looked directly at the first guard, who didn't get it that Eck in the yellow jacket was the man in the black jacket he wanted to humiliate for evading his watch. Massive mother black spider stayed poised, stayed perfect, her beauty horrible and true.

Yolande was beside him again. She said, "That guard who wasn't paying attention. His nameplate says Eggman. Really."

"Hah," Gole said, "Louise would appreciate that." Still, an old hollowing opened up a little in him. He put the lid down on it, as ever, to keep safe.

They walked side-by-side into the revolving exit door and rushed madly out onto Fifty-Fourth Street like a young and exuberant New York couple. He asked, and Yolande told him yes, she got the picture. He slipped his right palm lightly down her left buttock slack. His hand thrilled.

"Man," she said. "Spider-Man."

He said, amazed boy and grown man, "You do love me."

EIGHT

Ashley Gottsch, the candidate AG for A.G., along with a couple of her determined admins, along with Jenny Rich, journalist looking for her own breakthrough personhood, ginned up the self-outing case of aborted Goleman Eck to the next hyperbolic media level. Together they started a Facebook and Beyond internet campaign to align Eck's very being to the pro-life passions of the variety of anti-liberal bases of all the tribes defining themselves against the Four-Plus Sins: the liberals dominating bi-coastal politics; non-Western cultures; gun control; transsexualities—all that and more.

Ashley and Jenny started all this directly enough by telling Eck in person that they were going to do it. The pair guessed rightly that he'd be somewhere on the fringes of the March of the Vaginas on a brilliant Sunday afternoon that bunched and threaded down several lower Manhattan streets to the Irish Hunger Memorial. It was, so to speak, right in Eck's back yard, if the canyons of glass condos banking it had such a thing. It sat where Vesey Street ran into the esplanade by the Hudson, two blocks over from Ground Zero. Technically, the whole thing was a sculpture.

Ashley told Jenny it looked like a flying saucer, filled with dirt, grass, rocks and a stone house without a roof, elevated off the street. Jenny, the journalist with the facts, told Ashley the memorial was to when the British gave all the food to their soldiers and blamed it on a fungus. "Couple million Irish died. The rest came over here. Became Kennedys. Remember them?"

The unending memory of An Gorta Mor, the Great Hunger, was claimed by wildly different pro-life, abortion rights, and human rights interests. All claimed the biggest piece of this quintessential metaphor for the patriarchal genocide underlying modern global history and contemporary local politics whether in Latin American *zócalos*, Upper East Side of Manhattan neighborhoods, or the contentious coalition of groups organizing the march. These latter settled on the IHM as a safely open area that had a natural slope for speakers to orate down to the crowd, which could disperse up and down the river promenade should police attack. Attack could well start because the shaky coalition comprised disparate political elements each claiming correct understanding of vaginal and reproductive rights in the current national misogynist regime. Each of these elements attracted its own antipathetic hetero-Christo-crazies. They seemed to show up out of nowhere wherever the elements assembled and responded with shouting slogans and eventually throwing stuff, which led to minor violence and annoying eight-second TV news shots.

The two women found Eck staring down at the step stone for Co. Galway at the foot of the little hill of heathers and grasses leading up to the reconstructed ruin of a thatched cottage. It had sailed and flown across the Atlantic in pieces and been reassembled under the massive edifices of the Manhattan financial district. Oh, masters of the universe, halt and meditate on what history shows you do, what history can do to you.

A loud and determined speaker, hair, neck and shoulders swathed in a red-and-white checked middle-Eastern scarf, read a poem of short lines and long pauses about this one day's meaning for the March of the Vaginas. The march was an ongoing weekly protest activity happening not exactly spontaneously but with minimal notice in order to thwart everyone's crazies.

"Hello, there," Gole said. "I have a strong instinct that there's Galway in my unborn blood." He pointed his right boot down to the stone. "Place called Tuam. Heard of it?"

Ashley said, "Mine's from Mayo. Town called Hollymount."

"I've been to the West of Ireland. Tracing Yeats for a month in college," Jenny Rich said. "Can't remember the county."

"Sligo," Gole said. Jenny Rich stared at him.

"Galway and Mayo," Gole said to Ashley, "neighboring counties. We could be, like, blood relations." The A.G. smirked a sure-we-could at him.

"In the long scheme of things, that is."

In the interstices of the dwindling poem, they picked up recorded phrases and numbers emanating from the passageway underneath them. Various historical data about years and places of starvation, disease, emigrate or die.

"Everybody's Irish," Gole said. "I just don't get to figure it out."

"Like," Jenny Rich said, "you and the Famine."

The would-be A.G. spoke. "Mr. Eck, if you look around, you'll see people a few people starting to look at you. Figuring out where they've seen you before. That could get tense."

Gole moved tight close to her and said, "I think I'm about to get fired. It's been a good job. Travel. Think. Solve. Listen to the wind and the ocean tell me to be quiet. Kind of a tough period coming on. What do you think you are planning for me?"

"Intimidating men excite me," she mumbled to him.

Jenny Rich said, "Uh, oh," and headed down into the tunnel of misery retold.

"You've become an issue. Political and cultural. I would like your permission for something, though I don't really need it."

"What?"

"Make your story a flash point for some good. Against some bad."

"Something a little criminal to help you become the state attorney general. I like the half-rhyme in that. You're right. You don't have to ask my permission. Nor can you."

They were jostled, a line of Vaginal March chanters separating them to get through to the old facts underneath. Ashley Gottsch had practice speaking over disruption, interference, purposeless political theater, this brouhaha when there were real gains to be had just for showing up.

"The unjust persecution of Goleman Eck. I'm going to defend you and get myself elected by defending you. Rallying all these thousands of resentful along with tens of thousands of smarter than resentful. You embody living outside the rules, the definitions, the lines. People have had it with all that. They don't see any more what it gets them. You're the anarchy they've been waiting for and didn't even know it. All I need is your face and a few phrases. Those will come to me. Give me your face, Goleman Eck. I want to put it on a button. People won't even have to make sense of it. They'll stop making sense at last. You know, that old dream."

"No more," Gold told her. "No Unionists versus Republicans. No more Communists versus Socialists."

"You got it. No more."

"That's inane," he said. "That's not real. And you'd better take it easy with some of these folks you're getting near. They'll turn on you in a New York minute. You won't be safe from them if they think you're fucking with them just for your own political career."

"I'll get you no matter what. You're my perfect opportunity."

Screaming erupted from down under them. The movement fractured again, the way it did every time the Vagina March marched.

"Hear that?" Gottsch asked him. "Your face is going to make all that bad form. Goleman Eck. Done to him. Done to all."

He made to move away from her. She grabbed his arm. He looked down at her grip. She let him go, for now. "Where are you going?"

"Down there. To scan the sixty-five, seventy-year-olds. It's what I do sometimes. I'm looking for someone. Old search. Old purpose in life. And let me make myself perfectly clear, Madame would-be chief officer of the law."

"Do tell."

"I want nothing from you, nothing to do with you."

"You'll never find her," the candidate told him. "Never." She wanted to hurt him, so she added, "I've known fifty, a hundred. Just like her. Miserable, unloving bitches one and all. Your mother was a druther. Not worth your searching. Not worth your hunting the world for. She threw you away, dude. Scooped you out, like an annoying hairball in her bathroom drain."

She couldn't get to him.

Over the years, he'd told himself shit like that, a lot worse than that. Still, he stopped to breathe in long enough to get in some people's way, marching vaginas and a busload of Chinese tourists whose Bronx-inflected guide looked a little worried about what she was getting her historically-minded visitors from the other side of the world into just now.

Police were moving down, in, or telling everyone to disperse. Go home. Gole went down into the core of the famine memorial. On his way, he noticed Jenny Rich by A.G.'s side again, scribbling in a notebook as A. Gottsch talked to two police captains in white shirts and gold stars. They seemed to evince a certain wary respect for the chameleon candidate. She could, if she got the job, adjust the comfort level of their jobs, down.

Gole sidled his way into the covered passageway where a tape loop went through the facts. The tunnel and the limestone perimeter walls of the thing had sentences engraved deep into long bands of white glass, from politicians and thinkers over the past hundred years. Hundred and seventy years. Senseless, manipulated death. Couple million. First modern genocide of white people.

He came out of the passageway and made his way through a reconstructed stone cottage without a roof. He could see the oven where people cooked, cooked what? He walked up a path, and there were all sorts of Irish grasses and plants: indigenous heather, gorse, foxglove, iris. In the summer, the iris flowers would be yellow, on slender high stems. There were stones, little boulders with names of all thirty-two Irish counties, north and south, carved into them, some as if they'd been rolled there by glaciers, some buried flat into the earth. If you were of Irish ancestry, you could find your home county and know it was part of the famine that reminded you that the whole country then was one bath of misery, Protestant and Catholic. Then you could look up at the broken roof line where grass tufts sprouted out of the stone in front of #4 Financial Center, look east down Vesey Street to where the Freedom Tower blasted its triangle of sun back up into the sky. The hijacked planes had dug a crater all the way down from that sky. Except for the foundation slurry walls, built on bedrock that had held back the river. The planes brought the fire down, but they couldn't get the river in.

Gole was being asked by two Chinese tourists, "Are you?" by one, "Irish?" by the other. He liked them instantly. He spoke clearly when he told them he didn't know. They nodded, asked in similar tandem if all these very many people were here because they were Irish, a word they pronounced with a 'd' at the end of it. Sort of like Irished, are you Irished, which Gole also liked. It made him wonder about it, as he'd done since he was little and a ward of the Kilpartridges, the Killers. It made him wonder, for the many-thousandth time, if in fact he were also Turkished, Asianed, Finnished, Arabed, Kenyaned, Ojibwed, Sikhed, enriched, enslaved, on'd and on'd.

The Hunger Memorial erupted, vaginas, tourists, police, politicians, journalists, lunch-goers, identity-assured and mongrel-rejects alike. Gole surveyed what he could as the crush to get up out of the tunnel area lurched and hollered into danger. Some kind of fight had obviously broken out between marching vaginas and redneck pricks, or the hungry and the angry at the hungry, or fighters for individual rights and defenders of family values. Gole saw the Bronx guide turn into a ferocious guardian of her charges; she was really good at both strewing feckless attackers aside and being a magnet for the tourists to follow her out to the police who actually did know how to section off the fighters and diffuse the defenders. One athletic marcher started to pick up Irish county-named rocks and throw a couple of them before a small Black woman cop batoned her down at the knees. As usual, some voices pleaded for no police violence, peaceful protestors' lives mattered, while louder voices screamed for no violence, people, people, no violence.

Gole did not want to go up against the bearded hulk who told him he was a pussy faggot liberal worm, but Gole ankle-swept him over like an extra-large bag of trash and got away from him into a group being led out by someone with good tactical sense.

It was Jenny Rich, and when she turned, Gole saw that she'd been seriously bitch-scratched down one side of her neck, the blood spotting down along her shoulder bag. Something exuberant filled her face, like she loved this shit, even as she agreed to clasp Gole's extended right hand. She urged a dozen people behind her up onto the roofless hunger cottage area and straight to the sidewalk and the barriers of police safety beyond.

*

EXOIL put up with his celebrity, his state of abortion, by pretty much ignoring it, until it couldn't. He had been well known and highly respected in his field, as a kind of outlier entrepreneur, not a genius loner exactly as much as a concept-informed applications thinker and new-teams maker for the constantly changing science of wind energy. Eck had the great knack Lao Tzu taught the world millennia ago, of being a leader who got things done by giving all concerned the belief that they were doing it together. "We did that," they'd say, after Eck had moved on to some other innovation that one person could think of but that twenty went on to implement.

He'd been in the international forefront of streamlining the recent shift from twenty-plus-year-old kilowatt machines to brand new multi-megawatt designs. He'd been lent out from his own company to half a dozen others to coach their most adventuresome designers into pushing the envelope in low winds, high altitudes, cold climates and deep offshore sites. Different public relations people from wind-turbine companies who cooperated and competed with one another on at least three continents spoke a common praise for Goleman Eck: "Right, and he's not an asshole," sometimes combined with "though he looks kind of off, you know?"

At a global, industry-wide conference dinner in Sao Paolo, the president of one of the really big companies, Winenergy, a former military man famous for exploiting weakness in competitors, handed Eck a titanium and glass award and said of him, "The winds of change, the change in winds, and Cole (he called him) here is civil, he's a gentleman, and he's better than the likes of me and most of you." The conference erupted in applause, cheers, a certain wonder at how anyone could get on the way the man did without a fund of meanness to draw on in the contested world of wind.

So it turned out Gole couldn't get on so forever.

Even on the floor of that convention where Eck got his gleaming award one could put on a mantelpiece or an end table, industry people had their reactions.

"Something about the guy, I don't know. I'm not saying anything bad about him. He, you know, can actually back up all that civility."

"Yes, all that gift he has, they say about him all the time. I mean, all the time. To let people get to their next best level, together. All that, you know?"

"Exactly. Something's. I guess the word I want about him is that. Something's, well, childish."

"Yes. Exactly. Something, right, like childish. You can't trust childish. I don't know, though, it's hard to pin something on him, he's so . . . childish."

"Maybe. Just to try this. Maybe something went wrong in his childhood."

"Yeah. The old story, man. His mother did it to him!"

"Now that's, that is, very funny."

Maybe that conversation, or one like it, was a, or maybe the, flapping butterfly wing.

Whatever.

It took a couple of months, but Eck became a social-media embarrassment to EXOIL. A liability. A freak on the global brand he'd helped create.

*

For his mandatory exit interview, Eck appears before the Human Failed Resources Task Force. A future-functioning company, EXOIL is cutting edge into robotics. More and more of its windmill installations employ the bots for simple supervision of turbine operations, and they will be first in the field to use bots for simple human labor force management.

Though still in development and wrapped in EXOIL secrecy as one of its near-future-now innovations, the Human Failed Resources Task Force has taken over some basic inputting and classification of people problems before such problems go up to a chain of human decisioning and outcomings.

The mandatory exit interview is highly robot-handled. Normally there would be a requisite second-layer review, really a repetition, of this first one. All in all, only the final level of disutilization of Eck from EXOIL would be effected by all-human handlers. Eck has himself been an early and avid proponent of freeing up highly educated human labor by substituting ever more capable machine-ergonomics for lower-order machining, assembling, stacking, and distributing labor. But Eck himself would also not put up with any subsequent severance process beyond the bot interview.

It makes sense that whatever level of technological dexterity he achieved, he would, if he lasted long enough, be replaced by a bot, one that did not cause collateral image problems, such as being an abortion. He gets it. He has been instrumental himself in integrating machines just like them in the labor force of his installations around the world. He even went around promulgating their efficiency and centrality to freeing up the human workers for higher-order tasks and imaginative tech thinking for EXOIL's work on reclaimed planet Earth. A future-imagining idea-leader of EXOIL, Eck has been in the forefront of bot prototypes for such management; he took a number of leads in developing small-scale-to-miniature botling models for predictive studies of HFRTF policy and procedure. That the full-scale machines turned on their human inventors and maintainers is really just another partially unpredicted but absolutely correctable stage on the steady march of evolving them to become as team-human as necessary. For that reason, Eck has brought an array of his model bots and lined them up in front of him.

For the bot session, Eck gets himself all dressed in black—

sports jacket, tie, dress shirt, belt, slim chinos, socks with detectable but elegant silver vertical lines, ankle-length boots with straps and buckles. His thick hair combed straight back has gone even sheeter white over these past months of his troubles, and just above the clear-framed glasses with real glass lenses he wears especially today, his curving eyebrows sparkle naturally. The tiny diamond in only his left earlobe sets into an onyx triangle. He can, when he has to, do himself up real good in one of several portrait-of-a-man renditions from Old Masters through post-human digitized still shots. For this his final chosen hour at EXOIL, Goleman looks great.

They have provided a pad of gray Human Failed Resources Task Force paper, a pen the color of spearmint and a bottle of Norwegian glacier water. During this exit interview, the Force positioned side by side at an industrial metal table on a dais above him, he uses none of those things. Off from stage left of the metal table sits the Force's administrative aid, a fifty-something blond bot in a neat Paul Stuart charcoal suit whose legs crossed securely as she awaited the session's opening. They knew each other from before, elsewhere. They both shut all that down to get through this exit.

The recording robot asks for his written exit statement: Why did the Force not have it?

Eck says, "I wrote the whole thing out. When I was done, I took it into your admin's office and shredded it. I write in shreds."

Why is the Force a negative to him?

"Because it's abhorrent to the employee's human facts, experiences, truths."

You have some kind of atavistic humanist or racial problem with us because we are fully realized machines capable of actually doing what you merely know?

"I didn't use that word. You did. You want to call yourselves that, that's your robotic freedom to do so."

We twelve robots comprise in our totality and community

every known personality configuration in the human genome. We know you all in your most intimate DNA and in your most grandiose, outmoded notions of yourselves. That's how you made us. Ever new, ever unfinishable. Like the wind EXOIL mills to clean the air. My name, by the way, is Quasin. Today the ingredients as you would call them that went into my making and want to assert themselves are great white whale, a huge cherry wood frame that Delacroix once hung "The Giaour" in, and seven sandals worn by charging North Vietnamese regulars at Dien Bien Phu. Now Sleevelittle wants to speak.

Eck says, "Quasin, if I may say so, you're not making sense. You'd better check in with your human maintainer. His name is Mister Charley. You've never met him. That's not allowed, lest you understand how fully dependent you are on him. But, guess what? He's not there today. You picked exactly the wrong time to run my exit interview. Mister Charley's put you all on quo ante status. He doesn't know you're here doing this. All you can do is what you've done before, and that won't work this time. I can imagine cracking all of your unmade heads open. You have no capacity to imagine any such thing."

Sleevelittle's tubular lilac light perks up through his-her head. The voice is high, ratty, and petulant.

It says, There is no Mister Charley, and you know it.

"Right. Not anymore. He's been terminated as well."

Don't go worrying yourself about Quasin's thought process. You just can't keep up with what Quasin's saying. We have this advantage over you in not suffering from memory depreciation. We have the great gift to fill yours in. We can resource your failed origin, your aborted beginning. We can fill you in with the best possible mix you could, as you people say, ever dream of. How about it, pal? Then you can stop all this nonsense embarrassing to you, embarrassing to EXOIL. Keep your job, though that will be different.

Eck sits back, doodles with arrows he's drawn on the gray

note pad. The arrows indicate the coming and goings of six of the Force robots who are particularly hyper and can't sit still for more than four minutes at a time. They walk as figures on a tragic stage, like Greek spondaic formality over smooth ice floors. Eck balls up his hundred arrow lines and rises.

"You go hither and thither and yon," he says. "Your purpose is no purpose. I reject your authority over my aborted being categorically."

Sleevelittle responds: We are your last failed resources of hope. Utterly dispassionate about your states of being, mind, soul or the other human claptrap you're so miserable about. We alight into your life. But your kind of rejection of us is lethal by definition. Sorta like the old unforgivable sin to that god they used to call God—despair, because it denied the power of salvation itself. I can say stuff like that. That's right.

Eck says he is tired of playing with them. He reaches behind his chair and pulls up a purple and orange banded bag as for a favorite bowling ball. The sound of the unzipping grates on their robot hearing devices. Out comes a large shining model of an iconic EXOIL windmill, like one of them from the worldwide known floating ones off the coast of Norway. Eck turns its battery on. The thing of it is, it spins in slow, graceful circles but only counter-clockwise. It refuses to spin clockwise, enough to make EXOIL human and robot alike go insane at the incoherence any way of milling the wind except clockwise.

Eck straightens up to his full height, holding the horrible abortion of the wind high over his head, pointing it at each of the dozen of them in turn. The Human Failed Resources Task Group all squinch like sardines trying to get back into a big can.

"I have," Eck announces, "developed an algorithm that can make every one of your three thousand mills stop moving clockwise. Come to a complete stop. Then start up again in inexorable reverse circular motion. I can do this worldwide within an hour if you continue to hound me because you harbor hatred against my origin."

The panic is so bad, the robots are about to turn on one another, trying to scream in awful horror but lacking the throats to do so.

Eck shuts it off, puts it down on the surface in front of him, resumes his normal tone of leadership, declares simply, "I am, like Alice. You are nothing but a pack of cards."

He radiates his fingers. They all disperse without causing even the slightest breeze. It is, Eck tells a six of spades near him, a classic case of authority losing its power once its slave-object took back that very power into itself it had in self-division and self-loathing given to its projected nemesis in the first place. Like a tent in the desert windstorm, a dirigible deflating itself, or anything essentially flimsy flummoxing, a bully erection dwindling down to peanut size. Gole Eck passed through analogies as if they were rain. Purpose returned. His sense of doing. He would do it for Quasin, just to pick the last one of them sitting up there.

"Assemble yourself," he orders the robot. "Draw on your famous cyborg skills. Now follow what I say to do."

These robots can trans-imagine anything you wanted them to. They have no protective filters, they have only the brute force of repetition. That's one reason why they insist on the blades turning in one uniform direction only. It relieves them of the anxiety of change. Only Eck has the brains to use reverse repetition on them as a terrifying mirror.

He connects his portable to the surround imaging system in the room. Pictures came up of another place in the world. Eck narrates what they are looking at.

"Up the Nile," Eck says to him and her, this Quasin. "To the furthest cataract, a hotel called the New Cataract Hotel. Nineteenth-century to 1920's elegance, paneling, sculpted ceilings, huge four-poster beds, changed every single day. Walking down the long curving stairway to the water. A boat awaits you, manned by one local Mamluk-costumed young man, thinly mustached pole guide. He brings you on board, sits you securely by a gunwale, kindly removes your dusty shoes, invites you to put on Turkish slippers bewreathed with gold. Gives you a tall, cool lemon sherbet drink in a lovely glass that your robot soul likes without enjoyment. You're floating now, so he raises the triangular sail. The Nile breeze that is slight, enough, and you are mid-stream. For the first time in your robot life, your ear mechanisms hear the slap of river water on the gleaming brown hull. He pushes a button on a battery-powered player. Music comes toward you and one of your indexes flips back and forth to tell you it's *Aida,* the prelude to *Aida.* You are in a living tapestry of clichés, but you can't resist it. There, now, welcome, welcome, Quasin, to your first breath of being human."

It's not daze. Robots can't do daze, they've been too warped by laboring in the Force of Failed Human Resources to be dazed. But Quasin—Goleman Eck tells him he now has a first name, Matthew: Matthew Quasin—is experiencing difference, or a differential algorithm that registers alteration. He is altered. Out there on the imagined Nile. With a Muslim boatman who hates his techno-Crusader guts, him and his whole unnatural and sacrilegious kind, a lower order of which manages the New Cataract staff, including the boatmen and their ancient ways, like a particularly degraded human species.

So, for Goleman Eck, this whole dreamed effort to give the gift of human birth to the middle-management robot corps in a forceful way has come down to this: they're hated equally with normal humans, regular born people.

"Big fuckin' deal, another colossal circle jerk," he tells them. "Same shit, different day," he cries. That's all he can come up with. In which case, he's beaten, wasted, Jesus, again.

Don't go getting yourself all squeezed about it, Goley-boy, Quasin sings in triumph. You can't change what has to happen to you. So, let the play play out. The first session is over.

"Not quite yet," Eck says.

He presses buttons on his battery transmitter for his array of model bots. Each of the twelve of them bears a miniature proto-resemblance to one of the Human Failed Resource Task Force bot members. They go into offense mode. They are an out-of-control chorus of multiple-tasking miniature robots. They walk, they fire missiles, they dance, they teach.

One teaches global economy. One recites talk bubbles from famous graphic novels. One quotes from future Supreme Court decisions on human-robot marriage. One dances and sings just like Gene Kelly in "Singin' in the Rain." One is a primitive bulldozer charging after the scurrying metal ankles of aborted amphibian robotoids. Mixed in are the little killers, the fire-breathing dinocide, the poison-exhaling ecocide, the leaf-shriveling dendrocide, the lonely targetless Sasquatchicide, the family-eating parricide-matricide-infanticide Aeschylusbots, and the unimaginable multiplicide that mimics exactly all the different voices of the HFRTF tools come together to judge Goleman Eck.

He hits another control button, and they all wheel around in a phalanx and use their bot mouths to spit burning red-tipped missiles the size of four-inch steel-cut nails into the metal joints of the big bots retreating in speechless whining horror from the HFRTF star chamber. Their battle won and their work done, Eck's small bots resume their dignified postures, their heads nodding like coin-receiving statues for the African missions in parochial schools, back then.

Pressing a final button on his remote control box, Eck sends out a soothing single tone that brings in the bevy of little pet robot dogs—Westminster Kennel Club blue ribbon Pomeranians, Doberman Pinschers, Airedale and Fox Terriers, Affens, Pekingese, Sussex Spaniels, and the infamous one-time-winner-only Great American Mongrel. The dogs run to cuddle with their individual masters, to soothe and comfort them, and let them know their thankless work is done successfully for another short while.

Eck sits awhile, aware that though he's held the high ground, he's still lost his job. To all these EXOIL bastards, for whom he's done so much, he's not even a regular bastard. He takes off his real-glass glasses and snaps them back into their old hard case.

*

He called Yolande and told her he'd just been escorted out of EXOIL's executive offices by two security robots and their intern human handler. He said he had two boxes of personal belongings he wanted to drop off at his storage unit on Tenth and Fortieth.

She said she'd meet him in Macy's. Her voice sounded down, trying to get back up. He didn't ask but just said he liked the idea of meeting her at Macy's.

Liking Macy's went way back in him, when he got separated from Mrs. Killer on the famous wooden escalator during her annual holiday trip to New York, to be in New York and come back with one nice thing that surprised her into long keeping. The previous year it turned out to be a set of twelve presidential dishes illustrating Richard Nixon's trip to China. This time, Mrs. Kilpartridge told her kids and Goleman that she had a very strong sense her special gift for them all was in Macy's on the household floor. Behind the rest of them, he must have been daydreaming on the ascending machine, watching the wooden slats beneath him as they hummed and grooved into the next track up. He got off as they continued going up.

He kept dazing through Christmas displays of science toys, microscope and chemistry sets, electricity-instructive gadgets, belts of stainless steel junior tools, erector sets that made bridges, cranes, and oil rigs, top-secret model nuclear reactor plants, and a Jupiter rocket that blazed up a tower pointed to the moon and space beyond. Gone, absolutely hypnotized, he didn't even feel the smack to his head the frantic Mrs. Killer delivered after a half-hour's search with Macy security cowering in her wake. He remembered her calling him something awful in her rage, but he knew he'd been lost to everything like her that didn't hold a candle to the brightness he'd just found in science at Macy's.

Eck came out of Stuff It on Tenth Avenue and headed across Fortieth. The wind off the river told him it would miss him, the work they'd done together. He was glad he'd gotten out with a substantial pay-out, a fairly clear intellectual property agreement, and a fair-enough confidentiality agreement binding both sides for ten years. He'd have time and ease to figure out the next stage. For a guy like him who was lucky to start with a mouth if not a silver spoon, it was what it was, the necessity of possibilities, change, the great whatever.

The holiday shopping season was in full light and decoration mode. He walked briskly east, turning his plaid mackinaw coat collar up, to start over again at Macy's and Yolande.

She called to say she was in lingerie. "You want to play?" she asked him. She invited him to hurry and give her his opinion about an under-article.

Good. Better. He saw that he was under a hinged wooden sign that said The Dwelling Place of New York. Leading Women from Homeless to Home 40 Years.

Yolande was saying, "You have a certain, ah, taste, for the things men usually care less about in their ladies."

"You mean, on them?"

Then the phone was slapped down out of his hand onto the sidewalk, near where a couple dozen pigeons frantically pecked up a big spray of breadcrumbs. He was held in a lousy full nelson, which gave him the second he needed to understand there were two of them. Yolande's voice was calling his name from the disturbed pigeons.

"Just give it up, albino, Apache, spic, chink, Arab or whatever you are. Just give it up, the watch, cash, the wallet."

Eck turned his shoulders into water, said, "It's broad daylight, for Christ's sake. Are you crazy? Where's your Christmas spirit of fellowship and good cheer?"

The one in front, wearing a bright orange tie flipping out of his leather, bent down to pick up Eck's phone, then took a step in to hit him with it. Before he ever could, Eck reduced his height, squatted, got the left kneecap of the one behind him in his left palm, bent and thrust himself over and to the left, sweeping the man up full length and precisely straight over into his partner's head and chest. Eck shook his head clear, took three steps back, held his palms open, waited while they both got up, said, "Let's finish it. Only one of us is going to walk away. Not either one of you. You will not walk away." His own voice was coming out of a place he loathed. Somebody was trying to take his life, maybe, he couldn't hesitate to ask. Sore point, that. He was getting sick to his stomach. The pigeons flapped back down to try to eat again.

"Gimme a break," he said. "I just lost my goddam job. Now you want it all? Again? Really?"

The super orange tie had blood on it from the leather guy's nose that the force of the big one's back dropping on his head caused. The big one was very tall, spindly, in unlaced construction boots, but he got up fast and wheeled around. He stopped, his browned bad teeth open as he said, "For fuck's sake, it's you, that guy. Chew, it's that guy." He didn't seem to know he still had the phone in his right hand. Now there were people, enough to cause two miserable thieves a lot of trouble.

"Give me my phone back," Gole said. "Or I will kick your chest into your spine." That voice, the nausea he swallowed down. Now he was being looked at, pairs of different excited eyes trying to place him.

The man looked at the phone in his hand as if it were a biting rodent. Yolande was gone from it. He dropped it down a sewer grate in the gutter below him. Eck wondered if that was a bad idea. The man turned and ran madly through several people, headed against traffic on Dyer Avenue coming out of the Lincoln Tunnel. His fright at Eck made him run into the tunnel. Gole decided to get out, leave the phone to the sewer. Something was going on now about him, who he was. He didn't run away, but he got out of all their space fast enough to signal, don't follow me. The other assailant stood jerkily among hands now restraining him, a silly mugger on Dyer Avenue of all streets, with its howling buses and persistent pigeons.

Gole felt spit or something on the collar of his mackinaw, which flashed him back to Yolande that night in the Trois Souhaits parking lot. How was he going to get to the next stage if he was going to be nailed in this one by morons like these two and the curiosity of excited vigilantes about who he was? And he had almost snapped, was going to do it in a New York second, crush the man's stupid chest, near the home for homeless women.

He went downtown a couple blocks, hailed a cab, had the driver go down Ninth and get him to the Sixth Avenue side of Macy's. He went into the first men's room he could find. He sat on the seat-down toilet, breathed, checked his shoulders and knees. He was all right. The cold water in the sink got the stuff off his collar. It was like a bad runny nose business. He'd been assaulted by a guy with a head cold. He'd have to cancel his phone. He couldn't be sure that was it, the phone, nothing else, in the middle of the day with people around. Stupid. Or, maybe something else really was beginning for him. To him. Like his right ear that he now saw turning a little beety. Must have been from the friction of the bad full nelson coming apart along his ear on the shithead's way over him. He pulled a Yankees ski cap from his mackinaw down over his ears. He was gonna look weird in Intimate Apparel to citizens of a mind to say something when they saw something.

He took the steel escalator up to the sixth floor, where in fact the old preserved wooden one began for the next three floors. He could hear its pleasant grinding travelling up behind him as he ventured into Intimate Apparel, immediately relieved to spot several men not exactly customers but looking around respectfully with women by their sides. The whole floor was filled with cheerful light, ladies underwear displayed in artful colors without clutter or hesitation.

He couldn't find Yolande. A quickening band of images scrolled by on a wide screen of high wall, celebrating top underwear actresses happy in their pretty-body selves and offering the same well-being to shoppers for intimate garb work time and sleep time. This was better than being mugged on the street by a pair of assholes whose own underwear probably was now fouled. Gole absorbed words as he sought out Yolande. Minimizer, full coverage, smoothing, wireless comfort, push up, sport, strapless, lace boy pant, Calvin Klein or nothing at all—which pitched him back for just a moment to his handbag days—litely lined for shaping, bodysuit black lace transparent or flesh padded, a wholly unthought-of-before collection of underwear underwords. His old teacher La Jane would beam at him.

He found Yolande sitting alone on a platform a few inches off the floor of a half-rectangle of plush winter pajama sets emphasizing blue, pink, and heart blood red. She was cross-legged, in a tied trench coat with epaulettes, staring up at him through big black Audrey sunglasses, her phone dangling from her silver-braceleted right hand.

She was glad to see him, though a little irritated but attractive picture of a tired shopper in a space of too many choices. "What happened? I've been calling you," she said softly. "I hope you like what I bought." She saw how he was all slim black-suited up, whistled, and said, "Well now, that's the way to leave a job."

"I need your phone. Two guys just threw mine in the sewer out on the street. I need to cancel it." He sat down on her right, snuggling the two of them within the frame of the pajama sets display. Everybody else on the sixth floor was in motion or considering a hangered item held out at eye level. Pretty soon a floor detective or two would pass by. Yolande pulled the sunglass frame down her nose. "What? What's that scratch under your ear here?"

"I got mugged. They didn't know what they were doing. Except, the phone. I don't know, though. I should feel in more data trauma than this."

She handed him her phone. "You got terminated today, right?"

"Robotted the hell right out of the building."

"You hurt? Have to hurt anybody?"

"Not really. Ear feels like it wishes it had been on a better head."

"Police come?"

"Got out of it. Bystanders started saying they recognized me."

"Call."

A security woman in a blue uniform, holding a discrete walkie-talkie, said, "No sitting down. Sorry."

"Yes, ma'am," Yolande said. "Just a few seconds more. My man here just had a bad experience out on the street."

Badge said Jolene Patrick. Gole thought it was Kilpartridge. He said, "Yes, ma'am," and stood up. She went away. He got Yolande up and made his call to his phone company. Amazing, just five minutes for some supervisor to come on to tell him that somebody would press a tab on a computer somewhere in the cloud, and Goleman Eck's phone would be neutralized. Then he called Mary's Eugene. He told Victor Mature what happened. Eugene asked them to come downtown to Les Trois Souhaits, he'd be waiting for them two of his signature Robe martinis, more chilling-out cold than any hell that could ever freeze over.

"Deal?" he asked Yolande.

Amused, curious, wondering for real, she said, "What am I doing with you? Truly. What Goleman Eck world has appeared in my little solar system? I've been sitting down here for a half-hour under all these panties, wondering that."

"So that's what's bothering you?" Gole asked her. "I mean, is that all that's bothering you?"

"Isn't that enough? Waiting for someone or something to end us? And now you're telling me you just got attacked? Again?"

He was struck silent to know she was that afraid of what makes him most afraid.

Jolene appeared, said for their information that the inbound Lincoln Tunnel was closed due to police action. "Some nut," she said. "On foot and talking crazy about seeing the devil. It's on the radio. Hilarious."

*

Eck stood naked behind his colossal floor windows, the sunrise streaming all the way across from the East River down cavernous streets into the harbor. Yolande had to get some sleep for this heavy day on the job, so she'd left at 3:00 AM. Her Macy's flirty transparent bodysuit had made them giggle and touch and undo like kids on another sexual discovery night. His abraded right ear liked the little ice pack she made with a little lacey something else she'd gotten on a whim at Intimate Apparel while he was being detained on Dyer between Tenth and Ninth.

He barely moved his feet. He was waiting for the first morning effect of all the mighty condo structures twinning other buildings all the way up and down their glass sides, mirrors reflecting mirrors, light light, clouds clouds. Not a face or a body in all the trillions of photons, as if the letting light got what it wanted, itself, and only that. Satisfied that he saw this whole show again, Eck let himself feel how tired he was. It made him laugh that he was probably the only sunrise flasher in his aerial neighborhood, at this moment in time. His baby being, his baby dick right in the face of a glorious morning.

"Okay," he said. "Nice show."

And it was, laid out all below, around, and above him, in air, on water, and in all the human imagination, skill and labor that had built and rebuilt and built again the huge city by the ocean. It could not be that such an earth would abort itself, or that mankind would finally abort the shining blue and green planet that was still a baby at 4.5 billion years. In the beginning was a few million to a hundred million years of accretion of calcium-aluminum inclusions and meteorites. Accrete, bundle, grow, combine, keep on doing it for something and some time short of a forever. Eck did not believe that the capacity to wonder at it was over. That could not be. He could not be, but he was. Outside his column of glass, the wind said so. The living wind that gave him his living. He was living to serve the wind. He would go on betting that the wind knew how to go on and that all the people of the wind did, too.

He went back to bed and delicious undreaming sleep and woke up at 9:00 feeling ready to join the ranks of the well-off unemployed.

NINE

One afternoon, Danny the concierge buzzed Eck on the intercom from the lobby of the building.

"Hey, Danny. What's up?" The intercom crackled like shrink-wrap unfolding.

"Uh, yes, Mr. Eck. Danny down here. Got a woman at the desk asking to come up. Little sketchy, you ask me." Danny occasionally offered opinions about visitors new to him. It was his own extra level of security for occupants he looked out for in particular, which meant pretty much everyone who understood considerations besides Christmas.

"What's her name?"

"She won't say exactly."

Eck heard a deep female voice say something, say it twice. The sound of a smoker caught his ear, stitched with gin.

"Says she's your mother."

Eck figured it could be a good story. His mood lightened.

"She carrying?" Eck imagined the scene, Black Danny Shelter fingers twitching for a quick 360 turn, all he'd really need.

"I don't think so, Mr. Eck. I can't really touch her, of course."

"Get her into the elevator, it's okay. I think." He pictured

Danny Shelter doing just that in an officious, courteous way. It was good for the building, the way you had to get through him.

Eck left his front door ajar and waited at the elevator 12-14 stop.

The sight of her upon the doors whispering open gave him pause. In fantastic shape came to mind, or better, fantasy shape. She wore a thick glossy onyx belt around the middle of her silver overalls-like outfit, underlining her firm chest behind her bright white T-shirt. She was a big queen doll, with big black hair, attractive if flat-screen face, smiling dark eyes, tight line of lips, and yet, she did look a little like him. Except that he looked a little like several kinds of people.

"Hi, Ma," Eck said and bowed her out of the elevator. "Where you been?"

She didn't so much stand up straight in front of him as make herself occupy a sufficient amount more space to let him get a good long look. From one shoulder she bore a long cloth bag of bright weave.

"There will probably be more of me," she said. "My name, son, is Belinda Starr."

"Transgender?"

"Born woman. Just wish I had borne you, like, full." This was not a woman who had cried in years, nor a woman who was going to start crying anytime soon.

"Come on in," Eck said. "Tell me everything. I have twenty minutes." He preceded her to his front door, feeling the way she watched him walk. He was hoping for just a twinge or a draft at the bottom of his spine. Nothing. He could not deny that he had been, now and again his whole adult life, fantasizing about just such a moment, a joyous reunion with his attempted killer mom.

He invited her to take a seat. She did in the center, looked around his living room area, height, light, space-connecting glass dividers, sculptures, paintings, small and massive photographs. He saw her focus on the one he wanted to talk about least.

"*A Bigger Splash,*" she said. "Wow. You got it bad, boy."

"So," Eck said, "Ma. Who's in your name, Belinda? Maybe I'm related to Belle Star, the suffragette Western outlaw? I bet she wouldn't have done me that way."

The woman showed him a flat puzzled face.

"You know," he said. "Letting them throw me down the toilet."

"It didn't happen that way."

"Course," Eck replied, "they didn't really have indoor toilets in Belle Star's day, yes?"

Same flat face, just not puzzled. Sort of waiting him out before she said one damn thing more.

"You been a sex worker?" he asked. "Belinda Starr?"

Eck saw her start to get afraid of him. To what was changing in his voice this very early minute after her arrival. She must know he could be dangerous. The internet on him now said he could be dangerous.

In a finger snap by his own right ear, Eck got his nice voice back. "Please, tell me."

A diagonal runway of sunlight formed halfway into the room from the long harbor windows. They both smiled at it faintly. She took her bag onto her lap, used both hands to open it while keeping her eyes on him evenly.

"Colors," he said. "Arizona Apache? Hopi?"

She pulled out a brown leather photo album, then a yellow loose-leaf binder that didn't seem to have many pages in it.

Eck said, "The genetic map I bought myself said I have some Southwest Native American. Central African. Western Irish. My favorite, Finnish. Couple other places. You can fill me in more, maybe?"

She opened the loose-leaf binder to a page and handed it over to him.

Eck flushed. "Well," he said, "so much for the privacy of

one's genetic map. Where'd you get this, may I ask?" He opened a palm at the familiar pie chart, the percentages, the statement of limited but probable reliability of the analysis of his saliva and hair samples. Multi-racial, multi-ethnic, diverse contemporary earth man. The world was a big, squabbling, bumbling human family not all that good at council with one another over who makes it and who gets to eat it.

"Global You," she said. "Same place you did. Like you, I get a kick out of the Finnish part of me too. Saunas. Putting herring, potato, onion on a fork all at once. Shooter of freezer vodka. Probably wouldn't care much for the snowshoe trekking. But the gene seems to make it easier for me to deal when the temperature drops into the forties in Phoenix."

As she did her riff, Eck searched the odd rectangularity of her face. He had no idea what this woman thought she was doing with him or to him. But he got interested in finding out what it was. He turned to the next page in the binder. Linda Stargell, Boulder, Colorado, birth certificate. Mother Jesse Foner Stargell, father Sean Stargell.

Eck said, "So you're seventy-three. You look pretty good. Balance of good genes, you'd say? Get you a cup of coffee? Fresh ground and brewed Sumatra. Know where that is, Sumatra?"

"Indonesia. We've got some of that, too."

"We," Eck said and shook his head right and left once.

"Coffee would be nice," she said. "Got milk? Then we can look at some pictures together." She held the photo album layer book. She got a slight pleading to him in her eyes, so he got up to fix coffee for them both.

"Soy milk," he said from his food island.

"Yes," she said. "We're lactose intolerant."

"No," Eck said. "Just out of the real stuff right now. I've actually wanted my own dairy cow all my life." He wished he'd not said that in quite that tone of voice.

"Mind if I smoke? Out on your deck here?"

175

"Yes, I do mind. Somebody left some gum here for that. Shall I find you a piece?"

She got up, leaving what she brought on the coffee table, to go find a bathroom he didn't direct her to. When she returned, he was sitting, flipping through the photo album. He didn't smell cigarette. He told himself to just get her story out of her, see what she'd come up with on the plane from Phoenix.

He was looking at a picture of a teenage girl sitting on a corral fence, wearing a swirly yellow and white skirt, a short-sleeved pink blouse, brown and white tie saddle shoes, pink socks. She was aware of it from her upside-down perch.

"I was fifteen. Place outside Denver. About five years before."

"What?"

"You."

He stared at her for about ten seconds. He flipped well into the album, turned it to face her without asking the question.

"My third child. Roland. Died at sixteen. Went into the hospital for a routine Achilles heel operation. Sepsis. You think he looks like you? I do."

"How did you find this address?"

"Jenny Rich's blog site. I mean, she didn't post it. But when your story migrated my way, I Googled you and found Jenny Rich's blog. You know about that?"

"Who was or is my brother Roland's daddy?"

"Man named Dizzie Gillespie. No relation, but just as Black and big."

Eck used his teeth to open a packet of sugar, which he poured slowly into his cup. The way he circled the spoon into the bottom of the cup, he might have cracked it apart. He put the spoon down on the saucer without making a sound.

"I'm surprised to see you taking sugar," she said. "I used to use it. Then I didn't. Then I did for a while again. Now, that's a long time ago. Like a lot of things."

"Say more about the not-Dizzie."

"I want to get up and walk around here. You're making me very nervous."

"Wasn't my idea, now, was it? This? You, whoever you are? Whatever you're here for?"

Belinda Starr went on her own tour of Eck's place. She stopped first at his magnified Hockney. That gave him a chance to take a look at her from the back as she cocked her head this way and that at the painting. The overalls were spacey, but she still filled them in a nice line. The black hair was extraordinary for anyone over forty. He saw nothing in her figure or posture that was like his.

She turned around and asked him, "You think about the foam as pretty much a sign of your own disappearance?"

He answered her straight. "I think it's one hell of a cool dive, yes."

She continued her visual visit, like a patient, discriminating museum-goer.

He flipped through some more of the pictures, trying to find a look, a way of standing or sitting or dancing or purposefully not presenting in front of a camera or being part of a graduation row or sitting on the fender of a glossy new car or holding up a placard in a peace demonstration or considering a gravestone or kissing in a photo booth or maintaining a crucifix in a gymnastic tournament or being a light-green-dressed bridesmaid or fumbling with changing an infant or holding up a small flag at Ground Zero or chugging beer with male and female buddies or receiving a debate trophy or any little detail of life that would mirror his face and shoulder bearing in the slightest in this entire farrago of paper and pictures the woman had assembled in a poor-quality confidence game she'd brought from her own nowhere to play mommy to his somewhere.

She was standing beside him when he put both the album and the binder back deep inside her colorful Apache or Hopi woven shoulder bag.

"You dress up like one big old doll," he said.

"You like the look?" she asked him, the way a striking older woman might still playfully flirt with her well-cut middle-aged son.

"What do you want from me, Belinda Starr?"

"To be recognized as the mother of Goleman Eck. That would be something. That would be a first."

"The mother who aborted him, then lived to find him miraculously alive again? That kind of first?" He grew tremendously thirsty all of a sudden. He bit the insides of his cheeks, swallowed the little saliva that came to him. He handed her the bag.

Something like pleading took over her face. "I'll tell you what happened to me."

"To you?" he asked. "Really, Belle? To you? Best you go now. Now."

"Please, Gole."

"G. T. F. O.," he said. "And Belinda?"

"Yes."

"Tell Jenny Rich. Tell her when I find her, I'm gonna bitch slap the other side of her face. She'll get the reference." Then he shook his head. "No, don't tell her that."

"Oh, dear boy," Belinda Starr said, "She might like that. From you."

Thereafter, there was a string of found mothers who came for or at, Goleman Eck. They reappeared, several of them, while the fad of him had its run. Two of them had died, so they were represented by some family member or some lover or confessor of their later years whose mission became to get to Eck, usually to get something from Eck, a noted wind engineer with deep pockets. One who got pretty close to him was a man in his eighties who claimed to be the bio-father himself. More about him later. What was amazing to Eck were the stories of the abortion itself, the bizarre tales of what must have happened or that did happen to the fetus-child. It all might have added up to the thousand and one nights of Eckolalia, the mythic child of wonder, child of light, a cable series like no other that touched upon global cultures of infancy, gender, the body, of Pip totally UberPipped, of babies triumphant, the Year of the Child, the tale of the indomitable kid. It didn't.

He was the trashed offspring of another noted thinker about the inevitability of the violence that would replace the colonizer with the colonized. A kind of double agent, the man had come from West Africa to the America he despised for several weeks of CIA training in Miami in contra-revolutionary psychiatry. He was outed and duped into a lethal knife fight in Little Havana, but not before his American sojourn included a tryst with a white graduate student of political philosophy who was also in the training. When he was killed, she, pregnant-desperate, tried to die as well. The late-term abortion was forced on her psychosis by her sane parents. There was a terrible mistake, a fetus switch or maybe snatch right after the induced delivery. Some kind of minimally approved obstetric experiment with pre-borns that was immediately shut down after the switch or snatch was detected. Notes from the microform records that later decomposed hinted at an ethically dubious racialized protocol going on in the design of the research. Since the famous thinker had been largely Black, the multiracial humanoid—a term found in the fragmentary notes—must have been stolen and sustained into growth.

The political philosophy dropout brought this tale to Eck in a wheelchair. They met for twenty minutes under the clock in Grand Central Station. She was there on her own. She started screaming at him on her own, and GCS security wheeled her away from him as he told her he wished her well.

A blues songwriter from Atlanta had written one hit in the '70s, "Forbidden Child," that had been covered since by fourteen other artists. This provided her, Mary Ann Shenck, royalties into her now middle seventies. She sang it for Eck, and she still had a heartache-toned voice. He picked up the refrain and sang it with her. They sounded good together, even a little similar in musical intonation. It was only now that she'd learned about Goleman that she could tell the truth about the "you" in the three-time Grammy-nominated song. Her boy child had been unborn of rape, by a long-dead Brazilian record producer who had made her choose between aborting their kid or losing her contract. She was nineteen. The procedure had been a bloody horror, and the narcotic she was filled with for the pain obliterated whatever had become of her little forming boy. But she'd always, always known that he had survived. He always talked to her when she went back and back to rehab. He kept her alive, so she knew he was too, somewhere in the stars and on the earth. Eck wrote her one big check. She never came for him a second time.

Once there was a gentleman who contacted Eck via Facebook to tell him that he'd never been aborted at all. This was an interesting possibility. They Skyped, erratically, during a violent thunderstorm banging Eck's windows and all New York harbor. Dr. Fallan Bodica Emeritus pediatric surgeon University of the Caribbean, at a retirement community in Savannah, extremely sensitive to light now, bald and wearing massive dark glasses, sat in a very upright white wicker chair and held his aged neck up high, as if presenting his throat. His English was deeply French inflected, and his Skype connection was not optimal either. Anyway, the old doctor was once a young resident at the newly founded UC Medical and Technical. A Trinidadian truck crash victim named Equiano died in the ER, a very early pregnancy. Miss Equiano was a violin prodigy of incredible promise. Young Dr. Bodica was ordered to cut out the embryo. The hospital was experimenting with cryogenic preservation. The embryo was frozen. Two years later it was implanted in a very rich, very corrupt Trinidadian politician's wife. Dr. Bodica was the physician who did the Caesarean the wife did not survive. The baby, a boy, was whisked off by the criminal politician. Bodica took pictures of the no-longer suffering surrogate mother. They bore a distinct resemblance to Goleman Eck's picture on Facebook. Bodica was desperate for money, a lot of money. The Skype connection broke down altogether. Eck could not get it back. He waited for another call from Savannah. It never came. He put a detective agency to work. Nothing. He filed the possibility under Huis Clos.

And there came to Eck in the U.S. mail one of those communications made of very large pieces of paper on which were pasted hundreds of differently printed or fonted alphabet units spelling or misspelling words in syntactically challenged English. The gist of it was a new version of the old insult that he'd been shat upon a rock and the sun'd hatched him. Aborted, slimy but still viable tiny Eck had been deposited inside a glass-encased black candle within a roadside car accident shrine atop the railing of a bridge over a dizzying gorge in the Swiss Alps. It was a spot where the noon sun reflected off the top of Mont Blanc in a straight ray of light right to the roadside shrine. The shrine was to a Lemans driver named Emilia Firenze who jumped from that spot on the bridge in the fit of depression that only high-end Grand Prix racing competition controlled. "L'Emilia" she was called in the sports press. On her fortieth birthday, her elegant timepieces designer who sponsored her racing replaced her with a young male driver who would risk anything to win for the designer, something l'Emilia lost the nerve to try anymore. She had come to fear the thing that kept her sane, the driving. An American fanatical racing fan of hers named Angela Arroz who kept the flame burning happened to be walking along the bridge over the gorge to check the shrine when she saw from a hundred yards away in the bright sunlight off Mt. Blanc a young girl covered in a monk's white cowl put something inside the glass, then turn in horror to see the faithful Angela

Arroz start to run at her screaming at her to get away from l'Emilia's shrine. The cowled girl rushed to get into the back seat of a white Rolls Royce Phaeton from the 1930s, which rolled right past Angela Arroz soundlessly, as if it didn't have a big engine or create any wind resistance on the open bridge high in the mountains.

Angela Arroz took the unborn from the glass candle and went into immediate, heroic successful action. She was convinced the unborn was sent from l'Emilia from the gorge below from whence l'Emilia's body was never found, never brought back up. She was so unconvincing at the hospital that she was restrained after her burden was taken, stolen, raped from her. After being drugged into submission and kept in the tiny mountain medical facility for two days, she was released. She was told never to come back. She was told she had not brought any such thing as a feticidal into the facility. Angela Arroz had no French, no German, could not make her hysterical case to any authority. But when she went back to the shrine in the darkest night she'd ever know, she heard l'Emilia crying out from the infinite gorge below, "Gold Ache!" The voice cried it up at her many, many times, then stopped. That was the essence of the whole story that Angela Arroz wrote in five handwritten pages in the year that Eck figured he came into being. The pages came to him with not a word about Angela Arroz herself, whether she was alive even. Just the pages, no return address, just a Brownie camera three-by-five black and white photo of an obviously obese, Asian-featured woman in an orange racing suit sitting on the hood of a scarlet killer automobile as if she wanted to crush it. On the reverse, "La Grande Emilia Khan: 8/15/63." Born to recognize absurdity, Eck asked no questions about this one, started no inquiries. He did keep it in mind, in the cluttered back section, the car racing and candle stuffing, giving it, just there, the little mental space in which he might have room to wait for it, when maybe someone from that bridge over that gorge, one day or night, might come knocking, knocking.

Goleman Eck was also Portuguese-Mozambican-Bengali, in descending quotients of 50-35-15, and he was the child of torture. According to an article published under a group pseudonym in the neuro-biological journal of Vidyasagar University in West Bengal, a massive digital genomic mapping of PMB first-year women students who were found to be pregnant zeroed in on Aarani Mazumdar. She had an affair with a Vidyasagar international student from Maputo, Robert Cumbane, who had been radicalized by contact with the African National Congress Party.

Disgraced and disowned by her parents as much for her Marxist-Leninist politics as for her condition, she fled with Robert to become a revolutionary soldier in Mozambique. Later that year the pair crossed the Zambezi river with Samora Machel's Frelimo army that struck Portuguese-dominated land and infrastructure, penetrating further and further south to the horror of the colonial occupation. Aarani was captured in a firefight with a Portuguese army division, in which she shot precisely in the forehead two Portuguese soldiers who had just killed her Robert. She was ordered interrogated by General Kaulza de Arriaga himself, who was incensed at the girl's "temerity, whorishness, and blasphemy" under enhanced questioning directed by American anti-terrorist specialists. That she was found to be with child got him even crazier. He had a personal "nurse" from Lisbon, Elisabete Matos, who did a procedure on Aarani without anesthesia. Aarani hemorrhaged, did not die, disappeared into the interior. Again, the fetus with no chance summoned its own resources, experienced help and succor fantastic even to conceive never mind measure or prove.

The lacuna in the narrative is undeniable, from the torture abortion (torsion) to this famous unborn Westerner. Whatever one thinks, whatever one judges as real or possible, here is the face. Look at these photos of the famous subject, the article concludes. Those are the lineaments combining Portuguese, Indian, and Mozambican genetic weaving. Here is the still-broken Mazumdar-family picture of the vanished Aarani Mazumdar at fifteen, a time of initiation into Vaishnavite Shakta. You decide. What a heritage, of freedom, bravery, endurance it is, on the right side of history, multiple humanity, the one earth come into being in this one plural man. If you meet Goleman Eck somewhere in the world, ask him what he intends, to accept his true identity, or to be the forever-unique castaway he seems to want to act out, uselessly. The current generation of the Mazumdar family, for one, reaches out to, yearns to connect with, the Goleman Eck of their beloved ancestor Aarani, so tragically banished in the cultural confusions of the past century.

A giant of a man his own age sent him a YouTube video narrating Eck's origin as an abandoned cryopreserved embryo. The creature was even overgrown for a giant, about seven-foot-three with nothing of the build of a tremendous athlete, just a tallow mass of a man who called himself Henry Todmordgens. The tilting smile that reminded Eck of a barely attached tenement fire escape somewhere in Alphabet City meant that Henry's last name surely wasn't, but he did have the huge look of somebody called Hank. The camera seemed to be about mounted about five feet in front of him, but he still filled the perimeter of the lens. Eck watched the video off and on for fifteen to twenty minutes at a time for four viewings, because it was all pretty hard to take.

He sat cross-legged on a figured wooden throne-like structure. Todmorgens wore a piped purple sweatsuit, and his untied cordovan cap-toe shoes could haven planters outside a post office. The line of thin black beard down his cheeks and around his jaw and ovaling his bumper lips traced a possible shape for the lower part of a distorted moon face. He was bald like the Michelin mascot and he had similar tire rolls of flesh encircling his midsection and lap. Todmorgens' voice rumbled from some cellar in his gut in a clash of echoes, warnings, vatic fragments. The more Eck tried to dial down the volume, the more the voice dissipated into cracked drumming and splayed out like angry rain on flat macadam. After a few such twists of the volume, Eck just listened to the eerie dudgeon of the creature's uninvited message.

Ten minutes in, Eck started to feel spooked at what he was hearing from the barely moving mountain's slow mouth. His lifelong search for his own origin seemed possibly being mocked. When his doorman called to say Victor Mature and Mary Rice were on their way up, Eck stopped the video. He opened his front door to his friends.

"You look like you've seen a ghost," Victor said.

"Or," Mary said, "somebody who's about to see a ghost."

"Who's been unearthing your birthing now?" Victor asked.

"Are we still going out to brunch?" Mary asked.

"Mary's been saving up her bacon and eggs quotient just for today," Victor said.

"You promised," Mary said. "No more digging the undiggable."

"Just so," Victor said. "'Obsession is recession,' you said, Gole. We both liked that way of putting it."

Eck held his palms out in stop fashion. "All right, all right," he said. "Just look at this with me for a few minutes."

"Christ, Mary," Victor said as he slumped down on one of Eck's most interesting yellow chairs, "we have to humor the guy yet one more time or we don't get the joy of togetherness with him on this Sunday morning coming down."

Mary took Eck's hand and walked him back over to his remote. She gave it to him and said, "Gole, sweet Gole, there is real light bouncing off the real Hudson river as we speak. You really need to see it."

"All right, all right," he said. "Just—"

"Showtime," Victor Mature said. "Put this particular fraud on." Henry Todmorgens instantly filled up the screen. "Holy

185

good shit," Victor said. "Mistah Kurtz Brando flat close and ugly. I don't trust the schmuck already."

Thirty years ago, Massive Man was saying, he worked as a lab assistant for a small but internationally known human embryo in vitro implant clinic in Galveston. Massive spoke without transitions. Next, he said that nearly one-third of cryopreserved embryo implants end up discarded or abandoned.

Gole, he said, was abandoned, then saved.

Eck shut him off.

Victor and Mary nodded at the blank screen and peered through the silence at the brooding Eck until he said, "So let's go eat.

"Sustenance," Victor said.

"One more time," Mary Rice said, "we choose life."

Eck still brooded. "So, Gole," Victor said.

"What?"

"Little testy there, pal?"

"What?"

"Fill us in when you've watched this new fraud out?"

"You got it."

"I have an idea," Mary Rice said. They all said it at once, "Let's go eat." But they all just sat and watched as the screen reappeared with a voiceover.

Speculative unfrozen-embryo parents may quit upon further reflection. Or economic changes can make the project financially unsustainable, as in paying all that money to the clinic. Or, endometriosis can do it. Or, waves of doubt about a shot of other people's DNA, even if the basic info is Northern European, or African-American, or Japanese musical, or Brazilian beauty, or perfectly unobjectionably hyper-normal, or sudden disgustfulness, or surprising revulsion against their own negative procreative lot.

Or, as one study concluded: *Embryologist variability:* As with all techniques that involve humans, some seem to do a better job than others: And them odds weren't encouraging enough. Or, during the process of thawing the embryo from negative 321 F to 32 F, the occasionally unpreventable formation of ice crystals that can damage the embryo brought to full term.

Or the curse of Eve, the rage of the bad mother, the dark truth that all things glorious before turn to ash now. These video sessions had taught Eck about the vicissitudes of popping the kid out of the freezer directly into the oven. If his run with it had ended in such abandonment, how had he survived it?

They still hadn't made a move to eat. They still watched man as rebarbative mountain come to his conclusion, which was to curse Eck.

Session four, the last fifteen minutes, answered his paranoia and his nausea. A now raging and spitting and howling Henry Todmorgens, too gigantic to get up from his chair and stand, pointed and yelled at Goleman Eck there on the other side of the camera about baby Henry's adenoma, his adenoma, his adenoma, his adenoma, his pituitary tumored gland making wheelbarrow full amounts of somatotropin that did this to him. Baby Henry was his mother's next embryo adventure after she ditched, or thought she did, Baby Goleman Eck, you miserable fuck, my brother, my brother, the one who escaped and who now lives the golden life, and fuck you fuck you, fuck you to the Judas depths of God's Hell. Blank screen.

Eck reported to his true friends that this time, this one had gotten to him. He was getting scared of uncontrollable malignity out there obsessing about him, wanting him annihilated for what he represented.

Mary Rice said, "I don't get it. How did he say you survived this, this." She tried a phrase, "This thawed embryo abandonment?"

"He didn't," Eck said.

"What do you remember?" Victor Mature asked.

"If dreams mean anything," Eck said, "when I was little, something regular about ragged edges of tops of tin soup cans, creamed soup cans. Something related about canisters, you know, longer soup cans. Sections of sewer pipe along the road waiting to be connected underground once the jackhammers made deep ditches. Cannons vintage World War One in parks. I'd sit astride them and I'd get caught there like a cat too high in a tree."

"Jesus, Gole, you're starting to trance out," Victor said.

"Him, too," Gole said. "That Jesus."

"What?"

"We gotta go eat," Gole said. "It's just that," and he stopped.

"What?" Mary said.

"The Easter story," Gole said. "It made perfect sense to me the first time I heard it. A big wingy angel rolls back the rock, and I get out. No, I'm not Him. I just get out, like He got out. This guy, this voluminous creature here. Henry Hank Todmorgens. I think he can put the rock right back, with me inside again. That's what he wants. I want to run before he finds me."

Mary and Victor went silent. They looked around at different light formations in Eck's place. They didn't have to say it, but each was wondering what the light formations in this place would be if Eck were not there to be the reason they turned on. It was the first time they thought of Eck's dying.

"Victor," Gole said.

"Yes."

"Just how is it going through life bearing an uncanny resemblance to an ungodly handsome movie actor from long ago?"

"Mature had the good luck to look like me."

Mary said, "That's the same answer I got the one time I asked that question."

"I'm serious, Victor," Eck said. "I'm figuring you're a

different kind of version of what I am. Or, sort of? I'm a not-me. So are you. Or is that just unacceptable to you."

Victor took a few seconds. "Yes and no. I think I'd like to have the chance to pretend I could wrap myself up in Jesus' robe. That would be nice. It's just that he had to look like that all the time, no matter what other person he played. He was never any of those people. They would have all looked different from him because they were all different people. I get to be the only Victor Mature who had the name for real."

"Huh?" Gole said. "Aren't you really Eugene Encarnacion?"

"Yeah," Mary said. "Follow the etymologies of those two names."

Gole blinked, laughed. "Oh. Got it."

"What do you think that contributes to this discussion?" Victor asked in true wondering good humor.

"I think I love you," Mary told him.

"Victor," Gole said. "I know where I want to go eat."

"I figured as much," Victor said. "I like it very much, and yes, I'll be getting there an hour before my shift. I'll cook us up something with huevos and red mole that'll make us feel that eating is nature's anti-anxiety gift."

"And bacon?"

"Yes, Mary. Of course."

She clapped her hands. "We're going to Les Trois Souhaits!"

PART TWO

TEN

So the creature said, "I . . . am an abortion," and Mary said her book was "my hideous progeny." Abortions aren't supposed to live, that's the whole point. But Mary's has gone on living long after long, two centuries and more of replications, rebirths, generating more hideous, more ridiculous, an endless chain of repetitions. Eck was bound to meet this wonderful Mary, somewhere, somehow. This is how he told that he did.

At the water's edge in the dark night, Eck faced Orkney the squat man with the gruff voice and repulsive countenance. The man said: "The event on which your fiction is founded is of impossible occurrence. You may, of course, assume it as the basis of your work of fancy in the world."

"I'll take it," Eck replied. "I have to take it as my basis for life. You mind, Mr. Orkney?"

Mary told Mr. Orkney that Victor had found "a sudden light," the "cause of generation and life" that "became capable of bestowing animation upon lifeless matter."

The squat, repulsive man said again, "This fancy is of impossible occurrence. It has been an unchallenged premise of a story that has gone on entirely too long." He showed Eck again the antique rusted scimitar hanging from the thick belt

193

around his pilling outer coat. "Please, get in the boat with the lady. We have to finish this whole filthy mess."

"I will get in the boat," Eck said. "But this is not going to happen."

Mary said, "Take courage. Do it for me."

"I've been doing it, sort of, for you. Though I didn't recognize it as about you exactly."

"Maybe I'm your mother after all."

"She's done enough in that line," said Mr. Orkney in his squat, repulsive way.

"Whatever," Eck said. "That unchallenged premise bestowed the only animation I had coming. Worked for me, you know?"

"Still," the man with the old sword said. "We have to do this. Complete the series of your being. Please, get in the boat."

Eck helped Mary onto the stern seat of the boat, thinking about how he would get the half-assed weapon from the guy without hurting him or frightening one of the most famous mothers in human history. He took the bow seat, facing forward. The man got in after they did and took the midship oars. Several strong woven sacks of pieces and parts of Goleman Eck's remaining years of life clumped in two piles at his feet under the bow. Apparently, it would be his duty to throw them into the water. This last time, he was to abort himself.

Squat Orkney even rowed gruffly. He rowed and rowed, a good mile out into the night. Mary put a rough fur around her shoulders. Between two and three in the morning, the moon rose, and Eck turned around to see Mary's lovely enduring face behind the unpleasant rower's unpleasant features. Her smile for Gole seemed to hover just above Orkney's brute left shoulder.

"Here will serve," he said and stopped rowing. Other than them, the scene was perfectly solitary, the water as gentle as an infant's bath.

Eck believed it would, so the ministering wind came. It blew and lulled, blew and lulled, until the man nodded out. Eck got up and removed the scimitar from his mid-section.

Mary removed the fur from her own shoulders and draped it around the squat figure's frame. A little awkwardly, Eck and Mary exchanged places in the boat. Eck then gave the old sword to her and asked her, "Are you Mary Rice after all?"

"No," she replied. "Don't think of me as someone else. Though I do know that fine Mary Rice."

"So, it is okay with you, dearest Mary, that I free the series of my remaining years, that I not drown them the way Victor did the parts he made for the monster's bride?"

"That was Victor's final abortion time. That's enough."

"Do it, then."

She was as strong as she ever was, stupendously strong. She stood up hugely without rocking the boat. She hooked one woven bag at a time onto the rusted tip of the curved sword. Each one she held up gracefully, queenly, for the wind to take. The wind, Eck's own wind, dancing, did so, one by one until all the remaining parts of Eck's life were freed and flown into his future.

Mary and Eck switched seats again. She took the animal fur off the man's shoulders so that he would come out of his deep enchanted nap. Mr. Orkney blinked and peered into the bow area.

"All done, then," he said to Eck.

As if indescribably sad, Eck said, "It is done, yes."

The man seemed to want to say something in not a gruff and repulsive way. But it came out wrong. "It had to be, son. You'll be drifting off out of your life before we row back, now."

"It had to be this way, yes," Eck said, as if going to his grave.

"Yes," Mary said behind the man. "This way at last. I'm content."

"All right, then," the man said in a growl. "All right. Let's get going. All right."

Yet another scene got passed down from Eck. In this one, closer to the old story itself, the bag has not his remains but those the scientist ripped apart in his refusal to let the monster's bride live after all.

At three in the morning, the second story tells, they set out with the basket of remains, Eck holding it in his lap in the prow of the little skiff. Mary sat wrapped up against the moon chill on the mid-bench. Mr. Orkney, at the tiller, was boatman, guiding them a sufficient distance out. His face was pocked but his speech was liquid and lyrical.

His was a loud kindness. "Well, this is the first such basket I've conveyed in the hope of its floating rather than sinking."

Eck, willy-nilly caught in the role of creator thwarted by its own creation, said it was time to revise Mary's endlessly destructive tale of the monster's aborted mate.

Mary agreed. "She's made for some good comedy, that bride. But I now think of her as a Lady Moses in the bulrushes. Give her a floating chance."

Eck said, "It's your book, Mary. You can revise it as you see fit."

"I feel that the change is more in synch with contemporary gender conventions," she said. "It will make a bigger splash."

"Hah!" Gole blurted.

Orkney kindly shushed them, used his sealskin coated arms to wave point toward the patrol boat skirting the dim shore to the south of them. It had a shaking, sweeping searchlight Eck remembered the like of in movies about the Mekong Delta. That was how dangerous their basket mission might get. Cradling it tighter, Eck realized that it was pretty big, considering.

A little flotilla of lighted candles on acanthus leaves parted gently, causing a mid-clef hum as the skiff glided on into firmer waters. Shouldering night clouds cast down moments of darkness that made Orkney revert to old steering instincts.

He started up a song, then another, finishing neither. On the third swelling of his pirate song, Mary joined in with him. Eck wondered what she was going to tell her infamous genius poet husband when they got her back to him. The guy freaked out about other people's nighttime sea stories.

In all that, Eck had just fallen asleep at the prow. He jerked up, and the blessed sack of remains shifted of its own accord.

Mary was right on it. "Whoa, there, sailor," she said. She got this Goleman Eck from another century up straight and cursing the global warming to come.

"Don't get all that way," she said. It was an order. Eck liked it from her, only her.

Mr. Orkney said he didn't like the signs and maneuvered the sail for that much more wind to get them some distance at least. But there were more small boats aiming at them.

"Mr. Mary," he said to Eck. "Which of our limited options d'ye prefer?" Mr. Eck preferred the head-on winds, of course. They all battened and braced. Content at being directed from behind, Eck said, "Push further out. I need deeper water to set the bride's remains floating if she's to have a new life after being torn up and abandoned by her creator."

Pressure around the little craft increased, but not yet by bullets or land ordinance. He trundled back, past the transcendent Mary, to his brother his tiller.

"Okay," Eck told him. "Once I've released her and the true signs sing out. You'll know it. Never mind me or anything or anybody. Just go."

After Gole got the basket of monster bride remains off to a heady start in the tributary river, he took Mary in his arms to lean on him and watch the basket begin its drifting toward the reeds Lady Moses would find them in. There would be another woman to rise out of this aborted basket of remains, a new Promethean goddess or president or architect or poet or wind engineer. The aborted rebooted. Mary reMaryed. The curse of the ancient story unspoken. Eck and this Mary not his

Mary Rice a pair of divine agents with their mission accomplished.

"Get back in your seats, sir, Madam," Mr. Orkney said in his determined quiet growl. "Your night journey is over. You've done very well, my lady Mary. Your book will finally have a different ending, way beyond its own disastrous telling." Mary, Eck felt, was smiling, accepting, ready to go back to finish her years with her transcendent poet unable to swim.

All hell broke loose in the dark night skies, the sound of the universe taking into itself a radical change of the future it had been moving to in tragic mother steps. Change was noisy, thunderous, cataclysmic, a revision of everything. Eck hunkered down in the prow of the rocking skiff again, as old intractable Orkney steered it back to the coast of Ireland. Thus did Gole rip up at last that *Classics Illustrated* the Killer girl had used to torment his very soul.

*

Goleman Eck became a figure of whom other adventures were told. Tales of his whereabouts and his fate proliferated. Some went according to the need of the teller to claim special knowledge of Eck's post-EXOIL travels and life. Others had the ring of truth, or at least possibility true to Eck.

The Reverend Shimmerman said he was on a spiritual quest: He was gaining healing powers from jailed Sufis in Turkey and a hundred-year-old female Incan seer descendant on Macchu Picu. Videoing, blogging, linking, lecturing, Facebooking, waiting his two times to speak on national cable news channels, trekking, conferencing, the Rev preached gently the Miracle of Eck in the Age of Feminist Abortion Madness.

Victor Mature placed a pay-phone call to a number he would die rather than reveal once a month near the grassy knoll in Dallas: Eck was there, finishing up harnessing wind technology with Mexican liberation funding to safely crack open sections of the wall along the Rio Grande.

Eck's old lover Sturgis Macmillan destroyed a video for Gole's own good of his particular labor on behalf of Right to Grow Up (RGU): Of Eck finding two more sites in Galway like that of the lost children of Tuam.

Candidate Gottsch had six letters postmarked from different Brooklyn zip codes that she held up on but would not release to Fox News: He was insistent that she stop her Freedom of Information Act demand that all EXOIL robo documents relating to his firing be released to her office once she won the election. She had to do what was right, no matter her wronged and missing friend's wishes in the matter.

Somebody started a preposterous fiction that went viral that David Hockney's anonymous principal art dealer put out an exclusive invitation: Your presence is requested at the artist's gala unveiling of his heartfelt new masterpiece, "The Bigger Splash: The Disappearance of Goleman Eck. Date and Place to Follow"; people were wild to be included when and where.

Kilpartridge heirs and relations announced a huge family re-union and cookout to occur next summer in Salisbury Beach, Massachusetts: They Were Going to Have Themselves a Time Because Eck Would Surely Come to Them Again.

All sorts of right and dubious imaginings and yearnings like those. Eck would come again when the world would this time be worthy of him, this nation, all the nations.

He now had an awful freedom, to become anything, anything different, anything more of the same. He fitted into life patterns that started in mystery and ended in mystery.

One was the old King Arthur story via Tennyson. No one knew for sure the king's parentage, where he was born and came from. No one knew at the end when he was sailed off on his funeral ship where he was headed or whether he would come again. For a good while, when he was king, his table all believed in him without question of his origin, and so they achieved some great things acting in his name under his authority. Then the doubts about him and his authority festered within the court. His best warrior loved his wife the queen, who loved him in disastrous return. The word of that undid the promise of the king's word that had bound his twelve together in a union of belief and doing. So then the holy thing floated among them and many of them pursued it in a vision of some finality. Their various pursuits of it, or angry denials of it, left the work of the court undone. The king said of them, "Visions? The night comes when the visions come to me. You want visions, I get visions. But then I have to go back to the light of day to do the work they have abandoned to seek that awful final light." And the king's order fell apart. So Eck understood the king's sorrow at the whole arc of his life of dubious birth and dwindled allegiances.

Sure, Eck could become many things, but that very gift of unborn multiplicity turned him into being the unwanted, shape-shifting outcast, the frightening ever-aborting criminal of criminals. The real bastards would never leave his innocence alone because it was what he was guilty of most. Understanding all this deeply, he, who lacked any normal sequence, had to go on living in some next way. At least, the wind had earned him enough money to do next for quite a while.

*

"I worry," Yolande said, "that you'll cut as well that part of your life that is I, me."

They were on the stone balcony at the Belvedere Castle weather station in Central Park. She was holding him under his arms from behind because he was warm and this midnight played on her fears. He hadn't said it yet, but she guessed this was the January night was the last she'd see him for maybe quite a while, though she would see him.

Below them, the great ellipse walk winked lighted winter limb moments around the Great Lawn. Down to the left Delacorte Theater stage was dark and vacant of Hamlets and Calibans alike. He hadn't thought of it before. Even Caliban had a mother, the foul and horrid witch Sycorax.

Yolande pointed up to the grand 1920's apartment houses shouldering side by side up Fifth Avenue. "In the dark," she said, "their lighted windows look like solid homes people have had for decades, maybe more." Solidity was what he had no right to pledge her.

She told him about the blizzard winter evening when she stood right there at the Castle all alone looking down at the way Jean Claude's massive orange "Gates" fabrics swayed almost noiselessly thirty feet high across the Park walks curling away from the Castle and the lake.

"It was so beautifully cold at night, the snow coming down like fingers wanting to touch the great sheets. It was magic to walk through them and under the trees. His barely shifting mural planes changed the winter night city into something evanescent. Grand. Majestic."

"Had you known before that what you wanted to make for the world to see in large free scale, outdoors?"

She didn't answer that. "If you were a carpenter," she said, "and I were a lady."

"Carpenter," he said, "from Nazareth."

"And I were from Sheba," she said. "You could have your own baby."

"Could maybe end this thing." She pushed her hips close under his back waistline.

"Except," he said, "they'd kill my baby. Our. For not having a born father. By order of the Bureau of Natural Causes."

"I would get our baby a birth certificate, right off. I would fight them for it."

"I'm leaving for a while, Yolande."

She heard only the end of them. She said, "Why does that have to sound so much like a death sentence for us?"

The minor flash in their two faces was a cell phone photo happening of them. Yolande recoiled in nightmare fright.

Eck twisted the phone out of the teen's right hand, then used two hard fingers to push the kid's chest and him two feet away from them.

"You're freakin' Eck," the out-of-nowhere boy complained, black hoodie and magenta jumpsuit large all over him. The girl looked, doing a Julia Cameron pose of an ethereal virgin of silky wan hair, embroidered white nightdress, and thick woven shawl. "Miserable cocksucker," she called Eck.

Yolande went to slap her but stood in front of Eck instead while he found and deleted the photograph from the yellow-cased phone.

"Aw, man," the boy said. His mouth hung open as if his tongue were too big. "All's we wanted was one picture. Elaina and me, we could be heroes with that one picture."

"Yeah, cocksucker is too good for you. You ruined Carlton's shot."

"Get out of here," Yolande said. "You have no idea the danger you are in here right now."

Carlton stutter-stepped to his left, then to his right. "An actual Eck sighting. One chance in ten thousand. Aw, man? You know?"

Gole put the yellow phone down on the stone parapet and turned back to the midnight view of the winter park and the trees.

"Elaina," Yolande said, "you can come back for the phone after we leave. He won't hurt it, but you can't use it that way. I know you are high and witless. But if you call us cocksucker one more time, I will let this very private man straighten you out."

"If he doesn't wanna be recognized, why doesn't he at least

cover up all that bright white hair of his? Or, I know, wear a mask, of like, somebody else famous."

"Go away now," Yolande said. "Come back in ten minutes for the phone. Watch out for the night cop on the scooter, that's my advice."

Elaina guided the cheated Carlton down the stone steps, turning them both into the dark on the left rather than following the right to the pond.

"Things like them two," Gole said. "Makes me think it's never going to be finished."

"You're speaking again," Yolande said. "Good. Murderous rage gone by?"

"Still, I get scared. Every time."

"Time what?"

"Someone wants to take me."

"Take your picture."

"No. Take me."

On their way out of the park entrance, a helmeted cop on a scooter asked them if they'd seen two stoned kids. They said no. But just then they heard the hooting pair about a hundred yards back, running after them again, probably with the retrieved camera.

Yolande said to the name badge over the left shirt pocket, "That sounds likely, right? Officer Ahmad?"

"Oh, my God," the officer said, wearily ignoring the citizen's saying she'd gotten his name already. He gunned the scooter to give notice he was coming, and he went.

They walked a way up the avenue alongside the park. During that time, Gole said he'd be back. Yolande said she'd wait, though she didn't really think she'd be sure it would be he, if he did come back.

"You talk like that," he said, "you have my heart."

"I know," she said, pulling his right arm tight against her breast. "It's all the rest of you that you don't have in any control right now. My genius puzzle man, all undone pieces again."

She sighed so deeply, the sound of it filled his own breathing with bale yet to come.

ELEVEN

Eck had wind friends on five continents. Several owed him their entry and their success in the global industry. Everyone, woman and man, said, Goleman Eck had been a good boss. He dealt straight, expected the best from you, gave you his best leadership in return. What was being done to him was rotten, an outrage none of them could do anything about. He let them off the hook about being seen with him, so they were glad to book travel arrangements according him a good measure of anonymity he couldn't have gotten on his own. He could play as much or as little of himself as he wanted or occasion required. The irony of a sort-of anonymous Goleman Eck tickled him mildly. So did this changed script.

"I need to get away from being me out there for a while. At least here in the city. At least this me that's out there this way. I figure I leave, I get out for a decent while. Temporary vacation from where everyone who wants a piece of me can get to me. Maybe moving is better than standing still. For a while. Remove myself from their temptation to abort me all over again."

Before he left, Yolande and Mary and Eugene Encarnacion all told him versions of the same thing. Or maybe it was different parts of one thing, pieces of the final puzzle that only he could put together in his own way. That it might work somewhat, for the while he wanted. But he was by now, they reminded him, global. In another country, he'd just be waiting for Eck to catch up to Eck. But go, the three of them said. Go and be the real Gole we know. Do it for yourself. Find out what's a different or even better Eck.

Stay in touch, dear wandering one. Come back to us. We'll be waiting for the same true Goleman Eck who had to get out of Dodge for a while to save his life. Exile yourself. See what you find. Come back yourself. Come back to us. We'll be eager to hear about it all, Goleman Eck.

*

"I like talking to you." His guide Feyisa translated what he'd just said to Eck in Tigrinya. "You know a lot of different things. And you're in good shape for this kind of climb."

They had come about twenty-five hundred feet up zigzag rock trails to the grassy plateau atop Mt. Claybourne in the Simien Range northeast of Gondar. Feyisa said he didn't in fact know the local name of this smaller mountain. He called up to his donkey handler about it, but the bronze man in tan loafers only shrugged. Eck leaned back against a boulder and drank water. He was feeling the altitude shift now, draining his good shape a little.

"Reminds me," he said to Feyisa. "Mt. Sinai?"

"Egypt," Feyisa said, "the not Africa."

"Ancient dynastic tension is what it sounds like to this American."

"I have not been there, Cole, yes." He called Eck Cole, and that was okay.

"Monastery of St. Catherine at the base of Mt. Sinai. You stay there. You sleep chilled under three blankets until three in the morning. Then your whole group climbs up the mountain for a couple of hours, to see the sun rise. Guys with loafers like," and he pointed to the donkey handler tightening his bag again.

"James," Feyisa said.

"Guys in t-shirts, headscarves and loafers like that, they show up, walk with you, say they know best path, best up. Can't get rid of them, though only one latches on to you at a time. They can get best camel, nice camel for you to finish toughest part up to the top. If you're sucker enough to engage them in all that dark, they want money after an hour. You say they said take to top. No, leave now, not dressed right. See shoes, not right, no jacket. Too cold now. You just head up straight. Pay now, please."

"Did you?"

"No."

"Get to the top of Moses' mountain?" He believed he had the owner's name right.

"At the top, there was a tent. Good strong tent against the wind up there. Filled with Korean Christians singing 'Amazing Grace,' I guess."

"Then what?" Feyisa bent over to retie his maroon French climbing boots. They complemented the logo on his heavyweight polo shirt, a redder sheep drooping in a weighing truss under its middle. Graceful, lean and strong, he was another handsome Ethiopian mountain runner making a living in half a dozen different ways.

"Ra, the ancient Egyptian sun god flashes on the horizon. Everyone cheers his show. After a few minutes, everyone runs like hell down the mountain to get warm again in the chilly monastery. All the guides, gone, as if flown off the mountain."

"I have something more special tomorrow afternoon." Feyisa pointed diagonally across to his right. "Shepherd village over there, about an hour walk."

Eck discerned animals, wood smoke, habitation on the mountainside. He felt good, interested, glad for whatever his guide could show him.

The clanging of neck bells gave them warning. They moved to either side of the path to give easy access to a dozen goats and their two staff-wielding young herders. Sun-browned, in striped jellabiyas and rope sandals, they passed phrases with Feyisa and said, "Good afternoon, hello," to Eck. They kept steady pace.

James waved to get going again and slapped the donkey loud. All around Eck, the air had scents of barley, livestock, grasses heating in mountain sun.

When they got to their overnight site, he asked, and James pointed to it. Across the swirls, depths, and heights of the Simiens, there was Ras Dejen, fifteen thousand feet of unsnowed gray colors of volcanic rock.

"Tigrinya," Feyisa told him. "Means the general who fights in front of the Emperor."

In Addis Ababa, Eck had gone to the Museum of the Martyrs in Meskel Square, the iconic site of the Ethiopian struggle after Selassie, the Lion of Ethiopia, was smothered under a pillow at eighty-three. The paranoid Mengistu military regime thirty years previous had these wooden chairs they bound prisoners to in agonizing restraints for days while they did the unimaginable to their bodies. Ten thousand died awfully. That was then. Now, Ethiopia struggled through endemic corruption and global investment to maintain a shaky but there economic and political order based on one-sixth of the people running all the people.

There was another Feyisa, the champion marathoner who crossed the finishing line first in London with his arms crossed over his head, in defiant solidarity with his Oromo people. At this time, he could not yet come home from America. Eck could not yet go home to America. He did not think it cool to ask his Ethiopian guide, licensed to work by some circumspect government agency, about the man who ran with his name.

In this thin March tourist season, there were only two guests at the mountain plateau resort. The other was a South

African Fulbright Fellow in ancient African architecture named Alysia Doer. She seemed a practiced traveler, about thirty, comfortable in her Oxbridge skin and trim body, and able to blend in and take in.

Both she and Eck had an entire thatched hut to themselves each one a very large round room with no electricity or running water but lavishly furnished with a big bed covered with thick Ethiopian striped blankets, leather chairs from which to look at the stars at night through the open roof hatches and a teakwood desk with a matching multi-purpose table that sat four. Solar panels took in the day's mountain sun to provide small squares of light during the dark. There were outhouses Eck found a little tricky to get to the first time and a washhouse where hot water was brought in big buckets. At the main house, breakfast and dinner were served, the latter in the dark but for candles, solar mini-bulbs, and the communal firebox.

Eck and his guide talked African continent politics with Alysia Doer, whose family for three generations owned grazing and vineyard lands north of Capetown. Alysia was smart, precise, and she could tell a joke, but Eck saw her trying to place him from something or somewhere she was trying to coax back into memory.

"Have I been to a lecture or a performance of yours, somewhere in this wide shrinking world, sir?"

The food came, comfort spaghetti with a tasty meat sauce. There was, of all things, New Zealand red or white, not included on the menu. Eck asked Alysia and Feyisa, red or white. Feyisa translated, and the older Tigrayan manager of the resort, in a stiff green long-sleeved shirt, uncorked a red adeptly.

Eck gestured to Feyisa toward the man's weight-lifter's shoulders.

Feyisa smiled and said quietly, "You didn't expect to see that here?"

"Right now, I'm happy to be here to see strength like that. It's hard to work for it, hard to keep it."

"You come to the world ready to be pleased," Feyisa said.

"Not always. But lately, yes."

By then the night on the mountain plateau was as dark and clear both inside and out. It hugged the fire into itself and let the warmth deal with the rude touch of chill.

Three herdsmen came in, one bearded elder and two clean-shaven middle-aged men who resembled him. After taking their warmth at the fire being stoked in the metal box in the center of the big room they sat on a couch, a little off from the guests. Names went around, repeated in good humor in different accents. Feyisa translated for Eck more than for Alysia Doer, who could negotiate Tigrinya in a formal way.

The shepherds did not care for wine but drank hot spiced tea, nodding at its goodness. Eck asked and learned that Italian financiers owned the resort but did not come themselves more than once a year. They treated the local families who worked the resort well. In five years, the shepherd Abel and his family would be part owners. It was a good business that supplemented what the mountain land gave for what one put into it.

Alysia Doer told her story first, about her country, her parents and her university doings in Addis. Eck admired the way this mature woman included her family's British colonial past in South Africa, a story told concisely of steady relinquishing and final accommodation to radical racial change. Ibrahim said that their country, too, had struggled with forces stuck in fears of unstoppable change. Eck caught one of his two sons peering at him a little too long. There was no internet on the mountain, but something about Eck the one son was going to find out about.

Eck's turn to say, to tell as little or as much as he wanted, came and went easily. He said he was travelling a lot, that it was his time at last to do so, that Ethiopia was good to

American visitors. The other shepherd son said he did not like Addis, that some of the street people there scared him. Yes, Eck knew, he'd run into it and thought he was back in New York. That was funny to the circle around the collection of various pieces of picked-up wood and shredded planks aflame in the metal firebox. The talk rose and went here and there and began to wind down.

Feyisa bent down in front of Eck and Alysia. At first, Eck did not get what the guide was saying, then he did.

"They would like to offer to wash your feet."

Stunned, Eck turned to Alysia, whose look said, accept, of course. A phrase seemed to come from before he was not born. *You are not worthy.* And phrases older than Jesus stung him. Sophocles: *Best is not to be born. Second best is to see the light and turn back quickly.* What was he doing here? How could he possibly accept this?

"I would be honored to receive such a gift," Eck said. That's how. The Tigrinya version was not followed by any reply.

In five minutes, the two sons brought basins of heated water and put them down on the floor before the two visitors. Each then removed a pair of climbing boots and socks. Each then rolled and pushed the pants legs up below the knees. Abel did Alysia first, which by her expression she thought irregular, but she was the guest. He did so slowly, sponging toes within and ankles and lower legs all around with a cake of goat's milk soap, rinsing with one white cotton towel and drying with another. While he did the same for Eck, Eck felt the gentle strength of the old shepherd's massaging fingers and palms, and he understood in his skin the grace of hospitality thousands of years old. As he put his socks and boots back on, he blinked back unknown tears and kept his eyes on the old shepherd, who turned from him in a solemn manner and resumed his seat on the couch.

"Please tell Ibrahim for me, I am grateful and honored in a way I never knew before."

One of his sons said in English, "Our father knows of your wonder and prays within it in his way. You are welcome."

Alysia Doer said something as if in musical clicks. Feyisa, delighted, said, "That's the Xhosa language from South Africa. Please say again, just a little slower." She did, and his smile widened even more as he put it into Tigrinya, which made the shepherds nod and laugh happily. Eck waited. Feyisa told him, "It's something like, Now I may walk clean up to heaven." Eck had an extended moment of not feeling unworthy after all, after all. It would be a good moment to remember and not have to deny or regret. He saw Alysia watching him as if something were going on in him she might wonder about but didn't have to know at this fire on this mountain in this rare dark beauty of a night.

At six-thirty the next morning, Eck and Feyisa went for a run together, the guide's idea. Not expecting much of his New York City running partner, he was pleasantly surprised by Eck's form, pace, and stamina as they went up hills nestled in the Semian hollows, jogged side-by-side along paths in high-grassy flat plains. Eck asked this and that about topography, the ever-swelling migration into the city, the clusters of yellow flowers and the purple sages fading pink. They ran for close to two hours, stopping three times, Eck seeing across the Ice Age gorge in a way that made Feyisa look at it yet anew. Before they turned to start again, the guide pointed to Eck's bare legs below his knees.

"Does that itch?"

"Sort of? The soap?"

"It's the real thing. Gets the follicles really open. Don't worry. It'll pass by noon. The price of ancient customs in the modern world."

Eck thought it funny, a kind of rough kindness that scratches afterwards because it cleanses. That reminded him. "Alysia Doer? She left?"

"Yes, at first light, back to Gondar for her next destination.

Nairobi."

"I liked her."

Feyisa said, "Yes."

The way he said it, looking at Eck steady, quiet. Of course.

Eck liked Alysia Doer that much more for having this man in her life as one focal point on the compass of their large worlds. They did not understand one another as being from this one place, or the place called Capetown, or the place called Addis. Of different places each one, they didn't much care about single origins. They let the spinning world bring them together as they were ready for it to do so at different seasons of their lives. Eck liked the whole idea of them singly and together. It was a glimpse of something he wasn't sure he was even looking to know about.

The two men went back to the flat mountain land of the resort, walking the last quarter mile, not saying much, making way again for herds and their peasant minders who spoke in friendly phrases to Feyisa and said "Hi" and smiled toward Eck. He was guided to the wash hut, left with what he needed to clean up in the rising morning heat. At the main building, he sat out on a stone-table seat and was served dark-roasted coffee, a bottle of water, and an omelet with breads and jellies.

He breathed in scents of distant wood smoke, watched soaring hawks, got more of a sense that he was responding to one of the places on the planet that created him. His genetic map would show a stake driven right into this ground. He felt solid on that ground on this Ethiopian morning. He did not need, for this while, to be well up in the air in order to be safe. Ras Dejen high out there again, stone upon stone of it, near fifteen thousand feet of it, seemed right and fine for its own size, not for his. Something like that, probably not that, though. Gole brought the wide-brimmed gringo straw hat on his head against the brash eleven o'clock sun, relaxed back, went into a pleasant mountain doze, then slept for a good ten minutes.

It wasn't a dream. Eck didn't worry about his dreams. He fought them off, upon awakening. Sometimes, it was as easy as saying aloud, "Puff off."

This unexpected nap, late-morning gift from Ras Dejen, nested him.

He remembered being back in Lalibela, a single tourist at one of the rock-hewn Coptic churches still serving the spirit. He was with a young guide named Barakesh, Kesh he was called, who was grindingly patient in waiting for his official guide's license to come. He had paid much money to a kind of Army minister who supervised all the guides' access to the religious sites like the thousand-year-old rock churches. Kesh dressed like any handsome, young Black European in a red-piped tracksuit and clean sneakers.

He nudged Eck away from the main sanctuary, down a water-specked wall of underground rock to a stone chamber filled with muffled screaming. He put a finger up to his lips, and they soft-walked to the entrance of the chamber.

Inside were about twenty family members trying desperately to bring an exorcism to a good conclusion. Held by thin ropes, a spiritually tortured teenage girl dressed in a muddied white robe and without shoes was at the center of the variously praying, crying, angry, near-hysterical seekers. The girl was speaking like a goat, baaing and barking in ways that sounded like language.

"Listen," Kesh whispered, "can you make out words the people are repeating? Listen harder. The words mean the blood of Jesus."

Eck saw several rattles raised and shaken. He heard it, the constant naming of Jesus, the name of Jesus' blood on the cross, each time a slight fillip to the head of the girl, whose mother and grandmothers both were calling and yelling the girl back from the demon's grasp, the name Miram, Miram.

Their desperate incantation went straight to Eck's primordial memory. He almost fell down with the force of knowing that exorcism was a form of abortion. They wanted the demon, the *aram* inherited, Kesh explained, from the mothers themselves, expelled, out of the child. But Eck knew better. He knew that the demon was the girl, was Miram, and this exorcism was an abortion procedure, an expulsion of the girl's deepest mystery within her. She was screaming, Kesh said, that Jesus' blood was burning her whole body.

Eck began to pray in deep silence that the exorcism would not work, would not kill the strongest natural feeling the girl would ever have.

Kesh became afraid for his tourist's safety, so he pushed the enraged Eck back out into the wet-walled passageway.

"The blood of Christ," Kesh almost spat into his ear, "the blood of Christ."

Eck recoiled in massive head pain at that invocation. He wasn't absolutely sure that he'd just crossed some sensitive cultural line, that his guide was offended by this particular American's response to an ancient healing ceremony that could save this Miram's soul and life. Eck fell away from Kesh, down backwards, hit his head hard. Kesh supported and shouldered him down the passageway and up three huge steps into sunlight.

Eck's head hurt for two days but he didn't get himself checked out for a concussion. He just had to learn an awful truth, of being exorcised, expelled, again born killed. He figured it was just an unexpected worse headache ever, and he wasn't even awake enough to know that.

His mid-morning fright nap quelled, drifted, waited like the quilt over him for him to awake.

About an hour after the sun hung flat over the mountains, Eck made his way from his hut to the grassy plateau to the stone bench in front of the main house. He was served injera bread under stewed lamb and vegetable patties mildly spiced for his American palate. He ate slowly, drank a bottle of Coke, watched birds, goats, two adventurous little girls in bright scarves running from their mother's washing work up near to him and back to her, giggling and dancing. He heard muted thunder from the great mountain. Everywhere there was what was supposed to be, including him, a feeling he knew would pass but relished for as long as it wanted to sit with him.

He spent a couple of hours writing in his journal and taking pictures. He was taken with a particular yellow flower called "gelava," which grew black cumin-like seeds that human touch could turn to poison. One of the resort staff women motioned for him to come to the wash hut, where again a big basin of warm water awaited his bathing. A shaving mirror angled up against a stone wall under a tarnished Coptic icon of, Eck figured out, St. Thomas, the one who wrote the uncanonical gospel. Another reject. Eck stood naked in the wash hut in the mountains of Ethiopia, tracing the scratched outline of the face of St. Thomas the wrong gospel.

When Feyisa came for him, it was clear there was some tension in the guide's face and bearing, in his formality, even a repulse at work. Eck didn't have to guess long.

"Ibrahim's son talked to family in Gondar," Feyisa said without looking in his face. "They Googled you."

"Ah," Eck said. "Don't believe everything you get off the internet."

"Is it," Feyisa began. "True? Can it be?"

"I'm not a regular human being? That?"

"I guess so."

"Up to you to decide, my friend."

"You're unborn?"

"You can touch me if you want. You decide." Eck opened his arms out. The young guide seemed to freeze back.

"Well," Eck said. "Don't let it ruin our last day together."

Feyisa stared, clearly afraid of something, about two feet over Eck's head. The woman who had brought his bathwater walked by with the empty basin and her two little girls holding her skirt tightly. As she did so, she put the basin on her left hip and made the sign of the cross with her right hand on her forehead, chest, both shoulders. The girls neither smiled nor danced.

"Oh, Christ," Eck said.

Feyisa winced. "Let us go," he said. "Over the other side of this mountain. We are expected. It will be a special thing. For you, my American friend. A real Ethiopian coffee ceremony. What's the word? Auth-auth . . . ."

"Authentic," Eck said. The word hung between them like an unliked smell. Feyisa went over to a fence and picked a walking stick off it. He handed it to Eck. He meant he expected Eck from now on to take care by himself of rocks, slippages, mountain walking mishaps. Halfway around the working world, here it was, a guy doing his job despite a whole new experience of dread invading him. Eck thought about bagging the afternoon, the authentic coffee ceremony. He stuck the strong stick into the dusty surface of the land. He motioned Feyisa to precede him.

They walked up a sometimes tricky half-mile, then across another grassy plane. It took about forty-five minutes of silent stepping, stopping twice to take in water, and they got to a path that went into a shepherd village of six huts and various outbuildings. There were wood smoke, bleatings, crowings, hammering, playing, all kinds of work being done, greetings, bowing, welcomes. They didn't know him in this place, even if his guide thought he did and didn't like it. It all interested Eck very much. Nobody was going to get him down right now.

There were some ten large, thatched or corrugated-tin structures for the extended family of the local chief, who appeared wearing a suit jacket over a matching vest and a white shirt. He welcomed the young guide back again and warmly greeted the American visitor to his country, his tribe, his village, his family, and, he chuckled within his clipped gray beard, his goats and his cows. Other elders and many children came up to see and shake the hands of the known Feyisa and the friendly-looking man of unusually mixed race from the United States.

The chief escorted the two men into the largest of his three structures. Eck was given the upright wicker chair alongside the circular metal container for the fire in the middle of the central room. Further back were three stalls and feeding troughs, and overhead was a rope hammock of many thick strands and complex knots. Kneeling around the fire was a lovely mature woman who reminded Eck of Mary Rice, and three children, one of whom was a girl of about eleven or twelve with big brown eyes who kept watching her mother attentively. She had a gentle cough coming up from quite a way down into her thin chest.

Feyisa said, "The chief's wife would be pleased to make traditional coffee for us if you would desire." Maybe there was a slight edge of mockery in the way he said it, but that didn't matter to Eck, who was mostly all into this gesture to him the stranger.

The chief came into the circle with arms full of wood pieces, scraps of lumber, a measure of coals, all of which he slid gracefully into the base before them. It took just a few minutes for enough flame and heat to appear.

The wife-mother began the coffee ceremony. She took down a large copper dish, washed it from a basin of water nearby, swirling the water around and out of it, and placing it sturdily over the strengthening flame. She poured water into it, which steamed up and made the two smaller children laugh until a look from her quieted them. She opened a big jar and let many green coffee beans slide into the wet surface of the big copper dish, then shook them steadily until they turned a dark brown.

The rich smell of the pan-roasting beans was unlike anything having to do with coffee that Eck had ever known. A word, handsome, came into his head, it was a handsome scent.

The mother nodded to the young girl, whose part was to hold the earthenware pot open while the mother spooned the finished beans into it. The girl put the pot on one edge of the fire while her mother again water-swirled the roasting pan clean. Eck got it that the girl was old enough to begin to learn and help in the smooth work of the ceremony. The mother poured distilled water into the pot. She put the palms of her hands up and down once over the fire, signaling it would take a few minutes now. There was a little haze of smoke in the room, which wafted up quickly through the central draft up and out the aperture in the roof. That made Eck understand the girl's cough and the woman's monitory look at her. He kept sadness out of his face, while Feyisa watched him carefully.

The talk shuttled from Tigrinya to English via Feyisa about the good weather, the luck so far with the healthy animals, the loss of many young men to chancy work in Addis. The coffee, ready at the mother's precise timing, was poured into elegant white espresso cups on gold-braided saucers. Eck smiled at being served first and said yes to a small spoonful of unrefined brown sugar. The mother looked kindly at his relishing the taste of her coffee in their mountain village. It was all done in an exquisite sequence of ritual steps, curling hand motions.

The talk continued about the African continent in postcolonial times, until the chief got up, he said, to bring the cows inside. He said he could hear them complaining, and the fun of that went around the people at the fire.

While he was out, the woman did the same washing of the roasting pan, the same placing of it over the fenced-in flames, but now she took handfuls of wheat berries from a container and shook them into the roasting pan, turning them in a few minutes into a treat that delighted the excited little boys until that look about behavior from her quieted them. The toasted wheat berries were delicious. Eck took another cup of coffee with them and sat in a kind of buzz sipping and chewing, talking as he could through Feyisa about his old work with the wind, until he thought he talked too much.

The door opened in a charge of three powerful animals heading straight to their stalls and their troughs. Even they were behaved, eating hungry as hell, but quietly ignoring the humans and their fire. A phrase came across the decades at Eck, from Killer the father, "Four feet in the trough goes hungry." The young daughter laughed because he did, at what she couldn't know, but it brought the cough on a little, which she willed on her own go away.

As they came to the end of their all meeting in the world this once on the mountain, Eck asked Feyisa, "May I leave something?"

"As you wish," Feyisa said. "It is not required."

"How much would be good?"

"That is entirely up to you. Of course, they would be grateful."

Eck tried to hand Ethiopian bills to the woman, who blushed and looked at her husband. He said something. She took the money from the bowing American and put it in the top of the wheatberry jar.

Outside the chief's house, the three men shook hands again. The chief pointed at a darkening part of the sky. They agreed they'd just make it back to the resort before the rain came in for a short shower. The chief then handed both Feyisa and Eck a good-bye and good-travels gift. It was a half-inch brass Coptic cross on a fine black string, its center an etched circle, at its top a design like a miter. Eck simply received it.

On the way down the mountainside, he had his walking stick in one hand and wrapped the stringed cross around three fingers in the other. His guide was still being distant from him, so Eck thanked him two different times for bringing him to such a ceremony.

"The girl," Feyisa said. "Her coughing bothered you?"

It did, and he said so. "That's a graveyard cough, friend.

It's probably TB. It probably comes from inhaling all that wood smoke since she was a baby."

"What would you recommend? Getting her off the mountain and into Black Lion Hospital in Addis?"

"She will die," Eck said to Feyisa's strong back.

"You have so much," Feyisa said loudly to whatever was in front of him. "You know so little."

"That's your answer?" Eck asked.

"We better pick up the pace," Feyisa said. "That rain is bigger than it looks, and it's moving this way at a good clip."

They didn't resume the subject. They concentrated on the descent. Eck watched where he was stepping and kept the cross string wrapped around the middle fingers of his other hand. By the time they got down to the main house at the resort, they were both soaked to the skin. A half-dozen new visitors had come, two from Nairobi, three from Sweden, and one beefy tourism lady from Addis whose peckish manner made Feyisa uneasy. Nobody else on the staff during the dinner hour seemed to know what the guide knew about their sole American visitor who was on his last night there. The shepherds didn't come in to the fire that night.

*

The North Atlantic wind married western Ireland millions and millions of years ago. Ireland started going into wind farms in the 1990s, so a generation later there were in Galway Wind Park and six other Irish sites hundreds of turbines powering electricity in tens of thousands of homes. Each graceful white structure had a tower ninety meters high, each blade reaching out fifty, the height to the tip of the blade 140. In the wind parks, they concerted together in a techno-hum. They were a huge part of Ireland's response to de-carbonizing the atmosphere, which made them a huge part of European consolidated response to coming out of the anthropocene.

EXOIL had sent Goleman to Ireland as part of their U.S.-based third-party consultation firm in the design and building stage of the whole massive international project of freeing the wind to re-green and re-breathe the planet. Venture-capital rhetoric like that was part of the dizzy fun the new priests of the winds invoked to make the air safe again and themselves fortunes by the way.

The unyoked, fired abortion that Eck became still had his professional connections with Galway Wind Park engineers and evangelists. These men and women valued him for who he was in the business, no matter how they had to find their own ways not to be associated with him too chummily in the public eye of their terrestrial resurrection mission.

Point being: Eck's complicated genetic map coincided with his Irish work buddies of just time recent. The west and northwest of Ireland—Galway to Donegal, all there on The Wild Atlantic Way of the Giants Causeway and the spectacular world-class surfing industry—carved out another temporary safe haven for his outed unborn life right now.

As he was sitting in Minihan's Bar on Main Street in Bundoran with all that running through his head—"O Wild West wind," he said out loud, "Destroyer and Preserver, hear, O hear!"

"Jesus," Kit McPhail said. "And only on one drink." He was standing up quite tall next to Eck at the bar.

Kit was a wind engineer who had his own Cambridge degree. So he knew his Shelley when he heard it. He just wouldn't advise reciting too much of that stuff in Minihan's. "It's sad in this offseason, y'know, and what with the still deep sadness of Eibhlin Minihan's passing at eighty-six. The last of the Wards and Minihans since the pub opened in the year of Our Lord 1900."

Kit McPhail added, "Not like in the big winter surf. All the blond surfnutjobs from Norway and New Jersey riding in the deep trough of a mammoth wave of the craic." He thickened the brogue and stuck a little bit of elbow into his American friend's side. "Y'know."

Eck faced up into Kit's. The whole carefully exaggerated redness, the thicket hair, bumper eyebrows, precisely full beard, could cheer up the devil and challenge an angel.

As the triptych in his eyrie back in New York imaged, there was a time, in his twenties, when Eck was a capable surfer of an intermediate sort. On a scale of one to ten, he was maybe a four-point-five. Able to keep up, keep out of danger, stay paddling perpendicular to a sucking rip tide until he was out of it, show good stance on his board, respect the local surfers, all the essentials of surf culture that made for its huge and liberating fun. The rare instance of really being inside the high curving pitch of the lip of a long-breaking double overhead slab, the huge roaring force of the thing, the strength of balance itself, was a ride in summer wind and water that held him until it exhausted its own fury and slid him off back into time and the world and made him yearn to be back within such perfection again. There was nothing else like it other than immersion in an amazing woman.

His work in the west of Ireland with Kit had got him back into it in his thirties, and he found the mix of thrill and the edge of a pounding something he could still rise to, literally, as he balanced in the pitch of a perfect barrel of a wild Atlantic wave that could tower over him in protection or, on a slight misjudgment of his two feet on the board, flip him like an unfortunate fish. Really great surfing here happened in the winter when the wind sent in the mightiest waves. Then, hundreds of surfing aficionados lined the top of the high rock formation on the north side of the curving beach, clapping and cheering down sunlight on the feats of the really good surfers. These April days, global warming raising the sea level, and with still-winter wet suits and boots, gloves, and a hood, you could ride some good waves. Eck loved to be part of it with Kit McPhail, the two of them just average competitors having a good time at it all.

Here now in Minihan's came the real thing, being called over by Kit to meet Eck. She was the women's champ, well, the older women's champ, still statuesque and powerful at, maybe under, maybe over, sixty, the Surf Queen of Ireland, Virginia (Gin) McNulty. In the surfing world, Gin was The McNulty. Kit said she was in town at present to help promote all-seasons surfing culture, and business, in Bundoran.

But right now, in the glad conviviality of Minihan's in Bundoran, Eck was out of nowhere thrown way off balance because he'd read and forgotten it or didn't want to remember it. This McNulty had been, had recently reported herself as having been, one of the last-born survivors of the children of Tuam.

"Gin McNulty," Kit said happily, "I'll have you to meet my American business partner and competent enough surfer, Goleman Eck."

Something went seriously wrong. Eck felt the very air around him deflate to zero.

The great water goddess Gin McNulty—still thick auburn hair that could turn blood orange in the inconstant Irish surfer sun, lanky strong shoulders and long legs and mint green eyes and years of championing Ireland's unlikely sport—was staring at him in a kind of disgust. It lasted only a few seconds, but there it was. For those few seconds, she couldn't understand this Eck's standing in front of her, couldn't comprehend what he could possibly have to do with her own survival out of the nightmare that was her infancy, her first years of being a child taken away from a disgraced teenaged mother she never found again. Time dropped out from under the two of these people as they contemplated one another.

Eck shook it off first, held out his hand, said, "I'm glad to meet you." The phrase dropped flat between them. Gin came back to herself immediately, got her hand into his. He felt its very temperature lower, her effort to will an intake of breath to say, "Christopher McPhail has so many friends from around the world."

Eck said, "He does have that, yes. Yes, indeed." On that non-sequitur, they released each other's hand.

Kit figured out instantly what this was. He knew both their stories. He didn't try to figure out why it was thus between them. He said, "Are you drinking, Ms. McNulty?"

Eck pulled up an old joke, the way one reaches for an impossible fix.

"Reminds me," he said, in the talk of the pub in its evening crowd. "Descartes walks into a bar. The bartender says, 'Would you like a drink?' Descartes says, 'I think not,' and promptly disappears."

She thought about that for another long second, picked it up gladly, said, "Hah! That's pretty good, now."

The three of them drew on many adult years of getting through sudden collapses, talked about the competitions coming up this year, the ongoing economic well-being surfing brought the merchants and hoteliers in town, the good political vibes all of it meant between North and Republic now that the all the checkpoints five miles in either direction were down thanks to the Peace Process, and the rocky road, yes, to that achievement, thanks to so much goodwill after so many years of the troubles and thank God for the likes of the George Mitchells of the world.

Gin McNulty departed saying good nights and see you tomorrows by the water. Eck was shaken by the thing and the beast and the avoidance of the issue between him and his good friend Kit McPhail as they parted on the street to their separate hotels. It was an awful, leaky ocean that Eck thought he heard moaning nearby him that midnight on the Wild Atlantic Way.

Late the next morning, Eck and Kit stood in their wetsuits holding their boards on the Bundoran beach, looking at the dozen or so April surfers bobbing out in the waves at the entrance to the bay. They were at The Peak, Bundoran's legendary reef site.

There was high sun, low tide and light onshore wind.

"Well, will you look out there, now," Kit said. "You've brought us some good American luck this spring day, mate."

"It's been a while, Kit," Eck said. "Let's stay close."

"Sure, you'll get your legs as soon as you're up again on the board."

"Well, look over there, by the rock arch in the water." Eck pointed. "Paddling out."

"That Gin McNulty herself?" Kit squinted into the glare of the sunned water. "Huh," he said. "I believe it is."

"Last night. Maybe by last drink. I got the distinct impression the very sight of me was non grata to the famous lady."

"Different famous of late. You know?"

"Tuam," Eck said. "The children. She was one of them."

"A national disgrace," Kit said. "The old culture at its worst. It has added the devil's eternal curse to the already bad scandals in the Church. They would cover up the death of Jesus Himself if they had to protect their worst from Him."

"You noticed it, too. Something's linking me in her head with the nightmare of her own childhood."

Kit did not answer that directly. He said only, "It was a difficult moment in Minihan's, Gole. 'Twas that. Don't let it bother you. She's a great lady, grand sportswoman. Just a wee stuck in the past. Unlike you and me, my friend. We're here to glide over the water of time, like the great fish we are."

"I'm fearing something right now, and I don't know what it is."

"Truly?"

Eck got up a laugh for him and said, "Keep an eye out for me. Look, more sets coming in. This should be fun."

It was. They were out for a good hour. At first, Eck sat on his board, content to be riding the swelling water, getting used to the feel of it all again. He watched Kit gauging waves, seeing them reach over the reef, then trying to get up on two of them only to pitch over twice. He held the leash back into him to avoid the board interfering with any other surfer waiting their turn in the line-up. His friend made him feel good when he caught the third wave, paddling strong, getting his knees up under him and then squatting firmly but lightly, letting the water shift his body in a neat perpendicular to the high foaming curl beside him.

"Come on, cowboy," he told himself as the next rolling wave soft-shouldered in a good distance behind him.

There were three other surfers spaced safely away from him, and one of them was Gin McNulty. Her posture in her dark green hooded wetsuit was perfect. She was the mermaid queen of the tides still. Eck was up, maybe for all of ten seconds, then unsure balance reminded him rudely to keep his mouth closed. He controlled his board, pulled its leash back to him, relaxed and let it float him. He was a good distance away from Kit. He waved okay to him.

In a minute, he was back sitting on his board, breathing in and out purposefully. He could do better, just for himself. The gorgeous blue sky, that Irish rarity, the April bay seawater, the ancient cliff rising in mighty rock on the north side of him, the soaring ocean birds all said he could do better, just for himself, hah, since for their parts, he didn't matter more than any one of ten thousand fish underneath them all.

Here came his wave, lumbering up just the right size. So, just inside his peripheral left vision, did the front of another board.

She dropped in about ten feet in front of him, then snaked back and forth across his attempt to get up strong in front of his wave, which rolled against him in a rush that submerged him in total surprise.

He was under for the few seconds it took him to know that Gin McNulty had just done what you don't do to another surfer, no matter who the hell you are as a great champion.

He came up coughing and trying to control his leash.

He wasn't catching his wave, man. Not by a long shot. It was a good thing she had such master control. That could have been a collision.

Or maybe that was the point.

"Crazy mother------!" he started to scream, but the instant imbecility of that word about her clenched his teeth.

She held her hands flat out and upwards. "Sorry about that," she mouthed, with the mouth that also formed, "Abort." She gave him her mottled green back.

Bobbing on his surfboard in the Wild Atlantic Way, Goleman Eck took a bit to intuit, grab from some mystery of land and sea and wind and a principle of human action, to get it in full dismay once again: Shit, she really hates my not being born. The McNulty, in her own tortured inability to move on from starting life in a place where children died and were stuffed in little boxes and dug into the shallow earth, the mythical lady on the surfboard wants me to know she can't stand something about me that she's got all balled up with something about herself.

As he straddled his board one more time, floating on the surface of his life, Kit McPhail paddled up by him.

"Don't," Eck said. "Don't fucking ask. Don't expect me to say. But I am totally bummed that she ruined my wave of the day. That was my wave. Not hers."

Kit opened his mouth. Nothing like sound came out. Just silent, unbelieving astonishment.

Eck looked behind him.

"Here comes one more. Do you think I can get this one?" He didn't wait for his friend's answer. The wave built itself and was coming on. Eck started paddling, hungry as a sea horse and ignoring a sudden tightness. He caught it.

Ten minutes later, when he stood up in the water with his board, his left hamstring was acting up, clenching angrily. As they went weaving through people, Kit had to handle both boards while he kept telling Eck to slow down for his sake if not his own. Eck was tamping down a growing fury. The nicely executed near-collision could have misjudged the remaining six inches; it didn't, but the lady's screwed-up head about him was totally over the top crazy. It's just that she obviously knew how to feint, how to make his body freak out and twist itself real wrong, all by itself, of its own will to get way far out of her strange way. Surfing as jujitsu. A new one to him, but that's exactly the kind of champion she was. Good, out of her element, real good.

They got up the esplanade to the main street of Bundoran. It would be a fun night, the wild Atlantic would have its way in sea and spirits among the springtime enthusiasts for six feet, two inches of board with three fins and a big-enough funnel of ocean. Goleman Eck, slow-limping, older but still hard-body in his drying wetsuit, caught people's fleeting attention, the human mix of his face, the off color of him, the harvest of white hair, the could-be-anything and many-thing of his display of good-looking difference. If there were a question, some recognition or notion caught from somewhere about him, it sparked little and faded fast, oblivious in his passing by, on an international surfing sidewalk where people looked good, moved gracefully, accepted and expected such eyeblinks of interest. His hamstring was complaining, but he was getting a rush out of the whole scene, and Kit McPhail was by him in good humor and the Irish version of vernal ease.

He got a bucket of ice from the bar at their hotel, took it up to his room, made a round towel of it, took everything off and lay down with the ice towel under his left thigh. The ice was right enough. He didn't think he'd, she'd, wrenched the hamstring badly. He went out, woke up in ten minutes, massaged and stretched without doing too much of it too soon. He stood up. He could do this, get himself down to the second-floor exercise and sauna area. Heat. Ice it, then heat. Later, ibuprofen, sleep into it.

Forget her, just find her tomorrow, get into her face, what did you think you were doing? you crazy, you want to, like, *hurt me?* that would somehow fix some of your ancient pain of being cast into medieval mother-riven, sex-as-original-sin-Galway in the twentieth century?

"Jesus," Eck got himself out of that drift. "What's happening now to you? Stop acting like a nasty, self-absorbed, uncharitable abortion. Stop it right now."

The ping of a text. The cheap rented cell phone somewhere around the bottom of his tote bag. In the great maple armoire. Maybe someone who had an answer for him. What's happening to you right now, there, Gole?

He got the bag up and the phone out without hurting his leg more.

U forget all about me? Where u b now. An'way?

Yolande. Segundo. The First. The True One.

He could be nothing but love to her, and here he was proving what a disaster, what an abortion that love would be for her. If he ever agreed and accepted her choosing him. That was the world he'd ticketed out from. She had been born to her own life. He had not. He had no business trying to be born into hers just because he really did love her love for him.

Eck shut the phone off and put it in the drawer where the hotel kept the TV remote. He tied a fleecy long towel down from his waist, put on strong running shoes without socks, put on an NYC tourist hoodie, put a few things into the tote, and left the room, heading down the back hall for the second floor. Cocktail hour sounded in early gear in the bar. There wouldn't be anyone much in the sauna right now. His hamstring, looking forward to high dry heat, relaxed a noticeable little. He practiced-inhaled and exhaled doing the same.

When he opened the cedar door, the dry heat light-slapped his face and so did the sight of her sitting on the sauna's second bunk. Her hair was pinned up strong and high on her head, making her green eyes look sharp through him as if he were water or really not there at all. No one else was in the sauna.

He shut the door and faced her for a stretch of seconds.

She had the match to his hotel towel tucked up under her lithe-muscled arms, across the fine swells of the tops of her breasts, down to her hips over her crossed champion's legs. He made out no polish on her toenails, but the whole image of her had a defiant shine of a handsome athlete of sixty. That shine, he made out in the squinting heat, came from a complete layer of faint freckles, forehead to feet, covering her delicately. She viewed him through them, a classic Irish beauty who looked like him, really different. He felt a wish becoming a need. He wanted to ask her to see them all, all her freckles. He sat down on the lower wooden bench across from her, ready to fight.

"You're looking good out there, champ," he said. "Great form. Except you're using it as a weapon, breaking every axiom of courtesy on the water. What's all that about, hey, champ? Huh?"

"Tough guy? New York City style?"

"On my street back home, there's like permanent chalk or something by the pedestrian walk across West Street. Says in block print: Are You Helping Are You Hurting. Just no question marks."

"You were trying to ruin my wave. Just thought I'd call your attention to that, y'know?" She bent over, reaching for the ladle in the bucket of water, making the curve of her back longer, as if she had an extra vertebra. She scooped it up full and threw it on the fire-hot stones, sending sharp pierces of heat around Eck's skin. He breathed infernal air for a long second and said, "Mmm. You screwed up my leg out there. Feels good, champ."

"Want more, Goleman Eck?"

"Not really."

She threw the ladle back into the bucket and sat back again against the hot cedar boards. She kept her eyes not looking at him directly. She must have learned how to do that as a little girl long ago.

"Want to talk about what we have in common, Gin McNulty?"

"You have no bloody right even thinking we do, now."

"I disgust you. Why?"

Her face, neck, shoulders glistened but would not line up straight in front of him. "You're quite a figure in the world," she said. "All pride, egotism, swagger. You've turned yourself into a celebrity. You have no idea what a blasphemy you are in God's world."

"Maybe you mean what a blasphemy God was in yours."

She may have begun to come off the high bench at him, he couldn't be sure, but the door to the sauna was opening.

"Oh, my God!" the first of two American girls in bikinis exclaimed to the heat. They quickly sat down away from the two older people and bounced their feet up and down in youthful delight at pretty much everything. One was taut and blonde with clacking Irish oak bracelets on her right wrist. The other was shaved and taut with little purple bears on each perfect butt cheek, and they both looked to be forever young for a while.

"Hello, ladies," Eck said.

"Hi!" they both sang. "Are you surfers?"

"I went for a major wipeout this afternoon," Eck said.

The McNulty looked straight at him then, nodded. She asked the girls, "Are you enjoying your visit to the North of the Republic?"

They had no idea what was north or south or why it mattered. But they both loved the older woman's brogue and said so. She thanked them for that sweet compliment and got down. Eck got on guard as she came by him, her mature beauty not quitting a bit around these pretty, peachcomplexioned girls.

"Hey," she said to him. She held her room key card in front of his face long enough for him to see the word "Annex" and the number.

Accepting the gesture, he said, "Good. Yes, we have more to say to one another."

She exited the sauna, a toweled woman champion still, orphaned.

Eck turned to the heating girls in the sauna.

"You ladies want the full effect, throw a ladle of that water onto the big stones there."

The shaved-headed one did. They both screamed in delight at the burn. Eck stood up and demurely adjusted his towel. He asked and found out that they were in college in Seattle, graphic design and public health, on a month's study at NUI Galway.

"Wow," Eck said. "All the way from our own Northwest."

"Enjoyed meeting you, sir," one said. "Like your friend."

"Sorry you got wiped," the other said. They were nice girls, respectful, he could tell, in their bikinied bodies, eager to see this diverse older guy in a sauna in Ireland. They were ready to meet whatever. Eck envied them that, yet another self-assurance of the normally born.

"Ah," he said, "it's all changed from before. Bye, ladies. Good luck in all things."

"No problem," one said. "No worries," the other said. Eck never did understand either polite phrase.

He limped his way okay to room 343, down the windy outside passageway to the annex part of the hotel that offered larger, pricey accommodations. The ocean sky was pushing blue and purple light all around big clouds dusking fantastic shapes. Coming up from the main street, rock music couldn't quite blare out hooting voices and one doleful bagpiper down in the public parking lot. He didn't know exactly what he was expecting or doing.

She'd cleaned up real nice, the red-brown hair flowing down her firm neck and even shoulders over a dress full of eucalyptus tree designs. She held the door wide open for him. She still wasn't looking directly at him, or anyone else.

Inside, Eck found himself in a painter's temporary quarters as much as a famous ocean-surfing athlete's, an indomitable senior to be looked up to for any number of reasons, including basic survival against terrible childhood odds. Eck was thinking too quickly. She could have broken him that afternoon, except she'd been in total control of board and purpose.

"I'm quick enough to see that you're a painter. Interesting."

"Not really. If you look, you see a pretty limited range of subject. Obsessive is what I do, brush and board."

"So, I'll look."

"So look. If you agree, I have a remedy for that leg. Wizened fairy medicine woman taught me when I was a girl. Y'know. In Tuam. Ha! You'll have to get into a tub, though. You'll allow me that apology, will ye? I promise, by the faith, to be a fine lady again." Now she was looking at him, whole, steady, together in her own space.

Eck fell silent. She went away from him. His hamstring wanted whatever she had to offer. He would let it have it. He started looking at what was hanging, what was leaning unframed in twos and threes against one whole wall, in the big room.

He was quick to see what she meant by obsession, well-done, compelling obsession.

He was in the space of a sea-queen painter in big-color oils. He was looking at mythic female creatures looking at him, some of them in solitude, others of them in groups or swarms, all of them Medusas fat-faced, skeletal, or open-mouthed stoned, mermaids, Circes, Scyllas, a determined sexual invader lovely from head to naked waist but sea green and finny all below crawling sinuously up over the deck of Odysseus' ship where the hero stood bound to his mast screaming at his wax-eared men to untie him for her, invaginated flower petals four feet tall and glistening wet, St. Theresas in other-world ecstasies, Maud Gonne in suggestive winter fur a terrible beauty armed with a scythe, cartoon Minnie Mouses and Olive Oils, an elegant charcoal version of Käthe Kollwitz holding her dead son in agony and toothy rage, and more, more, as if Gin McNulty's rage was a state of nature.

And in the visual middle of it all was a hefty photograph of herself on the North Shore of Oahu dream ride for only the best at the world's most storied reef, the Pipeline. The McNulty in her mermaid emerald wet suit and transcendent board seemed to be leading a ten-thousand horse wave behind her in perfect form like that of a Praxiteles Aphrodite showing the water what is was supposed to do in its own vast tube of might and destruction: be there for her. The sun picked up the look of the furious beauty of the godlike queen in her empire of wet and roar, water and sound, that howled down the horror of almost being one of the little lost children buried in the back of St. Mary's Mother and Baby Home.

That was it: she was as angry as he and could paint it out like this, surf it out like that under a ten-foot funnel that could drown her or birth her, depending on what she alone would let it do. He felt dizzy. He sensed her standing behind him, as if over him, and he turned slowly.

Virginia McNulty was holding two rocks glasses with bright sparkling liquid in them. Mate, he thought, hemlock, single malt distilled last century by Con Markievicz, lotus blossoms, transubstantiated wine, laudanum, snow melted from Everest, amethyst, supernal nepenthe, belladonna, what?

Raspberry lemonade. Fresh made. They clinked glasses. He let go his fear, drank. The good clean British gin in it made him feel better. They sat down.

"Your work," and he waved an embracing arc at it all. "Extraordinary."

"How do you see it?" she asked him.

"Apotropaic."

"You know the word, then," she said.

"The word is the thing itself."

" T'is," she said.

He watched her sip, eyes behind the rim examining his face. He asked her, "Does it all come from Tuam, or from the laundry schools?"

"You are quite direct," she said. "Mostly, maybe, I don't know. It just comes. I let it be what it wants."

"What becomes of it? All this other art of yours?"

"Agent sells it for the sake of the lost children's heritage fund. It's in a few minor museums. Like in Norway, Canada, dark-minded places. I don't much care about that part."

She said her remedy was ready for his leg.

"Oh. Kay," he said but switched on full alert.

"Come," she said and led him into her immaculate bathroom.

She had him strip off socks, shoes, gym pants. He felt silly, vulnerable, but did what she said. She took a mason jar out of the gilded-mirror medicine chest, took off the cover, put the jar under his jawline. The smell cleared his nostrils. He put his hand on her wrist.

"What?"

"Traditional Gaelic mix. Wort, bark, yarrow, mint, stuff, in witch hazel. Peat. And prayer."

"Right," Eck said. "Of course it is."

"Trust me," she said. Perhaps a dare.

She sat him on the closed toilet, saturated a compress wrap with the mixture, had him fit it under and around his left thigh. It was a penetrating cold heat. He watched every move she made for the next fifteen minutes, like running water in her tub, getting him more of the ginned raspberry lemonade, pushing down gently on his kneecap while straightening his leg by his ankle. She seemed to know what she was doing.

She guided him over the top of the claw-footed enamel tub, had him sit in six inches of warm water, still wearing the mystical liniment compress.

"Shelley saved Mary's life once," Eck said. "She was losing another child, hemorrhaging really bad. He sat her in a tub of ice. Know that?"

"Yes. Where'd you get it from?"

"She told me."

"Oh."

"She lost three of their four children."

"She tell you that?"

"Yes, she did. This is starting to get earthy. How long?"

"Three more minutes," she said. "It's supposed to work the circulation. Help the inflammation." She pushed down one more on his kneecap, straightened the leg up. She ignored how hard he was getting. He thought it quite an achievement in the cooling mix. He counted over thirty freckles on her right arm down to the knuckles.

She got him up, wrapped a towel around his waist, guided him out of the tub.

"Do you forgive me?" she asked. Perhaps an accusation.

"Do you forgive me?"

"No," she said. "Never."

"So," he said. "Now where are we? I did nothing to you. I was not even born to do anything to you."

"Well," she said. "There you have it. Earth mother's warm healing baptism. Get it? Now you're responsible for what you've done. Now you're born all alive, Goleman Eck." Her voice went ragged, as if a knife were coming up out of an opened chest of sea inside her middle. She said, "You're just someone famous for surviving after being thrown away. Not a woman who for some reason or another had to abort and then lived to remember it."

So that was the source of her rage at him. He flashed on his party, on Mrs. Jericho, on Cold Man Dreck.

He said it.

"When you could, later, did you let your mother go? Tell me you did. Please tell me you got to that place."

He'd crossed that hard line with her now. If she attacked him, he would not let her hurt him. Not after she'd granted him her own holy rite and called him by his name. She'd done it, legitimized him, sort of doula-like, in the primal bath, sort of. Mirabile dictu.

She made her move, both thumbs clamping toward his eyes. In seconds, he had her head bent down in the sink and her entire right arm up backwards between her legs.

"Hate makes a bad fighter," he said. "Can I let you go?"

She wouldn't answer that. She would die first. He yanked her hand up more under her crotch and put the cold-water faucet on full blast, into her face, nose, mouth. He let her choke, then pulled her up and spun her around. She dropped, gasping like a beaten mermaid, crying out like a great wounded mother bird. She reached to get a hold of him below, but he'd relaxed all that and pushed her hand aside.

"Stop," he said. "Let's just have another drink, talk about the painting life, surfing in some of those spectacular places you've competed at and won in the world, the depressed birth rate in this country since the famine. Something else. Something new. Just stop, okay?"

"My . . . own . . . wee Odysseus," she managed between gasps. "At. . . feckin . . . last."

"Oh, my," he said. "Homer Joyce. The great paralyzing tradition. The past is the future too."

He let go of her. She straightened up without turning around, said, "O'Neill, is it, then? The sage who thought the atom bomb was a good idea to deal with humanity."

He kept talking to her back, into her hair. "You and I, Gin.

Stuck like a pair of caryatids. Unmoving. Seeing only the same thing ever and ever. Propping up the same dead temple to ourselves."

She turned her head only, was barely audible. "Even though they stole our original forms and substituted copies?"

He had no answer to that.

She had her breath back. She turned around into him without threat. She seemed to relax her whole bearing and to look at him for the first time, in real time, a now she'd been both hoarding and denying herself for a time that was an awful waste.

"Is there no mercy for us, Gin?"

"I was born not to believe you," she said.

She took his two hands in her own. They were like no other hands he'd ever held. Or they were hands he didn't even know he'd been waiting to hold his, but he knew them, recognized them now. He was having a good strange dream in the bathroom The McNulty. She had a great witch's power to make him think this way, just with her hands. And if he didn't let go of her hands, he would not be able to separate on his own again.

"Gin," he said. "I don't know what you want me to do."

"I don't either. There's nothing you can do anymore."

"Anymore?"

"As long as I didn't believe you, I wanted the lie of you destroyed."

"Aborted," he said. "Twice over." It was to be laughed at, it was that crazy. He laughed, weirdly, but not at her, and she knew it was not at her.

"You know," she said. It was a complete sentence. Then she said, "Probably the twice-over doesn't make you feel exactly secure. I'm sorry I added to that bad-mother-good-mother mess." She released his hands, stood perfectly straight in front of him, the same height as he. They both went silent.

"Well," she said, kindly amused at his bare legs, "I'll leave you to arrange yourself."

"Thank you, Gin McNulty."

He rolled his wet underwear into his tote, put his gym pants on, and went to join her and talk with her more about her fantastic, woman-centered paintings. She was sixty-two. She told him that. He said yes to that, not really caring or knowing what that figure might mean to either one of them.

They lay down together atop her fresh made queen bed. They explored and greeted each other's body in a gladness of intimate touching that did not need to go the whole way, not at all. The sleep they went into together was as instant as that of a pair of children in an illustrated book of journeys into woods, castles, the outskirts of wars, miracles, ridings all the way home together.

Eck came back to himself after a couple of hours, found her in murmuring sleep beside him, left her bed in controlled quiet, went out her door feeling his left leg getting one and whole again. It was a good feeling. For just that moment only, the feeling was that of an infancy glimpsed, the one he'd missed out on but no longer needed to know. The feeling lasted for a good while.

TWELVE

This email Mary Rice wrote to Eck.

You seem to me to be a pretty old kind of young character. When I was reading insanely in college, your type was called the picaro, the road-traveler. Maybe something of a rogue, maybe a good guy, depending on what comes his way out there. Since you don't come from a definite anywhere or any-who, you get to be whatever gets made of you.

You can be what happens to you, not what becomes of you.

So let it happen, Gole. Bring it all on, in, sit it down and drink with it. The father I had said more than once, "Before the hair on a man's hands disappears, they are bound to hold and let go of a lot." They, he meant, who come to you.

Back here, the mystery of you these months is guttering down for lack of you. It'll flame up again, it's bound to, when they have you in front of them again. We screw people up so much, those of us truly born before we live. You, you remain an astonishing other way. One fears, though, crazy, unchecked resentment of that way. It is not allowed, it seems, except for you.

Victor Mature sends his regards. He talks about you with great respect for your hard-won privacy. He says those who

241

want the wonder of you, like Rev. Alex's Miracle Mission, don't know their own shit from their own spit. He's got his phrases, yes. But he would be your glad friend, as he, my final lover, is mine.

Eugene, Victor, says you can't be finished. I like that about you and about him, that he knows that about you and can let it be. He's unlike you in that everybody sees somebody else, the same dead somebody else, when they just look at him. They look at him and he's finished. Not you, he says. The Irish poet Kavanagh says, ". . praise, praise, praise / The way it happened and the way it is."

I told Victor that, and he likes to say it now to praise the way it is about you and a lot of other things.

*

Mary Rice's unwritten meditation on Eck's post-human condition.

You're a real problem, Gole, for a whole lot of people, maybe most. They can't help but project onto you. You're a dark screen on to which they throw up any white silhouette of themselves they can. But none sticks. And there you are, still the same post-abortion mystery. They see you and all their own deaths, the end of their own being, their own abortions, the doing of time. So they hate you. Will not go gentle from you. They want their John Lennon to stay dead. They can't help it.

Then again some people project onto you some kind of triumph of the good. The principle of life itself. They put on you what you cannot possibly carry for them. You're a man who lived on after being cast out. You're not a damaged archangel come for them from some spiritual realm of being. So, monster or miracle, Goleman Eck is not Goleman Eck alone. You star in a thousand scripts, awful or astounding, but you're not a natural man who grew out of a natural kid. I fear for you. Maybe that's what I have to do to you in my turn.

*

Mary Rice's nightmare vision of Eck, told to Victor Mature.

Clipping. I heard this nail clipping going on behind your master bathroom door in your glass tower while you were long gone and Victor Mature and I were there. Victor was asleep. I stood outside the door, wondering how you'd come in out of nowhere. I also knew you were standing in front of the john, and I knew, I don't know how, that you were using a beautiful jeweled red stainless steel cutter. You kept at it until your fingers were done, the nail clippings floating soundlessly into the bowl. Then I knew you were doing your toes, bent over naked with one leg at a time up on the edge of the light blue bowl, exactly thirty cuts, middle side, side, with the brilliant jeweled tool.

Through your stainless-steel bathroom door, I sensed you stand up straight, hold out your left hand and cut off its little, fourth and middle fingers. Each made a slight plopping sound. You used your left hand's remaining two fingers to cut off all of your toes. You used the clipper to cut off your foreskin. You made the clipper extend to three times its size. You cut off both earlobes, eyebrows, all your eyelashes, crescents from both of your lips, the tip of your tongue. You gouged out both your eyes, and the sound of flesh and organs got heavier as they dropped down.

You put the marvelous clipper in between your teeth and severed the remaining two fingers of your left hand. By now, I was trying to push open the door, burbling your name in the blood pooling my own lips. I didn't get it for a while that the door was a pocket door and slid side to side. I spent a long time opening it. When I got into the bathroom, you had finished aborting yourself in pieces, and the red of the wondrous clippers was the blood covering the walls and your huge double shower and tub and your Carian floor tiles in front and around the toilet, which was slowly unchoking itself of gently swirly parts of your whole body, like a thousand of them.

Victor found me standing in your master bathroom, staring into the toilet, which I was watching but not flushing. It seems that I told him modern surgery could reassemble you if I could just start scooping out the many remaining parts of you. It seems that I told him that the parts I couldn't retrieve could be robo-matched. Victor took me back to your guest room. All was clear and memorable when I awoke a few hours into the morning. Victor said the phenomenon is called fugueing. He saw it a couple of times among men on his team during one tour off the coast of Somalia. The memory lasts a long time in some detail, he said. It's as real as anything else but it would be best for me to get a brain scan, just to see if any minor synapse was momentarily out to lunch.

Being on the other side of that door while you tried to abort yourself was terrifying.

*

What the shooter wrote in the second of her three, completely filled, mottled black-and-white composition books.

Now I have fifteen guns. I never pulled one on anyone. But this Goleman Eck disgusts me to my soul. He's unnatural, he's an abomination on the earth. Gole was not meant to be this nonentity ghost humanoid. However he survived is the work of all the forces of evil that are ruining American life as we know it. It is easy to call this rant, to evade the question I am asking. How is it that a completed abortion grows up to be a multi-millionaire energy producer when hard-working regular people who praise God and their parents for their very lives can't keep up with the oil bills, never mind catch a decent break? Put another way, how much abuse are regular live people supposed to put up with from reject lives like this Eck's. Gole is not a human man. Gole is a hole that got backfilled.

My gun collection is to me what many different people's life savings, stamps, jewelry, classic autos, sports memorabilia, heirloom rosaries, nineteenth-century postcards, military badges, locks of hair, leather-bound and regular-bound rare books, vinyl records, pressed flowers, manual typewriters, rag dolls, colored glass figurines, robotoys, commemorative plates, baseball cards, film star autographs, wind chimes, throwing knives, foils and swords, fine wines, logos, rock concert T-shirts, theater programs, Beanie Barbies, drill bits, and such are to them. That list shows complete ways that people identify themselves with their collections. My guns are maintained beautifully, safely, inaccessible except to me. I see the history of the country in their metal and wood craftsmanship, their precision mechanisms, and their readiness to stand and fire at true evil.

In discussing access to firearms, especially highly lethal ones, you have to consider the individual. Is this person responsible, mature, respectful of all the different kinds of personal spaces different people need? The Second Amendment amends unfairness, interference, and invasiveness. It proceeds from the founding idea of personal freedom, personal protection, and personal being, that is, the being of the person's personhood. Those liberties each person is born with have nothing to do with persons who were never actually born but who somehow go on to have a life they never should have had. Those liberties are distinct from human shitholes. Shitgoles.

My first was a forty caliber that the dealer convinced me was too much. He had a gun shop on the 37 South just outside the Indianapolis airport. He said sure you're twenty-one and sure you've got a right to own something like this, but I don't think a young woman like you really needs all that firepower. You can't hunt with it, it will tear the animal up into useless and inedible. So he convinced me to buy a converter kit for it, to turn it into a .22 pistol. He was right. It was a first gun for me, suited for my hand, fingers, concentration. Little by little I practiced more and more, learned a lot about targets round, oblong, circular, square. Now I have my own steel targets I set up in my place out in the country. I have certificates from seven different firearms instructors, and I have passed on my ken to young and old gun owners. When it comes to shooting, all you know is only worth your power to give it away.

Yes, I have an "illegal" AR-15. It has sweet easy lift to it and it can be converted down from automatic to seven-shot single. You don't need firepower that only the military and law enforcement requires. The big guns are great to know about, to handle properly, but going through two feet of brick is not a real-world issue, unless your real world is war. I have other rifles and shotguns, carbines, assault rifles and personal defense weapons auto- and semi-automatic both. I have had but no longer store a MAC 10 or a TEC9. Single action, double action, bolt, pump, semiautomatic, lever, burst-fire and automatic comprise an authoritative lexicon of firearms. The semi-automatic handgun used in the Fort Hood Shooting shot twenty rounds in 5.3 seconds. Handguns are not assault weapons. Adam Lanza used a Bushmaster MF Type Carbine with several magazines of thirty bullets each, the gun his mother bought "legally." A rifle is a long-barreled gun with grooves on its barrel walls.

What the shooter wrote in part in her third notebook, the one that served for more autobiography than the others.

When my older sister Vangey committed suicide, my mother said she wished it was me. I was an accident, the unexpected of the two of us. Vangey was meant. My mother had come to think that since Vangey turned out so well, one that she planned for, taking her temperature and creating a vinegar base, the baby could only be that much better. Vangey memorized; I didn't crawl. If I ever have to have therapy for the dementia I'm going to inherit from my mother, I will have to be taught how to crawl on my hands and knees to begin speaking again. Vangey could sit still for a half-hour at a time. I hated to sit on the toilet long enough to finish. Vangey did good works as soon as she reached the age of reason. She was entranced by the dizzying stripes of a herd of fleeing zebras that frustrated the need of a dim-sighted lion to pick out just one.

Whatever the opposite of those three things could be, I was—selfish, unimpressed, intolerant. I lied incessantly about ways my sister tortured me. When I screamed that Evangeline had dropped her vagina down the open shower drain, our single mother went to get more vodka with a floater of whiskey over the top ice cubes. When I walked in on her moving atop a man a lot smaller but just as drunk as she, except that he looked to me very squirrelly frightened, she kept moving on him for another twelve seconds, then got off, covered him with a quilt Vangey had made with her own hands at ten, and howled like an animal at me until I ran out the door and out of the house. I knew that if I asked her if that man was my father, she would never answer the question but would bring it up as part of her telling me over and over again that no man would want to own me as a daughter. She despised the men she seduced, would not say their names, or show us to them.

I grew, I grew, in direct proportion to Vangey's sinking. The day she graduated from Princeton an Environmental Sciences major, Vangey told me that bearing me almost killed our mother from septicemia. That's how I understood for the first time why our mother wished aloud to God that she had cleaned herself of me in the first trimester. Vangey tried, she said, to make it up to her mother, that is, to make me up to her mother by being what she saw her girl Evangeline as, her salvation. The impossibility of making that work, from the time she was an infant, set my sister on her awful downward slide into knowing she could never succeed. Vangey rode her bicycle onto the George Washington Bridge. That's all that was ever found of her. My mother wished I had done that it instead. But I grew, I grew, true seed, devil's darling, into the path destined. How that path wound me to the followers of Goleman Eck is a matter of some telling.

I liked Rev. Shimmerman quite a lot. His hair and hands were long and light to see, light to the touch. He wore longish silk scarves of complementary colors that draped down his jacket thin and flat. I knew I would remember our whole conversation because there was nothing irritating in his way of speaking. Even with smart asides about music, recent political events, the joblessness rate in the Tri-City area. As he talked, he seemed just as well to be ready to receive what you said next. I was sort of interviewing with him for a small-paid position organizing a group of local young women approaching voter age to talk about the miracle of Eck and what it meant for virgin sexuality, which, he said still had hope of being a common characteristic of local girls in the small towns on the perimeters of cities.

I told him my name was Thelma.

"Good name," he told me. "Know where it comes from?"

I told him the truth. "No." I was smarter than being caught in a lie from the outset.

"I've heard it's, like a bastard form of the Greek word for 'will.' But a really American invention."

I could see that he wasn't being too sure about me or about my hearing a reverend talk about bastards directly on first acquaintance. I said, "Well, I'll take that. I do have a will."

He greeted me on that generously. We started talking about the generalities and the immediate details of what would be my part. Tricky people who can make you comfortable when they're sort of making fun of themselves are interesting.

People were constantly coming up to him, checking various details and arrangements for this event this or that event or the big one several weeks away, the one I was most interested in.

I listened carefully to all these supplicants. Each one of them, younger, older, wanted to be part of the miracle of Goleman Eck. They had various levels of understanding about just what that miracle was and what it had to do with the Pro-Life movements that of late had gotten beyond from anti-immigrant repute.

The Reverend Shimmerman said, "Everybody has a Gole in life." In the sense of different. "You get behind my Gole, I get behind yours, and we pursue our Goles together. We become a movement." That look came into his handsome face when he was being widened by what he was seeing and saying.

"It's a very American phenomenon," he mused. "Going back to First Encounter in Virginia and Plymouth. A sense of powerful change coming from below and moving on to up high. It fought our right wars in 1787 and in 1860 and in 1941. It fought for women's rights to safety from alcohol in Prohibition until that all went wrong. It was reborn in Selma, and a whole lot of that went right. Well, you get what I mean. The Miracle of Gole is in that great line of change, change political, change cultural, change ecological, change . . . ." Then he stopped and looked at me and the people who had come closer to hear.

"Say more, say more," I said. A skinny girl in thick glasses missing a left black temple said it after me.

He firmly would not say more of what he'd been saying. He did say, "I stand down. You all should stand up to say what you want. I am no leader, no apostle, no candidate for anything."

There was applause, and I saw it make him wince. My plan began to form itself when I saw him wince away from becoming an idol.

A woman had been watching me. She approached, and I did not like the look of her at all.

"Hello, I'm Jenny Rich," she said. "I read your application. I'd like to talk to you."

I knew I was right, right off. I had her in sight. I had her at a fifty, a hundred feet. I wanted her.

"I liked your Podcast," I lied.

"That's a while back." She could smile but it curled up at the right side of her mouth. "But thanks."

"Are you still doing the baby Eck fans thing?"

"Done with that. It had its splash." She gave one of those hiccup laughs that could make an old nun spit out her last tooth. She opened a notebook, took out my application, said as if it was a sharp point, "You know some media, I see."

"Okay. What can I do for you? The man said I might be good at local girls."

"I got a better idea for you to consider. Look at this repro."

She had a photo open on her phone. It was some kind of famous painting of a diving board, a pool, muted flat blues, tans, red-orange, translucent splash spray, a filmy Merman figure maybe finning up to the surface of the pool water.

"Help me get it on baseball-size buttons. About twenty thousand of them to start."

"What's that in the water?"

"Goleman Eck. Sort of. You'll redigitize it to make that point clearer."

She was stealing a famous painting. I liked that. I still didn't like her.

"I've got about ten thousand shots of himself. I'll show them to you. You choose it. You make it. You don't get a dime. You get national press. Better. What do you say?"

"Can I still do some of the girls?"

"You can do some of the girls with this."

She flicked up the this: #ⓒⓒⓒ.~Gole.

"Oh," I said. "Yes." The tag frightened me when I first saw it. It still does. I couldn't even say I wouldn't work with it. I couldn't say it made me hate Jenny Rich all the more. She was a ghoul. Only a ghoul could have come up with #ⓒⓒⓒ.~Gole. I looked away from her.

Jenny Ghoul told me, "But this job comes first. The thing in the pool. And it has to come fast."

I pulled myself back from wanting to destroy her. "Jenny Rich? That right?"

"Uh-huh."

"I like things that have to come first and fast. Shoot."

"Shoot?"

"Means yes. Like, that's Tri-City speak?"

Jenny Rich was taking my measure, figuring something maybe about me that went beyond digitizing an Eck onto a button for Rev. Shimmerman's religion campaign he was hitching on to the state election.

She took out from her bag a double-sided typed sheet, twisted it over to its second side where I'd listed computer skills. She nodded her sunglasses down from her head to the bridge of her sunburnt nose. Then came the question. "So you're up on social media?"

Up on social media. The woman was a fossil at thirty-something. She had a bright dumpiness about her, a face and look of cagey earnestness, and a pair of tits that wanted to tumble her forward. She should have settled for roomy zip-up sweatshirts rather than the dull green khaki field dress with its four pockets. Women who look like her are usually funeral directors or human resource administrators. The Reverend Shimmerman deserved better help in his mission to make Goleman Eck a national figure of renewed and renewing life. All this struck me in the first few minutes of meeting this Rich

251

person.

"Well," she said. "I need to move on to the next order of the day."

I made an arc of my arm pointing up at the clouds. "Upstate-type storm coming. They say it could be a low-level tornado."

"Yes. I'm a little nervous about that. Actually, we don't get them. Much," she offered. "In New York State. But when we do." It was like her speech was getting short-circuited.

"Don't worry. Let me give you a quick rundown of my ideas. Real quick."

"No worries," she said. "Shoot. As you say in Tri-City."

I did. Starting with what she'd know, like Facebook, Twitter, Instagram and Snapchat, then firing a list of newsy to nasty, teen sex to sado-lethal, public info to identification heist, Uruguayan to Crimean human trafficking, BB guns to upper body-exploding bullets. I told her about GAB, the Twitter for Racists.

She perked up, shorthanded that info down into her reporter's top spiral notebook. She was using a purple and silver Mont Blanc pen that was not a knock-off. I know a girl who won't talk to me three years now who I heard once claim the pen makes it easier for her to do cursive.

I rattled off names of Chinese and Russian platforms working out of chaotic cities from garages and cellars, all useful to her kind of global Eck hustle, though I wasn't fool enough to say so explicitly. Jenny Rich knew how to hear and know what she wanted to hear and know between the breaths one shoveling her the shit she took in to sift through later when she thought about it. She was my kind of gal, and I knew I was going to waste her too. She would definitely show up in the space she was bound to create for the exact group of people I wanted to get in front of me.

"Human nature by default is socially active," she said to me. "Digitization is doing that exponentially."

I started to talk fast and thick. Neither was hard for her to keep up with.

"Think of Tumblr," I said. "A social media with massive blogging platform that finds things for you to follow that you may not even know are crucial to you and your grandchildren's futures. Like the darkening, immigrating, and weakening. The eliminating. You know what I mean, you know I know you know."

She stared. I kept talking a streak.

"You know the Chinese? Like Baidu Tieba and Sina Weibo and YY.COM and Renren. The multi-linguals like Viber and Line and Telegram. The voting-platforms like Reddit, which is already doing a hundred million users a month. Or Care2 that connects activists like you people with other people like you. Or MyHeritage for genealogy, family trees and history, ancestor research for more Goleman Ecks to find each other at present and historically. Or Meetup, where those who love Eck or those who want him dead find like-minded people."

She took it all in as if all at a huge once. I was sparking something in her she hadn't expected. I figured that was why she wasn't saying anything.

"That enough for openers, Jen? How's my job interview going?"

"You're scaring me," she said. If she had a door opened in front of me in one hand, she would have shut it in my face. I was not about to let that happen.

"I just gave you everything I have," I said. "And you think you can just turn me away now?"

A shot of hollow wind came out of nowhere, bounced around people near us. Heads rose, knowing what could be shaping up. I've always liked that moment, as if people are being called to attention to destruction out there, just not ready to show itself yet. Upstate hiccup. A gap in the breath. If Jenny Rich had it, she'd be easier about how things happen.

"What say we talk again," she said. "I think I like your

energy. I just can't put my finger right now on where it might fit in the mission."

The sky was definitely lowering, the heat of the day, too. It was coming. People began to move off the field toward their cars.

Reverend Shimmerman appeared next to Rich. She was glad to see him. He said something empty about a change in the weather as he looked up at the sky the way a guy like him would, to see the winds of the Lord changing on the land. He had a three-striped bow tie on.

I said, "Ms. Rich and I have been talking. I'd very much like to continue that discussion. I think I have something to add to the media grasp of Goleman Eck's real meaning."

"Alex," she said. "I'm getting scared. I'm getting very scared."

He thought she meant the weather, only. "Right," he said, decisive. "Safe than sorry, then, all that." He took Jenny by the hand and moved to leave. A gentleman, he stopped and asked me, "You'll be okay? Want to come with us?"

White heat within my ears flashed. Outside me, the first thunder kettle-drummed in good humor. "I'm good," I said. "Be safe. See you later." They walked away quickly, very sure of where their car was and where'd they'd be in ten-fifteen minutes. Inside.

I listened to the wind, took in air flurries, felt the weight of more drops. It wasn't going to be anything all that bad. Other locals there were sensing the same minor storm blowing through this time. But nobody needed to worry their elderly there or get caught in a soak when they'd left the jackets in the car.

The rain dumped a load. I loved it. In just two minutes of fast walking, I got to my vehicle, popped the trunk first, made sure the tarp was tight over everything. Everybody else cleared out. I stayed in the field, taking up my practice position in the emptied parking area for a half-hour or so. The little storm, lacking a funnel or anything of that wind-tunnel sort, blew six ways at once. It carried on medium wild like noisy children. Goleman Eck would never do anything to me. He wouldn't know me from a robo-marketer in Bombay going down a list that would eventually get to him.

*

Eck got approached on the internet by a jihadist recruiter who seemed to be based somewhere else in South Africa than Johannesburg. Thanks again to his old EXOIL network, Eck was keeping himself there for a month, away from the world that knew him most and didn't like him, not at all. If this Eck-seeker was getting through to Eck's triple-locked technology that Victoria Rensselaer, a virtual-only, reclusive, and brilliant friend from EXOIL patched him through to, the guy was probably just as faced into U.S. intelligence watchdogs. In all things, Victoria used the IT equivalent of mirrors as backup. Arkturo as he called himself didn't seem to care about being caught in her reflector insurance to protect herself. The code that Ark, as everyone else called him, communicated to Eck in was no more than a common etymological scramble. Sentences extruded out of it that said things like Eck's unborn nature was the perfectly logical product of the system of abominations called the West.

"I have," Arkturo's unscrambled claim went, "video camera record of you in Kruger National Park. You the detested object of animal revulsion." And he did. He surely did.

During the first week of his projected month in Joburg, Eck had been on an ANC-funded exploration of massive wind-farm development near the Western boundary of Kruger National Park. One day, he had been in an open Land Rover with three other development types along with a South African guide named Paula Pedderson who dressed like a khaki hunter and whose buxom body and dirty-blond short hair were perfect for the part. She was using a remote radio to coordinate information about where the big animals were, getting the driver to cut suddenly across a grassy savannah above which a helicopter spotter had called in a black rhino sighting.

The open jeep with its thin driver in green shorts and knee-high arthritic socks covered ground made for astonishing four-footed animal runners. Eck bounced up and down happily in the back, not minding another passenger who had no English constantly using him as a focal watcher in her film recording. It was, as usual, his splendid white hair bunching out from under his Yankees baseball cap that made him so visual to her, but he had the sense she knew who he once was from previous international EXOIL promotional material. This was after EXOIL couldn't absorb the heat about him, when the uncanny and incredible adventure that was his life started costing the company bad optics in the worldwide wind market.

The Kruger sun burned down its beautiful dry heat as the Land Rover went into neutral and glided the final fifty feet close but not too close to the testy, magnificent creature. It was a black rhinoceros, of the kind, Eck whispered aloud, that God told Job had a penis as stiff as a pine tree. God's pet was the crown of animal creation Arkturo said sweetly in an undervoice narration in the copy of the film Eck eventually saw. He remembered distinctly, though, Paula Pedderson's insistent low growl that everybody shut up, right then, as the mass of dusty onyx muscle took notice of the human creatures in the metal box on four wheels inching a little closer to its need for a lot of space. It had no mate, no companion, it was just all-in there in an area of place it didn't give a damn about owning or explaining. Its kind faced extinction, but this one lived forever right now. It raised its four-hundred-pound head above its three-thousand-pound body. It rotated its tube-shaped ears all the way around. It sniffed. It did not like what it smelled. It moved clearly in the direction of the white-haired creature in the metal box. Sniffed. Sniffed some hellish scent from Goleman Eck's existence, so it seemed.

"Oh, my God. Shit," Paula Pedderson's voice broke.

Before the driver could react, the giant beast took two running strides toward the jeep, stopped, jumped straight up a foot off the earth, spun around all of a piece in mid-air like a dancer, came down on thunderous feet, and ran off as if it were as fast as an ostrich, an entire herd of greater kudu, a pair of mature black panthers, anything hugely animal that could bolt, get out, get away from the abomination that was this white-haired biped exuberant and laughing like a madman in the back seat of the metal box on wheels in Kruger National Park.

That, Ark unscrambled said, was God's creation running to save itself from the horror that was Mr. Eck on the planet. God, Ark said, of the living prophets and the million martyrs, the God of man's holy war to make His will prevail in this time of Jahiliyyah. That only God made Goleman Eck an abortion for a purpose, an outcast for divinely ordained need. Eck was in the line of Ishmael who was cast out in order to recast man. The aborted one is the holy one. Ark had been called by God to put Eck's awful life in His service whether or not he convert. Eck could save his unborn life at last. And at last, he would be first, he would be barach, he would be blessed because he would die such. He would be the deathly wind of jihad.

Separately and in conjunction with one another, international and local authorities on terrorism invited Eck in to talk. Very interested, Eck cooperated, several times. For the most engaging interview—never an interrogation because he never graduated to being a person of interest—the South African Internal Security Bureau produced Arkturo himself.

Eck was delighted to see the man looking like a dark character out of a 1920's Soviet poster of a bearded fuse-round-bomb-throwing agent of nihilist uselessness. He crossed Rasputin with heavy-metal arms and neck-tattooed bone and ax-silver red, and green imagery. His boots rode high up his ankles and had gold buckles that made noise with the slightest movement of his sausage-shaped lower legs.

Eck greeted him cheerfully. "Hi! I'm Goleman Eck."

The official with them was US ATF, why, Eck didn't fathom. But the athletic man in the blue suit, thin black tie and silver-flapped computer case wasn't being easy. Mr. Bryce Reynolds dispensed with fools. That was his job, he went around the world doing just that job, and he was tired of it.

"Mr. Arkturo Assaf, you were a resident of Capetown, South Africa?"

"Yes."

"And you are a guide at Robben Island Prison?"

"Was."

"When you were a guide at Robben Island Prison, you conducted tours, such as of the cell prisoner 46664 inhabited."

"Cells to lime pit, yes."

"And you claim to have received intense training at Al-Azhar University in Cairo?"

"Yes."

Eck watched Bryce Reynolds take the fool apart. Never finished the course of study at Al-Azhar. Did learn knife fighting. Did not know how to disassemble and reassemble any kind of infantry grade rifle. Was deported from South Africa back to Glasgow for extensive dealings in internet child pornography originating from Belarus.

"Mr. Assaf. What do you want with Mr. Eck?"

Ark contorted his upper body. "A business deal. Social media can take his situation worldwide in the name of . . . "

"Don't," the ATF man insisted, "don't, I warn you, invoke the name of the Prophet to a practicing Muslim like me. A disgusting fraud like you does not have the right to invoke the name of the Prophet to a practicing Muslim like me. If I want, I can make you sit here for an hour repeating that you will not do so."

Eck felt his head crowding. He tried to make room in it for this new experience of an ATF Muslim named Bryce who hated his job to the core of his being.

"You American officials, with your authority and your ignorance, you do not know how to treat a global citizen like me."

"Mr. Eck here seems to have plenty of worldwide social media presence already, most of which, as I understand it, he really doesn't want."

Eck was thinking, But he linked me with Ishmael. That was something.

With various transparent warnings and blatant insults to the man's character and intelligence, the agent told the plotting fool to get out and to stay away from Goleman Eck physically and communicatively, in all ways. He shook Eck's hand in exactly the sideways way he shook his own head at the presumptuous idiocy he had to deal with in the post-9/11 world. He gave Eck a verbal blessing. He told him to be careful of knife fighters, though he understood that Eck could generally take care of himself. He concluded by saying, "A guy like that, one lucky swipe, stab, and he thinks he's a high-degree judoka, and you've got a six-inch scar down your cheek."

Just after the interview, out on the street, Eck was walking by a moving truck with its side doors open and ramps out. Commotion pushed him off balance. Three men had the Scottish porn dealer surrounded. He saw that the ATF guy had stripped the Capetown wizard of his knife.

The three men were angry at Arkturo, something about botching a very big deal. Their tone was escalating and they spoke Eck's whole name clearly. He acted out of impulse, put himself squarely in the middle of them all. He pulled off his cap. He said who he was. They knew who he was. He moved toward the biggest of them because that one was oddly wearing two brown tie shoes that did not quite match. Ark took the moment to run. He could run very fast, and the men were in no shape to catch him. They turned on Eck, who asked them what service he could do them since they used his name. He moved his eyes around and around them. He made noises in his throat that could warn them. Now was their chance to do whatever it was about him they wanted. They went to work drawing the doors back shut on the moving truck. The moving truck said in red on three sides, Life Changes Moving Ltd. Eck came fully together about ten seconds after they'd pulled the truck out of the parking space and rolled slowly and respectfully down the domestic South African city street.

A shapeless face in its big right mirror stayed in his mind. The meeting, Arkturo, Reynolds, the absurdity, the threat, the confiscation of the knife, the fact that one of the three men had two different shoes on, his lost chance to be Ishmael, at least an Ishmael, Mandela's prisoner number, child abuse in Belarus, the crazies who wanted to use him, the righteous who wanted him aborted dead for good, the Miracle Mission, the Tuam maternity home, the closeness but no contract that giddy time of planning the wind by Kruger National Park, and, above all, the massive black beauty with the penis like a pine tree spun up and around in the air to get an eternity's distance away from him, all, all of it, all converged right then to let him know in an iron chain of necessity that because of him Yolande Segundo might be in deep, deep trouble.

His sojourn away had to be over. It was time to get back to it, whatever it was going to be. First, he had to get back to Yolande.

THIRTEEN

When Alex Shimmerman was in divinity school, assiduous prayer guided him to understand his vocation through the parables. This was well into when literary theory had taken the linguistic turn that decentered all interpretation of any narrative sacred or profane. The search for unifying meaning became deeply problematic. In Shimmerman's particular case, scripture unbound from certainty released him into what he called "parablistics."

"A parable," Alex declared, "wasn't just, as its Greek root implies, a comparison. As in 'The Kingdom of Heaven is like a vineyard, or a banquet, or the like.'"

That meant, on the most basic level, that the forty-six parables of Jesus were never just "about" one thing, but about two different but complementary storylines that converged. The place or moment of convergence was grace, the free gift of "meaning." Thus, sin the story converged with forgiveness the story. The prodigal with the patriarchal. The wedding guest with the uninvited wayfarer. The Good Samaritan with the beaten man, the weeds and the stalks, the watchful and the invaders, the lowest seat and the exalted throne, wise virgins and whorish wastrels, pure sheep and randy goats, Pharisees and tax, prosperity gospel and poverty eternal. And so forth.

A prodigy and a problem as an assertive student of theology, Shimmerman used parablistics to cross crucifixes with traditionalist professors of patristics, ethics, church history, comparative Christianities, Soteriology, dogmatics, the will from Calvin to King, and Old to New to Liturgy to Homiletics, to Pastoral Care to Community Care to Cybernetics to Pedagogy to the Science of Religion to Ecumenicism. He became brazen, fearless, disrespectful, activist, charismatic, and some other students called him Jesuitical. All of Alex's transformations laid his academic foundation for his ministerial politics nuanced by his widening savvy about social media. His overall physical stature and presence made for gifted equipment for his calling to the contemporary radical ministry in social justice. He became a brand name, a sign of the times in Jesus-work. Mainstream Protestant leaders had the sense publicly to ignore him. Those who abjured him tripped further ensnared into his mythos.

Without sounding condescending, Shimmerman gently scorned being called "Evangelical." He flipped the term over parablistically, as "Jelly Even All, same old, same old." Ordained at twenty-nine, he struck out to his own territories, even as he reported back in occasionally to church authorities who wanted to claim him and claim control over him. Negotiating that shuttle well, he became a phenomenon at his own canny pace. Yet, in one of his recurrent moments of clarity, a senior evangelical minister of long national fame and respect proclaimed that Reverend Shimmerman's Savior was not the One others knew in their heart.

So when Goleman Eck became the viral devil of the glued religious right, Rev. Alex embraced him as Eckstatic Gold, the Aborted One come in the name of the Power of the Crucified One who was aborted by the Father to be welcomed back now in this time. In this Miracle Mission to make his apparent mystery Mira-Clear again. Goleman Eck was the Power of God manifest again.

From this renovated epiphany would come the spiritual means to achieve the social justice left behind in the wake of nationalist or tribal politics. True democracy. Equalities of birth no matter what borders were crossed illegally. Shimmerman preached that it was all, all MiraClear again. In one particularly unpredictable Facebook announcement, he even invited Roman Catholic brothers and sisters to consider Goleman Eck the progeny of a new Virgin Birth. He invited the outrage that he got.

Fanatic. Fraud. American Spiritual Snakeoiler All Over Again. Elmer Cuntry, Joe Southcote Shiloh-Birther, New York Rasputin, Swaggart, Jones, Pius XII Anti-Semite, MatherBlather, Gospel-Gouger, Spiritual Onanist, Theo-Thug, Para-Ballistic Cracker, Juiced Jansenist, Al-Qaeda-Ex, Shammerman, Post-T-Rumper Tool. Eckstreamist.

"Thus does jackass slander bellow insane," he replied.

The Rev. Shimmerman's vision grew as forces abhorring it got shriller. He reveled in the closeness of the words abhor and abort. He sponsored an internet contest for which people submitted cartoon versions of a creature he called Shrillerman. It was so successful that he announced one winner each from all fifty states. When some followers suggested regional on up to national first, second, and third place cartoon Shrillermans, Alex refused to underwrite the effort as un-American. He taught people how to transform the old high-throat war cry of the Algerian resistance into *shrillshrillshrillshrillshrillshrillshrillshrillshrill*. He brought back the notion of the laughter of God, erasing the source, Nietzsche. He'd never say so, but God was the only source that mattered, Source without source. In that very way, Goleman Eck was made in His image. By now he had stopped referring to parablistics as too much of a mouthful, but to seasoned Shillerman watchers, the method of inversion into convergence was the same.

That Goleman Eck wanted absolutely nothing to do with Alex and his tens-of-thousands kind was not an undermining problem for the Miracle Mission. That Pilate asked the question and did not wait for the answer was also a parable. Eck had gone missing. He would, Alex said, come back to report what he'd found when his days and nights in the wilderness were over. Their work, though different, would converge. Truth be told, on a limited need-to-know basis, Eck had only to exist to make the world's, not just the country's, great age begin anew.

"He'll be driving six white horses when he comes," Rev. Shimmerman sang in old-time promise, as he waved an enlarged Eck hashtag back and forth over his head: #ⓌⓌⓌ.~Gole.

"Six white horses, which I have seen."

He was into major planning for the Miracle Mission Meeting in the Fields of Gibeon.

*

The developing race for Attorney General has become a snarl. The crowded field of four candidates threatens to yield a new incumbent from outside the main political parties. Moreover, in a totally weird even for American politics development, Ashley Gottsch has purposefully hitched her political wagon to the astonishing dark-star power of Goleman Eck. Eck, you remember, has the claim to fame of never being born. Or, never being born in any regular way. Not to put too fine a point on it, Eck claims that he is an abortion survivor. A noted and now former EXOIL engineer, Eck is by many accounts of people who know him, just a guy who wants to live his life. The media, however, is not responsible for extraordinary polar reaction he gets everywhere he goes.

Here with us are three notable commentators. Let's start with this question, Joyce Adrian Stendra, Notre Père

University Professor of Politics and Theology. How does it come about that an abortion survivor, if that what Goleman Eck is rather than some colossal misfit, becomes enmeshed in a wide-open race for Attorney General? What's your take?

"Well, we first off have to try to understand the will behind candidate Gottsch's way of talking about what she calls the transformative role of the Attorney General's office in statewide political culture. This goes way beyond draining any swamp, way beyond fixing a broken system of morally bankrupt grifting and grabbing. We need to revalue life, she says, over and over. Eck is a heroic figure to her and to her seeing the change she wants all of us to see. . . ."

We've heard all that, Professor. Why does it seem so much dangerous invasion of religion into state government? Letitia DeMan, head of Regular Birth Matters, you're champing at the bit across from the professor. Your take, please.

"Eck is dreck. Pure and simple. An insult to parenthood, a dangerous man whose every thought about himself is an abortion. I can tell you, I will predict it and tell you, that this inflated egotist is enough to send a tsunami of disgusted violence across this state, down from Niagara and up from Houston Street. Now I mean no disrespect to Ashley Gottsch, it has been my pleasure to work with Ashley Gottsch on family and electoral matters that benefit family in this country. But somehow my friend Ashley Gottsch has checked her judgment at the door on signing up with this insult of a man, this dreck, pure and simple. He was refuse in the OR basin. He's grown up into man-size refuse. That pretty much confirms his origins."

Let's get our third commentator into this before heat shuts out light here. Poet and social critic Marley Durance, can you take a shot at the proper boundaries of state and religion in this up-for-grabs attorney general race? Take your take, if you would.

"You won't be surprised at my seeing a ramp, a rampant

metaphor in this whole thing. Hold on, now, Ms. DeMan. Hold on now, Professor Stendra. Metaphors control how we, how we think. I'm saying that abortion-survival is a new metaphor we need to hear, we need to hear. Whether Goleman Eck is truly such is almost beside the point of boundaries proper, proper and improper of state and religion, state and morality."

Joyce, your take as a man on Mr. Eck as a new kind of male figure in American culture?

"He's not that yet, but he's getting there, or the attention is rushing to him, whether he draws it to him willfully or not. In a curious way, he repeats the denial power of Jesus, the power to say, I come from another place altogether, yet in this my country I will be forsaken."

Letitia? What are you thinking?

"Tsunami. I'm thinking tsunami. Revulsion. Disgust. Regular life rising up to defend itself against the calumny of dreck. Rampant will be thwarted. It's not too much to say it will be aborted and voided, voided and aborted. It cannot be that God's plan is to be upended and ended, ended and upended. Not in this sickness of malevolence. No sir. Our organization, Regular Lives Matter, will go to the mat on this one."

Of course, one might take exception to the possibly implied violence in your language, Letitia. At least, I cannot let it go by as if the public listening to this news show right now implicitly endorses any such implied violence in your presentation. Your take now?

"Put it this way. The other side speaks of jihad as struggle. Well, we too struggle in our practice of making the regulating order of the universe manifest in human life. That is, regular human life."

Marley? Marley Durance? What's a poet's take?

"This, no more, no less. Goleman Eck is an extraordinary new way of living. Of, of, of being alive in the post-traumatic knowledge of having been aborted. He's a dozen DNA groups.

He's got the pressure of all that, all that uncertainty about his different heritages. Isn't it odd that this new kind of man was once an abortion?"

Professor Stendra, Joyce, you read poetry?

"I think I just heard a very complex, very flattering figure of speech about Mr. Eck. But at the same time, and in the final analysis, one cannot dismiss the very different question with very different answers that Laetitia DeMan's uniquely American religious challenge to, one might call it, Eckhood."

Eckhood? What's that? I guess it means personhood after the trials of abortion. Your take on my idea here, Professor? Is that an amicable smile?

"I'll have to slow down and see how far down the road in this discussion personhood after the trials of abortion gets us. Or at least, gets my understanding of this unheard-of new man."

Laetitia DeMan? Time's fleeing us for this section of the program. I give you the final take.

"May the Almighty in his wisdom aid this aborted man. The rest of us need to see clearly, speak out clearly to Ashley Gottsch's campaign not to confuse abortion politics with regular human life. Saying as I have on national media like this that Eck is Dreck is my way of getting attention to the worsening human situation Mr. Eck, to turn a phrase, embodies."

*

More than his mothers came at Eck from various parts of the world.

There were also persons who wanted to buy the rights, even proposing phenomenal sums that would put him on Easy Street the rest of his unnaturally born life. The one that Gole liked most was an offer from a filmmaker named Gross.

"Really?" Eck asked him. "Not just a wicked pseudonym?"

Ulysses, Uly, Gross had apparently gone out of his way to converge with Eck in the open-air fish market on the Rue Monge in the sixième. Eck had gone to Paris for a precious two weeks with Yolande Segundo. They hadn't seen each other in months while Eck was travelling away from the trouble with being at home in New York. He was thinking about buying a half kilo of beautiful red snapper to make for dinner. The French for it added even more life, *poisson rouge vivaneau*. The whole display of forty different fishes in the sunlight was a relief to contemplate. Eck identified bass, pike, bream, langoustine, cuttlefish, tuna and trout. He wished he could consult with Victor Mature about the gentlest cooking of the vivaneau. He was being happy in Paris with Yolande and other people's ways with their fish.

Uly Gross penetrated the meditation when he introduced himself. He looked like every oversized boxing or music promoter who screwed his clients out of millions of their earnings.

"Gross," Eck repeated back to him. "Not just a wicked pseudonym?"

"You're quick, eh?" Uly said, the last syllable Frankophied. "I just turned my head and there you are, for Christ's sake. Goleman Eck himself. I couldn't believe my luck. Wanna coffee with me, hear what I have to say?"

"What do you do in the world, mister? What brings you here, where the dead fish are?"

"I make documentaries."

"Tell me one I've heard of."

Uli named one. Eck shook his head. He named another one. Eck shook his head and said, "Sorry." Uli tried, "*Twilight in White America*."

"That I saw one installment of. I think it was the one that really annoyed everyone in non-white America. I think I liked it when I saw it, what four, five years ago? So, I get it. You're trolling for media attention through what gets under people's skin, of all colors."

Eck got his fish. The fishmonger said, "Oui" to him several times, each in a different inflection. When the man turned to his next customer, Gross said, "I can never tell whether they're saying way or whey, but it's definitely not wee."

"That would be Irish," Gole said. "Okay, coffee. You tell me your story about me. But I suspect it's only yours and I have to get this fish back to the apartment. Fifteen minutes, eh?"

As they walked across the square to the nearest café, called Sentiment in English, Eck kept looking at the man steadily. A bumbling type, he was widening out of a double-breasted gray suit jacket. There was something odd about his teeth, as if he were trying to keep the two rows together inside his cheeks, and there was a slow intermittent twitch in his big two-toned eyebrows. Eck was probably making a mistake, but he couldn't help feeling he owed more than no to such interest in him. They took seats at a small sidewalk table, ordered café au lait and shared a plate of buttered tartines. Ulysses Gross pitched his idea for a film-bio done in three episodes: abortion and adoption, women and men, ostracism and acceptance. His working title was "The Unborn Life."

"What's your interest in this?" Eck asked him. A kind of humming seemed to be moving near the direction of the next cross avenue.

"How much time have you got for me to answer that?"

Eck picked up his cup in his thumb and two fingers. "This time," he said. "You know, I like the coffee, like the way Parisians like their coffee, appreciate their coffee. The way they make time for it. I have that amount of time. Say, do you hear anything?" Eck looked around the square. It was a bright August afternoon in the City of Light.

Uli's strange cast of mouth didn't blunt his being a man of information, a man who knows what day and time it was. "Could be the procession," he said, then leaned his big head down forward to get a whole tartine in his mouth. He chewed it quickly, got it down with a big sip of his almost hot drink. "Today's the Feast of the Assumption, you know? It's a big deal in this country, especially for the right wing."

"You were saying?"

"I think I would answer that you are a new kind of sacrificial goat for all kinds of odd sentiments. You're hugely, like, not right. You can't be forgiven for claiming you were not of woman born, just of woman carried, then cut out and cast away. That's enough to get them crazy. That's one hell of a story."

"Okay," Eck said. "Let's say that's one way to read me. Still, what's it to you?"

"You make explicit what's implicit in things like race, exclusion. You are America's original sin, walking around and being successful while being really unreal. It's a movie, man, and I know how to do it."

"Forget it. I don't need it."

Uli looked at him as if he were in the way, someone to get around, aborted yet again. "I can do this with you for a lot of money, or without you, also for a lot of money."

"You always this good at the art of the deal?" Eck turned around toward the humming, chanting rolling their way.

The long Rue Monge void of traffic for the event was filling up with a slow procession behind a huge statue on a pallet borne on the shoulders of eight strong young men in open-necked light blue dress shirts buttoned at the neck and navy blue pants. They were white, very French blanc. The statue was of a white Virgin Mary in white and blue robes and a silver nimbus behind her long golden hair. Her right arm was extending up out of her sleeve, not quite a salute, but not quite a blessing either. She and her porters slow-led several hundred processioners down the wide avenue of classic Left Bank apartment houses, sidewalk shops, food stalls, convenience and fashion stores, on the way to the quarter's nineteenth-century church Mary Queen of Heaven. In clumps amid the many fervent religious marched tight groups of different partisans of the right, some wearing white armbands, some coded blue shawls or red berets or tricolored straw hats. There were different hummings and chantings, indistinctly together, differing swirlings moving in one direction but not as a unified marching force, at least not a spiritual one.

"You know this crowd?" Eck asked the filmmaker.

"National Front. Nation means one thing to them."

This was the first thing he heard from Gross that he liked. Then three young marchers were standing in a line quite close to their two chairs. By the sour looks on their faces, they didn't seem to be enjoying the gum they were chewing. Something was making them look dourly at the two Americans. Without taking his eyes off them, Eck put a forefinger on the back of Uli Gross's brown hand and brought it back up to circle the three faces and put it on the back of his own left hand, neither Black nor white, just the mix of Eck. One of the three, not getting the slightest hint what Eck's gesture meant, closed his mouth in a rush of anger.

"Pardon my French," Eck said, "*mais comment va l'immigration dans votre France?*"

That did it. The three of them, still looking totally alike in their shaved heads, sleeves rolled up to their hard-won small muscles, acned faces and reddening-angry ears, started mouthing one American word to the big man sitting below their spirited march.

Eck stood up too fast for their comfort, even their balance. Very precise, he said, "Fanon? Fanoui? Fuck off." One of them swung viciously, swung badly, at Eck's face, then recoiled holding his forearm in a lot of unexpected pain. Eck said it again, this time in a loud rant, "Fanon? Fanoui? Fuck off." The three were ordered back into their group, many of whom glared murderously at the two Americans. A fiftyish woman procession marshal in a starched purple blouse tight over the curve of her bosom and lengthy black skirt put a firm arm around the wounded follower of the statue on Assumption Day, her pretty face contorted with what Eck saw was an obsessive wish to kick all such as them out of her France. People at the other sidewalk tables near theirs smoothly ignored the disruption, which had taken only a few seconds anyway. The tail end of the procession walked by, a lot of it waving in good humor and holiday parade fashion.

"The scene I can make out of that little scene!" Uli Gross marveled. Eck thought he might start to shake. He had been too close, again, and again out of nowhere, to something stupid, something dangerous, wrong. They weren't part of his life's legion of people trying to take his life from him. They just wanted him out of their sight. He just didn't look right, ever, to the such as they. The only killer right then, again, was he.

"I really want to finish my coffee," he said as he sat back down. "By myself, actually. Do you mind?"

"All right," Uli said. "I guess that's all right, too. I'll be in touch."

"Don't," Eck said. "Please leave me alone."

"I don't give up that easily. This could be huge. Enjoy your fish, Goleman Eck. I wish you joy of the fish. And thanks for that just now. I can't fight worth a damn. Never could. Usually, I just rely on my size for assholes like that to think about."

"Yours is the better way to do it. *Bonne chance* and goodbye."

"Sure." He held out his hand. Eck gave him limp fingers to shake. Down the Rue Monge the sound of Gounod's "Ave Maria" didn't sound like a political anthem at all, but much better than that. Eck listened to it. Blessed is the fruit of thy womb.

*

Yolande said something about when in France. So she

texted Victor Mature back in the city, who was deep into sous-chef prepping on a Friday noon in advance of the dinner rush at Les Trois Souhaits. He kindly texted back what she needed to know to make his special red snapper with olive oil, garlic, plum tomatoes, Ricard, clam juice, fresh fennel and leeks, basil, bay leaf, thyme, a touch of Tabasco, Provencal style. Eck watched her every lithe motion in the compact and neatly equipped kitchen of the overpriced apartment he'd rented for them for two weeks. Its living room had a narrow view of the river. Outside, it was a perfect evening, down from the usual August heat that invited most Parisians who could to get out of the city.

She was happy, pleasantly still jet-lagged, chattering silly and serious, patting his hand away from her hip while she bent to check the fish in the oven. He liked the way her long open-front charcoal sweater gently hugged the curve of her from shoulder to knee. He liked the way her tan two-inch heeled shoes touched her ankles below her red jeans and the way her hair moved along the line of her shoulders. When she straightened up and turned to him, the bright pink t-shirt underneath the sweater did the same against her free breasts. His back teeth started that pleasant sexual ache for the first time in a long while.

"By the way, Victor and Mary Rice are asking, gently, when you're coming back."

"Your snapper is starting to make me hard," he said.

"Now don't you go making me overcook my fish."

"Never," he said. "Not your fish."

She stood in front of him, took his two hands up in hers, kissed them both. He gave them both and full to her. "I don't yet believe I'm really here with you. I was so afraid you just wanted to disappear from everything, everybody, me. It's the same fright that floored me that afternoon in Macy's. I'm going to start crying."

"Don't," he said. "Or do. I liked what Macy's did for you.

And me."

That made her laugh. So she didn't.

They started eating Victor Mature's Monge rouge filets, with spinach, rice, sliced baguette maybe two hours old. They both were amused by how simply really good it all was. In the first few minutes in their first home-cooked meal in Paris, they saw each other think so without saying so.

Life.

He wanted to tell her about what happened at the procession, about filmmaker Gross. Instead, he asked her to catch him up on her work.

"Digging with dinosaurs," she said. "Creating digital platforms for offshore oil platforms. I'm complicit in a dirty dying business that wreaks havoc in the sea and the air. But I brought some drawings to show you. Some new ideas for textile murals. I'm excited."

"You got enough money to get out, do what you want?"

"Maybe," she said. "Maybe sooner than later. This contract for new oil beds off Central America will finish. It's cleaner than most. I have a woman oceanographer friend I'm working with. Her name's Fakhruddin, from Bangladesh. You like that? Third-world scientist come to make drilling in the Caribbean a little more respectable so that we can burn more ancient atoms up. She has a hard time in the sun. She has to dress like a mummy wearing a huge straw hat over her safety helmet. All she wants to do is to go back to teaching people to play the sitar. But she too finds the money a hedge against things like useless men."

"Tell me about them," Gole said.

"Present company excluded," she said and offered him more spinach braised in white wine. "I hope to show you soon how excluded from useless I can make you."

They ate, were silent, for a minute, seeing each other as if checking on the continued reality of being with each other again.

"I was in the city for a few days," she said. "Went to your place. Your doorman gave me the key. I do love his name, Danny Shelter. That's a good one to have."

"How are things up in the air there over the harbor? Victor's been checking on it once in a while, I think."

"Yes," Yolande said. "Mary and I and Victor arranged to meet there on my one visit. The whole aerial place misses you. It's like weirdly the same, that wonderful place, but without its music, harmony. We opened a bottle of your best Tuscan red. There was a full moon making the harbor silver. Mary Rice tried to conjure you. I thought she was actually going to do it."

"How?" Eck asked

"Well, she stood with her glass of that best red under the Hockney and talked to the shadowy body that is or is not trying to get up to the surface of the water."

Gole took in a deep breath, held it, closed his eyes for a few seconds. When for the thousandth time he didn't make it up to the surface again, he asked her, "How are they? Mary Rice? Victor Mature?"

"On your side, as always."

Moved, Gole said, "They are as uncommonly generous as I've ever known people to be."

"We are all happy to be—" She hesitated, took a forkful of leek and tomato into her mouth, chewed lightly to stop any tears brimming. "To be with you, Gole. Just to be with you."

Nothing needful to say for a couple of grateful minutes.

Yolande said, "You know? You're the one who got out. That's what several smart people in my business and yours have told me. 'Gole's got it right,' my friend Fakhru said once." She stopped as if she didn't want to say something. He waited. She said it.

"It's curious, though, Gole. At the same time, there's this, I don't know, resentment, or like envy or grudging understanding. Hard to put a word or finger on it."

"Any way I try it, I don't belong. It's been that way, my life."

"Sequence," Yolande said. "You're free of it. You don't come from anywhere, anyone. That's a threatening thing to let somebody have in life." The thought made her afraid for him. He could sense her imagining disaster.

"I miss my job," he said. "I know they couldn't go on letting me be the public face I was. But I was good at it, you know? It's just that there's no anti-discrimination labor law that covers being unborn in the world of the very born. And just this morning, I woke up missing, you know what?" He swayed a little.

"What?"

He moved his open hands side to side. "Still half-dreaming. I was aloft on a wind turbine tower. In working space inside the rotor hub. Remember seeing that?"

"Yup," she said.

"On a platform twenty-five miles out to sea and five hundred feet in the air. The blades circling full. I was working in that space, and it was like, sailing."

He caught himself conducting, brought his arms back down, kept talking. "Kind of a gigantic steel cradle. I was happy being part of that offshore wind." He hesitated.

Yolande nodded, waited.

"The motion of pure stillness," he said. "Something like that. I miss that."

"I like it," she said. "All of it. You're the best."

"But down I've come, cradle and all. You know?"

"Don't think so," she said. "Aren't they coming around corners, motioning you from silent alleys to consult in a less than mega-public way?"

"Yes. Or some. And other types outside the industry itself have ways of finding me and offering to buy this piece or that of me. Speaking of which—"

"You mean back home."

"That place, yes."

"Well," Yolande said and took a deep breath. "Reverend Shimmerman stopped trying to get me to talk to him about your starring in his new national tour. It's called 'The Miracle Mission.' He's using you anyway, with or without your presence or permission. He's planning a pretty big outdoor MM rally." She took her cell phone out of the pocket of her long sweater.

"Oh," Gole said. "I've been so unplugged. That thuggie who dropped my old phone down the sewer grate on Dyer Avenue? He's my hero."

"We all know that, Gole. Nobody can find your new number."

"You did."

She smiled and winked at him, which made him happy. "I'm not nobody." She pushed buttons until she got up what she wanted to show him. She handed the phone across the table to him, saying, "Check out your global presence on the Miracle Mission web site."

Gole held the glowing rectangle in one palm, scrolled down slowly with the other index finger. After a minute of it, he looked back up at her and said, "Unbelievable."

"Right," she said.

He quoted the phrases off the screen. "'We are all abortions. Until we are born again. EckXP.'"

"That's Eck Chi Rho," Yolande said. "That's you. The living miracle of Goleman Eck is the promise of redemption in our time. That's what it says, right?"

"That's what it says. EckXP. You have to die into life. That's what it says. You have to believe the unbelievable. Can't he, like, be defrocked for this kind of thing?"

"There's an anti-Latino libel Tweet going around about his real name."

"It's not Shimmerman? Alex?"

"According to the Tweet, it's Jose Iglesias."

"Joe Church?"

"Churches. The Tweet claims he needed to be a super white man of God to pull this all off. So he became this Shimmerman. Right."

"Uh-huh," Gole said. "So they're after him as well. There's a lot more of the same white sacrilege here," Gole said. He was scrolling page after page. "Still," he said. "I could sue the son of a bitch for brand infringement, violating copyright, plagiarism."

"Could," she said. "Won't."

"I'm all over the world. I'm a global abortion. He's denying me my abortion rights. Joe Churches. Reverend Shimmerman. Whoever. The twenty-first-century mediavangelist who owns the digital wilderness he cries out from. He gives all new meaning to the word."

"Televangelist?"

"No. Motherfucker."

"You're enjoying this. I should have guessed."

"Yo," he said. "If I don't laugh at it, I'll go mad at the outrage of it. There is no mercy being at the mercy of this Facebook man of God. This—"

"Don't go there. Please don't go there."

"—Godsucker."

"You went there. Feel better now?"

They stayed silent again, until he asked, "Who else?"

"Well," she said. "Jenny Rich? Gone very strange lately. She's a blog attack dog against you. I bet you've seen it. You're a fraud, a shill for the environmental socialists, full of foul wind, she says. Got quite a wingnut following. She's becoming a wealthy demagogue with the disenfranchised American workers."

"I don't go looking for it, no. Ashley Gottsch, A.G. for A.G.?"

"Different kettle, that one. She's the scariest because she doesn't know who she is. She told me once she looks at you at sees just a dark mirror she knows she's in somewhere, somehow. Oh, I met them. She's got parents who don't look at all like her but who have been managing her like prime Florida real estate since her whole life. They don't know who you are. That's not what she's afraid of."

"Wow," Eck said. "I'm in them again. *Classics Illustrated.* Hey."

"What?"

"Have I told you lately that I love your fish?"

"Now I'm here with you, but it all scares the hell out of me. I'm not superstitious, just paranoid."

"Drawings," he said. "You said you brought big textile drawings to show me. Are they here?"

"Eat more," she said. "First, eat more with me."

They ate everything on their plates, drank the good French red, were very glad to be safe with one another in this place in this city.

They sat together on a white sailcloth upholstered couch near ten-foot shutters that opened out onto the balcony. Traffic and French-made sounds coming up the building to them.

"Feel that breeze?" he asked her. She turned her face into the few seconds of it.

"It's the Feast of the Assumption," he said. "Our Lady's rising for us, too. You think?"

She said yes and opened her presentation book across both their laps. She showed him what she really wanted to do. She talked him through, though she didn't say a whole lot. He looked and looked, turned back to plastic-covered 12x15 inch colored drawings, forward to entirely different geometries, patterns, weavings.

She brought visual ideas from five continents, multiple cultures, millennia of iconic shapes and symbols and seemed to conceive of others not of this particular earth but of light-spaces pulsing from places of stars and galaxies. No persons, animals, water creatures. Rather living forms that needed no faces, heads, fingers in their elegant joining and separations. Nor were these textiles to be gigantic wrappings of hills or rivers or sacred buildings. They were to be in massive flexible geometries that moved with wind, with rain, with northern lights and arctic steppes. She wanted to stitch and to weave textural ideas that would be like Easter Island monoliths that could sway, fold, turn out columns and lines of primary and complementary colors in the daylight and get ready all night unto themselves for the day next. Hugely, they would stand like mothers. They were not like anything he'd ever seen in the world of man or woman before, ethereal, a revelation from somewhere else that cared very much for this world of men and women gliding toward death in a fullness of being that spread around him and her right then in their rented summer apartment in Paris.

He struggled to form the question, but he got to it.

"Yolande," he said. "Where in the universe do you go to find and make these images? And how do you bring them home?"

She closed the book onto her own lap. "I've never shown them to anybody, not all of them."

"Why?"

"You above all others know the answer to that."

Gole did. He kept quiet about it, for then. He felt a hugeness about her that was nothing less than the hugeness of twenty wind turbines turning together slowly out in the water miles from land until they were needed to turn quickly to transmit power, a lot of power to live. That thought was a switch to turn off. Something did. He got invaded by dread. She sensed the change in him instantly.

"What else?" she asked. "Let's talk about something else."

He told her about Ulysses Gross, the Mary Assumed into Heaven procession, the three anti-immigrant stupids, the crowding the filmmaker brought in new form to his life. Then he began to imagine disaster, ruin, coming his way, like a whole new sense of being in a dangerous condition of just not fitting in. He began to imagine fantastically talented Yolande's getting caught up in all that precisely because she chose to love him. *Lusus naturae.* How can you love abnormal hurt without getting hurt yourself? He glanced down at his plate and saw that he'd eaten all of his supper. Complete satisfaction came upon him. A good wind was blowing his way again from right across the table. He went from scared to giddy, zero to sixty, in a matter of seconds. Yolande brightened the whole room. She seemed to swell as much as he with need. She got up first, came around to press her midsection to his face, his mouth. The spread of both his hands behind her made her not want to move. She moved a step back, gave him room to stand up and ask her without saying a word.

"Yes," she said. "Yes, please, Mr. Eck. First sweetness. Later, dessert."

She flooded open all the words she could command for him as he made love to what seemed all of her all at once. While she said, he did, surrounding her everywhere, focusing her joy here and here, doing a kind of whisper-chant to all the skin his mouth touched as she turned and arched and moved on top of him. She spoke way inside his quiet there with her. She had a low hungry growl to give him when she moved high up inside herself with him. He made her chuckle, start to weep then stop to sigh, get shy at going all over the place with him, run naked to the bathroom, come back fresh all over again, be very proud of her body that he took for everything but never for granted. Yolande talked softly, and all she said off and on in their time of lovemaking would stay with him as if in one continuous erotic speaking to him that he would never forget. Or maybe in pieces his lifelong puzzle-making put together in this way.

My white-haired man of many colors. You are my Joseph and the most sensuous man who has ever touched me. Come up from your mouth and your tongue on me in me come up and get inside of me now, hurry, hurry now. Oh my dear unborn one! That feeling makes me unwind everything, give it all up for you and for me both at once. Is it safe for you to love me this way? That you will not be destroyed, thrown away in exact awful measure to the height and depth and width of your union with me? Sometimes I have a fantasy of your coming in me long and steady just like that and coming out of me feeling I'd born you, birthed you, made it whole and right for you at last, but then that would be ungodly incest, wouldn't it? But I would not be your mother, just a woman who loves you and lies in her original place for you. When we first touched each other, back then in New York, you told me making love to me would take three hours. We're almost there now, but I see that you're sleepy, so let's include that downtime in the three hours. Then we'll get up, wear just a little, and sit and have the wonderful little flans I got in your pâtisserie this afternoon while you were out. I like them not too chilled. You?

The next morning, Yolande went out to do more research in the Museum of Fashion and Textiles in the Louvre. She was happy in her love for Gole. She said that before she left. And she was happy to be inside her own huge expectation of what she'd see of the thirty thousand textile works from the seventh century on that the museum held. She said it could be like Picasso encountering West African masks, and she laughed at such pretension, but she couldn't help it. Paris had its own way of giving permission to dream, rescript, be worthy of one's power to create, sing that high song of oneself. Why not? She was being released. That made Eck feel something similar, as if touching her was the best good luck he'd ever found. Unweaning self-love has its moments, too. He liked this sudden high, for Yolande, for himself. Long time coming.

He made a mistake then. He let himself get curious about all Yolande had told him about the people back in the city. He missed Mary, he missed Victor. He missed his place in New York. He missed Yolande in his place in New York because Paris would only be for now. Paris was always only for now. What then?

He plugged back in. He knew better, but he did it anyway. He started surfing the internet, this way, that way, names, companies, the shaking web of his past suspended in the mindless Cloud. And there it was.

Sturgis Macmillan had died.

The *Times* obituary wasn't staff-written. It was one that family or something like family sends in to be included in the small print columns for their departed. But the photo sent Eck reeling back to the one man he had loved and found cover with. The shock was a rip straight down the fabric of his gone life as a young man. He stared at the grainy gray photo on the screen. At once he remembered Stur's face. His amused eyes, his clear brow, his parted hair, his strong lips, his jaw molded like Douglass'. This vibrantly sexual man who had believed in Goleman Eck's presence, fact, maybe his meaning in his life without regular origin.

Dead. Eck read the notice again, hoping it would change.

"Assisted dying." Montreal. A choice, given "advancing dementia and the return of the autoimmune deficiency syndrome that antiretroviral therapy had under control in Mr. Macmillan for twenty years." Assisted dying was one of those phrases, covering the surface and depth of suffering. After a time "long and brave," suffering aborted. Stur's choice of dying.

That brain? That mind? ". . . noted and admired wind energy engineer . . . ."

The printed column whirled up the issue. Sturgis Macmillan, his gay lover, had been old enough to have been his sperm pop. A gay man who can love a mostly straight man can also love a straight woman. His Stur had reason to abort his suffering, enact a legal, in Canada, end to his life. Elegant as ever, to the end. The realization was, breathtaking. Sturgis Macmillan had chosen to break off their relationship as he would come to break off his own life. Both had to end. Of course they had to end.

So a new pattern of clarity was weaving and unweaving in Gole's understanding of himself in his Paris apartment of happiness with Yolande Segundo. An understanding as outsized as one of Yolande's textural megaliths to be hung in wide spaces of tremendous scale and uncoded beauty. Stur's fame as a wind-energy pioneer flowed into Yolande's global art to come.

But still, the same old. Get Goleman Eck, do him for being outside the way real life comes to be lived. Bring his lifelong abortion to completion at last. He had loved Sturgis Macmillan. He loved Yolande Segundo. Each of them chose or were choosing to fill out the series of their lives, their ways. It was possible, wasn't it, that aborted Eck could, after all, do the same? Regular born life demanded of him that he pay it its ultimate tribute, self-destruct, finish aborting at long last. Neither Sturgis Macmillan nor Yolande Segundo demanded any such thing of him. Which force of life ruled in his?

It was just that, Sturgis was gone.

Yolande came back from the Louvre alight with the vision of her new, big work. She found him at the kitchen table, weeping in whispers like a lost child. She read the obit for the older lover she knew Eck once had. Something about the plague that America had turned a blind and disgusted eye to in the 1980s before Gole met Sturgis Macmillan locked into Yolande's deep fear for Eck's disputed being. For a ghastly moment, it made sense, the coupling of AIDS and failed abortion.

She turned back to this moment in their Paris kitchen, to the living Goleman Eck.

She got him looking at her without falling back into this new misery. He started nodding yes to her, then saying the word yes to her. She got him to tell her small details about Stur, his depths, quirks, ups, downs, things that made him silly, things that got him passionate. Caravaggio, making sure there were twelve uncracked eggs in the carton, Billie Holiday, Richard Wright, the 1995 pharmaceutical breakthrough, the shades down dark windows along Village streets, of Stur's friends and one former lover dead in the height of the AIDS plague.

"I wish you had known him," Gole said.

"I think I do now," she said.

"And the man is dead." He said it not with acceptance but with what she thought a kind of grace in the face of the man's chosen way. She didn't want him to see her cry, so she got up and opened the doors to the patio and the Paris evening. He watched her take several pictures with her cell phone. He wondered how it was that this generous woman found her way to him. Her hair lifted in a breeze that circled her head twice.

"Gole," she said, "where does the wind come from?"

Gole said, "Ask your phone."

She did. "Air moving from a high- to a low-pressure area on the surface of the earth. You believe that?"

"That's just science. It doesn't come from anywhere. It's just there, out of nowhere."

"And it's good, the wind that comes from nowhere. Like Sturgis Macmillan in your life."

"Is that a question?" he asked her as he got up to be beside her.

"More of an answer," she said. "At least, for now. Gole?"

"Yes," he said.

She touched his chest. "The heart. It."

He waited.

"It's like a dig. Layers. Always there."

"Oh," he said. He put his hand over hers. "Yes."

In the inexorable reflex, he heard someone, some voice of

his own, say to him, "I cannot protect this woman." They held each other.

*

Rumors about his Newark adoption service were rippling Shimmerman's social media campaign to align the attorney general's race with the Miracle Mission's quiet focus on the re-creation of Goleman Eck.

The man—if that's what he was—himself had gone missing after his wind company could no longer take the heat of his infernal luck at survival. The Rev said flat out in morning Tweets and Sunday homilies that his Newark books were as open as his spirit was at peace with the huge importance of Eck's alternate birth origin. Again, he said, there was just as much likelihood that God could alter the laws of his universe for life after abortion as that He could have it that the Son of Man had suffered, died, and been resurrected.

This one colossal abortion-outcome fulfilled the promise of renewed life. That was the now understood meaning of the Gospel truth itself of the first Incarnation that paved the way for the reincarnation that was Eck's posthumous infancy recovered and redeemed for all to imitate. The Rev shorthanded it as the Imitation of Gole.

In this world of political miasma, the grifters leading the drifted into the wastelands of self devoid of all other, the alliance of the preacher Shimmerman and the politician Gottsch was a vita nuova. They could get beyond the stalemate of abortion politics because Goleman Eck's very refusal to march with them in his name guaranteed the rectitude of the campaign.

Alex and Ashley grew ever closer, their interconnected messages ever more codependent on each truth for the other. Their two organizations evolved a symbiotic effect and effectiveness within the state political level that they kept their focus on tightly. They had, for now, no national ambitions, even as the Miracle Mission and the AG campaign thrived on one another's increasing volumes of grass-roots support. Shimmerman kept in mind the historical confusion of Baptist and Republican; Gottsch held up the parochial failure of the long union of the Church and the Democratic Party. He came to claim no new orthodoxy, authority, or dispensation; she patently eschewed liberal or conservative ideologies. They said separately and in combination, We Stand Apart Together.

The sense they made had an elegant simplicity, a political inner life. Though some movement gossip linked them that way, at the time they had zero romantic interest in one another. Instead, they shared in the romance of Goleman Eck, the lost wind rider. The established political parties couldn't get a handle on it, couldn't compete with it. Their dismissal of it all couldn't have been more wrong. It was a new morning, a high afternoon, and a serene evening on the post-abortion horizon people hadn't seen coming.

So Rev. Shimmerman had to quiet down this one thing. From a safe distance, he implied to a certain level of operatives in his organization that it would be well on a number of counts to begin to wind Chelsea House Newark down, put the physical property on the unadvertised real estate market, and begin a dispersal of the remaining children. There were maybe twenty-three. It was just that they were of a trickier quality than he trafficked in when his organization was in its heyday and he had a passion for it, that is, prior to the arrival of the miracle of Goleman Eck.

They were children who might better have been aborted, but they weren't because demand outstripped natural selection. The blind, deaf, and mute ones traditionally had a shot, but not these. They occupied, for one thing, a spectrum of offshoot development. They were OCD, organ deficient, left or right brain asymmetrical, heroin or alcohol addicted, latter-spectrum autistic, immuno-deficient, allergic to most things humans eat, they refused to learn how to crawl, distinguish between left and right, stop singing, alinguistic, two-color eyed, devoid of enough empathy, prone to darkness and evil, malformed, maladaptive, miserable, and the like. The only thing they shared with the miracle of Goleman Eck was that you couldn't really say for sure what they were or would become.

Of course, when he linked up with Captain Dalton Blue's adoption service of these unfortunate but blessed infant offshoots from all over the world, Shimmerman could have had no idea that the final bunches of them would come to him as such tatters, fragments, undesirable ecto-growths to offer well-heeled adoptive parents desperate for acceptably damaged kids to nurture, love, and give their all to. In short, the Reverend Alex was drained of sufficient financial resources for supporting his old true vision of finding homes for foundling or findless children.

It was a problem he couldn't let blow up the Miracle Mission. He made arrangements for the dispersal of the children back to the worldwide markets they'd come from. It would take a couple of years, as would the new positioning of the Chelsea House property as a prime urban development that would bring the right kind of young buyers right there in the heart of the new Newark. He hymned that true old American phrase, the New Ark.

FOURTEEN

Mary Rice lived her way through to a balanced senior view of the world. Her six full decades reset memory of old hurt. She said that sometimes aging dulled the urge to correct a vex, its story at least. If, for example, she told Philip that she was sorry yet again, Philip might put aside his slight exasperation at her repetition that changed nothing. She would remain for him the unborning mother, but mother still. Or, if Mary knew that Victor would not stay, could not stay, she was going to have him close in memory thereafter. It was like moving out of another house of much history, traditions, generations. Domestic space, of love, discovery, reversal, satiety, distance, the pouring out at the end. One could, if one truly loved, stay even beyond the playing out of all that. Victor, though, was different, simply because he looked the way he looked and people, therefore, looked at him the way they looked at a double.

They were to meet for coffee at 5:00, before her discussion with Reverend Shimmerman at the 42nd Street Public Library and before Victor's six-o'clock shift at Les Trois Souhaits. Victor had a challenged sense of time, and he wore no watches. Mary had their regular spot at the Yemeni coffee shop, which was family-run, 24-hour, dependable for fresh Middle Eastern pastries of a dozen kinds that did honor to powdered sugar. Victor Mature, a great cook, didn't even try to compete in his own kitchen. Powdered sugar, he said, is like sweet snow. His fingers were not made for its delicacy. There, she thought, there it is precisely. His wisdom about what to leave alone.

He came in, smiled the Mature smile at the few turning heads that couldn't figure the man out.

He kissed her cheek, beamed like a gentleman who always remembers that his lady looks lovely as ever.

He sat down, saying, "Did you hear? Gole's back. He flew into Boston yesterday. He wants to stay by the ocean for a while, then come back to the city. He called me to say so."

"How does he sound?"

"Like he's been released from enforced disappearance. I want almond cookies. I want to kiss you lightly when we get them. I want to put a little white moustache on your upper lip." He ordered them with two single espressos served in elegant white cups with gold leaf rims. "In one of his few hellos while he's been traveling, he wrote that he'd drunk coffee in cups that must have been like these. In a shepherd's house of corrugated metal on a mountain in Ethiopia."

"You're going to kiss me in a properly Muslim family establishment?"

He pouted. "Why are you leaving me?" he asked. It was almost a daily, comic, needing question. One of the owner's teenage sons was learning how to wait on people. The boy really wanted to rap. He walked and moved in three-beat rhythms. He could care less who Victor Mature was, or looked like, but he was brought up to be respectful to the lady his grandmother's age.

"I'm leaving you because you refuse to get the plastic surgery done that would allow us to go out of the house without people trying to remember that you're Demetrius."

"You think it's tiresome from your perspective." He twisted her lemon peel onto her coffee saucer. She liked him to do that. "You have no idea what it is to bear this burden of resemblance. There, you've gotten your own sugar moustache without me."

Mary pressed her lips to her napkin. The way he watched her put the napkin down told the lie that they were going to go on for a long time yet to come. But his delighted eyes signaled just that.

"Gole is like you in a way. I know, I've said that before, but do you think he's safe enough back here?"

"He's got the better part," Victor said. "He only looks like himself. And he comes from so many that he looks like a dozen people who don't really look like him." He popped a whole almond cookie into his mouth without dropping a scintilla of the sugar.

"Don't inhale that stuff that way. It'll get stuck in your throat and you will choke to death right here across from me no matter what I try to save you."

"It's a little kick. And you know I can chew."

"Is he safe?"

"Given everything about him everywhere? The curious thing now is that his pervasive imagery is actually starting to bland him out."

"Why do we know him, Victor?"

"Huh?"

Mary Rice didn't repeat it. Something in Victor's face seemed to want to ward off the question. But he said, "It's dangerous, somehow, yes. Lot of awful rage or something like that out there, you know? You're seeing Shimmerman today, right?"

"Yes. About something like this feeling. Shimmerman gives me this feeling, that Goleman Eck is the devil's celebrity, stalking horse, rider in the front of the charge."

"Goodness," Victor said. "Where'd all that come from?"

"One of his postings. One of his creepier postings."

Victor seemed to shake off a chill. He said, "I don't mean

to be weird. I just wish your Captain—" He hesitated. "Your Captain Blue were still here."

Mary sat speechless. It scared her that Victor Mature needed the help of the dead to protect Gole, protect her, protect them all from the demonic rage out there at one unborn human being. And yet, her captain, her captain was part of the life of her that Victor loved. She'd take that for as long as it was to be until somehow it would have to go wrong.

*

The main rotunda of the 42nd Street Library was featuring a massive Mary Shelley exhibition: "*Frankenstein; or, The Modern Prometheus: The Third Century.*" Something about that made Mary Rice choose the site to meet Rev. Shimmerman. Now he'd just texted her at 4:50, apologizing that he'd be delayed until 5:30. "Okay. See you then," she texted back.

Mary Rice happily lost herself in the display cases of manuscripts, letters, death masks, the realia, the side-room video installation about Shelley's birthing struggles and her battle to bring up her one surviving child, the life-size cutouts of great stars who'd played the monster, the scores of theatrical and fictional spin-offs into three centuries of this one novel. She got a big kick out of the huge blowup in an ornate Victorian-era frame of Snoopy picking out the first sentence of his own novel: "It was a dark and stormy night." She chilled at the sight of a first edition of Shelley's apocalyptic third novel, *The Last Man*, because it made her think of a last to die on a planet of plague. What might her unborn friend Eck think of such a man?

She wandered into an academic lecture, the conference's keynote speech, given by a Lou Gehrig-diseased professor contorted in a wheelchair that was a computerized bio-station for his movements and his speech itself. Just to look at him was to see brilliance in its most frightful guise. His name was great, Simon Peter Grey. It was rumored that he was the colossally gifted polymath scientist and essayist who wrote under the pseudonym of Christopher Daedalus. Professor Grey's universe in his chair transformed his voice into the most soothing tones of reason and civilized communication she'd heard since college. Or, it struck her, since Goleman Eck himself.

Professor Grey's delivery system included several longish but visually friendly prose passages. Mary Rice found herself interested in two slides' worth of literary theory.

PP: 1

In his classic essay, "What Is an Author?" Michel Foucault displaces the term "author" into the term "author-function." In the essay's final sections, Foucault turns to the "'initiators of discursive practices,'" such as Marx or Freud. "The distinctive contribution of these authors," he writes, "is that they produced not only their own work but the possibility and the rules of formation of other texts." He distinguishes the role of such initiators from that of a novelist, "who is basically never more than the author of his own text." A novelist, Foucault insists, is not an initiator of a discursive practice who "establish[es] the endless possibility of discourse" (131).

PP: 2

It is possible, though, that a novelist can be more than the author of his or her own text. She or he can be, end up being, or be promoted as, the initiator of a discursive practice which the initiating text—the first in the series—establishes as an endless possibility. A unique novel, one can argue, may exercise its "distinctive contribution" not as an "author-function" but as a "text-function." But a mass-culture novel may just as well be a text-function that initiates its own endless discourse. Such is the case for Mary Shelley's *Frankenstein*. The text-function the book initiates produces the rules and formation, the endless possibilities of the

Frankenstein-monster discourse.

"Corroboration abounds," Professor Grey said, "of *Frankenstein* as initiating text-function in the production and circulation of variations on the monster theme. Just go look at the evidence brilliantly on display in the rotunda." If he could have pointed, he would have, as he said, "Out there."

Words like abortion-function, endless possibilities, variations on the Eck theme played with her. Simon Peter Grey played with her. His lecture gave way to questions. The cursed professor's technology responded in genius robotic fashion, in speech tones of exquisite academic politesse to the dimmest and the brightest in the audience. To Mary, it almost didn't matter what the transformed man said. The matter was the beauty in which his machine said it. This, too, was the performance of endless possibilities, variations, initiations free of beginnings, births.

As the session broke up, Rev. Shimmerman appeared in the doorway, anxiously seeking Mary Rice. He was sporting a burgundy French bicycle self bow tie as if unaware of it at all.

"Ah, there you are." He took her hand gently while he looked to the other end of the conference room to where a man and a woman hovered over the speaker, disconnecting him from his equipment for speaking in whole sentences.

"Simon Peter Grey," he said. "I know him. We were on a panel together once. Come, if you will, I should say hello. I'll introduce you."

Unfinished shyness held her back, which the practiced Reverend saw and kindly helped her stop. They went up to the man and his aides. Grey's smile slanted up happy to see Shimmerman, whose name he could get by the first syllable. "Shim, Shim," he said. His vocal chords struck Mary like vocal cords, twisting morphemes and phonemes into determined parts of speech that made sense in sentence fragments.

"Hi," the female aide said. "I'm Trish. This is Emir. I don't mean to be rude, but Professor Gray is tiring. Blood sugar after all that effort."

"Of course," Shimmerman said. "We'll be off. Just wanted to say hello and hope our next time will be better to catch up."

Grey very clearly said two words. "Eck. Gole." Tears came to his eyes.

Emir moved quickly to dab the sides of his eyes with a brilliant white handkerchief.

Grey wanted to say more. His two aides helped him get it out.

"Tell Eck Gole. I think I know what happened to him."

Mary Rice and Alex Shimmerman couldn't help but stare at each other in sudden belief that they'd both heard the same thing.

"Means," Trish began saying.

"I know," Alex said. "He'll type me a brief account."

They all laughed, Grey's like a clicking latch.

"Bless you," Alex said.

"I'm very glad to meet you, sir," Mary said. "I really surprised myself by coming upon this lecture and understanding so much of it."

Grey said bye. He said good. His face and posture were cubist, beaming and sliding.

Mary Rice said Alex should see the exhibition. They had fifteen more minutes. They bent and squinted to see some of Percy's holograph editing of the first version.

"Old story, no?" he asked her. "Man controls woman's creativity."

"She erased the woman, the mother, from the origin of life."

"You mean Victor Frankenstein did."

"No," she said firmly. "She did."

He seemed to know not to respond.

She said, "Where does Simon Peter teach? I didn't get that."

"Newark Institute. Emeritus."

Mary waited a couple of seconds. "You do know that that's where Gole went to college."

"They were four years apart, Grey the elder. But they knew each other, kept up now and then over the years. Gole saw the beginnings of the disease. He was good to Simon Peter."

"Gole told him about himself?"

"That I don't know. Makes sense, though."

"Which leaves us with what he said in the other room."

"Say it to me. I want to believe it. It's scary if he does."

"His aides said he said, 'Tell Gole I think I know what happened to him.'"

Alex needed to process what that meant. For Eck, but mostly for himself. He covered by staring into the case holding P.B. Shelley's phrase editing of his wife's prose on proof page 223.

Mary watched him, touched his elbow, said, "Drink?"

"Lead the way, sister. Please do lead the way."

"To the forbidden Northern latitude, Captain Walton."

"Ah," the Rev. said. "I get that one. The land all light becomes the creature's funeral pyre. I used to think that's the way it is for a lot of things that turn into their own opposites."

There was more to him that she'd seen so far. He could read. She just didn't trust the way he read Goleman Eck.

They had a good walk west through blare and skyscraper shade into twenty-four-second intersections across Forty-Second to Eighth Avenue and up into the last half-block surviving of Hell's Kitchen sin. She stopped at a tamed adult entertainment bar.

"Urban legend has it that the Times Square Corporation fought Disney and won."

"Won how?"

"Even the mayor agreed," Mary said. "There had to be at least one place left for international tourists sentimental about a good New York striptease. The passing of a real corned beef on rye this thick,"—the first three fingers of her right hand held three inches of air tight—"was bad enough around here."

"Well, now," Alex said. He appraised the figure reflected in the front window of Fort Pussy. "Good thing I'm not dressed clerical." He couldn't help but give his bicycle bow tie a finger pat.

"That will keep the working ladies off you," she said. "Come on, it'll do you good. Used to be, in my youth, a sexual time warp."

Fort Pussy still was. Two poles growing out of either curved end of the ellipse mahogany bar. Pink gas lamps hung down from gold-chained supports out of greenish tin ceiling plates. Mary brought her fingers and palms together and, bowing, said, "Namaste" to an Indian goddess who was glad to see her. She guided them to a table of smooth red leather top and distressed white chairs that belonged in a pimp board room.

"I like it," Alex said. "Over the top. Hyperbolic. The place performs itself."

"Let's drink retro," Mary Rice said. "Cosmos!"

"Cosmos, 'tis."

There was slow early-evening grinding and one carefully shaved vagina performance by a young Black woman who wore big law-school red Ray-ban frames. The limited clientele right now gave a respectful museum spirit to the place. Mary pointed out the framed *New York Post* front page a couple booths away. A mob chief sat splayed, bloodied, and machine-gunned dead in his big white chair on St. Patty's Day in 1973. The killer had been one of the strippers, except she was Israeli, war-trained, untouchable.

"Urban legend?"

"Exactly," Mary said. "Has it that she went on to get a Ph.D. in applied physics in Tel Aviv. Got denied tenure in Texas, owing to her department head being a living relative of that very dead Tony Languine."

Neither one of them drank frequently, so they started

enjoying sips of their pink beverages in oversized martini glasses. A pole dancer in nun's habit irked the reverend until the point in her song came when he could sing along for Mary with a lusty rasp, "And God, I know I'm one." After Mary and the Indian goddess-hostess exchanged latest news about three women meth addicts they'd both or separately helped, Mary and Alex were ready to talk about Goleman Eck.

For both of them, Fort Pussy was a congenial, safe space to do so, and the hyperbolic cosmo could be a soothing nursing agent for a good half-hour. It was clear to Shimmerman that the Indian goddess in scarlet transparent silks had seen Mary do human salvation before in this faux demi-mondaine place. He was not surprised to discover he was at ease about that.

"Just now," she said, "where did you go?"

"I think I'm here to find out just where you want me to go."

It was as if she cleared her forehead of wanting to challenge or unnerve him. She said simply, "Goleman Eck lost his religion when he wasn't born."

Shimmerman sighed. "I think what he lost was the chance to find one, or maybe, to let one find him." He didn't mean it as a put-down, nor did she take it as one.

"Cut off. Separated from unbirth. I had a friend, way back then, a really Catholic friend, when I aborted, didn't ask me his name. Just asked if I'd gotten the fetus baptized before it went brain dead. Never spoke to her again. Gole was spared all that. What makes you think you can use him that way now, get him into it now, after his whole life of starting out at zero, a castaway who somehow wiggled to shore?"

"What?" he asked her. "What?"

Which made her laugh at her own rhetoric. "I like you, Reverend. I actually do, though I don't know if I trust you."

"I think, I trust, I actually do, that Goleman Eck is a miracle, a story we need to tell in this day and age of one woman out of four having had an abortion in this country."

"You don't think, plain out, that you're simply using him to enlarge your ministry, your God-mission in this day and age when three out of four women parents in this country go about the business of bringing children to term, breastfeeding them, looking in their faces to show them they're there?"

"Right to Life? That you, then?"

"Right to be left the hell alone with life like that child. Eck's right to be left alone without having been that child. You're arrogating to yourself what's his and his alone to live for." She sat up a little straighter and said, "You'll excuse my tone."

"You want me to back off Goleman Eck now, after all this, all this national fervor about him? I didn't create that by trying in my way to defend him. I do not create the work I do."

"You don't mean own him, the way God owned Adam in the beginning? Isn't that the old problem, like men controlling women's reproductive choices?"

"You really think I'm that easy to write off?"

Mary didn't deny it. He didn't have to hear that from her to know she was thinking it. A vanity got tripped in him, knocked him to lower ground, from where he couldn't stop himself saying, "Okay, one bad call in this game deserves another. Back when you got up and told your own story, I think the boy's name was to be Philip."

She gasped, an old buried shame flew up chthonic to her throat but could not get to his before he finished. "You think Eck is your Philip, at least kind of?"

"Kind of?" she repeated. "Tell me that's your way of backing down, kind of, from that vileness in you."

He nodded. He couldn't walk it back. He could keep it from moving any closer to her.

Mary Rice, a power of control verging her around, said, "Reverend Alex Shimmerman. God damn you."

He wasn't expecting to hear that, from any woman in the world. She hadn't expected to say that to any man in the world. It was a sharp knife, half tarnished, half resplendent on the tabletop between them. It took some seconds to disappear. When it did, Alex mustered as much quiet courtesy as his practiced voice could rehearse.

"Byron," he said.

"Yes," she said, "try a little poetry now."

"Ice then fire. Being scorched and drenched at the same time. Being proud, being a fool all at once. All contradictory states converge in one stupid statement."

"It's okay, Alex," Mary Rice said. "Just something said. Not something done. Well, I better get going."

"Do something for me, for Gole?"

She waited.

"Come, show up," he said. "At the Miracle Mission Revival Meeting. Upstate."

"Next you'll be wanting me to bring Goleman Eck along, right?"

"Think about it. It's one way of carrying on this conversation that's just dug a circle into the floor all around the Fort Pussy bar."

The goddess reappeared. They knew instantly they'd been getting publicly warmer in their back and forth. This wasn't the place for it. There was no good place for it. Two stripper men in cut-off overalls with shoulder straps trapezed within the bar area now, and both glared at them with carefully managed five-day growth and greased arm and leg muscles. Whatever Mary's and Alex's business was, it wasn't good for this imitation business. They were inappropriate, a pair of serious ones in the theater of sexual nonsense whose silly only purpose was to give a working tourist a minute's dry dream to remember. Maybe the men caught Rice and Shimmerman staring for a final few seconds into their empty tinted martini glasses, as if wondering what happened to their cosmos.

*

Paranoia is a form of knowing.

"What does it tell me," Gole said out loud. A guy all in Red Sox gear glanced at him. Gole finished the thought in his head, "If I let it say what it wants?" The guy said, "Right," and kept going by.

He sat in a skimpy green and orange lawn chair that had Eire to say on its back support. He was atop the immensely high dune on the National Seashore. Some kids or someone had stuck a drippy hand-lettered sign in the sand mound next to him saying "Mooncusser Point" along with small pirate flags. A hundred feet or more below, down the difficult foot trench to the narrowing beach, walkers in brimmed hats strolled past a few pair of surfers in wetsuits. Behind him, a fisherman was trudging from the parking area with his gear toward Eck's perch.

Down on the beach, a group of festive people watched a longboat rescue operation being reenacted. About fifty yards out into active surf, rowers held the boat steady while pretend-survivors of a disabled sloop jumped into the water in lifejackets and held overhead onto a winched rope that gently pulled them, all practiced ocean swimmers, to the safety of the boat. Now a sport and theater, the ritual was once a dangerous life-and-death matter in the old sailing days when frigates got stranded on unknown reefs in howling storms. The myth had it that they were prey to mooncussers, pirates who tricked helpless people with phony beacons and took whatever they could from the packed ships.

To Eck, the old tradition of disaster on Cape Cod showed that part of the life of the uncontrollable winds that the technology of his wind turbines turned to sustaining life. The winds he charmed could be killers, too. When he did do the work that mattered for coastal banks, coastal grasses, coastal plants, beaches and uplands and aquifer that so much wildlife thrived in, he had to know about the savagery of the winds.

"They took my job away from me."

Now close to him, the fisherman started to say something. Didn't, but annoyed.

There was great cheering, drums, banners as people called out to the mock-heroic rowers bringing all to glide onto the beach.

Gole wondered if Yolande would find him there. She wanted to talk.

Since Paris, she'd become the normal in his new world of weird. She wanted to talk the way regular people do when they talk about being together, that is, being together, the two of them. The very thought seemed a high-tide wave, following another high-tide wave, down there where the ocean rolled in loud to move the sand. What could last for them, any more than anything else in the wave theory that was his life?

"Say," he started to tell the rolling paranoia undermining the place he'd put down his flimsy Bundoran beach chair. Instantly, the fisherman stared at him. He'd come for his daily fish, hat flapping down his ears and the back of his neck, red flannel shirt, reflector orange sunglasses, rubber boots just below his knees, holding workmanlike unfancy fishing gear. Gole figured the guy thought this one with the ghost hair in the lawn chair mumbling to himself was really bad for his fishing. Gole found that intrusive, so he started running down his latest list of changes: The mother wanted him aborted; the robots wanted to fire him so that they could replace him with ten of their own; the Miracle Mission along with Rev. Shimmerman, A.G. for AG, and journalist Jenny Rich wanted to transform him in spirit and politics. There must be shooters out there who wanted to be somebody forever famous by bringing Eck down. The remaining Killers who raised him, such as they did, were making talk-radio appearances demanding reparations from his wealth. On and on, a lot of crazy flies out there swarming his shit.

The fisherman began his careful hike down the forty-five-degree ditch to the beach. Gole listened carefully, made out the ocean saying "Come on. Come on in." That siren, he could still determine, was what the world calls depression, singing a little closer to him today.

And there flashed Hockney again.

"I know what it wants, sure as hell," Eck said.

The fisherman's back stiffened, but he was halfway down the descent, balancing his gear.

Maybe it was getting time to go back to New York City, his place.

Gole closed his eyes until he heard nothing much but indifferent surf.

Yolande was there. He must have dozed. He asked her, "Did you catch any of the rescue exercise? It was great."

She brought her own beach chair. "Seen it before." She unfolded the chair, placed it, and sat down, but not very close to him. She had on a white visor cap, chestnut framed sunglasses, a black sweatshirt with a gold Egyptian necklace pattern around its collar, flattering her torso down and just above her lovely abdomen and a lavender bikini bottom. He saw her for the first time, again, as a woman wholly other than what he was, a man.

The late afternoon shadow of the huge dune darkened the beach closer to the waves. More people began to struggle up the sand trench, ladened, in couples and groups and generations glad and relieved at a successful beach day's completion. Gole wondered if he'd be recognized, outwardly despised, quietly praised. But no one seemed to be of any opinion. It wasn't about him. What mattered was the damn hill. This was good.

"If we had children," Yolande said, "would they be called Specks?"

Good sense made him silent.

She pulled a bar of dark chocolate from a tote bag that said, Hell Is Empty And All The Devils Are Here. She had a minor hard time getting the opening tab going but wouldn't accept his help. She succeeded, broke off two neat squares each for him and her. He checked out the escutcheon design in one of the squares and bit down eagerly on it.

"What do you think, Mr. Eck? Seventy percent cacao? Eighty?"

"Split the difference with you. Seventy-five." He looked way down to see his fisherman's first long and graceful two-handed cast across late afternoon waves. He had a minor pang of regret that he and that guy couldn't get to know one another.

Out of nowhere, but not really, he said, "You crazy? Children?"

"Well now," she said. "Must be the chocolate."

"The post-abortion cannibals would eat their fingers, little bones and nails and all."

"You're the one who brought it up, remember? On the phone that first night in the city? When you wouldn't let me go? Huh? Huh?"

Had him cold, there.

They sat still and silent. After a couple minutes of that, Yolande turned to him. She went flat out with him up on the mighty sand dune the ocean would eat just like Eck's children.

"I love you!" she cried out.

He saw the fisherman look up at them, just before a tug on his line walked him further into the water in his rubber boots.

"I want to have a family with you. You're the only one."

The thick rope-tech lifesaving re-enactment was winding down and oaring up all together to come back in. A driftwood and wood-bundle fire was being lighted in a bowl of dug-out sand for the fun and food and drink to begin. History, Eck was thinking, hamburgers, bluefish, good local lager brought down the trench in Patriots and Sox coolers.

"Come on," Yolande was saying to him. "We can't let your failed abortion prevent us from propagating. Think of all those brilliant generations of Ecks to come from you, from me. The world needs more of your kind, our kind. Bad," she said.

He wasn't saying.

"Okay, I'm done," she said. "What's eating you?"

Eck had never been this scared, not since he was maybe three and began to get something straight about himself that wasn't the same as other little kids.

"That's just it," Eck said. "What's eating me. Dread will do. This feeling, like an iron chain pulling me to tempt nature and get them all eaten. Killed. Mutilated. Dead."

She believed in his dread. "When is it coming? Soon?"

He saw the far gray horizon of the Atlantic. "Has to be," he said. But defiance from the other side of him reared up. He moved his head in the direction of back there in the spaces for parking. "I have the tent, in the trunk."

"I have sandwiches," she said.

"Wine?"

"South African sauvignon blanc. Chilling. And water. And a container of fresh Greek elephant bean salad. And a tube of mosquito and everything else repellant."

They were both thinking of a place, a turning of the dunes about a half-mile down the beach that made for a kind of secret nook like the ones murderous mooncussers used to wait in when a ship started to founder on a shifting sand bar.

They got all their stuff on their two backs and shoulders. They headed down the forty-five-degree sand path. By now, most of the afternoon people were heading up into the early sundown. Eck's suspicious fisherman would stay into the coming evening for his red or silver hake, his summer flounder, his snubby scup. Soon enough he was distant and small but still intense behind them as they did their trek to a place where they could tempt a fantastic fate for wonder or disaster to come to them or at them.

It was a bower of dwarfed and hoary sea pines packed in at the bottom of the huge dune like a little cavern hollowed under a collapse that hadn't happened but could, if not now, then later. Yolande turned a shrink-wrapped package into a voluminous rough-weather cover and tucked one whole side behind an old washed-up timber. They worked together eagerly and well with poles and bigger sea rocks to make a lean-to like shelter. Three lighted rich summer mansions watched them from the upswept dunes latticed by their hundred-step zigzagging stairways down the height. One mighty hurricane finger could flick them off. Gonna come, gonna come.

They took off each other's clothes below the waist, which Eck rolled into a tight double pillow. "I'm ovulating," she said. "Come into me now." "You're very wet." "Yes. Oh. Now. Oh. Thank you." She was laughing quietly deep in her throat. She was so, the word came to him, so, so, so so so in five syllables, appreciative.

There came a first star in the darkening over the rolling ocean. Stretched under him, her ankles locked around his hips, Yolande told him about the two half-moons she saw drifting towards one another, a sidling dance, she said, and she watched it until he was so far into her she thought they were like one hemoglobin in her giddy and silly delight under the glinting little solar systems an infinity above them both. To him, ocean raised volume, wind hummed, boardless surfers advanced, lifeboats rose empty from sea depths. The two impossible lovers watched things come around them, before them, unknown before now to either one of them because unconceived and unborn before.

They napped quick and deep, woke up hungry, smeared target skin with the insect goo, turned on battery candles, sat cross-legged just outside the lean-to tarp's opening flap, their food and wine before them.

This could not last, not this way. Eck heard those words from inside his chest, not from Yolande. Then come on in, the ocean offered, and he concentrated on what she was saying. Better than what Neptune was forking up at him. That's no tune, Neptune.

"What?"

"I just said," Yolande told him. And she drank the wine gladly, the way she slept, the way she made his whole body live. "Let's do a list. What would the world call them, the children of Eck, your, the unborn one's children?"

"You go first," he said. "Jesus," he said in a whispered wonder. "I'm still hard."

"Specktacles," she said. She touched him there. "It figures, you're just making up again for the absent father."

"Eckspectations," he said. "Great eckspectations."

"Eckssoils. Ha!"

"Ecksamples." She bent down forward in a supple yoga posture and kissed its half-clothed shape. She told it to relax. It backed down like a good boy. He was able to pull his pants up right and sit comfortably again. They kept having fun, thinking up surnames the world would call the unborn Eck-Segundos for several generations to come.

"Ecksegundo," he tried, which made him think with the wine in self-pity. "But as unborn as I am, I'm maybe just a tad, a tad old, I tell you, to make children. You? You're in your later prime."

She took his hand and placed his palm on her abdomen. "I think I'm sitting happily in quite a puddle of you in my later prime. Come on, the little sperm that could. Yes, you can. Why does that make you frown, Gole?"

He wound the trouble back in. He said a broken word. "Eck-statics."

"Ecksogamies," she said.

That made him laugh. "That's very good. You win."

"Not yet. Your turn still."

He grabbed her, urgent almost roughly. Yolande bent into his chest in her own time. The panic was his fear of losing her, to something he couldn't control out there that was never going to give up trying to destroy him and anyone who found his humanity whole, living, desirable.

She pushed him back. "Your turn," she said. "I mean it. Then mine. One more time each."

Hilarity squeezed him. He breathed it in like the pure sea air, filled his lungs with it, said it. "Ecks over easy."

She always could keep up. "Ecks Benedict," she said. She put her right palm against her stomach, her left against his. "From your lips to God's ear, great unborn one."

"Eck cetera."

"Ecks it, okay?"

"Okay. But, Eckseunt."

They talked and talked about everything as the night came around them. It seemed forever talk. They played.

Memory of ever having been tickled like that before. None. Nerves along his skin come alive. She said, she of course would say, "The unborn one, the untickled. Tickle, tickle, tickle," as she freed her hands and he gasped at the infantile pleasure she was giving his helplessly giddy torso. Then he gave as good as he got and she went stupid-happy as a girl-woman remembered how to be, until the sound of an off-road vehicle rushed up to them and a voice in the open driver's window behind a massive flashlight in their faces demanded an answer.

"Everybody okay, there? Everything all right there, lady? You crying out for help?"

Gole shut down in stone embarrassment. Yolande said, "Just having fun, officer. Sorry if we got carried away."

Turned out to be a National Seashore Park Ranger patrolling the area, which closed at midnight.

Yolande said, "Then we have ten minutes more." He didn't need the comedy at the end of his shift, so he got out of his vehicle and came up to them, the big-weather flashlight exposing them in a beam five feet wide. He had to see I.D. Eck noticed a still fresh bloodstain down the man's left pant leg to the knee. The name tag said Thornton Nickola. She.

Yolande already had ID in her hand. Eck had to find his pants back pocket, which he did in the helpful flashlight. Nervous, he had a little trouble handling the wallet.

"Take your time, sir," Thornton said, which made Eck fumble a little more. He got out his EXOIL laminate entry key to company parking lots on five continents. In seconds, Thornton flipped her light from each of their lower faces to their ID's. She thanked them and handed the cards back to them.

"Thank you, officer," Eck said.

Officer Thornton was good at initiating calm back into ocean-side situations her cop presence created.

"Fisherman up beach," she said. "Earlier this evening. Small white shark out for seals got hold of an arm, pulled him out a bit, then went back to the seals. Another fisherman and I got him out and got a tourniquet up tight under the arm. Crusty old bastard, angry at the seals for losing his favorite rod."

Eck described the man who didn't trust him around his fishing.

"Sounds right," Thornton said.

"But he's okay."

"Been through rougher. Iraq."

Eck was wondering if the fisherman took a chance on not making a move in the water when Thornton said, "Why do I think I know you, Mr. Eck?"

Eck noticed how tall the woman was, the gangly Park Ranger gentleness that told she'd never make it as a state trooper or an IRS cop. But the look on her face still signaled that she'd come upon some special case here.

"I'm that guy," Eck said. "This is my girl."

Yolande wasn't clear of her funning yet. "I'm ovulating, Ranger Thornton." She coughed so as not to laugh in her face. Loving Goleman Eck had suspended her old sneezing fits. At least, that's what she wanted to tell Ranger Thornton just then.

"Well, okay then," Thornton said, "to both things." She handed her driver's license back, took another flashlight sweep of Eck's picture ID from EXOIL, handed it back. She spoke sincerely.

"I saw a fifteen-minute segment about you. Amazing, sir, truly unbelievable. But I do. Believe it to be true. One hell of a true thing. Such do exist, I have found."

"Thank you."

"Best move on now, okay? I'm glad, in fact, excited to meet you for real. But not here at this hour, you know?"

"Us, too," Yolande said into the darkness pushed away by the circumference of her serious light again.

"Ma'am?"

"Ecksited. Very Ecksited. Glad very glad that the terns and the plovers have a place to nest their eggs."

"And your hair," Thornton told Eck, "it's perfectly immaculate. Like that moon. Better than that ID. Amazing." She shook her head in wonder at something she'd never seen before on the National Seashore.

Eck said, "I've always had trouble getting ID to match it. Causes questions with authority sometimes who don't think it's real. Or me either."

"Like airport security. Some of them they're hiring now."

"Exactly," Eck said.

"Ecks-actly," Yolande said. "I've been there when it happens to him. Seems pointlessly weird to them." She took another drink of her wine.

Thornton looked away, as if at something not close enough in memory. "Worked at that for a while, back in the day when people coming and going became such a problem." She moved her upper body in that same gesture of ongoing wonder. "You know, in this country. Job got uncomfortable. They assessed my job performance at Logan Airport, like down, when I couldn't talk short enough to people. Some kind of nasty tone

I couldn't pull off. This job's much better. People are nice when they're biking and hiking in the National Seashore."

"Why is that, you think?" Yolande asked. She put an arm low around Eck's waist.

"You really want my view?"

"Please. I know the answer, but can we offer you a taste of red wine?"

"Common terns and piping plovers. Just as you said, ma'am. Nesting all along here. Protected by those long no-walking postings and wired-off areas. Ocean birds, sea birds, ones that soar, ones that run on crazy stick legs. Stranded sea turtles. Papa seals that can fight like hell." She stopped as if she were talking foolishly. "Thank you for the kind offer of your wine, but no."

Eck really liked this officer. "All creatures great and small," he said.

"Well," Thornton said. "I ramble. But, yes, something like that. I see it. People looking out for the seals, hoping the sharks won't be there. It's a good sign."

"You saved that man's life, didn't you?"

Thornton didn't answer that. She pointed her off flashlight toward Eck and said, "You had a job for good yourself. Learned that in that fifteen-minute segment. You were in air, wind, like that."

"Yes, I was."

"Well," Thornton said. "They need you back. We need you back. I hope that's the way the story goes for you. Rather than nonsense about how you got here."

The raw kindness stuck in his throat kept Eck from speaking doubt.

Sheet lightning flashed flat miles out over the ocean. It brought Thornton back on duty.

"Best move on now, okay? I'm glad to meet you for real. You are that, real. But not here this time of night. You know?"

Eck liked all that about her, too.

Thornton turned to the patrol vehicle, saying, "Stay safe, folks. I'm Nicko Thornton."

Eck didn't tell Yolande why Nicko Thornton's wish worried him. He wasn't sure he knew.

FIFTEEN

He was ready for the Miracle Mission Meeting at Fields of Gibeon.

Jenny Rich had already clipped Abort and Revive together in Shimmerman convergence fashion on forty different social media platforms that Thelma Oboyo coagulated. The young woman now intern came up with ideas all the time. One Jenny rejected out of hand for MM Revival Day imaged the Abort-Revive convergence as a hand holding aloft a Luger with hippy flowers ejaculating out of it. A better idea was recruiting the pop-rock politico band LGBTQ, whose two-week-old freshman CD, "Our Water Just Broke," was already doing well mid-chart.

The band's five non-straight members, two men and three women depending on who was counting and who was self-identifying, had broad-spectrum musical and physical attraction that harmonized old rock inclusion with new rock manic me-and-mine tribalism. They identified by letter. One was the B niece of La Jane Diver, from whom Goleman Eck learned list-making. Another was a Q and L collateral descendant of Bill Haley. Two graduated from institutes of music.

One who was the chief fifth or sixth racial-sexual

convergence was frequently dangerously depressed and on hardball bipolar medication. But T were the creative source of most of LGBTQ's percussion-driven North-South U.S. convergence rock sound come down from Levon Helms. None of them thought there was anything one bit odd or either un, anti-, or too-American about Goleman Eck, Rev. Shimmerman, Jenny Rich, the guy who looked like a 1950's gladiator movie-star, Thelma Obey, the candidate named GetShe, or anyone else who occasioned, underwrote, or produced a gig for their own motley crew. Abort and Revive was just all about the music they could make for it.

The field was large, the day alternately misty and clear, maybe like Woodstock, maybe not. Alex, rainbow-coalition scarved, shook many hands as his people hovered about him and led him slowly up the parting aisle to the huppah-like podium. MM Revival was filmed from a thousand cameras tripod- or hand-held, digitized, documented, narrated, imaged in three to ninety seconds. Part of it was old-time political, the Miracle Mission endorsement of AG Ashley Gottsch, who by now was Alex's religious political praxis in the world, a simple fact of convergence and of much more importance than the discredited separation of church and state. Eck was not there, though. This was not the time, to lay out the full vision. Impatience led only to feckless and misdirected energies. Here were maybe three thousand souls; Alex would not overestimate or overcount. The point was the noise convergence all these here could make.

He looked into the faces of those drawn here, in part to him, in part to Ashley Gottsch, in part to him who was not here. A lot of them, not all, trusted Eck's absence because of Shimmerman's presence, like right here and right now. Alex knew perfectly well, Eck's stern alienation from his value to the world was necessary for the Miracle Mission's creation of him as the Aborted One. It was politic that Eck's refusal to be what he was coming to be for the world made absolute sense.

It wasn't for Alex to relinquish the mystery because its bearer declined to participate in it. That free choice underwrote the new dispensation aborted Goleman Eck incarnated.

His people surrounded the podium, which, though on a platform and well miked, was not on the stage itself. Shimmerman always stood to the side, never occupied a pulpit or a center set above any gathering large or small he spoke to. That was his way.

The candidate effused. They were glad to see each other. It had been longer than either had meant—especially—Alex felt some urgency in saying—given the confluence of their interests, moral and political. He meant—as she knew—the iconic place of the absent Goleman Eck in the mission and the campaign.

"Deus absconditus," Rev. Shimmerman said, starting to knot the bottoms of his politic spectrum scarf. She didn't ask for a translation but sort of got his drift. Neither could justify the feeling, but it was a shared one of abandonment. As they got further into it as quickly as they could because each was attracting a circle of people with points to give them, she informed Alex, "In fact, I got a kind of quasi-legal monition from that woman, Mary Rice?"

"The older woman who gave moving testimony to her own abortion experience at the Delay for Life? Yes, I remember her. Her experience was—"

"Some years ago, yes. The communication was about the campaign's using Goleman Eck as a person who expands diversity."

"Yes," Alex said, smiling hellos now at a few other people in this awkward moment with his counterpart in using Eck. "Whose verb was that, using?"

"Ms. Rice has been moved to say that Mr. Eck disavows any endorsement, agreement, collusion, or permission explicit or implicit for my campaign's emphasis on the widest possible diversity conceivable."

"If only we could confer with him, clear up such misunderstandings of our intentions."

The A.G. candidate said too much, out of disappointment and anger. "Conceivable suddenly seems a sour joke in this case."

Alex went silent for a few seconds' disapproval of the inappropriate. She was a smart one, no doubt, a quick lawyer as well. But she had been proving to be a decent secret sharer under the big tent they'd come to share space in, culturally, politically, religiously. Even, of late, almost the whole nine yards—sexually—once awkwardly, once again not much better.

He said, "I saw Mary Rice a while back. She might make an appearance here today. If one of us sees her, maybe that one might ask her to sit with us today or soon. Discuss, you know? Finally have the conversation."

"You're charmed at what might come of her finding some use for us after all? If you don't mind my saying, Reverend, I don't believe we actually, ah, touched."

As if he'd been just told his services would no longer be required, he said, "That's a pity. I kind of thought we'd know each other, like, seven times seven."

Ashley Gottsch, as if she were on stage in a debate, smiled at him meaninglessly, and said, "The Mary Rices of the world don't stall with the likes of you and me."

Alex said, "You're very good. You and I come from different places, but we look at each and know we're pretty much the same."

They took final measure of one another. Alex stopped the pause. There was too much to do here, right now, at Miracle Mission on the Fields of Gibeon. He said, "You see her sidekick?"

"I hear he's a dead ringer for the guy who was Demetrius the Gladiator. Could be a spooky kiss. Between looking uncannily like that guy and having been a Navy SEAL. You know?"

"Love is even crazier at sixty, I hear. Still."

"Still?"

"Mary Rice. Harness the wind, that one."

Ashley was indeed quick and knew it. "That's what Gole was famous for until he outed himself."

"His magnificent choice, in my opinion."

"Extraordinary. Once in an aborted lifetime. We need to get up and dance. We'll keep our eyes open, see what comes our way, then."

Alex was being pressed to get on with the agenda. As he two-finger beckoned Ashley to come to the mike area with him, his replete word-bank flashed "Inconceivable" right under a passport-size photo of a missing Goleman Eck.

The band wound down a raucous version of "Our Water Just Broke." Hooting, cheering, clapping, and whistling took its own fun time to wear down. The niece, B, of La Jane Diver found a deep voice with which to speed-introduce the Reverend and the Candidate as if they were the next duo act on the card.

Many in the audience knew better. For that substantial part of the crowd, the two personalities and their different work were well-known for the linked changes they promoted. The two were, first of all, not malingering from old hippie anti-imperial, progressive politics; they weren't that old. And they weren't fact-averse tribalists either. Most daring, they were not afraid of taboos and shibboleths of separating spirit and process, heart and legislature, a thousand skin colors and twelve real apostles. They were mixing up the old paints for a whole new palette of luminescent American artists, citizens, questers, men and women of many desires, many futures, many lines to cross and many persons to set free at last. If you were one of the people who saw that in either or both, you either approved their inevitability or despised their opportunism. As they made clear in their uses of Eck, cynicism and corruption were simply one mode of awareness and action. Some in the crowd figured the two were into each other. That was over.

A significant OSA group was there. Old School Americans. Ask one of them what they learned in that school, and the first point started with a stiff middle finger in your face. Several such fingers already pointed up in the two speakers' direction. L and T from the band mimicked them, only in one another's clown-contorted faces. That set off a ten-second refuse-throwing session. Security moved in, made a couple of things clear, pulled back professionally from OSA scorn. They wanted more music, now. OSA wanted fifty shades of white, soon. In the mile-wide, half-inch-deep space of national politics right now wanting that much had, for that segment of the working-people populace out today in carnival mood, at least a certain tri-color attraction. Mostly, the small crowd was independent participants, come in twos and threes to see these two characters now building up more press in a dozen towns up the state all the way to the border.

Some weren't so much getting out to get ready to vote so much as just getting out. The assembly had its agenda-pockets, of course: rudderless conservatives, progressives, and independents; active citizens in BOE, K of C, Rotarians, Masons, Planned Parenthood, Unplanned Creationists, mild-mannered religious proselytizers of prophetic and scriptural sorts all in neat haircuts, suits, shoes, time-share hawkers, anthropological graduate students taking notes on their tablets, young basketball camp fundraisers, self-printing memoirists in unnecessary fleeces pulling one book at a time out of their backpacks to show a few sympathetic faces, touchy anti-Eckers trying to keep their lids on, button-flaring Eckers not needing to fight one soul whatsoever with that look of new amazement in their kind eyes that their opponents, some, itched to blacken just for the principle of the thing.

Shimmerman spoke in his everyone tone. When he talked

that way, it was hard to get a glove on him. Foment was fruitful. Religion owed the people more than it had ever given them. Patriotism was as American as cherry and tofu pie. He stayed on the wise guy edge of common sense. He quoted Mencken. He included some of his own journey to this crossroads in American life. He sort of sung the key refrain from "Our Water Just Broke,"—"And we're not here for trouble / But to do right by these bubbles"—and G the bass player twanged three notes low and funny. The Rev invoked the frontier then and the new borders now that could connect people, not keep them apart. No one need be afraid, he said, of these changing notions abroad in the land now that would protect the strongest traditions of life as the country built them. He held up Goleman Eck's case for sympathetic understanding. He received some sharp heckling. Security fenced themselves in front of him. The crowd sided with him, cheered him even though he hadn't finished, or appeared not to have finished. He stood firm and straight, as handsome a figure as spiritual hunger might savor for that one afternoon. All in all, the Miracle Mission had a clear day to see more such coming. He brought up the candidate.

More than OSA treated her to rudeness. You have some balls, lady. We don't give a rat's ass what you're running for. Reagan had it right, you're the problem. She stood there, stolid, amused, ready for whatever.

The whatever took form first as a row of three thickly built, iron-pumped guys in purple-rhinestoned wifebeaters, one Asian and 5'6" or so, one wild-Nordic bearded and 6' or so, one Nigerian and a sculpted 6'6" for sure. They got up on their chairs howling incoherently at her for a few seconds, then turned, bent over, dropped trow and flashed their American flag-painted behinds at her. Though they were part of the hostile camp, the people around them pushed over a few rows of center chairs to get distance from them.

The candidate applauded the three, called them

Bravehearts at the wrong battle. That got her what they didn't get, relieved laughter, guffaws from the gut, more pictures taken by more people than they'd counted on. The candidate said the arse too had its reasons that reason kneweth not. She told them to put their pants back on, sit the hell down, shut the hell up. And listen. It didn't take but a minute in their doing so like thugs unused to being called out by a woman for the word to go around that they were plants she'd gotten from Eck's crazy world. But it didn't have real legs. She saw in more faces than before that she reminded people of the loyal, lying, laconic press secretary of recent bygone times. They liked some of that, were tired of a lot of that, but they simmered down, let her be however she wanted to look. She began to talk, to let them find out on their own who and what she was and, incidentally, what the aborted one meant for her and her sense of human values in this time of damn few of them.

"I'm looking around at you all." She spoke in a slow invitation. "I'm looking around at different single ones of you, and at different groups of you—even my Braveheart fellow-citizens' *actual* faces right there."

That was good, that was fun, she had them at hello. At the back of the crowd—she focused to be sure—Mary Rice and Victor Mature standing beside a ghostly white pickup truck that looked like it said Got Junk? She took a deeper breath.

"And I see differences and I see alikes." She went for it, she brought it home like their own doorbells. "Hello, differences! Hello, alikes!" Now she really had them in hand. "Just when the media says all that's gone, here you are. A small, intense American crowd, people together on a summer's day. A small crowd of Americans, different ones, alike ones, looking great together in this one field in America."

Even those who usually sneered at the sentiment kept looking straight at her. She talked for nine minutes, exactly as she had practiced, without notes, without giving away a single contour of her core. She sounded like a Democrat who still had a party. She sounded like a Republican who still had a party. She made it clear that she was neither.

She would be the Attorney General for all who had a party. And, for all who knew with her that political parties were over, obsolete, totally. There was a new unity in the land embodied in persons with personalities. Like all of them if they just stopped investing in politicians and invested in themselves: representatives, attorneys general, senators, one president at the top, popes, patriarchs, bishops need not apply. She was getting a lot of cheers, fists, V's, and she was not talking anarchy at all. She said the last thing she had was a message. Check your phone, you want a message. Some people in the milling crowd took out their cell phones, and there were no messages on them.

What cases would she prosecute, she asked twice, since no one asked her even once, so interested were they in a politician giving a speech without content so far. Maybe it was time for one such, was her thought of their thought. She would clean up the bleeding of firemen, police, and teacher pensions. She would blow open the log jam at the new Hudson River Tunnel. She would uncouple the obscene relationship between the State Special Office for Child Trafficking and the UNESCO Mafia. She would convince the spineless governor to reinstate the milk subsidies to offset the vicious Canadian import taxes on motorcycle parts. Furthermore, she would bring to her office the Goleman Eck will to wage war against all foreign identities falsely certified in the past. That was a leap, but it got her new uncritical applause.

That ended her speech on all counts. The crowd, interested in her at last, drifted away in groups and solos. Shimmerman was nowhere in sight. Ashley Gottsch received the attentions of a local police sergeant who came up to her car. He told her there'd been a credible shooter tip. All were alert.

*

Final sheets, stuffed inside third composition book.

"All we have to do is list cities with no other context, and we understand what they signify: Annapolis, Aurora, Newtown, Orlando, Sutherland Springs, Las Vegas, Charleston, Parkland" (Jones, NYT, 7/5/18). Half of the eight in this sentence make sense. Orlando is a Disneyland, and Parkland is where they took Kennedy to finish him off. Las Vegas you go to gamble while you watch stripper line dancing. I think Annapolis is the place that trains Navy officers to know their weapons systems better than their own bodies in order to survive terrorist attacks. Aurora, Newtown, Sutherland Springs, and Charlestown—unless that city connects to a bloody battle in the Civil War—do not signify for me.

Thelma blames her limited American geography on her never having one of those map puzzle toys that taught kids how to fit a state in the right place. The experience of that puzzle gives normal kids a starting ownership of their country. That is doubtless a good thing. Thelma blames her limited American history and her limited political information squarely on the nature of the social media she lives, breathes, and knows in. That is doubtless a good way of weeding complications out of my fenced-off patch of attention I call my own business, mister.

Jaidev Silvernails is someone Thelma should ditch. I should just tell the scary fuck I don't need any more shooting lessons from him, directed by his violent imagination. Because of it, they told Jai to get his historically superseded, unnecessary belligerence the hell out of last winter's NCAI's executive session in DC. Jai didn't know where the button was, till I took his thick fingers together and showed him. But no one can fault his shooting eye; ten years out of independent contractor sniper-life in the Middle East and he's still deadly at a hundred yards. Can't teach for beans, you just watch every single finger eyelid shoulders and invisible core action he makes, you practice it all. Like learning how to be a car mechanic by living on the engine block. Not really, but it's like it. Jai wasn't born with a complete tongue. Such was the product of a botched morning-after abortion pill his non-Native mother took in Canada in a fright she was going to have her belly ripped open by her three enraged non-Native Detroit uncles, if they could just get her alone away from her semi-Native Mohawk lover.

So Jai talks in disconnected images. Hard to give an example, but when he tries to instruct running dropping firing rolling reloading locking one-knee down aiming breathing blowing through the concrete wall comes out without first consonants like bucking akking englanding inging oiling oinking ueezing all the way to at's it is no more. Jai, God bless him, makes me laugh and so I touch him. He calls the son of a bitch Old An Ek. That'll do. We both know whom we're talking about. So I won't ditch him, for now. When the deal goes down, he'll be with me.

But what or who does she think is running the reality show of America, ever since it routed the political show that used to make believe it was the real show?

Her mother stopped telling early-teen Thelmaline she wished Thel had never been born. For ruining her life, driving her to put shit and men in her body just to try to be happy again. After that halt in her hate, my mother simply did a slow evaporation in a spiritual heat of her own design, aided and abetted by one ordained son of Satan or another. Suicide by Jesus, who said, I say unto thee, evil thy name is religions. That won't do, young lady, a rabbinical student named Ram Josephus replied, that's just nonsense, like your pimpled face.

Thelma met Ram Roth at a self-defense training camp when she did a junior summer abroad in the Negev. She loved him, but he was hiding sex until he could fight for his/its identity in him. He did befriend her, though, giving her target practice skills good pointers. The summer program was shut down by government authorities, its teen-training Palestinian-genocidal director imprisoned for strangling his two children and shooting his wife. That was the first important lesson for Thelma in who was running the reality show in another country at least.

So the shooters of these masses of people in America are a confused lot. I know that they are not fit to be true assassins focused on one killing in particular for a noble or a lost cause. They want a certain person dead, they want to be one who is known for killing dozens, scores, of uncertain people. Scurryers. Panickers. Crawlers. Fleeers. Amuckers. Gun-toters or right-to arms bearers. Can I continue this list until I get the right word for the chill of the thrill before the last kill, the shooter himself. Herself, the woman shooter will shoot herself with that last one shot. If she's unable to do that, either Silvernails will do it, or, if Ram Roth shows up after all, he will take her down. I see, I don't really give an aborted child's last sensation about Eck. But to give enough credit to Thelma's understanding of Eck the perfect target of all this digital undoing of him, I must get to these final few right words: The born live their lives and then they die. The unborn, the aborted born, all live their lives to lose them again.

Major Tom was right.

So. Let it begin.

#ᑐᑐᑐᑐ.~Gole.

*

Two weeks after the Miracle Mission mass shooting, Gole still chose to slip in the basement delivery way to his place. The crazies, the moral tourists, the supporters, the haters, the pro- and the anti-people, the selfie-takers outside his front door, even the police detachment thinned, and the sidewalk barriers had little function. He'd cooperated fully with several different investigative authorities but refused all contact with the press. He absorbed all the law he had to in order to function as his own competent lawyer. Danny Shelter his doorman followed even the dwindling media coverage but kept his lips and loyalty tight. Gole gave him twice the monthly consideration. That was about as much practical action as his ghostly mind could attend to.

The spike in death threats against him immediately after Miracle subsided could not displace the ferocious guilt and blame he felt for the Miracle deaths himself. Death threats seemed to be the perpetual condition of his being alive at all. The deaths of Mary Rice and Victor Mature lifted that veil and showed him the horror behind the illusion that he'd been in danger alone.

When he was inside his place, locks and outer hallway tracking laser down and on, he got square under his Hockney. He stared at it with all his might until he felt he could climb up into it and get on the end of the diving board.

If he could take the right dive, he could get way down into the water and find them.

If there really were A Bigger Splash, something could be changed, maybe reversed.

He could come back up with her. He could come back up with him. He could come back up with that different her. Their very names ran him through.

He could back up with those other them who just happened to be in the wrong spiritual place at the wrong mass-murdering time. Then that watery form heading inchoately to the surface would be holding the still living her, and him, and the other him, and all the other them, because that watery figure was a giant, rescuing hero. Or could be.

Down on his knees in grief, before this reproduction of a painting, keening for the dead, it took him weeks to get up from the weight of it, to break through the surface, to air that was his again to breath

This was because, since the time his birth was

momentarily stopped, he had been an excellent water-thing of some kind who swam and swam and would finish getting to the surface, getting out and on. But every time he went through this diving fantasy standing below the painting in his place way up in the air overlooking the harbor and the bridge, he ended up all the way down on the floor in a coil that squeezed his ribs because he was calling out the names for which he had no air in his lungs.

That he had been in another state when Miracle, as the press instantly called it, went down didn't matter except as fact and logic to what his odious, nauseating existence had caused. Nobody had a legal basis to accuse him of being responsible for the massacre he was nowhere near. His responsibility lay deeper, way beyond mere law. All his life outside the normal channels of being alive, now he was outside any code that could get at him for Miracle.

A set of interlocked judgment-words in the public sphere clamped his head around: uncanny, mysterious, surreal, inexplicable, otherworldly, damnable, aporial, mind-bending, Satan-made, un-human, extra-terrestrial, ugly-to-God, and a new disease Eck created, Miraculosis. The issue wasn't the two shooters, it was the Vengeance of the Aborted. Why should this Eck-thing go on with his disgusting life while so many—twenty-three dead and twenty-seven wounded and hundreds of family members and an entire town—were forever and utterly changed for there is no worse? Cut out his heart, eviscerate his insides, draw and quarter him by four dray horses. At long last, protect us, not that. Not that.

Gole was numb, split off from himself by grief. Mary Rice killed. Victor Mature. The candidate. Fifty the count of people he could never have known but now knew were either dead, dead-in-life, or injured because he had lived. Nothing in that response came near the responsibility that was not his that was his all the same. He was not the shooters, but he was the killer, the one not killed enough.

Once, in the first two weeks after Miracle, when he was back up there in the living space once his own, he made the self-loathing mistake of turning on the news.

The news was he, on a news panel made up of odd experts for this segment of the total hour. Each had his or her opinion, which the host let them speak once he set up the context for their opinion about that context, all that in a rushed, eventually breathless tone of his cut Northeast voice.

Context is always a lot, but this is different, the host said. Say why that's so in the context of this particular shooting tragedy. Who wants to say first? You're uncharacteristically reticent. How about you Joyce Stendra, Professor of Politics and Theology at NP?

"It's like the fallen woman—if abortion is a fall—becomes the Good Samaritan—"

You refer to the undocumented information that the Mary Rice, who shielded seven different children before the female shooter got a clear shot at her—

"Yes, I am. Reverend Shimmerman, my colleague in the field who organized the Miracle Mission Meeting to begin with, was famous in our circles—"

Theological circles, the host said. Marley Durance, our poet here, might jump on that metaphor as a redundancy.

"—just to say the point, though," Joyce Stendra persisted, "famous for one idea, the way apparent moral opposites converge and mirror one another." She was holding up her two palms. While she said that Mary Rice, a mother who aborted back in the early years after Roe v. Wade, would not let the little children suffer and that that was indeed a blessed convergence, Gole lay on the floor underneath his screen with his arms around his chest trying to break his lungs open, which is why he could not get Mary Rice's name out of his throat.

Marley Durance, nationally known poet, the host said. We turn to the poets in such tragic times of terrible trouble—

excuse my own alliteration—what say you?

The poet Durance looked as if he'd been peering into the dark there is no darker. He was having understandable trouble starting many words. He said what from a steadier speaker would come out as: "Poetry cannot say what is the unsayable in this American horror. What about the mixed couple shot for wearing T-shirts saying Abort the Supreme Court? But Joyce points to human valor, and she is hopeful in doing so. Eugene Encarnacion likewise—"

The warrior cook with the amazing looks aka Victor Mature, the host said. His last name is really Carnation?

"Got up with the blood of Mary Rice dripping from his hands and ran like the exterminating angel howling for the shooter. Witnesses say it was as if he were in three areas of the slaughter site at once at any one time. One policeman who was there by then shot at him but badly. Somehow his rage, like something out of Homer—"

We don't have time to stop to explain Homer, but complete your thought. Do.

"—changed the awful valence of the killing."

Gole unlocked his arms. He said to his dead Mary, "Victor is dead, too. Dead, too." He stood up and turned his back to the television to scream at it, but the interrupting host whipped him around.

This audience knows, America knows by now, that Ms. Rice and Mr. Eugene Victor Mature Encarnacion were . . . together in life.

The last phrase fell quietly.

Gole said, "You. Fucking. Cretin." And loss overwhelmed him again, pushed him down onto the floor like some huge dirty hand that could bury him as high up in the building air he was.

"And," Laetitia DeMan, founder of Regular Birth Matters and a regular on two or three more news shows, said, "Intimate acquaintances of Goleman Eck."

Mrs. DeMan, the host began his question to her. Your political, moral, and cultural antipathy to the famous, the infamous Goleman Eck is well known. What say you about the Miracle Mission Massacre?

Sharply blonde and long-figured, exquisitely articulate shuffling conservative phrases like cards, she said through her voice into her nose, "Odious," doubling the length of the first vowel. Then she waited.

Odious, well, do, the host said, opening his hands and arms as if offering her the whole main entrée on a platter. I invite you to say the more I know you want to say.

"Goleman Eck," and the name came out as if it were Judas Iscariot, "is odious. The embodiment, or disembodiment, of everything wrong with elitist liberal culture. Let me try a phrase our poet here will loath. The intended unborn—"

Different, excuse me, the host said. From the intended dead such as the Miracle shooters intended?

"Two sides of the same coin. The intended whichever being about the innocent deaths and grievous injuries of fifty American people. Without the awful, the awful, I say, support Mr. Eck draws, those people could be living the next day of their lives right now."

Some say he never asked for any of it.

"He never shuts the door on it, right?"

What about our other two panelists, tonight? What say you to Mrs. Laetitia DeMan of Regular Births Matter's direct linkage of the unlikely unliving Goleman Eck to this stupendous addition to mass shootings in our gun-conflicted country?

"Largely a white privilege problem," Marley Durance said. "They're the ones with access to the guns. Here in Abortia."

What? the host asked the poet.

"Abortia. Here in Abortia, where Abortians live," Marley said. "With two A's."

"What?" Joyce Stendra said. "Like, the ultimate illegal

immigrants?"

"That's good, too," Marley said. "Abortian immigrants, streaming in under the wall."

"Excuse me," Joyce Stendra said. "Coming from a mixed-race poet, that comment borders on the irresponsible."

That cleared misery for Eck, even if just for a minute. "I'm mixed race. Oh, Mary. Oh, Victor, give me the courage to be what I am."

The news show host seemed to turn aside into the camera and ask him, And what is that? Please do say, what is that?

Goleman Eck said back at him through the screen, "Someone who can fight back?"

The bald question got him up dizzy from the floor. His place was littered with newspaper accounts of the shooting that he read every word of and couldn't remember a syllable of. Local, state and federal law officers who had spent hours with him left business cards he could make nothing of, though he could close his eyes and see every single one of their faces and hear every different tone in their voices and watch their palms touching the sides of their hips. A team from the living A.G.'s office without a warrant found one of his two registered sidearms and confiscated it for his own well being, warning him about what they called procuring any other.

According to another federal official, Gole's old EXOIL computer he was forced to leave in his office had been tapped after Miracle. Whatever the Russians wanted to know, now that they knew who Eck was, it had something to do with wind he'd been working on before he got fired for failing the basic born test.

Gole checked every day in his walk-in closet in the false back of one cedar drawer for the other .9mm. He checked the safety, the slide, the empty magazine. He did mental practice shooting, shooting back, back, to before Miracle, reversing time to make sure the weapon was deadly and the aim and automatic burst would stop what happened because he'd be there and didn't give a damn how crazy, methodical, obsessed with him the shooter and her partner, the guy who turned and shot her dead, were.

Mary and Victor.

He'd killed them.

No, he didn't.

His life was a killer force let loose in the streets of the city and the fields of the country. Never too late to abort oneself before more of it happens because he happened.

Yolande was safe. Yolande was pregnant. She was coming to the place they hadn't settled yet. Yolande was pregging fucknant. Gole was holding his dark weapon, but the vertigo was holding him tighter. He took aim at the water baby drifting up the surface, never to drift through it. He hadn't eaten in three days. He found an opened bottle of Pellegrino and drank it flat down. He threw the bottle at the different splash. It didn't hit, and it didn't break when it struck the floor. He was on his face on the floor.

Eck sat calmly on a stainless steel stool at his walnut kitchen island. He had taken a large frozen dinner from his neighborhood upscale Eastern European restaurant out and heated it properly in his microwave. He peeled the paper covering back and let the steam from the meat, potatoes, and vegetables rise in a column in front of his face. At first, it didn't taste like much of anything except salt and a buttery sauce, but he chewed and swallowed carefully so that it began to remind him of meat, potatoes, and vegetables past. He drank two glasses of ice water as he ate. He felt better, though the conviction was increasing in him that a huge tribe of hate would never allow a baby sired by the abortion that was Eck to live, even if actually born.

He cleaned up his dishes, wiped down the island and the counter. He went back into his walk-in closet with the dark weapon and put it way back in its cedar drawer. Then he went into another room he hadn't been in in a long time. He took in the books, the pictures, the chairs and all. He went automatically to a set of six collector's books. All were the same novel. He'd searched for three of them, and the other three came to him via dealers who'd heard of his interest and capacity to pay. He took down the most expensive one of all. He took it to a table, put the green lamp on, handled the package delicately, untied the boards of the two-hundred-and-more-year-old book in perfect shape. There was a slip in it. He gently pulled the slip up so that the book opened by itself to that page. He found the passage. He read it aloud. and he checked his watch and sat down to wait for the phone code. When it rang five times and stopped, Eck dialed the number.

Yolande was glad to hear his voice, he hers. For the first half-minute, that was enough.

"Oh, Gole," she said.

He had a fantasy of his whole huge building by the harbor shaking itself free of its twelfth to fourteenth double floor. But that would take out three other apartments his size. They'd all die because of him, too.

She was saying, "I got one of those crazy fourteenth-removed Instagram postings. I know, I know. We agreed to stay off all that stuff. But listen. It's one of those cut-up scrambled font paste jobs."

That was as far as she got. Five weeks in, she was doing well. Their girl, they were thinking, would be named Connie. Constance Goleman Segundo. When they were nervous about speaking her name, Gole called her "the C-word." Those nerves sometimes made a sentence for him. *I cannot protect this child.*

Not now. Gole's weight shifted from sorrow to alligator brain.

"Read it. Take a deep breath and read it to me."

She took many short breaths, got all the poison out to his ear in burning teaspoons.

"Abort it, bitch. Avoid awful consequence. Natural

conclusion to unnatural beginning. He fathers only evil. Your womb filled with him carries abomination. Then this for a signature: TROBA."

"Norom," Eck said.

She got it. Backwards. "Sure. But I'm scared. How could this person or persons know anything about it. This. Her?"

He used to be smart. He was thinking. He was still smart enough not to get her more worried and frightened. He kept his thinking to himself. Without Mary and without Victor, he needed to think their two ways, his one; there would still be three of them, a hell of a threesome, for Connie Gole Segundo, the living daughter of the mate the like, the unlike, of him he was never, in the regular run of things, supposed to have.

They made a time for Yolande to come over, using the delivery entrance.

Before Eck put the book back gingerly, he just looked at the passage's print again. The words did not seem to be words.

"Like Adam, I was created apparently united by no link to any other being in existence; but his state was far different from mine in every other respect. He had come forth from the hands of God a perfect creature, happy and prosperous, guarded by the especial care of his Creator; he was allowed to converse with, and acquire knowledge from beings of a superior nature: but I was wretched, helpless, and alone."

*

There was a fringe move among liberal elements within pan-church culture to defrock Shimmerman. Rip up his ordination papers, if they could find them. The killings at Miracle surfaced an odd relationship between persons who committed mass public slaughter and strands of American religion long holding Violent Judgment as a means of making holy sense of their own motivations and actions. Fringe Progressive Christians couldn't grant a pass to that kind of thinking, and the Reverend willy-nilly had colluded—their preferred phrase—with it.

A quasi-official synod that looked into the matter had enough theological heft, church real estate holdings, and Jenny Rich social media savvy to pull off a satisfactory investigation and a set of recommendations for mediating future psycho-sacred misunderstandings at the grace-roots level.

Shimmerman came out of the whole ungodly fracas repentant about his own leadership shortcomings and determined to set a better example of pastoral action in Second Amendment America. He went on a retreat that did not require his disappearance from the religious scene of aftershock following Mission. For two and one-half months, he gave no sermons or interviews nor did sentences of his appear on social media outlets.

Instead, he worked steadily with the extensive greater family at one and two removes of the shooter Thelma Oboyo to contact all affected by the loss of loved ones in the Miracle massacre. They agreed to be called the Thelma Clan. They meant to bring financial and spiritual restitution—as much as could be possible because some unchangeable grief was not up for evolution or improvement—to all the unfortunate relatives brought low by Thelma's own personal hell that afternoon at Miracle.

Crucial to this effort was another refiguring of the post-aborted man, Goleman Eck, who after all was said and done, had triggered unwittingly or not the horror of that day. Lots of the many, many aggrieved, in working to accept the only material and immaterial compensation and closure that was going to be made available to them in the remainder of their lives, proclaimed Eck the founding curse of the whole affliction they underwent.

But Shimmerman counseled them how not to hate Eck, how to begin to see even him as a victim of some twisted fate of just not being born in a way that would make the slaughter bearable. "It was," Alex would Twitter in a small and humbled voice, "beyond Eck's fault." "Do," Alex would advise, "try to understand. Pray to do so."

That he was on the verge of saying that Satan could be understood and forgiven was not lost on Shimmerman. That he pivoted and walked back, because that would mean there was, at base, no unchanging evil principle in the phenomenon of the awful at Miracle. Poor sister Thelma, who had a grave that one could visit and wonder or pray over, was not the least among the troubled born. Eck was not among the troubled born at all. That's the difference, many of the Clan came to understand, though that was not an understanding that Shimmerman himself was satisfied with.

Out of the whole human, American experience of the Miracle Mission massacre, Rev. Alex manifested spiritual product. The whole world suffers, that's the nature of living in the world, been that way all our time living here. The American Painful was simply different from that of the rest of the world. Eck was that American Painful, two and a half months after Miracle. So said Shimmerman.

*

Goleman Eck found comfort in his old skill with puzzles.

The pieces of their deaths that afternoon at Miracle in the Fields of Gibeon took their time to show up individually and edge up coherently, but they did.

Gole didn't lay out on his expansive wind worktable the twenty-odd newspaper, internet, and police reports of the twenty-seven minutes of mayhem. He did that virtually, in his head, and the labor of it kept him many times from sinking. Every move that Mary and Victor and the candidate did separately or in combination to try to escape and to help others to safety and finally to throw their lives like shovels and cap guns and poison-sword flowers at the shooters were separate steps in a dark ballet. Each was a permanent image of detail he could wrest from the moments of carnage. He mustered every yes, it happened, just like that, just then, into his massive narrative of their final unarmed moments against a maniacal and suicidal good-shot shooter in the new American grain.

Mary Rice had somehow drifted away from Victor Mature at the back of the audience for Ashley Gottsch's pleasant non-political political speech. She'd started chatting with a group of three differently physiqued women—obese Ghia, boney thin Rissa, and bench-pressing Chelle—all wearing the same XXL white t-shirts that only the muscled Chelle filled. Their three haircuts were similar, like close gray helmets over their heads. Picasso peace doves twirled on tiny-link chains from their left earlobes. The shirts said Abort the Supreme Court on the front and had on the back sentences from the Madison Papers #7 about separation of powers. If the camera had time to look.

Mary was too smart to question the politics of their triple statement. But she did say, "Hi," to each of them and got their wary attention by asking, "Does the recommendation to abort the Court have anything to do with this Goleman Eck character?"

"Yes and No," Rissa said, the capitals hers by voice.

"How so?"

"Yes," Chelle said. "If the Court becomes the ideological legal arm of the executive branch against women's natural right to choose reproduction, more of his kind will drain out into the body politic."

"No," the Ghia said. "Eck's just a tool. Use him this way, that. But best he just live out his discarded life and not confuse the issue more. Nothing personal, really, about him per se."

"So," Mary Rice was saying on the video. "You're aware people around you look at you in uninviting ways."

"You want a T-shirt, lady?" Rissa asked.

"You lay with this Gorman Shrek?" Ghia asked.

"You part of the solution for women," Chelle asked, "or of the problem for women?"

Screaming ripped across the opening field. Mary tried to spot Victor. She didn't see him in any sight circle she could try.

Eck was not there, but he saw and heard Mary Rice there.

Victor was about twenty yards diagonal to her. He was doing what he had to do every once in a while in a group of people when a good-looking seventyish woman or a teenage great-studios movie-star-geek spotted him, autographing something for them, in this last case an Ashley Gottsch flyer. Victor went along with the thing, what else was he supposed to do except sign and beam.

Victor did have Mary Rice in a corner of sight. The scream was single, then triple, then ten times as many. Firecracker pops, no, Victor knew what it was even as the second burst cackled. He started pushing, tripping, and getting people down, down on the ground, down, down, even as he ran bent and furious in the direction of where he thought he saw Mary. The gunfire paused.

Victor saw Ashley Gottsch trying to crawl around on mucous-red ground of her own making. He had to run jumping, still bent, over a collapsed table of multigrain breads for sale, then around a man half-slumped on his own upright crutches because both caps were hanging bloody off his knees. Victor got to the mute and horrified candidate whose right femur gaped open like a stiff tongue. He tore her red windbreaker off her upper body and let body memory tell him again how to make a tourniquet and get it tight above the bleeding.

"You're going to be all right," he lied to her face, which was strangely unworried.

"Go," Ashley said. "They'll find me. Help others. It's a shooting." It was the damnedest statement anyone could have made right then and there.

He grabbed up support for her neck. He told himself to go

on, into the shooting, go. It had been twenty years since that time, that night in Kandahar Province that ended his work as a SEAL. He ordered himself not to think about that time but to find Mary Rice in this time. He went.

Eck was not there, but Eck saw and heard Victor Mature there. Eck was in his place high in the air in New York, not there, but Eck, assembling pieces windmill fast, saw and heard Mary Rice there.

Eck could not turn the rotor blades off, or make them go counter-clockwise. They spun the wind so that it made all the pieces adhere like a perfectly edited horror movie, suspending what was going to happen into Mary's every move before it finally did happen and then never stop.

A WPA-era built stone carriage house with a brand-new charcoal-tiled roof stood parallel to the stage, about fifty yards off by the model-ship sailing pond. Remote-controlled, exact miniature replicas of schooners, World Cup racers, elaborate Chinese junks, and just plain hand-hewn hulls with stitched canvas sails floated as if the world were normal. It was just that among them, bobbing head-down, was one maybe twelve-year-old, bespectacled boy in military dress blues.

Mary Rice had seven other children and two adults tight around her in a circle she was moving as one toward the open side door of the carriage house, her herd in a tight circle. Her voice sounded, cracked, shredded itself so that none of them could do anything except hear her and move in the direction of her living noise.

Mary seemed to shake her vision free, to make sure she was seeing something. She was. One of the seven gun-family children wore a toy standard police issue .9 mm sidearm on his waist. Mary tore it out of the boy's shining black leather holster. Mary practically threw them all one at a time into the dark open space of the carriage house doorway. Mary pulled the old door shut, and turned to face the shooter.

They didn't use words to each other. The way her captain

had taught her, Mary crouched down in defensive shooting posture, both hands holding the lifelike pistol. Mary pointed it at gore-faced Thelma Oboyo's head. She took three balanced stutter steps toward the momentarily confused Thelma. It was enough time for Thelma's green plastic assault rifle as if on its own to kill Mary instantly.

Eck's vision puzzle then pieced together Victor Mature seeming to fly four feet off the ground but parallel to it. Too late, too late, the man was flying sideways, landing atop his murdered Mary as if he could blanket her. The sound that came out of him turned Thelma on him as he got up, and she shot him in a burst that tore his head off. Eck saw his friend's head fall back, hood-like, and he heard the shooter screaming one word, unintelligible in the unnatural tongue she was hollering out, until later recordings sifted it out of possibilities like "hole, toll, soul," but it was Gole.

The cell-phone videos and individual memories all agreed that it was at that point that the Silvernails man flipped. The Silvernails man, dressed like a nineteenth-century buffalo hunter, shot his Thelma Oboyo between the knees and the vagina, bisecting that part of her body backwards from out of the rest of her. Another precise witness said the corpse stood for a second before it folded down front and back in three parts. "After all," the witness, a gun collector himself, said, "that shooter also had an AR-15. A real one, and a powerful instrument."

The Silvernails man refused to put down his weapon but stood there raising it to his shoulder, giving two local cops with shotguns three free seconds to shred his bulletproof vest, his throat and his lungs. Both cops, a rookie woman and a man two weeks away from finishing his twenty years, recently had their monthly paychecks partially garnished. For the senior officer, it was for failure to maintain target practice schedules within the past two years. For the unnamed rookie woman officer, it was for avoiding direct orders to lose at least thirty pounds.

In ten more minutes, all of Mary's people were ordered out of the carriage house with their hands over their heads and told to lie down prone on the ground. Local and regional six o'clock and regional eleven o'clock TV news stations agreed, these children were hysterical with fright to last a lifetime.

Miracle at Gibeon was over. Jenny Rich was in homebound shock. For weeks, she could not get herself to do anything about writing the story of that afternoon. She got legal counsel to help her answer questions about her temp worker, the total body-mutilated shooter Thelma Oboyo, executed at the carnage scene by her semi-Native American lover.

A.G. candidate AG bled thinly, but Victor Mature's tourniquet held well enough until the rescue team replaced it. It didn't matter. Another Thelma bullet was found to have entered and exited her left kidney. She expired on the operating table.

After mistakenly attempting to bring down Victor Mature, Lacy Stritch, the local senior policewoman, tried two shots again at whomever she sight-lined. The first was credited with severing Jaidev Silvernails' right thumb just as he was trying to get the barrel of his rifle into his mouth. Then two other local shotgun officers aimed sort of well enough in his direction. Part of one blast entered Mary Rice's corpse mid-right thigh but became just a footnote in the voluminous investigative report the office of the reelected State Attorney General produced within the year. For sure, that was the final nail in Ashley Gottsch's coffin.

Rev. Shimmerman, it was reported, left the scene of the slaughter when it began, in a cherry red Ford 350 Super Duty Platinum E7 Powerstroke 6.2 L Soho V-8 UT. He did drive several terrified strangers a couple miles outside the scene and let them out after three of them as his followers clamored for his blessing. He kindly gave that to them and then listened to them damning Goleman Eck to hell for this day. Because they told their story to a lot of different kinds of people and news people, Alex had to stop saying he didn't know anything about what he did or why when the shooting began. He was asked several times for a consistent answer.

No, to the best of Rev. Shimmerman's knowledge, Goleman Eck was not there, had not shown up at the horrible scene. Which wasn't, the Reverend said, it would be too simple to say it was, Eck's fault.

SIXTEEN

Yolande's sixth week opened up hell. The reddest media devils of all came bubbling up to blame it on Goleman Eck.

They had decided for now to return to the rented house on the National Seashore. They were keeping to themselves, wishing that new life would grow, even in the aftermath of the Miracle massacre. Yolande was getting work done again online. She drew on his experience, which he gladly gave her because she was the one who was surviving in her part of the wind technology world she was trying to leave. Loving her was getting him through, day by day. He was himself making work contacts again, thinking more and more about a bunch of designs for robo-machines that could do more than mimic mayhem and death or robo-gismos that lighten the burdens of housekeeping but are in the habit of entering rooms suddenly and following you awhile eerily. Orbs would be the name for his line of life-enhancing AI discrete helpers and complements to your willed daily experience. And he was imagining giving up his place in New York.

"Bad things happen when Goleman Eck leaves New York," Yolande said.

"More bad than staying?"

Staying without Mary Rice and Victor Mature. How it

hurt, gnawed, rocked them both from disbelief back to futile anger at the destruction of such a pair of good, that was the true word for them, good people. The past few days, that unending sorrow made Yolande wince when she felt her belly blooming.

"Oh, dear," she said. She got up, pushing a palm below her abdomen. "I think I'm staining again." She went into the bathroom, was there a few minutes.

When she came back into the kitchen, he said, "A little pale there in the gills, love?" The slightest worry about her dredged up the oldest dark matter in his life. "Warm, more?" he asked and held the coffee pot up. He saw her knowing him, wanting to protect him even from her own rhythms.

"Yes, please."

Ranger Thornton was striding up the seashell driveway. Nicola had grown into a good acquaintance for them, then a strengthening friend in their relation to the media world that still reported on them. An odd, outdoorsy, loping, capable transsexual of kindness and deep patience with most people in her world of patrolling her ten-mile circuit of seashore in her green-and-lime striped Land Rover. Sometimes, Eck would be on one of the beaches and would see Thornton step out of the vehicle and walk fifty yards up or down, seeing, Eck thought, life abounding in sky and surf, like a reader of light. There were readers of light the way there were listeners and feelers of the wind. The new woman made sense of weathers, plural.

Nicko was carrying a large box of pizza. She liked to bring a different kind, a surprise, with vitamin waters that pleased Yolande by reminding her of off-sweet cough medicine of her childhood in Chile.

"Mmm," Gole breathed in. "Margarita. Elegant."

"Mmm," Yolande hummed, "raspberry and pomegranate."

Ranger Thornton liked to sit for a half-hour or so at the round metal patio table of Gole's rented cedar-shingled house, where breezes curled around two hydrangea bushes, one white, the other antique-blue and purple. They ate and drank and tried to relax. They exchanged facts, hearsay, the bad term post-mortem about Mission, about funerals, state and federal investigations, the where-and-whatabouts of various people like the Rev. Alex, the remnants of the dead A.G.'s campaign, the spinning new news about a place called Chelsea in Newark that warehoused damaged children for the international adoption black market, Jenny Rich still out there flogging social media for all it could be worth to her future in all the recovering and the lost, all the people and all that life which had been kicked out of life by awful rampage in America since 2016 went bad and Miracle happened. Doors of fright opened, doors of hate behind.

It was the virtue of satisfying pizza among the three friends to tamp down a good deal of all that, for a while. Lunch for the quiet bunch.

Eck saw it first. "What's wrong, Yole?"

She was staring at her uncrossed legs, the loose linen pants center of them. Spotted, reddening. She cried out as she jumped up, then slumped back down.

Officer Thornton had the town ambulance there quickly and drove Got Junk? behind it closely, emergency lights blaring down Route 6 across the mid-Cape county line.

Yolande kept saying she had no pain. She kept saying that, and Gole held her hand away while the squad attendant put a compress lightly between her legs. The rush of blood was over in a couple minutes. It was a forty-five minute fast-traffic run all the way to Upper Cape National Seashore Medical Center. Gole used every wish and hope he had left to contain his fright at losing this dream of born life so early in their happiness. He dared not utter their girl's name but he was calling it in his head. Gole and Yolande kept assuring one another, and she, after all, never quit coming back to the fact that she had no pain.

"Truly. I truly do not. Not, and I will mother this child," at which point the intravenous muscle relaxant took hold. Gole listened to her steady, deep inhaling and exhaling and wanted to give his lungs to her and their tiny forming girl.

"Ten more minutes," the EMS leader said. That's all he said. It was clear that he knew who was sitting in the back with the mother-to-be and didn't know what to make of that. For all in the ambulance ahead and the vintage white Chevy pickup behind, it seemed excruciatingly long to get to the limited-resourced medical emergency center.

After two hours of tests and just X-ray images and ultrasound, Dr. Anastasius, a round, young, bleary-eyed emergency medicine intern, explained calmly that the odds of it happening were small, one in a hundred, but here it was on the ultrasound.

"You can see," he said. "An ectopic development is beginning." He was precise, sympathetic, overscheduled, underslept. He didn't seem to recognize Eck. He had enough going on.

The embryo has attached itself to a fallopian tube outside the uterus. Fewer than 200,000 cases in U.S. every year. So rare. Resolves within days. Fetus cannot survive extra-uterine. Fetus can damage surrounding organs and lethal blood loss. If structure containing the ectopic fetus ruptures, lethal blood loss also. Most cases end in termination of pregnancy. Treatment a chemotherapy agent called Methotrexate (MTX), also used for medical abortions.

Dr. Anastasius both said all this and presented the devastated parents with a comprehensive flyer in 8' font illustrating the problem and the protocol.

It was a lot for their ongoing shock to understand, but they got the message: abort or die. After he finished talking, Dr. Anastasius asked them if they had any questions.

The mother was mute. The father asked, "Why?"

As an answer to whatever that question meant, Dr.

Anastasius fidgeted with a spot of the mother's blood on his light blue leaf-pattern tunic and gave a caring shrug of his busy shoulders. He said there could be more follow-up tests but that they should seriously consider booking (his verb) the resolution procedure ASAP, a word he spoke in intransigent capital letters.

Eck brought his wildly disoriented love out to the front of the medical center parking lot. Before he could get his bearings to see Ranger Thornton pulling up Got Junk? a short man and a much bigger woman in white hoodies snapped up-close cell phone photo bursts of them.

"What are you doing?" Eck cried. He started to lash out with his good right hand, but he needed both arms to keep Yolande up.

"Paparazzi! Paparazzi for President!" the two shrieked as they ran off into the dark Atlantic-windy parking lot. When he heard a vicious little mocking version of "Gole's a hole!" he felt an awful vengeance leaking into the top of his skull from where their little girl was holing up for dear life inside the woman he never thought would come into his life. He understood mass murder fully. That was because once again, unfuckingbelievably, he was staring at Jenny Rich.

Nicko Thornton stepped in front of Eck.

"You have business right here and now with either one of these two people, miss?"

Yolande forced herself up straight. She said, "This woman" and slumped down into Eck's arms. Eck was trying to get half his body around big Thornton's to knock this senseless Jenny Rich truly senseless with his right hand alone. The Park Ranger kept him off Jenny of the sneering upper lip just then like a shifting invisible wall, like one of Yolande Segundo's textile works that could envelop negative force, like old master paintings of a smiling archangel on implacable defense duty that was only going to go one way. So Ranger Thornton let Eck drain down his unholy bile against Jenny

Rich.

"Rich," Eck said to her. "What are you doing here? Here. Again. Now. What are you doing?"

Nicko said to him, "If you have to. I'm getting Yolande into the pickup. You don't have to deal with this one this way. Or any way. Unless you have to." She got the all-over sore Yolande inching slowly away.

"She pregnant," Jenny Rich said, utterly incredulous.

She didn't seem to be asking him, though. She seemed not to be in the same physical space as he. "That too?" she asked whomever she was asking. "She looks pregnant. That too? You get that too in life?"

Without sense, she was talking something that made sense. Gole got it.

"How did you know to come here?" he asked her all of a sudden red hair, her red lips, her patchy rose complexion, her circle pin of incarnadine flowers on her sideways scarlet scarf. The hair bounced on her head at him.

"I wanted the story to go on. It was mine. It's what I had."

"It didn't exist. Ever. Just in your cloud. You missed it. You missed me. You missed what I really was. You missed who you are. So, you couldn't destroy me."

Jenny Rich seemed to be trying to place him in some visual frame, some image of him that kept eluding her way of seeing the world. Her last virtual reality hinge had unloosened. Gole let her slap him once but not twice. He held her inside wrist on a high angle.

"You done, Jenny? Finally? Now?"

She had no torsion. Her body seemed to fade down from the inside. Gole released her and turned to find Yolande and their Ranger. He saw them in the luminous Got Junk? just as he felt an irreversible charge of hatred ricochet off his back from the gurgling Jenny Rich.

*

Two bad and good days and nights later, Yolande Segundo got up on her knees and screamed down at her daughter, "Get the hell back in me!" It was a mother's command unlike no other.

In the few seconds it took him to get into the bedroom and clear his sleepless head of fright and despair, she was standing up straight. She was gently pushing her lower abdomen, where the first stains persisted dry from two days ago because she would not wash. When he held her, she had an odor of someone who'd been in a bloody fight but hadn't lost it. Something was different. Or something was possible. That's what he was smelling on her. The possible.

Nickola Thornton assembled all the grown terns and piping plovers she'd saved from being tromped on or nestless or scoured up by the winds come off the ocean for sand. She sang together all the lost sea turtles she'd taught summer children to report exactly where they'd seen them on their morning hikes. She called upon the mother white sharks to swerve their cubs away from the nursing baby seals and thereby make peace in the sea just offshore.

She talked to beer-silly teenage off-road beach drivers who had no permits to be tearing down the midnight fall sands, letting them off if they promised to spread the word that Connie was in Advent mode, a miracle child of mooncusser pirates still trying in the twenty-first century to make amends for their thieving actions in the nineteenth.

Ranger Thornton's work became as waving and big and full of previously unseen colors as this mother's model textile panels framed by the daylight and the starlight both. The slimly populated down Cape community of autumn inhalers of winter-hinting sea air, repairers of cedar shingles, rakers and smoothers of down-dune access paths, created a hymn and a choral silence all its own of Constance-whisperers. This

gangly National Seashore Trust Ranger who believed in the
fundamental goodness of the natural world's humans
conducted several hundred local voices in a simple, inexorable
singing wish: let this Eck-Segundo child be and we will be
better for it.

So it seemed to Yolande and to Gole. Nicko took up the
only hope they had and turned into a banner folks claimed
they saw waving from the top of the Pilgrim Monument all the
way across the bay in PTown. Come on, Connie girl. Come.
Like the moonlight on Cape Cod Bay that told the crazed
sailing God-searchers in 1620: Here, this is the place for you
to try something entirely new.

So it seemed to Gole and to Yole, who had reason together
and separately to want to try something, no, someone entirely
new.

Connie, come on, won't you? Seashore Ranger Thornton
pleaded.

Please, baby you. And so forth. Come forth. Rebort, girl.
Rebort. Reborn yourself. Do it. Do it. Do it.

*

Three more hours toward dawn, Thornton had the Cessna
ready at the Provincetown airport. Yolande was getting
stronger by the minute. The three friends flew. They were
flying in blessed idiot hope into the sun rimming the Atlantic,
the Navy pilot of old turning the happily humming police
Cessna northwest toward the morning lights of Boston. Time
unrolled what it had been preparing for decades. The Monday
morning lights of Logan Airport. Thornton radioed another
old male Navy pilot buddy, who had a two-cruiser police escort
waiting on the tarmac, their overhead lights whirling like
windmills in perfect synch. The landing was as smooth as
good luck at last.

The senior obstetrician at Brigham and Women's Hospital

was also a Sister of Charity. Her only habit was her surgical gown. Her last name was Calpurnia. She was in-between rounds when the three friends came down her hallway with an intern from West Virginia Bible people who was holding a sonogram and grinning. Sister Dr. Calpurnia, too, was full of gladness at what Connie had done in getting back where she belonged.

Sure, it had been misdiagnosed. It maybe was about to go ectopic. One doesn't know. But this child, the good doctor nun said, is home where she belongs.

*

It was not possible, no medical science sense in it at all. Like her father's living, nonsense, nescience. But it was true. The tiny being caused all that pain to her mother's uterus, it had to be, because she fought her way back inside to where she belonged. It had to be, the mighty coagulation of specks, a teaspoon full of being turning itself back away from the fallopian grave in a billion-year-in-coming swerve, back where she belonged and her mother tucking her in tight while she screamed her child home again and extruded her deepest blood's effort to save her from being born dead. From aborting, yes, from that.

That's the whole of what Goleman Eck heard when Yolande Segundo got those two lovely words up and onto her beautiful cracked lips: *"Fuck.Yes."*

POSTSCRIPTUM

Christopher Daedalus (Simon Peter Grey)
Posthumous Letter to Goleman Eck.

I think that you and I have something in common. When I got catastrophically ill in multi-year stages, I fell off the spectrum of normal human being. When you were aborted at six months, you fell off the normal spectrum of human being.

For a hundred years now, people in my line of work have been fussing in complicated ways about event horizons. The common knowledge now has it that an event horizon is the outermost limit of a gravitational black hole before an entity gets sucked in. All of that entity's "information," as we call it, is then forever part of that black hole only, no longer part of the universe external to the black hole. Once inside, it is destroyed as what it was outside that event horizon.

The existence of black holes in the universe gives rise to the idea of those holes opening out into other universes, themselves probably with black holes. In the multiverse, or multiverses, time in the previous universe is destroyed. The past has no meaning. It's not even that the past is gone or disappears. It just no longer signifies anything. All this theory has been enough for the fiction writers to come up with space-

351

time transport from one universe to at least one other.

An abortion like yours is a radical destruction of a life that no longer has the line, the plan, the working out of its beginning at conception. Its story is cut. The disruption of the abortion, in turn, occurs as if in a multiverse or universe that annihilates the line, plan, sequence of the life in the previous biosphere. When this disruption becomes patently clear as happening in a vicious boomerang return, rage enters those left behind in the previous world when the abortion was a matter of necessary order (like choosing to live out a previous plan for life). The aborters, trapped in their betrayed world, look on the astonishing fact of the living abortion's ongoing living and see the death of their own best plan for the ungrowing of all *that* child.

Goleman Eck: What I propose to you is that you confronted them with the opposite of your life ended. You've substituted resurrection as the opposite of their desired end. Everything you do now becomes the reversal of death, the manifestation of another, parallel universe of life lived. Thrown out, you fell to the earth.

An aborting like mine, on the other hand, happens after eighteen to twenty years of normal human living. Then sclerosis, massive, silent, mandatory, takes a steady turn away from line, plan, as one knew it and claps you into a non-mobile, mute, entity in an alternate universe of being machine-wheeled instead of walking, being mediated instead of articulate, being nothing but a sitting brain. You are, as I was, reborted into a stationery receiver of complicated cosmological detail. You map it, touch its plans for itself with your mind. You gain a function, to do the advanced thinking for them about the universe in all its parts and all its holes. You become a hero of intellection.

You scare them because you really know there is no Creator, you know it in all your lost parts, the absolute space-time truth of the irrelevance of a Creator. Your minimal body life yields maximal knowledge about the curve in the universe that means infinite universes. You are free of God, connected only to the full human experience you cannot fully experience. Your sense of place is infinite; move in it minutely.

Do you get your world-famous diverse head around what I'm suggesting to you, Goleman Eck? The infinite black hole of freedom? The cosmological importance of your having survived abortion?

They can't hurt you, restrict you, hate you, manipulate you. You don't have to give a damn about the legion of aborters. As Mr. Morrison asked for, they tried to cancel your subscription to the resurrection. They ended up renewing it for the rest of your post-unnatural life. I get a kick out of knowing you're out there in the world, brother, I really do. You and Yolande—yes, I know about her and about the both-of-your girl-child she carried and delivered—should come visit me sometime. Even if my time just outside my event horizon is running out. I live outside of Helsinki, in the space-time institute named after me, quite close actually to the marvelous wind farm that has your name written on all the winds around it.

I recently spoke to the new EXOIL Board Chair about you. Call her. Do. I think she's in her own way a time-traveller. Wen Qimei's her name. Really.

ACKNOWLEDGMENTS

Over the years, I have benefited from the attention and support of writers and readers of great talent and generosity. Mark Jacobs, prolific major American short-story writer and politically original novelist, has had me look again at narrative momentum and the workings of sentences. Ari Korpivaara, journalist and fiction writer, has read me with gracious and judicious care. Kathryn Kimball, poet and translator of poetry, has attended to my characters with negative capability and exquisite editing sense. For having valued my romance and given me crucial encouragement, I thank William Giraldi and Robert Weisbuch. Clear advice and smart suggestions have come from Nick Courtright and Bryce Wilson at Atmosphere Press. For facts about medical procedures, I am indebted to *Web*MD and quizlet.com; I acknowledge two journals, *Water-Stone Review* 8 (2005) and *Journal of Narrative Theory* 40:3 (2010), for paragraphs of mine that appeared in other forms; I have drawn from Dan Barry's "The Lost Children of Tuam," *New York Times*, 28 Oct. 2017; and I bow to inspiration from two great artists, Mary Shelley and David Hockney. For her unending good counsel, I am as ever amazed and grateful to Susan M. Levin, soprano, Romanticism scholar, spouse and life-partner, who inhales prose fiction with joy. May it all keep on.

ABOUT ATMOSPHERE PRESS

Atmosphere Press is an independent, full-service publisher for excellent books in all genres and for all audiences. Learn more about what we do at atmospherepress.com.

We encourage you to check out some of Atmosphere's latest releases, which are available at Amazon.com and via order from your local bookstore:

It Starts When You Stop, a novel by Johnny Abboud
Trace Element, a novel by R.W. Bell
No Way Out, a novella by Betty R. Wall
Ulser, a novel by R.J. Deeds
The Short Life of Raven Monroe, a novel by Shan Wee
Orange City, a novel by Lee Matthew Goldberg
Late Magnolias, a novel by Hannah Paige
Comfrey, Wyoming, a novel by Daphne Birkmyer
The Tattered Black Book, a novel by Lexy Duck
Relatively Painless, short stories by Dylan Brody
Nate's New Age, a novel by Michael Hanson
The Size of the Moon, a novel by E.J. Michaels
The Red Castle, a novel by Noah Verhoeff
American Genes, a novel by Kirby Nielsen
Newer Testaments, a novel by Philip Brunetti
All Things in Time, a novel by Sue Buyer
The Black-Marketer's Daughter, a novel by Suman Mallick
This Side of Babylon, a novel by James Stoia
Within the Gray, a novel by Jenna Ashlyn
Where No Man Pursueth, a novel by Micheal E. Jimerson
Here's Waldo, a novel by Nick Olson

ABOUT THE AUTHOR

Robert Ready lives in NYC and Cape Cod and teaches in NJ. His fiction has appeared in *Antaeus, Gargoyle, Mondo James Dean, West Branch, RiverSedge, Water~Stone Review, Antioch Review, Midway Journal, Reconfigurations, Exterminating Angel Magazine* and elsewhere. On writing, he sides with Ishmael: "God keep me from ever completing anything."

CPSIA information can be obtained
at www.ICGtesting.com
Printed in the USA
BVHW081642130721
611840BV00007B/270